Copyright © 2017 by LOVESTRUCK ROMANCE PUBLISHING, LLC.

All Rights Reserved.
No part of this publication may be reproduced, distributed or transmitted in any form or by any means including photocopying, recording, or other electronic or mechanical methods except in the case of brief quotations embodied in critical reviews and certain other noncommercial uses permitted by copyright law. The unauthorized reproduction or distribution of this copyrighted work is illegal.

This book is a work of fiction. Names, characters, businesses, places, events, and incidents are either the products of the author's imagination or used in a fictitious manner. Any resemblance to actual persons living or dead is purely coincidental.

This book is intended for adult readers only.
Any sexual activity portrayed in these pages occurs between consenting adults over the age of 18 who are not related by blood.

CONTENTS

Rancher Bear's Baby	1
Rancher Bear's Mail Order Mate	61
Rancher Bear's Surprise Package	127
Rancher Bear's Secret	187
Rancher Bear's Desire	245
Rancher Bears' Merry Christmas	313
Join our group	353
Other books from Candace Ayers...	355

RANCHER BEARS COMPLETE SERIES

BOOKS 1-6

CANDACE AYERS

LOVESTRUCK ROMANCE PUBLISHING

RANCHER BEAR'S BABY

RANCHER BEARS BOOK 1

Her life is playing out like a country song. No job, cheating boyfriend, pregnant by a one-night stand. What else can go wrong?

Elizabeth followed her boyfriend halfway across the country because he wanted to get out of the city and back to nature. Giving up everything and accompanying him would cement their relationship. Or so she thought, until she found the bastard in the arms of another woman.

Down and out, Elizabeth is grateful when a handsome cowboy comes to her aid. Weird how she can't seem to keep her hands off of him. She's never been attracted to another man like this before.

Alex is one of the heirs to his family's billion dollar ranching operation. He'd rather party and play than fight with his brothers over who will gain control of the ranch. Alex actually thinks it's funny when the brothers find that their father has added a stipulation to the will. The first to produce offspring inherits the ranch. It certainly won't be him.

When Alex helps a woman in need, fate puts him face to face with his mate. He instantly falls head over heels for her. Fate is cruel though. She obviously doesn't feel the same for him because he can't seem to convince her to stay in town.

Each has only memories of their one night of steamy passion to cherish, until they receive surprising news that they'll soon have a little something else to cherish.

1

ELIZABETH

I kicked up dirt in my ruined ballet flats as I headed towards the sounds of screaming fans and country music. I wanted to find Sam and watch the rodeo with him. It was about time I tried to assimilate to the country way. We'd been in Landing, Wyoming for almost two weeks and I still hadn't seen the little town's nightlife.

As I spotted the small stadium, if you could even call it that, I couldn't help comparing it to the nightlife I was used to. DC had everything. Culture, dancing, and drinking. There was more, but at twenty-three, those three things ranked pretty high on my list of fun things to do.

What ranked pretty low was walking down a dirt path between the only motel in Landing and the little mud hole where the rodeo was held. My flats were label and had cost me a pretty penny. A penny I no longer had, so I had no hopes of replacing them. They'd been the victim of Sam thinking he was going to cheer me up about the dust I'd been tracking through to get to the local library. He'd tried to clean the delicate suede with a nice rough run through an industrial sized washing machine at the laundry mat.

The stadium was really just a big fence surrounding a bunch of dirt and a few sets of metal stands. There was a big wooden box set up on one end with windows revealing a few men who were giving commentary about what was happening in the dirt.

I passed by a few cowboys in their outfits and smiled at them. Of course, they just stared at me. If I had to say one thing about Landing's population, it was that they were the most private people I'd ever met. They weren't big on strangers. While it seemed like they'd taken a liking to Sam, even the sweet looking librarian clammed up when I walked into the library, looking to borrow her paper to job hunt.

The metal seating was mostly full, which was surprising for the small town. I never expected so many people to show up for something that didn't make much sense to me.

I stood at the bottom of the stands and looked for Sam. For the guy I'd moved across the country with, he sure had been hard to find since we arrived in Landing. I could feel the people in the stands looking at me, but I ignored it and just focused on finding my newly mysterious boyfriend. I made my way around the stadium with no luck. I couldn't find him anywhere.

He'd said that he would be there, so I found a seat and tried to blend into the crowd while I waited for him to show up. It wasn't easy, that much was sure. Landing residents seemed to scoot away when I walked by them. I wanted to like them, but I'd never felt quite so alone in my entire life. I didn't think I'd done anything to offend them, but they all seemed to want to keep their distance from me.

The country music screeched to a halt and a man with a thick accent started talking about the next cowboy up. The men were riding bulls, which just seemed dangerous and pointless to me. I was slightly concerned for the bulls, too. It couldn't be healthy for them to have such large men sitting on their backs. As I contemplated the cruelty level of bull riding, a man caught my eye.

It was different for many reasons. First, it was the first time anyone had really met my eye since I'd arrived. Second, because something seemed to sizzle in my lower stomach as soon as our gazes connected. Butterflies seemed too innocent and small a word to compare to what I was feeling. In all actuality, it felt like someone had released a thousand tornadoes in my stomach, that were all trying to escape at once.

The man was big. He towered over the tall men around him, making them seem average, at best. His shoulders were wide enough to land a small plane on, it seemed, and his arms tested the limits of the denim shirt he was wearing. A narrow waist and hips were encased in dark leather chaps that made me hungry to know what was waiting for my eyes in the back.

Tousled blonde hair fell almost to his shoulders and peeked out from behind a dusty cowboy hat. His lower face was all sharp angles and five o'clock shadow. I couldn't see his eyes as clearly as I wanted to and I found myself standing, my body desperate to get a closer look, to see them more clearly.

I bumped my ankle on part of the metal seating and the pain cleared my head. I blinked a few times and felt my eyes go wide. The cowboy was still there, standing in the dust right inside the fence, watching me with a half-grin on his face. He winked and I reacted like someone had set my ass on fire. I jumped about a foot in the air and then rushed towards the exit.

With my heart racing, I fought the urge to look back at the man. Something about him was calling to me, but I'd never been a cheater and I had no plans on starting. I had to just get away from him and pray that whatever I was feeling went away. I had to find my boyfriend and make him spend some time with me so I could remember why I didn't need to feel anything for anyone else. Sam was enough. He had to be.

I decided to go back to the motel and find my phone so I could call him. I would ask him to come home and then wait for him in just a nightie. Things were okay. I'd just have to prove it to myself, I figured. I shook out my trembling hands and tried to forget about the stranger. The tornadoes in my stomach hadn't calmed down any, but I could easily convince myself that it was just something funny I'd eaten.

I rounded the corner of the stadium and, from the new angle, spotted Sam's truck at the back corner of the parking lot. The shiny new chrome stood out amongst the other vehicles and I had a moment of anger at Sam. He'd just *had* to have a new truck. I'd poured more money into it than I cared to admit. It was just a part of his country western dream that I was going along with.

The closer that I got to the truck, the closer I got to realizing something wasn't right. The cheering from the rodeo drowned out most of the moans, but not all of them. I knew what I was going to find by the time I reached the front bumper of the truck, but it didn't stop me.

I trailed my fingers along the warm metal at the side of the truck until I stood beside the bed of it and could clearly see Sam with a woman bent over in front of him on the other side of the bed. Judging by the look on her face, she was really enjoying it. Judging by the look on *his* face, he'd spotted me.

"*Shit*! Beth!"

Dread dropped like steel in my stomach, crushing everything in its path, including the tornadoes and my ability to keep my lunch down. I bent over and threw up on the special edition rims that he'd wanted. They didn't matter much anymore, anyway.

2
ELIZABETH

By the time Sam got his pants up I was halfway across the parking lot. I didn't have a clue where I was going, but I wasn't seeing clearly through the tears.

I'd given up my life in DC to join him on his stupid journey of getting back to his roots. I'd given up my job and my beautiful apartment. I'd given up being near people who loved me and wanted to be with me.

The injustice of it all settled on my chest and I found myself so angry that I wanted to hit something, someone. I wanted to hit Sam. I'd never been violent, but I could feel my fingers tightening into fists at the idea of laying into him.

"Beth! Jesus, stop. Let me talk to you!" Sam caught my shoulder and spun me around.

It was the push I needed. I swung my hand out at him, aiming to clean his clock, but he ducked it. Frustrated, I shoved him away. "Don't let me stop you, Sam. Go back to fucking Daisy Dukes over there."

"Are you going to calm down any?"

I laughed. "Go to hell, Sam. It's over. This whole thing was a stupid mistake."

"We've been together for two years, Beth. You just moved across the country with me! You're really going to end it like this?"

"You're really going to fuck someone else while I'm waiting for you to come back to the motel?"

He tossed his hands in the air and seemed exasperated. "I'm sorry, okay? Let's just forget this. Come back to the room with me."

I sat down on the curb behind me and crossed my arms over my chest. "I'm done with this, Sam. Let's not drag it out."

He punched the car next to us and backed away. "I'm going back to the room. I'll be there, ready to talk, when you are."

I didn't watch him go. I was really done. When I made up my mind about something, I stuck with it. I was ending a two-year relationship in a matter of seconds, but strangely, it didn't feel the way it should've. I was pissed, embarrassed, and hurt, but I didn't feel crushed by the thought of leaving Sam. I'd get to go back to DC and bitch to my friends. I'd get to escape the country hell he'd landed me in.

I sat there for over two hours watching people get in their cars and leave. When there was just one truck across the lot and the lights flickered out, I realized that I wasn't as okay as I thought I was. I mean, I was still sure of my decision, but I hadn't thought about how I was going to get back to DC. Everything I owned was in the motel room with Sam. I had no money, no transportation, and nowhere to stay the night.

The tears that I'd been fighting off fell too easily as I realized just how alone I was, and just how dark it was in the parking lot.

3

ALEX

The rodeo had done nothing to soothe my nerves. Every muscle in my body had been tense since I'd seen the woman in the stands. My bear was pawing at me, telling me to go and find her. He wanted to devour the little human. I wasn't far behind.

It'd been a while since I'd felt anything besides anger and frustration. For over two months, I'd been dealing with the shit from Dad's death. He'd left the ranch in a fucking mess, that was sure. No boss, no back up plan, no nothing. My oldest brother, Matt had stepped in as temporary leader, but he wasn't exactly made for it.

Matt was no better than my other brothers. Lucas, Michael, and John were all money obsessed. They didn't give a shit about the ranch when it came down to it.

Despite the distraction that my family had become, everything had quieted when I spotted her. I'd fucked my way through every woman, bear and human alike, in Landing, and every town around, but I'd never felt anything like I'd felt when I laid eyes on her. My bear had tried to take control.

Her scent called to us. Honeysuckle with a little hint of something spicy. It'd taken everything in me not to chase after her when she'd left. My bear had roared in my head, demanding I go after her.

I'd stayed late at the stadium, using the excuse that I needed to make sure everything was locked up tight, but in reality, I needed more time to calm down. My fur was still just under the surface. I was too close to shifting to be able to hang out at the bar with everyone else. Adding liquor to my current state was a sure fire way to cause a disaster.

A hint of her scent wafted my way as I headed out to my truck. Damn. I shook my head. I was losing it, smelling her when she wasn't even there.

The farther into the lot I got, though, the more I was sure she was around. I stopped moving and tilted my head back to take in a deeper breath. Her scent came from the north end of the lot, the darkest spot. When I tuned into my senses, I realized I could hear whimpering.

Fur sprouted from my arms and hands as my bear roared in my head. He shouted that she was hurt and we had to save her. I was already running in her direction.

I spotted her, sitting on the curb, looking small and vulnerable. With a quick scan of the area, I saw that there was no imminent threat, but it didn't stop my bear from raging at the sight of her tears.

I was still a few feet away from her when she looked up at me. Her bright blue eyes widened and she held up her hands.

"What are you doing?!"

I froze in place and shook my head. *Great*, I thought, I'd scared the hell out of her by charging at her. "I heard you crying. Are you okay?"

She reached up and wiped at the tears. "I'm not crying."

I couldn't help but smile. "Of course, not. What are you doing out here, in the dark?"

She wrapped her arms back around her knees and frowned. "It wasn't dark until a few seconds ago."

My dick hardened into steel as her plump breasts pushed up. Her dress barely contained them and my mouth watered at the sight. "Need a lift?"

As she hesitated, I shoved my hands in my pockets, trying to look harmless. It wasn't easy. I was a big man, an even bigger bear, and everything in me was demanding that I grab her and claim her.

That gave me a slight pause. *Claim*? I'd never felt the urge to claim anyone before. I'd never even wanted to feel that urge before. Fucking my way through town had never seemed all that bad. Claiming someone meant having a mate to come home to. It meant responsibility. It meant forever. Forever for a bear was a long time.

I looked down at the small human and took a step back. My bear snuffed at me and demanded that I get closer to her. He was infatuated with her already.

"I... I don't have anywhere to go." The words seemed to break some type of barrier that she'd erected upon seeing me. The tears began falling again and it didn't seem like they were going to stop.

My bear was so close to the surface that I was sure my eyes were turning golden. I blinked a few times and tried to remain in control. "Alright. How about you just get in my truck for now and we can decide where to take you after? It's going to rain soon."

She looked up at the sky and then at me. "You aren't some pervert, are you?"

I couldn't help the sly grin I gave her. "Of course, not, ma'am."

4

ALEX

"I'm Alex, by the way."

She stood up and straightened her dress. Her hands shook slightly as she rubbed the fabric down across her thighs. "Elizabeth."

I walked beside her to my truck and had to fight to keep my hands to myself. She was too sexy for my own good. At probably a foot and a half shorter than me, she made up for her lack of height with the most delicious looking curves. Her waist dipped in but her hips and ass flared out, begging for me to bite at them. I wanted nothing more than to bury my face between her legs and find out if she tasted as good as she smelled.

"Why don't you have anywhere to go?"

"Because my boyfriend is an asshole."

My bear raged and I had to cough to cover a growl. If the bear was pissed, the man was irate. I'd been entertaining visions of sinking into her soft curves all night long. The idea of another man getting to do that set my teeth on edge. "Yeah?"

She shrugged and a lock of her long blonde hair fell over her shoulder. "I guess I can say ex now. I just caught him banging some red head over the side of his truck. So, that's over."

I opened my truck door and stared down at her. "He cheated on you? What the fuck is wrong with him?"

That got a grin out of her. "That's not even the best part. I just moved here with him. From DC. I moved across the country to be with an idiot who cheated on me within days of arriving. I quit my job. I sold my car. I sold my favorite bed set!"

Seeing her cheeks turn red and her muscles tense up in anger turned me on like nothing I'd ever felt before. I wanted more of it. "Sounds like a fucking asshole to me. What else?"

She tilted her head and bit her lip. "What else?"

I grinned. "I've had exes before. The lists of things they were pissed about were always longer than that. What else did he do?"

"Oh. Um... he had me help him buy a new truck. It's a stupid truck. It's like a shiny new toy. He wouldn't even let me take the plastic off the seats. And he didn't apologize tonight! I caught him screwing someone else and he still didn't apologize! What's even worse is that he's sure that I'm coming back to the room tonight. He's in for a rude awakening. I'd rather be homeless than go back to him."

I watched as she looked up at my truck and tried to figure out how to get into it. "Need some help?"

5
ELIZABETH

I looked at Alex and then back up at the truck. I knew the limitations of my short stature. I could climb into the truck, but there was no way I could do it without flashing him. "Um, yeah, actually."

He wrapped his hands around my waist and moved like he was going to pick me up but I made a squeaking noise and shook my head. I wasn't big, but I had curves and they weren't light. I didn't want to be mortified if he couldn't pick me up.

"What's wrong?"

I stared up at him and felt my cheeks go red. "You can't pick me up like that."

"Why not?"

"I'm not exactly a feather."

He laughed and picked me up. With ease, he sat me down in his truck seat and left his hands on my waist. "These muscles aren't just for filling up my shirt, ma'am."

I couldn't help but laugh. I didn't have a clue what I was doing with him, but there was something about him that made it hard to say no. The tornadoes in my stomach were back with a vengeance and every time he made eye contact with me, they seemed to get a little wilder.

"Thank you."

His eyes were honey brown up close. They seemed to glow as he looked at me. "You're welcome."

The silence between us grew. His hands were still on me and the air between us seemed to be alive. My skin was raised with goosebumps and even the light cotton covering my chest felt heavy suddenly.

Thunder rolled in the distance and Alex's fingers tightened on me. "It's going to be a big storm."

I looked past him and watched the night sky light up with a lightning bolt. Anxiety played at the edge of my mind until I couldn't ignore it anymore. I pulled away from Alex and crossed my arms under my chest. "This wasn't how things were supposed to work out."

"Fasten your seatbelt." It was all he said before closing the door and walking around the front of the truck to get it. He slammed his own door shut and then started the truck. "Ready?"

I shrugged. "Where are we going?"

"My trailer. This storm isn't going to be nice and there's no way I'm leaving you out here in it."

Heat blossomed south of my stomach and I shifted in my seat. "You don't have to do that, Alex. I can't go to your home."

"You can and you will. You can even take the bed. You've had a long night."

"You're being so nice. Thank you. I mean it. I don't know what I'd be doing right now if it weren't for you."

He pulled out of the lot as the first fat rain drops started to fall. "I get to spend some time in the company of a beautiful woman. Things could be a whole lot worse."

"And you promise you're not a sex-crazed pervert?"

He laughed. "I'm not a sex-crazed pervert. Promise."

I tried to relax into the seat, but it was hard with him sitting so close. "Thank you for giving me a place to stay. I didn't know what I was going to do. I just knew I wasn't going back to that motel while he was there, waiting."

"What *are* you going to do?"

I looked out at the storm that was just starting to pick up. "I don't know."

6

ELIZABETH

We were both quiet the rest of the way to his trailer. I was focused on how intense the storm was growing, while Alex hummed along to the country song on the radio. It was oddly comforting, considering my situation.

When we arrived, he ran around to help me down from the truck. In the few seconds it took us to get from his truck to the front door, we were both soaked. He opened the door and pushed me inside right as a massive boom of thunder hit.

I screamed and jumped, the sound shocking my already fried nerves. "Jeez! Does it always storm like that here?"

He dropped his cowboy hat on the floor and then kicked off his boots. "We get some big ones. Let me grab you a towel."

While he disappeared down a hallway, I looked around. His trailer was clean, for the most part. The coffee table was littered with a pizza box or two and a few beer cans, but for a guy who seemed to live alone, it was clean.

I stood on the small tile entryway and shivered. His air conditioning must've been on high and the water dripping from my soaked hair and body felt like it was going to freeze in place.

"Do you want to take a hot shower and get out of that dress?"

I snapped my head around to Alex and froze. He'd taken his shirt off and his pants were unbuttoned. The weight of the rain water was tugging them low, letting me see a lot more skin than I'd prepared for. His chest was something that I knew I'd never forget, his abs a dream.

I grew warmer just looking at him, but a shower would give me a chance to get away from his abs for a few minutes. "Do you have anything I could change into?"

He pointed down the hallway. "Last door is my bedroom. The closet is open and you can grab anything. The bathroom's through there. Take your time."

I slipped out of my even more ruined shoes and hurried to his room. I closed the door behind me and locked it. I took a fast shower, using his soap and shampoo, and then dried off. His closet was a smorgasbord of T-shirts, flannels, worn jeans, and flannel bottoms.

I knew the bottoms would never fit, so I didn't even bother. I pulled on one of the flannel shirts and buttoned it. It fell almost to my knees and smelled like soap and something woodsy. Feeling warmer, I finger combed my hair and then headed out to the living room.

Alex was in the kitchen, staring into the fridge. I must've made a sound because he turned to face me as soon as I stepped into the kitchen. His eyes traveled the length of my body and back up again. I pulled the shirt back onto my shoulder and forced a smile.

"I hope this is okay. I was freezing."

His eyes seemed to get brighter as he nodded and licked his lips. "It suits you."

I looked down at my toes and wiggled them as I thought about what I should say. "I really appreciate you letting me stay here. No one else in this town has been nice to me at all. I wasn't expecting it."

"Landing can be a pretty private place."

I gestured around us. "But you let me in your private space."

"The other option was to leave you crying in the dark by yourself. What kind of man would I be if I did that?"

I looked up and was surprised to find that he'd mostly closed the gap between us. He was close enough that I could, and did, watch a drop of water roll down his chest. "Aren't you cold?"

He shook his head, causing more water to sprinkle me. "I run hot."

He could say that again. I sucked in a breath and tried to remember that I'd just broken up with Sam. I was supposed to be sad and distraught. I was... I was in lust with Alex and something about the man was calling to me.

"Do you have a girlfriend?" I spit the words out while I still had the ability to speak. It seemed that being around him was burning up my fine motor skills.

He grinned. "No. Why do you ask?"

I gasped as the front of his jeans touched my thighs. I backed into his kitchen counter and realized that I was out of space to move away from him. Not that I wanted to. My body was just reeling. My hands shook as I grabbed the counter and my knees were trying to knock out a rhythm against each other. I'd never felt so much need or want for someone that my body vibrated with it.

"Elizabeth?"

I bit my lip and raised my eyebrows. "Huh?"

"Why do you ask?"

I stuttered as I answered. "Just wondering."

Alex leaned down until he was eye level with me and then lifted me onto the counter like I weighed nothing. "Something's happening here."

I nodded because there was no use denying it. When he moved forward, I opened my legs wider so he could stand between them.

"You can tell me to go fuck off and still stay here tonight. Just so you know."

Something about him giving me an out made me lose the little bit of doubt that was nagging at the back of my mind. I let my shirt fall off of my shoulder again and held his heated gaze. "I don't want to tell you to fuck off. Just so *you* know."

7

ALEX

The little spice in her words was all I needed to hear to convince me that she wanted me just as badly as I wanted her. I could smell the sweetness of her arousal and it was wreaking havoc on me, but I needed to be sure before I closed the gap between us.

I took one more look at her, sitting there in my flannel. Her shoulder was bare where one side of the collar had slid off, and the bottom of the shirt had ridden up her thighs. I had plans to run my tongue over every inch of her smooth creamy skin.

I ran my fingers through the hair at the back of her head and pulled her mouth to mine. The little moan she let out as I kissed her scorched every nerve ending I had. I flicked my tongue out and teased her lips before taking her mouth.

Elizabeth didn't just give over control. She pushed back, fighting for her own dominance in the kiss. She bit my lip and then sucked my tongue into her mouth. I pushed my dick against her core, unable to help myself. I needed to be inside her.

I gripped her thighs and then ran my hands up to her waist. "So fucking soft."

Her hands fumbled at the button of my pants for a second before she gave up and palmed me through them. "So hard."

I grabbed her ass and pulled her off the counter. With her legs wrapped around my waist like a vice grip, I carried us to my bedroom. I buried my face against her neck and breathed in her scent. My bear was roaring his pleasure, but with my mouth against the smooth skin of her neck, he beckoned me to mark her. He wanted me to claim the female as our own, to keep her with us forever.

Elizabeth ran her hands through my hair and tugged. "You stopped."

I'd been so lost in fighting the urge to mark her that I'd just frozen. I planted a kiss on her neck and forced myself to pull away from it. I kicked the bedroom door closed and tossed her on the bed. "I was thinking about how many ways I could take you before the sun comes up."

She raised up on her knees and slowly unbuttoned the top button of the flannel. I'd never loved that shirt more. Her eyes moved over my body, heated and heavy-lidded with desire. "Take off your pants."

I raised an eyebrow. "You're the boss now?"

The button gave way and her hands moved down to the next one. "Maybe. I'll show you mine if you show me yours."

I growled, unable to stop the response. I was seconds away from slamming my dick into her and she wanted to *toy* with me. She didn't understand how little self-control I had at that moment.

"*Woman.*"

Her grin was slow and her eyes bore into mine.

"*Man.*"

I unfastened my jeans and pushed them lower on my hips. "You first."

She worked another button undone and then dropped her hands to the bed.

"I want the pants, Alex."

I'd never been with a woman who pushed back against me. Something about her demanding her own bit of dominance rocked me. I wanted to fall to my knees in front of her and beg for a chance to touch her. My pride refused to allow that, though.

Instead, I shoved my pants down and stood naked in front of her. I watched her eyes go wide and felt my muscles flex in response. Her arousal scented the air heavily and I tilted my head back to breathe it in.

"Your turn, little one."

She went back to unbuttoning the shirt, painfully slow, with her eyes glued on me. When she got to the last button, she undid it and then held the shirt closed with her hands.

"Ask nicely."

Without thinking, I jumped on the bed and tackled her into the pillows behind her. I grabbed her wrists and held them above her head.

"You're a tease."

Her eyes flashed and her chest rose and fell faster. I could hear her heart racing.

"That implies that I'm not going to put out."

I bent down and nipped at the skin on her collar bone.

"And you are?"

She arched her hips and my dick settled against the bare lips of her cunt. Her wetness coated me as she rocked her hips back and forth.

"Yes. I'm yours for the night, cowboy."

And there it was. The night. My bear huffed and urged me to claim her. She couldn't leave us. It wasn't just one night. It couldn't be. I ignored him and took my time looking at her body, spread out under me.

Her skin was naturally sun-kissed and filled me with images of swimming in the stream behind my house, naked. She'd look good at any and all of my favorite spots, naked.

I cupped her breasts, unable to resist for any longer. They filled my hands perfectly. Her nipples were small and pink, and so hard against my palms. I dipped my head and took one into my mouth. Her taste exploded on my tongue, honey and sweetness.

"Alex!" Elizabeth's voice was higher as she locked her hands in my hair and pulled my mouth closer to her flesh.

I flicked my tongue over her and then moved to the other one, teasing it just the same. When I ignored them to move down her stomach, she whined. Her skin was soft under the stubble on my chin and as I rubbed it across her stomach, she shivered.

Her fingers tightened almost painfully in my hair as my mouth burned a trail to that sweet spot between her thighs. I licked a line up the junction of her legs and lips, wanting to drive her insane before actually delving into her. I sucked at a spot on her thigh and left a mark, satisfying the bear a little bit.

She lifted her hips, giving herself to me. "Please, Alex."

Hearing her beg pushed me over the edge. I ran my tongue up her slit and then parted them to find her clit. She tasted sweet and it sent me back for more over and over again. I teased her with long strokes until her nails dug into my scalp. Then, I slipped a finger into her as my tongue settled over her clit.

Elizabeth rode my face like a champ. Her hips twisted and rolled, putting my mouth wherever she wanted it. When I slipped a second finger into her, she damn near busted my nose with an especially excited thrust of her hips.

The bit of fight for control spurred me to give her more. I fucked her with my mouth until she was screaming out my name and coming on my fingers. Her thighs shook under me and as I glanced up at her, I saw how flushed her entire chest and face got as she came. It was damn sexy.

She used her grip on my hair to tug me up and then kissed me like she couldn't get enough of me. I kept my fingers in her, though, readying her for me. I scissored my fingers and then pushed in a third. I swallowed her moan and thought of anything I could to avoid shooting off early.

"Fuck me. I need you in me."

Her ragged voice called to me and I barely restrained myself from sinking my teeth into her shoulder and claiming her as my own. I slid my fingers out and then stroked her clit.

"Condom?"

I reached over to my nightstand and grabbed one before sitting back and rolling it on. I looked back at her and noticed the slightly annoyed look on her face.

"What?"

She shook her head.

"You're prepared."

I grinned down at her and then rubbed the head of my dick against her.

"Jealous?"

8

ALEX

Something in Elizabeth's face told me she was. My bear was satisfied. Our little human was already feeling possessive of us. Although, I knew she didn't understand it. It was different for humans. They didn't understand what was happening like bears did.

She reached down and grabbed me.

"Are you going to fuck me?"

My hips rocked into her grip naturally.

"Oh, yeah."

She lined our bodies up and wrapped her legs around me.

"I want you. Now."

I kissed her as I slowly thrust my way into her tight body. She gripped me like a vise and I had to push in harder to get all of my length in. When my dick was all the way in, I stayed still to let her adjust. My chest was heaving from the effort of not coming. I'd never been gripped like she was gripping me. Her hot little body was holding me like it'd been waiting for just this moment.

When I could move, Elizabeth came alive under me. She pressed her mouth to my ear and begged me for it as I pumped in and out of her. I rubbed my face over her neck and dragged my teeth over the skin there, teasing myself with the potential of tying myself to her for my whole life. I wanted to. I wanted to sink my teeth in. What had started as my bear telling me to had turned into the man wanting it.

"You feel so fucking good."

She moaned and nipped my ear.

I moved faster and harder, showing her that it could be even better. She tightened even more around me, tempting my body to lose control.

Elizabeth rocked her hips into me and tightened when I pushed into her until my eyes were damn near rolling back in my head. I knew I wasn't going to last much longer, so I angled my hips higher so every stroke would rub her clit. Just a few thrusts more and she raked her nails down my back while crying out my name. She sank her teeth into my shoulder and it was all I could handle.

I came harder than I ever remembered coming in my life. My body felt like it was being sucked through my dick as I jerked and spasmed inside her body. I grunted out her name and wrapped my arms around her while rolling to the side so I didn't completely suffocate her.

Several minutes passed before either of us moved. When I did slip out of her, she groaned and buried her head against my shoulder. I reached down to take the condom off and felt it hanging off of me in shreds. I looked down and cursed.

"What's wrong?"

I leaned back so she could see and watched her eyes go big.

"That's not good."

My chest tightened and I had a moment of panic, thinking the worst. My bear roared at me, telling me that it was okay, that this was how it was supposed to be because she was mine. Although, I knew she was my mate, thinking that she could potentially get pregnant with my cub scared the hell out of me. I wasn't ready.

"Are you by any chance on the pill?"

She sat up and fumbled to get the flannel shirt back on.

"No, but don't worry. I'll just take a morning after pill."

My chest tightened even more, until I wasn't even sure what I wanted or needed. I reached out and tugged the shirt back off of her shoulders.

"Come here."

Her body was stiffer than it had been, but I didn't know how to fix it in that moment. I just did what felt right. I wrapped my arms around her and pulled her into my chest.

"Rest, little one."

9

ELIZABETH

I woke up before Alex and squeezed myself out from under his heavy body. The man slept like the dead. I was used to that, though. Sam slept the same way.

At the thought of Sam, I felt sick. It wasn't the way I thought it would be, though. I thought I'd feel sick because of what I'd done with Alex the night before, but instead, I felt sick thinking of having ever been with Sam. The idea of Sam settled on my stomach about as easily as a brick.

I went to the bathroom and then brushed my teeth using some of Alex's toothpaste and my finger. My hair had dried into a weird mess, so I braided it down my back and then pulled my slightly stiff, dry dress back on.

The spark I felt for Alex had grown into a torch. I couldn't even look at him without feeling slightly unbalanced. He was kind and seemed like someone I would actually enjoy being with outside the bedroom as much as I did inside. I stifled a giggle. Inside the bedroom had been amazing. The sex was earth shattering. I'd actually lost my mind and bitten the man. I'd *never* bitten anyone during sex before.

It was all so strange, though. One night stands had never been my kind of thing. Meeting him and feeling comfortable enough to come back to his trailer with him and sleep with him all on the same night was so unlike me. I just instinctively trusted him and felt drawn to him. Everything about this sounded so stupid in my head, but it was real.

I pulled my legs under me and stared out of the windows across from Alex's couch. None of what I was feeling for Alex mattered, though. I couldn't stay. I had to go back to DC. Wyoming wasn't my dream, I didn't even have a job here, and now that things were over with Sam, it was time for me to go home.

"Come back to bed." Naked, Alex stood in the doorway to his bedroom, looking confused and grumpy.

"Sleep better with you there."

My chest ached painfully and I shook my head. I wanted to go back to bed with him. I wanted to pretend like I'd come to Wyoming to be with him instead of Sam, and that things were going great. I wanted last night over and over again. But that wasn't the reality. The reality was that this hot sexy sweet man and I just had an awesome roll in the hay which temporarily took my mind off of the fact that my life was a mess, but now it's time to put on my big girl panties. I had to rip off the Band-Aid, and face my future.

"I have to go."

He rubbed his hands down his face and then pushed them through his hair. It went all over the place and, somehow, he ended up looking sexier than ever.

"Why?"

"I have to go home."

He growled and stepped towards me. "To your ex?"

I shook my head. "To DC."

"No. It's too early. Just come back to bed."

"I can't. I have to go, Alex."

He went back to his room and came back out a few seconds later with a pair of pajama bottoms hanging low on his hips.

"You can stay here. Stay until you get on your feet."

Tears filled my eyes and I had to look away so he wouldn't see them. "There's nothing here. Everyone treats me like I'm diseased. I came here for my ex and now it's time for me to go."

He sighed. "I can't make you stay, but I wish you would."

I nodded and stood up. "I have to go by the motel and grab my wallet, at least. I have to buy a bus ticket and get out of here."

"I'll drive you."

Sam was gone, luckily, so I just ran in, grabbed my purse, and packed a quick bag. I held my tears in all the way to the bus stop. I was confused about how much pain I was feeling. I didn't know Alex well enough for any of the feelings I was having towards him to be genuine. I bet a shrink would tell me that it's some sort of misplaced something-or-other and that I had transferred feelings I'd wanted to have for Sam over to Alex, or some mumbo-jumbo like that. Regardless, I felt a massive amount of weighty sorrow at saying goodbye to this man I barely knew. He insisted on buying the ticket for me and then slipped his number into my purse while we silently waited for my bus to arrive.

When it did, I stood up on shaky legs and awkwardly backed away from Alex. I was weak and let the tears fall as I turned and got on the bus without hugging him goodbye. I'd never felt anything quite as intense and the entire ride back to DC was spent crying over a man I'd known for less than twenty-four hours. I was going home but it'd never felt less like home.

10

ELIZABETH

Three Months Later

I'd arrived in Landing, Wyoming the night before and had stayed in the same motel where Sam and I had lived for those couple weeks. Landing was exactly the same, although, I felt like everything had changed. I woke up early, feeling like shit, as usual. My body was revolting. I'd heard of people having easy first trimesters. I wasn't one of them.

I stood in front of the floor length mirror on the back of the bathroom door and stared at my body. In my floral sundress, my pregnant belly was slightly blending in. So far, the rest of my body had stayed the same. Except my breasts. They were exploding all over the place.

Pregnant. Pregnant after a one night stand with a stranger. I was living in a Lifetime made for TV movie special.

I'd gone back to DC and thrown myself into work. I had been offered my old job back. They really didn't need me but had hired me back anyway out of the goodness of the boss's heart. I'd tried to forced myself to forget about Alex, although it never really took. I'd dreamt of the big man every single night, and daydreamed about him every single day. I was living in a constant haze, a fog that I hadn't been able to lift.

The first month, I'd been able to act like my missed period was nothing. In my sadness at leaving, I'd forgotten to take the morning after pill, but I'd convinced myself that it was just the stress that made me miss my period.

The second month, I realized that something wasn't right. I started getting sick in the mornings. When I was finally able to get away from work, I took a pregnancy test and, sure enough, it read positive. I was pregnant.

I spent the next month arguing with myself about what I should do. The internal conflict was tearing me up. I didn't want to have to be the girl who showed up at some guy's doorstep with the stork news. I also didn't think it was right for me to keep this news from Alex. Maybe he'd want to know. A part of me just wanted to see him; another part worried that I was asking for more heartache. I couldn't help the fact that I really *did* want to see him. Something about him was drawing me back like a moth to a flame. I just hoped I didn't get burned.

It was scorching hot outside, but that didn't stop me from walking towards Alex's trailer. I passed a few different people on the way that stared at my stomach with wide eyes. I looked down and rubbed it. "It's okay, little guy. This town is just weird."

I didn't know for sure I was having a boy, but I just felt like I was. A mother's intuition. I smiled to myself and shook my head. As crazy as it seemed, I felt good about my baby. Everything was tense and up in the air when it came to work and Alex, but I was solid when it came to my protectiveness of my baby. I would be having and taking care of a little one.

Alex's trailer came into view and the little tornadoes in my stomach started turning like crazy.

His truck wasn't in the drive, so I didn't figure he'd be there, but just to be sure, I knocked anyway. No answer.

The next place I looked was the stadium. There were a few cowboys standing around outside, but Alex wasn't one of them. Sweat was rolling down my chest and face. I started feeling a little panicked.

"Ma'am?" A big guy sent a little wave my way and started over to me. "You looking for Alex?"

I tilted my head. "Yeah. How did you know?"

He grinned and cast a glance at my stomach. "Just a hunch. He's at the ranch today."

I looked around and wiped sweat off my forehead. "How far is that?"

He held out his hand and shook mine. "Pretty far. I'm Jason. Let me drive you. It's too hot for you to be out walking."

I started to shake my head but then nodded. "I should probably refuse to get in a stranger's car, but this heat has melted my brain."

He grinned. "I'm not a stranger, anymore. I'm a friend of Alex's. I also have a wife who's a little farther along than you, so you're safe."

I held my belly. "Is it that noticeable? I thought it was kind of hidden in this dress."

He laughed. "You're fine. Come on. Let's get some air on you."

At the potential for air conditioning, I shut up. I climbed into his truck and adjusted the vents to point right at me. Jason turned the air on high and then waited until I buckled my seatbelt before putting the truck in gear and heading out of the lot.

"How's he been?" I felt stupid as soon as I asked it. Was I really expecting to hear that he'd been just as wrecked as me?

"Well, I don't know. He's been a little distant from all of us lately. Cranky as hell, now that I think about it."

I stayed silent the rest of the way. I was desperate to actually see Alex and put my anxiety to rest. Either he'd want to be a part of his child's life, or he wouldn't. There was nothing more to it. I just needed to give him the news and accept the answer. I was also hoping that seeing him would calm some of these tornadoes. Maybe I had falsely built up the connection I'd felt for him in my imagination so much over these last three months and that seeing him would bring me back down to earth. I'd see first hand that he was just a normal man, not the demi-god my damned psyche had made him out to be.

Jason made a few turns and then drove us through the gates and under a big sign that read Long Ranch. I looked around and spotted animals and a huge barn. We drove past that and after a few minutes, a large house opened up in front of us.

I was shocked by the sheer size of it. I could see people moving around through the large windows in the front of the house and saw a big tent set up out to the side of the house. "What's happening?"

Jason laughed. "You picked a hell of a time to come back. The annual Long BBQ is tomorrow. Everyone is busy setting it up, looks like."

I opened the door and climbed down from his truck. "Where should I look for Alex?"

He pointed to the front door. "You knock on that door there and someone will find him for you, no doubt. Good luck."

That wasn't exactly reassuring. I waved him away and then headed towards the front door. My stomach rolled.

I stood at the door and looked at the doorbell, with my hand over my stomach. I whispered to the little guy, doing my best to settle both of us. I raised my hand to knock, but the door yanked open and then a young girl was staring at me with wide eyes.

She had the same sandy blonde hair as Alex and the same honey brown eyes. She couldn't have been any older than thirteen and the excited squeal she let out solidified that she was definitely a ball of energy. She threw her arms around me and squeezed me tight.

"Oh, my gosh! You're having a baby!"

I didn't feel uncomfortable with her little arms around me, so I just rested my hands on her back and let her hug me.

"I am."

"You're having *Alex's* baby!"

11

ELIZABETH

I pulled back suddenly and frowned.

"How do you know that?"

She grinned a mischievous grin and shrugged.

"I can just tell. Come on. I'll take you to him. He's upstairs, working. We'll get him up, though."

I dug in my heels, suddenly convinced I'd made a hugely stupid decision coming here.

"I think I'd better wait out here."

An older woman, just as beautiful and striking as the little girl, stepped into the entry way and stopped short. She looked at my stomach and took a deep breath in. Her eyes went wide and she screamed Alex's name at the top of her lungs.

I held up my hands and felt my entire body go red.

"I'm so sorry to interrupt. I'll just go. This was a mistake."

She rushed towards me and grabbed my hand.

"No, no. I'm sorry to startle you. It's just not every day a pregnant woman shows up at my doorstep. Bailey, go and get your brother. *Now.*"

"Really. I think I'd better go."

She held my hand in both of hers and met my eyes. "Sweetheart, stay. I was just shocked for a moment."

I let her lead me into a massive kitchen. "How do you know?"

She grabbed a bottle of water from the fridge and motioned for me to sit down.

"I'm sorry. I didn't even introduce myself. I'm Carolyn, Alex's mother. Now, how did I know what?"

I took a sip of the water and looked down at my belly. "How did you know I was here for Alex?"

"I have five sons, but I just knew that you were Alex's." She looked behind me and grinned. "There he is. Alex, you've got a special visitor."

I'd already felt him in the room. It was like my body could sense his presence. The closer he got, the more my nerve endings tried to stand up tall to be closer to him. I slowly turned to face him and thanked god that I was sitting down. My entire body seemed to sigh and a tension that I hadn't even realized was there left my body.

He was just as drop dead handsome as the last time I'd seen him. His hair was longer and the shadow had turned into a full beard, but he was still enough to make my body react instantly.

I blew out a shaky breath. It wasn't a fluke. He still affected me the same as before.

"Elizabeth."

"Hi." I clenched my water tighter and tried to remember how to breathe.

In the blink of an eye, he was across the kitchen, and had me in his arms. His hug was crushing, but I needed it, for some reason. I felt better than I had in months and, like some sort of magic, my queasy stomach settled down.

"Bailey, come on. I think we need to give your brother some privacy."

"Are they going to do it? Mates are so gross with the sex stuff."

Alex growled at his little sister from over my head. "Bailey."

"Okay, we're going. Come and find us when you're done, Alex."

Carolyn sounded happier than earlier, singing her words instead of speaking them.

Alex leaned back and looked down at me. "Hi."

I bit my lip. "Hi."

He grinned. "You already said that."

I felt his eyes dip lower and then felt him stiffen as he breathed in deeply. I knew he was seeing my belly and I knew things weren't going to be as nice as they'd just been. I pulled away and went back to the counter. "As you can probably see, I gained a little weight while I was away."

He stuttered out nonsensical words and kept his eyes on my stomach.

"Bad joke, you're right. I'm actually pregnant. I found out last month and I've been trying to think of a better way to tell you, but a singing telegram just didn't feel right." I continued on when he still remained frozen. "Another bad joke. Okay. Well, he's yours. I just... know. I've been to the doctor and he's healthy. Bigger than normal babies his age, but healthy."

"He?"

"The man speaks!" I laughed awkwardly and wrung my hands together. "I don't know for sure yet, but I just have a feeling. I'm sorry to just burst back into your life like this, Alex, but I thought you might want to know."

He shook his head.

My heart sank. I had envisioned a thousand different scenarios, but I hadn't been able to stop my hope from building. There *had* been something between us that night. There still was if the way he grabbed me meant anything. Maybe I was mistaken, though.

"Okay. I'm sorry." I turned to leave and tried to fight the tears back.

"Wait! Where are you going?" He rushed over to me and grabbed my arms. "I didn't mean no. I'm just... shocked. I didn't think I was ever going to see you again and then you're here. Carrying my baby..."

I rested my hands on his chest and felt my body respond to his. "I can't imagine how big of a shock this is. Why don't you take some time to process it?"

He frowned down at me. "I don't need time."

"You don't?"

"No. He's mine. My father made me the man I am today. There's no way I'm leaving this little guy-or girl- without a father. Absolutely not."

His intensity hit me right in the chest and I had to look away from him. I wanted him to feel the same intense possession with me, but I knew that was an insane feeling. Nothing was making sense with him standing so close. I needed some space to figure things out.

"I think I need to rest. I've been feeling sick lately. Is there a cab I can call for a ride back to town?"

"A cab?"

I shifted from foot to foot, feeling a little more than antsy to get away. "I need some space."

I spun around and rushed to the door. It swung open just as I got closer and I charged past the young man standing there. I just wanted to get away.

"Elizabeth!"

"Beth?"

I turned too quickly to the right and went down hard on my hands and knees. It knocked the air out of my lungs, but I still managed to croak out the one name I thought I'd never say again. "*Sam?*"

12

ALEX

My heart was raging in my chest. I'd been dreaming about seeing Elizabeth again since the moment she left. I'd been an idiot for letting her leave. I knew she was my mate and yet I didn't fight for her because I was too busy panicking like a pussy.

I'd managed to drink my way through enough whiskey to float a boat while she'd been away. I'd tried to find her, but I had nothing to go on besides her first name and that she lived in DC.

Then, she was there, standing in front of me, smelling like heaven. It'd taken me a few minutes to realize that she was softer and her smell had changed. She smelled like me. The little cub inside her smelled just like me.

I'd managed to fuck it up, though. I was still hungover and my head was throbbing, so I'd said the wrong thing. All I wanted to do was carry her back to my trailer and keep her by my side. Well, I wanted to sink into her again and again while claiming her, too. I'd smelled her arousal in the air and I was seconds from dragging her away like a caveman.

I chased her as she ran and watched as one of the guys working on setting up the tents called her name. She twisted and then went down hard. All I could think about was the fact that my mate was hurt.

I ran to her side and went to my knees beside her. "You okay? Talk to me, sweetheart."

The idiot who'd called her name came closer and I let out a violent growl at him. He wasn't getting close to my mate. She was mine and I'd kill anyone who tried to take her from me.

Elizabeth coughed and climbed back to her feet. I could smell her blood in the air and it made the animal in me a little wild. I was close to turning and letting my bear loose on everyone around us.

She rested her hands on my shoulders and looked down at me. "Did you just growl at him?"

"Just letting him know to stay the fuck away."

She tilted her head to the side. "You know he's my ex?"

I turned my head to face the little fucker who'd hurt my mate. I stood up and towered over him, reveling in the stench of fear coming off of him. "You're the fucking idiot who cheated on her?"

Elizabeth held my hand and tugged me towards her. "Come on. Just take me home."

My bear stood up even taller. "Home? The trailer?"

She nodded. "Yeah. Don't do whatever you're thinking of doing."

The little shit came closer. "Beth, what are you doing back here? How do you know this guy?"

She rubbed her stomach and looked every bit the mother bear that I'd pictured in my dreams of her. "It's none of your business. Go away."

His eyes trailed down to her stomach and I watched as he breathed in and scented me on her. "You're pregnant with this fucking guy's kid?"

I stepped closer to him and Elizabeth put herself between us. She looked up at me and rested both of her hands on my chest. "Take me home. Please, Alex. I hurt myself."

Immediately, I calmed and lifted her into my arms. "We're going to a doctor."

"No, I just need some alcohol and a-"

"A doctor. After that, I'll take you home."

She grumbled, but let me carry her away. "I know I'm even heavier now. You can put me down, Alex."

I opened my truck door and put her inside gently. I lingered next to face, breathing in her scent. My bear, who'd been pissed at me for months, decided to talk to me again in that moment. He demanded I mark her and refuse her if she ever said she wanted to leave again. He didn't understand that human females wouldn't like that.

"You're not heavy. You're perfect and pregnant with my baby."

She sucked in a deep breath and chewed on her bottom lip.

"I missed you. I looked for you."

Elizabeth's eyes went wide. "You did? Why?"

I tucked her hair behind her ears and cupped her face. "Because I wanted you here with me."

"You did?" She sounded shocked.

I planned to show her how much I wanted her at my side. "Let's get you to the doctor and then we'll talk tonight.

13

ELIZABETH

After the doctor's visit, where I was checked out and had the newly shredded skin on my knees wrapped up, Alex drove me to his trailer and insisted on carrying me inside. Only after he'd gotten me settled on his couch with a blanket and a glass of water did he sit beside me.

"Do you need anything else?"

I had to stop myself from rolling my eyes. "No. I'm fine. And I don't need this blanket, either. It's about a thousand degrees outside, Alex."

He pushed it back at me when I pushed it off. "Maybe the baby is cold."

I stared at him with a blank face. "You're kidding."

Alex sat back on the couch and shook his head. "What? It could happen, right?"

I sighed. "I'm having a baby with someone who thinks my baby can be cold inside of me."

He reached over and grabbed me before dragging me into his side. "Our baby."

I looked up at him and tried to contain the excitement that built in me. The way he was talking, it sounded like he wanted to be with me. My head spun from how crazy it all was, but I wanted it more than anything. I'd come hoping that he would want something with me.

"This feels insane, Alex. What is this thing between us?"

"I could tell you but you'd probably tell me that I'd lost it."

I stretched out and rested my head against his chest. "I just quit my job for the second time and told my landlord that I would let him know whether or not I'd be needing the apartment past this month. I got a flight across the country and then a bus to the smallest town ever, where people don't seem to like me very much. Just on the off chance that you could possibly want to do this thing with me. Try me."

Laughter rumbled deep in his chest. "We're meant to be together. You were made for me."

My heart raced against my rib cage. "You believe that?"

He caught my chin with his finger and turned my face so I was staring at him. "It's true. I believe it with my whole heart. That's just the way things work in my family, Elizabeth. My Mom and Dad were the same way. They were meant for each other the same way we are."

I could feel his sincerity and was overwhelmed with the need to sob. I couldn't fight it and ended up with my face buried in his chest. "I'm sorry!"

"What's wrong, Elizabeth?"

I sagged against him. "I'm hormonal and that was the sweetest thing I've ever heard."

He just held me tighter and pressed his lips to my head. "Thank you for coming home to me, little one."

14

ELIZABETH

The next morning, I woke up early and started my day by vomiting in Alex's bathroom sink while he was peeing. Thankfully, I hadn't eaten much the night before. I dry heaved into the sink after everything was out of my stomach and groaned.

Alex flushed the toilet and came up behind me and rubbed my back. "Are you okay, baby?"

I shook his hands off of my back and turned the faucet on to rinse everything away. "You just peed and then rubbed all over me."

"Sorry." After a second, he continued on. "Are these the pregnancy hormones talking?"

I stood up straight and glared at him through the mirror. "Don't ever ask me that again."

"Right. Good point." He washed his hands and then dried them on his shirt before wrapping his arms around me. "Is this okay?"

All of my anger faded. I sagged against his chest and nodded. "I'm sorry. I just slept terribly and this little guy isn't happy if he isn't causing me some trouble."

"Let me stay with you tonight."

I felt how sincere he was in wanting to stay with me poking against my back.

We'd spent the afternoon and night talking and getting to know each other. We'd gone over the basic things, anyway. I knew his favorite color was brown and was seriously worried about him because of it. I knew he loved sweets and kept a bag of skittles in his truck at all times. I knew that he was the youngest out of four brothers, but solidly older than his little sister, Bailey.

Despite knowing all of the things that he could verbalize to me, the good and the bad, I hadn't felt like I knew him enough to start sleeping with him. It seemed silly and I knew that Alex wasn't in love with the idea of sleeping apart, but I thought it would make me feel a little more in control. Instead, I'd tossed and turned all night. I could smell him all around me in his bed, but not having him there to touch and hold kept me squirming. My body wanted him and I couldn't fight it.

"Okay."

His hands moved up my stomach, stroking underneath the T-shirt I wore, until the tips of his fingers teased my breasts. His dick pressed into my back even harder and I felt myself go from dry to drenched in seconds. He cupped my breasts in his big hands and ran his thumbs over my sensitive nipples, causing me to moan and arch into him. "Pregnancy looks fucking amazing on you, Elizabeth."

I opened my eyes and watched through the mirror as he pulled my shirt off and took in my naked body. I flushed and wanted to look away, but I made myself watch. My body had grown and changed in those three months. My stomach was fuller and protruding, as were my breasts. They'd already grown almost a cup size and it was a cup size that Alex was enjoying.

His tanned hands holding my pale breasts was something I'd have a hard time ever being able to forget. He leaned down and ran his mouth against the line of my neck. "I want you to be mine."

I tugged at his hair. "Just yours?"

His teeth settled against my neck and slowly he added more and more pressure until there was a slight pain, but even more pleasure coursing through my body. His eyes met mine and flashed golden.

I gasped and spun around to face him. "What just happened?"

His chest heaved and he turned and left the bathroom. "Nothing. I'm going to get dressed. I have to help Mom finish up with the rest of the BBQ."

I watched as he left and then turned back to the mirror. My mind was racing because I was one hundred percent sure I'd watched his eyes change colors. I'd never seen anything like it. "Alex?"

He moved back into the bathroom doorway and crossed his arms over his massive chest. "Yeah?"

"I want to be yours. No secrets, though. Okay?"

"Of course."

Things were weird. I could tell he was hiding something from me. I don't know how I knew it, but I did. The connection I felt with Alex wasn't normal. It hadn't been normal from the start. I felt as though I was already in love with him and I'd spent less than forty-eight hours with the man. When he spoke of us being meant for each other, I believed him, no matter how crazy my brain told me it was. Because I felt it too.

I'd been drawn back to Landing, Wyoming. Despite not enjoying it the first time around, I'd been pulled back like an addict. Everything in me had itched to be back until the bus crossed the city limits sign. I felt pulled to Alex the same way. I couldn't make sense of it, but for some reason, that was okay.

15

ALEX

Elizabeth sat between my Mom and Bailey, listening to them go on and on about babies in Landing. Babies in Landing came sooner than normal babies. They were bigger and tougher and would be changing into a goddamn bear within a few months of being born. That was something I was going to have to talk to her about before it happened, because Mom and Bailey were leaving that out.

She'd almost seen the bear in me come out to play. I'd nearly marked her in the bathroom. I'd been seconds from sinking my teeth into her delicious tasting skin and leaving a claiming mark for the rest of the world to see. She'd panicked when she saw my eyes, though. There was no way she wouldn't panic when I told her about the rest of it.

My heart pounded away in my chest at the mere thought of her running from me when she found out. I already loved her. Talking to her, listening to her speak, hearing her soft whimpers when I touched her, I couldn't get enough. My heart was hers.

I kept an eye on her at all times, making sure no one got too close. I knew she smelled like me and carried my scent at a basic level because of our little cub, but any bear within twenty miles would be able to smell the honey scent she put off. They'd be able to smell her arousal, too. Just like I could every single time she looked at me.

"You really did it, huh?" My oldest brother, Matt, said as he stopped beside me.

I was leaning against a shade tree, enjoying watching instead of participating in the festivities. I sent a cross look at him and straightened. "Don't start."

Matt, as the oldest, always assumed that he would get the ranch when Dad finally passed. Dad had been gone for a few months and until Elizabeth showed up at our doorstep the day before, nothing had been decided. He knew how much his oldest sons cared about money, but he wanted them to care about family, too.

Bears didn't reproduce at the rate that other shifters did. Mom and Dad were a freak occurrence. Our population had dwindled over the years, and if bears like my brothers didn't learn to care about family, our population would dwindle to nothing. In trying to teach his sons a lesson, Dad left a stipulation in his will that the ranch would go to the first son to produce an heir.

I'd discovered that little bit of information the month after Elizabeth left. Her leaving wrote off any chance I'd ever have of inheriting the ranch by being the first to produce an heir. Without her, I'd never want to have cubs. Hell, I hadn't even wanted to look at another woman since I'd met Elizabeth. Not inheriting the ranch was of no consequence to me. I'd never been huge on responsibility anyway. But, seeing her show back up with my cub growing inside of her belly, changed something in me. It was as though a fire had been lit deep within. Now, I would soon have a family to provide for.

My brothers were furious. Matt and Luke had been too busy looking for loop holes in Dad's will to actually get out and try to find a mate. It served them right, groveling over an inheritance with Dad's body not yet cold.

Matt shoved me and stormed off in the direction of the house. He cast a glare at Elizabeth that had me growling at his back.

I looked back at Elizabeth sitting with my family. They would accept her, eventually. Humans always made bears uncomfortable at first, because they couldn't be themselves, but knowing she was carrying my baby bear would warm them up. Then, when I finally claimed her as my own, they'd treat her like one of the family.

Elizabeth looked up at me with a grin on her face and waved at me. My dick hardened in my pants and I had to shift my footing to remain comfortable. She glanced at my pants and then giggled before turning back to her conversation.

There was no way I was sleeping away from her tonight. I couldn't, even if I wanted to. I needed to be closer to her.

Lucas, my third oldest brother angled up to me, his eyes on Elizabeth. "As the leader of this here ranch, you have a job to do. There seems to be a gap in the fence up the hill. Someone called and said one of the cows got out."

"Keep your eyes to yourself, Lucas."

He shrugged. "Just trying to understand what you see in her. She's kind of fat."

I'd punched him before I even realized what I was doing. Lucas reeled back and tripped over a tree root that stuck out of the ground. "Fuck off."

I headed in Elizabeth's direction, where she was standing and watching me with her hand across her stomach. I knelt in front of her so I could press my lips to her belly. "I have to go up and see about an escaped cow. Will you be okay here for a couple of hours? I'll come back just as soon as I can."

She ran her fingers through my hair and nodded. "Of course. You don't need company, though?"

I grazed her breasts on my way up, just to tease her, and growled when I heard her intake of breath. I wanted to throw her on top of one of the picnic tables and take her then and there. "I wish I could justify making you trek up the side of a mountain, but I can't. You can keep me company later tonight, though."

Her grin said she'd be glad to. "Be careful."

I kissed her on the forehead and then hurried off towards my truck.

16

ELIZABETH

The sun was high in the sky and the BBQ was well underway when things went a little haywire. Carolyn and Bailey made me feel more than welcome. They treated me so well that I was starting to feel a little guilty for taking up all of their time. When they both had to go and check on stuff in the kitchen, I made my way to the drinks table and grabbed a bottle of water.

I'd been introduced to Alex's brothers very briefly when we'd arrived. They'd seemed distant and cold, without one ounce of the warmth that Carolyn, Bailey, and Alex seemed to possess. When I spotted the oldest one, Matt, approaching, I quickly turned and attempted to get away.

As my luck would have it, he was just as freakishly tall as Alex and easily caught up to me. He lightly grasped my arm and pulled me to a stop. "Where are you off to, Beth?"

I frowned. Sam had been the only person to ever call me Beth and I hated it.

"Elizabeth. And I was just going to see if your mom needs any help in the kitchen."

"She doesn't. I was hoping to catch you without Alex hovering over you."

A pit formed in my stomach but I tried to contain it. "Why?"

He frowned. "Well, I just wanted to make sure you're okay with everything. It's not every day that a woman agrees to become a mother just to help a guy take over his dead father's ranch."

I balled my hands into fists and looked around. "What are you talking about?"

He acted like he was shocked. "You don't know?! Oh, no. This is crazy. I was sure you were in on it with Alex..."

I felt the urge to punch him, but contained it.

"Spit it out."

"Our Dad wrote it into his will that the first son to have an heir gets the entire ranch. You're a little money pot, Beth. You and that little bear in you. You're bringing a huge fortune to Alex. It's no wonder he's been giving you sweet looks. I can just see the dollar signs in his eyes."

I didn't buy into it for a second. I'd talked a little bit to Carolyn about her husband. She told me that when it's right, it's right. She'd been drawn to her husband the same way that that I was drawn to Alex. Unexplainably. Inexplicably. Unrelentingly. As crazy as it was that I'd stumbled upon Alex, it was right.

"Does your ass get jealous of the shit that comes out of your mouth? If you're going to bully someone, I suggest you don't try to pull it on a girl who grew up in the streets of DC. Now, I'm going to excuse myself. Good luck with everything."

I walked away from him and headed in the direction that I'd seen Alex go. I needed to see him.

It'd been a while since he'd left and I figured he'd be on his way back before too long. I'd just meet him on the road.

I hiked up the road and found Alex's truck parked off to the side. His clothes were thrown on the hood of the truck and my heart began racing in my chest. What could he be doing that required him to take all of his clothes off?

With images of him having sex with someone against a tree, I let my pregnancy hormones drive me. I crept through the woods, deciding that I was going to catch him in the act. I'd been so sure of our connection just minutes before, and there I was, creeping through the woods in an effort to catch him with his pants down. Off. His pants were off.

I heard movement up ahead and stepped behind a big tree. I knew I looked crazy and I felt it even more so, but something wasn't right.

After a few seconds, I peeked my head around the tree and screamed for all I was worth. Standing less than six feet from me was the biggest bear I'd ever seen. Not that I'd ever seen a bear face to face.

It just stood there, staring at me. There was something in its face that read annoyed, but that had to be the hysteria I was feeling. I was going to die and it would be Alex's fault. If he'd just kept his pants on, things would've been different.

I made a movement to step backwards and the bear grunted at me. It reached its paw out at me and I had a vision of it hurting my baby. I snapped and reached out and slapped its paw away. "You're not killing me. Not today. I have a baby in here and I will fistfight a bear to keep him safe if I have to."

It backed up a step and then Alex appeared in its spot, naked and grinning. "You'd fistfight a bear for our cub?"

17

ELIZABETH

I blinked a few times, unsure if I was still alive.

"Wha... what just happened?"

He looked sheepish and ran a hand through his hair and blew out a long, slow breath. "No more secrets."

I leaned against the tree. My mind was slowly trying to make sense of what I'd just seen. The bear had just... become Alex. One second it was a bear; the next second it was Alex.

"I'm sorry, Elizabeth. I didn't want you to find out like this. My bear just smelled you and came towards you."

I shook my head to clear it and then looked up at him. At Alex, the guy that I'd somehow fallen in love with without even knowing it. Alex, the bear-man. Man-bear? Something in me snapped back into place and I reached out and smacked him.

"I thought you were cheating on me! I saw your clothes and your truck and thought I was going to find you out here with another woman!"

He raised an eyebrow. "I just revealed that I'm a bear shifter and you're pissed because you thought I was cheating?"

I thought about it. "Yeah. You scared the hell out of me. I just verbally whipped your brother for even suggesting you didn't care for me and then I come out here and thought I'd find you... the way I did Sam. I was scared. Terrified."

"Which one?"

"Huh?"

"You said you had words with my brother. Which one?"

"Matt. He's an ass."

"Did he touch you?"

I rolled my eyes. "Does it matter? Can we get back to the matter at hand? What the hell is a bear shifter? Am I dead? I feel like this whole thing is surreal."

Alex caught my shoulders and pulled me against his naked body. He wrapped his arms around me and held me tight. "I'm a bear shifter. And no, you're not dead. Feel my heartbeat?"

I pressed my ear to his chest and listened to it racing away. "Why is it going so fast?"

"Because I'm afraid you're going to run away from me."

I leaned away from him and shook my head. "I'm still here."

"I'm a shifter. I can turn into a bear..."

It all made sense. As much something like this could make sense. I'd seen his eyes take on an inhuman glow multiple times. I knew there had to be something special about him that would explain that. I just never in my wildest dreams could have imagined it would be this. I'd watched *True Blood* like half of the rest of the country. I knew what shifters were. I just didn't think they actually existed. Like in real life. "Do it again."

He moved away from me and in a blur of movement, his body contorted and he was a bear again. He huffed and went down on all fours so he was closer to my height. He was huge. Ginormous.

I reached out and slowly rested my hand on his head.

"Holy shit."

He made a sound that was so similar to laughter that I couldn't help but laugh myself. I stroked his head and neck, feeling the coarse hair beneath my fingertips. It was either real or this was hands down the most vivid dream I'd ever had.

"This is amazing, Alex. Can you understand me?"

He huffed again and nuzzled his face against me. A small flutter in my stomach surprised me and I looked down at it with shock on my face.

Alex was instantly standing next to me again. "What's wrong?"

"He just kicked, I think. It's early, though. When you put your face against my belly, he moved." I laughed. "Is he going to come out a bear?"

He looked appalled. "Of course, not!"

I laughed even harder. It was all so crazy. "I'm kidding, Alex. He will be like you, though, right?"

He nodded and watched me curiously. "He will. And one day he will feel the same pull towards someone as I feel towards you. My whole family is like this. I'll explain everything better later."

I nodded. "Yeah, you will."

"How are you taking this so well?"

"I don't know. I think all of this has just been crazy enough that I'm more stunned than anything. Maybe I'll freak out later. Maybe I won't. How do people normally take this news?"

He touched my cheek. "People don't normally find out. That's why the town was so closed up when you got here. It's a big secret to keep."

I pouted. "But they were nice to Sam."

Alex growled and pulled me into his chest. "Mine."

I nipped at his chest. "Were you trying to eat me earlier? Is that a thing?"

His laughter rang out loud and clear through the forest.

"No. We do not eat people. There is something I wanted to explain to you, though. About mates."

"Mates? Bailey said that before. Are we mates?"

"Yes. Mates are just like they sound. Soulmates. You were meant for me and I was meant for you. I could feel it the very first time I laid eyes on you at the rodeo. I knew you were mine."

I kissed him then, desperate to feel something solid. "What does it mean?"

He kissed me back. "It means that we're going to be together for a long time. It means that I love you, and that my heart belongs to you."

I grinned up at him. "This is all so insane and I'm sure you'll have to explain it all a million times later, but right now, I just want to be close to you. As close as I can get."

He ripped the straps of my dress and pushed it off my shoulders. With a predatory look on his face, he pushed me against the tree. "As close as possible?"

My body reacted instantly, the same way it had this morning and three months ago. Maybe it was the mate thing, or maybe it was just how hot Alex was. I couldn't be sure, but either way, I wanted him. "What did you have to explain to me about mates? I have about two more minutes of listening before I'm tackling you and having my way with you."

He pushed my dress over my belly and hips and let it fall to the ground. His fingers cupped my sex and his mouth landed on my neck. "This. Mates claim each other. I wasn't trying to eat you earlier. I want to claim you as mine. Everything in me is screaming at me to mark you so no one ever thinks they can touch you again."

His lips felt amazing against my skin and I was ready to agree to anything. "Is it a hickey?"

He flicked his tongue over the same spot. "No. I bite you. It's a bond between us."

"Will it hurt?"

"Maybe for a second or two. It'll be worth it, though."

I rocked my hips against his hand, trying to get him to rub my clit. "Do you still want to?"

He scraped his teeth there and made me gasp with pleasure. "Fuck, yes. I've wanted to since that first night. It took everything in me not to do it."

I tilted my head farther to the side. "I want you to mark me. I want to be yours. Do I mark you?"

He yanked my panties down and easily lifted me until my core hovered over his dick. "When I mark you, Elizabeth, everyone will know that I belong to you. You own my heart, little one."

I cried out as he dropped me onto his shaft and pinned me against the tree. I dug my nails into his shoulders and held on. I wanted him more than anything. Nothing else mattered.

Alex drove into me again and again, filling my body until I thought I couldn't take anymore. "I've missed you so much. Never leave me again."

"My bear, make me yours."

My body was close already. Alex seemed like he was right there with me. His thrusts were erratic and his grip on my thighs punishing. I tilted my head to the side, inviting him to claim me. I wanted to be tied to him forever.

Alex let out a roar louder than anything I'd ever heard and then sank his teeth into my neck. Stinging pain lasted for only a second before blinding pleasure filled me and I tumbled into the strongest orgasm of my life. I ripped my nails across his back as the pleasure shook me. Alex jerked into me once more before I felt his seed filling me.

I felt him licking my neck but my head was so light that it just rolled back. My body felt like all my bones had been removed. I slumped against the tree behind me and mumbled his name.

Alex held me tight in his arms and lowered us both to the ground. He laid me on his chest and held me tight. "It's okay, little one."

I lost track of how much time we'd been there, recovering, but the night had fallen without my knowledge. I idly played with Alex's hair and pressed kisses against his chest.

"How do you feel?"

I lifted my tired head to stare at him and gave him a satisfied grin. "Like I should've stayed here three months ago and kept doing that."

He grunted. "I should've tied you up and made you stay."

I flicked my tongue over his nipple. "You should've, mate."

Alex hardened under me and shifted us so that I was straddling him. "Are you too tired?"

I grabbed him and then lowered myself onto him, filling myself with my mate. "Never."

He reached up and filled his hands with my breasts. "I love you like this. Ride me, Elizabeth."

Who was I to deny my mate? I leaned over him and kissed him long and hard. "I love you, bear."

"Always."

THE END

RANCHER BEAR'S MAIL ORDER MATE

RANCHER BEARS BOOK 2

Matt Long has had a hell of a six months. Hiding out like a hermit in the little cabin at the top of the mountain, fighting with his brothers, drinking himself under the table, and sleeping all day. When he isn't roaming the woods as his bear, Matt is wallowing in misery and guilt.

Running out of time, and with a nasty ex literally nipping at her heels, Leila Harold makes a desperate move. She bribes her way into Beatrix's Buxom Beauties, a mail-order bride service. She just needs a way out of town. But, when Leila opens the door to the small cabin deep in a pine forest in Landing, Wyoming, instead of finding her intended, she comes face to face with a giant grizzly bear. Lovely.

Matt had forgotten all about the mail order bride website. It was a drunken mistake. He tries to scare her away with his bear, but she just seems more annoyed than anything. She's not new to the shifter game.

Both, however, are new to the magnetic pull of finding one's true mate. They try to fight it, but it's no use.
Not even a cranky bear like Matt can run true love away.

1

LEILA

I was wearing the same clothes that I'd worn the day before. Jeans and a thick sweater that'd seen better days. My hair was dirty and hanging limply from a ponytail. I hadn't touched makeup in years, so every dark circle and bag was clearly displayed, without a trace of concealer to hide behind. What I'd give for a stick of concealer. What'd I'd do for a chance at a hot shower.

"Next stop, Landing. Two hours until arrival." The bus driver announced over the static filled speaker system. He glanced at me through the rear view mirror and shook his head. "Sure you're okay, lady?"

I hugged myself tighter and nodded. "Never been better."

It was the truth, and wasn't that just the saddest thing ever? Two years earlier, I would've seen that bus as a big doom wagon. What a thing perspective was. That bus was a freedom wagon, carrying me straight to another chance at life.

I knew nothing about Landing, Wyoming, except that there was a man there named Matt Long who was desperate for a wife. My stomach twisted, but I knew that no man could be as bad as my ex. Even if Matt Long was a balding man who wore gold chains and referred to me as his bitch, he'd be better than my ex.

I stood up and made my way to the bathroom at the back of the bus. The only other person who'd gotten on the bus in Cheyenne had gotten off earlier in the trip, so I had no competition. The tiny room smelled like death and I prayed the smell didn't stick to me.

My reflection in the small mirror was sad and pitiful. The last fight I'd had with my ex showed in ghost-like prints across my neck and throat. A bite mark here and five finger impressions there. A real standup guy, he'd been. I pulled the sweater higher and tried to imagine myself as a beautiful bride arriving to meet her new husband for the first time.

Everything was wrong with the picture. Matt Long had ordered a bride. Instead of that bride, *I* was showing up. A beat down, beat up, smelly mess of a woman who'd bribed her way into a mail-order bride service last minute. The poor man.

I'd been on the run through a small town in Southern Louisiana when I'd stumbled across Beatrix's Buxom Beauties. The sign in the window read that she arranged long distance marriages and I'd rushed right in. Beatrix turned out to be a seventy-year old woman who didn't get many calls. She'd been more than willing to talk to me all about her latest bachelor.

Matt was a rancher from Wyoming who needed a wife to settle some family issue, but he was open to love. It'd taken Beatrix a while to find someone young enough for him, but she'd finally settled on a woman named Maggie. Maggie was a few years older than Matt, but she loved the country and had once owned a cow.

Beatrix was also ready to retire. I had twenty thousand dollars in my bag that I'd stolen from my ex when I'd left. I offered her half to replace Maggie. She'd given me a plane ticket and instructions on which bus to take once I'd reached Cheyenne and sent me on my way.

It had been dumb luck showing up there when I did. As I was leaving, the real Maggie appeared to get her plane ticket. I'm not sure what excuse Beatrix gave her; I didn't stick around to find out. It felt a little like fate. I'd walked into the perfect situation, at the perfect moment. Perhaps it was a sign that my luck was about to change.

I'd tossed the plane ticket in the nearest dumpster and had gotten on a bus right away. The trip was longer and harder that way, but it wouldn't leave a trace.

I turned away from my reflection and went back to my seat. There wasn't time enough to spend in any bus bathroom that would make me look more like Maggie Stevens, excited bride to be. I hugged my knees to my chest and settled in. Maggie, or not, I was about to land in Matt Long's lap.

2

LEILA

"**G**ood luck out there."

I nodded to the bus driver. "Thanks. Have a good one."

He drove back the way we'd come and slowly disappeared from sight. I looked around at the town and took in a refreshing breath of crystal clean air. It was fresh, but ice cold and I immediately started shivering, but the air was cleaner than anything I'd smelled in the past two days. By far.

The bus stop was in the middle of a tiny town, surrounded on one side by mountains and the other by a rolling river. Tall pines grew up around the place like a comforting blanket. I instantly felt safer than I had in longer than I could remember.

A woman walking down the street cast me a strange sideways glance and hurried past. I shrugged and looked around a bit more, after remembering that I was supposed to be meeting my new fiancé.

I spent the next couple of hours walking up and down Landing, going into stores, and asking around. No one would tell me anything. In fact, the town was so secretive, you would think that *it* was running from a dangerous ex, instead of the other way around. I was about to give up and rent a motel room for the night when a woman drove by in a pickup truck and stopped for me.

"You lost?" She tossed her blonde hair over her shoulder and sent a sweet smile my way.

"Do you know who Matt Long is?"

Her eyes narrowed and she blew out a sigh. "Unfortunately. You looking for him?"

Worry edged its way into my stomach. "Yeah. Should I not be?"

She pushed open the passenger side door and motioned for me to get in. "I'll take you to his cabin. There's no reason for you to be standing out there in the cold."

I climbed in and held out my hand to her. "Maggie. Thanks for the lift."

"I'm Elizabeth. I saw you making your way around town. The townsfolk can be pretty closed off to newcomers."

I stared out of the window as she drove towards the mountain. "Yeah, I noticed. It was nice to see your friendly face."

"I was new here not too long ago. I definitely understand. So, why are you looking for Matt?"

I looked back over at her and tried not to feel threatened by the question. Living with my ex had taught me to be distrustful of even the simplest of questions. "We... have some business to take care of."

She laughed. "You sound like you'll fit right in here. Maybe you can get the giant stick out of Matt's ass while you're at it. He's been a big bear lately."

"Why?"

"Just natural for him, I guess. The family's been going through some changes and he's been locked away in his cabin for months. Probably up there ranting and raving." She looked over at me and rolled her eyes. "I'm sure he's a nice guy, under all the broody bullshit, but I haven't had the privilege of witnessing it yet."

I sighed. As long as Matt wasn't a hands on kind of guy, like my ex, we would be fine for as long as I needed to stay there. It did suck that he was apparently a cranky hermit. Maybe, somewhere deep in the back of my mind, I'd hoped for a kind, generous, handsome guy to welcome me to my new home. Reality check.

I couldn't make sense of why a cranky hermit would invite some strange woman into his home. It did explain why he hadn't been there to pick me up, though.

Elizabeth dropped me off at the end of the driveway with a good luck and a promise to get together later if I was still in town. I waved her away and made my way to the front door.

"Here goes nothing." I blew out a breath and knocked on the heavy wooden door.

3

LEILA

A loud roar sounded from inside the cabin before the door flew open to reveal a huge bear, easily the largest bear I'd ever seen, standing on its hind legs. It growled and stared down at me through two beautiful, glowing, golden eyes. Its dark brown fur was ruffled and messy, and it looked dirty and unkempt even for a wild animal. The creature might have been in worse shape than even me.

I took a deep breath in and then blew it out slowly while putting my hands on my hips. "You're shitting me."

The bear took a step closer and huffed, sending little tendrils of spit flying at me.

I reached up and swatted its nose before stepping around it and letting myself into the house. "I don't appreciate being spit on, you big idiot. I should've known something was up when Elizabeth called you a bear. Just my luck. Just my freaking luck. Run from a gator and end up with a bear. What are the chances?"

"Who the fuck *are* you?"

I turned around, remembering too late that, of course, once he'd shifted back he'd be naked. Standing in front of me was *a lot* of really, really hot naked human male flesh. My body immediately responded to his well-built, large, muscular frame, raw lust building in me so fast that my cheeks turned red. "Maggie. And you're Matt Long, I'm guessing. Matt *very* Long." *Did I just say that out loud?*

He growled and grabbed a faded cowboy hat from the hook on the door beside him to cover his junk with. "Why are you in my fucking house?"

"Because you signed up for a wife. Voila, here I am." I waved my arms down the length of my body in a gesture meant to imply that this is what one gets when one orders a wife sight unseen. "I'm going to take a shower now. It's been a long couple of days and I need to get washed up."

He blocked the way into the only other room in the small place. "No way in hell. I signed up for that shit nearly eight months ago. No one told me they were sending me something."

"*Something*? I'm a person, not a thing. Check your email, buddy. Now, I'm going to be using that shower. Unless you want to pull out your little bear claws and try to stop me."

He let me pass, finally, and I breathed out a sigh of relief. That'd been my test to find out if he was going to be anything like my ex. I was still trembling from my act of false bravado, but it seemed like this Matt guy, despite the grumpiness, was cut from a different cloth than my ex. Thank god. Otherwise, I might've found myself with deep bear claw gashes across my back.

4

MATT

What the fuck just happened? And who just walked into my house?

I stared after her, unable to take my eyes off of the way her ass filled out those fortunate jeans. She smelled slightly of sweat and something worse, but under that, I could smell a sweet vanilla scent that had called my bear right to the surface even before she'd knocked on my front door.

Maggie? Jesus. What had I done?

I opened up the laptop I hadn't touched in months and jabbed at the little keys until my email opened. Sure enough, Beatrix had sent me several emails about my new bride arriving. Beatrix, the same woman who couldn't find me a single damn woman under the age of fifty when I desperately needed one to claim the family ranch as my inheritance. Beatrix, the woman who I'd trusted to help me through the loophole in my father's damned will.

I slammed the laptop closed and threw it across the cabin. "Shit!"

The last thing I wanted was a bride. I wanted to be left alone. I didn't need a woman sniffing around my place, complicating things. Why can't people just leave me the hell alone? I couldn't say it enough. Can't a man suffer in peace?

I paced around my cabin, waiting to hear the shower shut off. She'd been in there for too damn long. I hadn't even used the thing in months. I swam in the creek behind the cabin to clean off. I doubted there was even soap in there.

She hadn't been afraid of me. At all. She was all human and she'd had the audacity to slap me on the nose, like I was some toy poodle. And to top that off, my bear hadn't even minded. The wild beast had been insane and uncontrollable for months, yet when a little human woman shows up, bear practically just rolls over on his back and presents his belly to her.

I yanked the fridge door open and glared into it. Nothing. I'd been living mostly as bear, so I ate in the woods. There wasn't even a single morsel of food in the place. *Good.* She couldn't stay if there wasn't any food. Not that I was going to allow her to stay anyway. I'd pay for her ticket back home and wash my hands of her. I hadn't signed any contract. I didn't have to keep her.

She walked out of the bathroom at that moment, wearing nothing but a too-small towel. Her long legs were still damp and tiny droplets of moisture clung to her smooth, creamy skin. Her hips tugged the towel apart at the side and revealed even more leg to my hungry eyes. Her dark, damp hair hung down past her shoulders, curling around her chest in ringlets, drawing my attention to the plump orbs being pushed up by the towel.

Clean and fresh, she had my bear coming to the surface. I could feel the fur pushing to erupt on my arms and chest and I had to grit my teeth and fight to keep the change from happening. Her smell was intoxicating. Her sweet vanilla-like natural aroma called to my bear in a way unlike anything I'd ever experienced. What the hell was happening to me?

She cocked her hip to the side and stared at me, a pink tinge creeping up over her face. "You didn't put clothes on."

I looked down and spotted my dick proudly standing at attention in front of me. With a frustrated growl, I went ahead and shifted, letting my bear take control of me. I was more comfortable as a bear lately anyway and with a scantily clad woman in my home, I figured it was time to take off into the woods again. Bear growled something at me, but I ignored him. I huffed at her and moved to the door.

"Oh, no you don't." She blocked the doorway and wagged her finger at me. "We should talk. I'm supposed to be engaged to you. You can't just leave."

I growled low in my throat and used my nose to nudge her away from the door. Only, my bear didn't seem to want to leave her. He kept his head next to her, breathing in her scent.

She actually giggled and rubbed the top of my head. "You're cute like this. Much better than a mean old gator. Your fur is soft, too. Like a puppy I had once when I was little."

First off, *cute?* Lady, a 400 pound grizzly is *not* cute. Second, neither of us liked being compared to a dog, so we growled. Loud. Like a bear.

She rubbed behind my ears and grinned at me. "Okay, no dog references. Got it."

I rubbed against her side again, enjoying the way I felt in her presence. Calm. Soothed. Damned if my bear was putty in her hands. He grunted happily when she rubbed us and was almost as bad as a puppy.

"You're sweeter as a bear. Much sexier as a man, though. I'd like it if you changed back so we could talk."

My body acted on its own accord. Within a blink of an eye, I was man again, kneeling at her feet, with my face buried against her stomach. Her hands were still in my hair, pulling softly through the messy strands. I looked up at her and my heart started racing. I finally cued into what my bear was chanting and froze. Over and over bear was saying it.

Mate.

Running out on her wasn't my finest moment, but, I don't know, I just freaked out. I was bear again before I even stepped paw off my porch. I ran deep into the woods, despite my bear's will protesting, and vowed to stay away until the human woman left.

I didn't need a woman. I didn't want a woman. Most of all, I didn't think I could be with a woman. I'd become more beast than man.

Hell, I wasn't sure she'd even be safe with me.

5

LEILA

It hadn't taken me long to run the man off, that was for sure. I certainly had a gift where the opposite sex was concerned. I got dressed in one of his flannel shirts and the same jeans I'd arrived in before searching his cabin for food. He had absolutely nothing. I found his truck keys sitting under a few weeks of mail on the counter, though. If he wasn't going to stay home and talk to me, I'd just have to figure some things out on my own.

Mostly, I needed to get away from his scent for a while. My heart was beating like I'd just run a marathon, and my downstairs hadn't dried since I laid eyes on him. Weird. I was reminded of whisperings I'd heard about similar reactions.

While with my ex, Steven, I'd learned lots of things that had, at the time, made my head swim. Like the fact that shifters even existed at all. I didn't realize there were so many different types, either. But I had learned a thing or two about them, none the less. Steven and his family were alligators and they were as mean as the day was long. There was no sense of humanity in them that I'd ever seen.

They'd talked as though all other shifters were pussies compared to gators, and I'd been around enough to know that not all shifters were like Steven and his family. It was the only reason I hadn't run screaming when Matt opened the door.

I'd also heard a little about shifter mates. Women had once in a while whispered about shifters having true mates, others who they were fated to pair up with. Mates found one another through fate. The reaction between mates was sometimes, but not always, supposed to be instantaneous. Attraction like no other and 'love at first sight' was the phrase many women had used. A mated pairing was highly regarded and respected amongst shifters. I had thought it was a load of crap at the time.

After meeting Matt, I wasn't so sure. Something definitely took over my psyche today. While stroking Matt's bear's fur, I had experienced a warmth and serenity unlike any I'd ever felt before. I was enveloped in an indescribable feeling of safety and comfort, enough to want to curl up beside his bear and sleep. That was his bear; when he was man, I wanted to jump his bones. One large one, especially.

Matt hadn't reacted to me the same way, though. There were no sweet murmurings or holding each other. In fact, he'd run out of there so fast, it was almost as though his ass was on fire. Definitely not 'love at first sight'.

I tied his shirt at the waist so it didn't look ridiculous on me and then hurried through the cold to his truck. I had my own money and I needed a few things if I was going to set up camp in his cabin. And, I was definitely going to set up camp. Beatrix had done me a giant favor, sending me to Matt Long. I wasn't going to waste the opportunity.

Main Street in Landing didn't have a whole lot of options when it came to clothes, but I managed to find a little country western store that sold jeans, boots, and such. I bought some clothes from an older woman who just kept giving me dirty looks, and changed into a pair of clean jeans in a bathroom inside a little general store.

I bought canned goods and a few jugs of water, along with multiple bags of candy and chips to snack on before going back to Matt's cabin.

Matt was still gone when I got back, so I put my stuff away in his dusty cabinets and went in search of entertainment. When I found none, I just made myself at home in the middle of his bed and stuffed my face with a bag of gummy bears before falling asleep.

I woke up to a huge grizzly bear head hovering over me. My heart leapt into my throat and my body entered fight or flight mode before remembering that I was staying in the cabin belonging to a bear. "You gave me a damn heart attack! What are you doing?"

After a few seconds of his huffing and grunting, I reached up and caught his massive snout in my hands. "I don't speak bear. Turn back and we can talk."

Almost immediately, I had a very human, very naked, Matt kneeling beside me. I sat up so I had a leg on either side of him, his face was still in my hands. "Hi."

He looked up at me, through golden eyes, and grunted. His brown hair hung down to his shoulders, and he was bearded. I got the impression he hadn't worried about personal grooming for some time. He was at least a half foot over six feet tall and wide with thick, corded muscle. The man would've caused a riot of lust in any red-blooded woman, but the way my body was reacting had me wondering again about the whole fated mates thing.

His face looked almost innocent, despite the full beard, as he gazed up at me. He just stared at me, unmoving and eerily calm.

I stroked his cheeks and smiled. "You get tired of playing in the woods?"

With a shake of his head, he frowned and scooted away from me. "You're in my bed."

I grinned at him and nodded. "Our bed. Didn't you hear? We're getting hitched."

6

MATT

I stood up and reached into my closet to get pants. I couldn't remember the last time I'd worn clothes, but considering how often my dick was hard around the insane female, I needed something to at least pretend to hide it from her. I yanked them on and then turned around to glare at her.

"We're not getting hitched. I hadn't checked that email in months. I didn't know Beatrix was sending someone and I neither need nor want a wife anymore."

Genuine pain flitted over her expression for a second before she blinked it away. Every instinct in me demanded I comfort her, and it took extreme effort to fight it.

"Doesn't matter what you want now," she snapped, "I'm here and I'm staying. Get used to it, bear."

I was under no delusions about myself. I knew I was scruffy looking, my bear was unmanageable, and I was a grumpy pain in the ass on a good day. Why in the world would a woman as hot as her want to be anywhere near me? She could have men lining up around the corner to date her. What the hell?

I pondered for a moment. She'd called bear 'cute'… and she knew about shifters. Maybe she was some sort of shifter groupie. I could show her that bear wasn't cute, and neither was I. It could work. I'd scare her into leaving. I grabbed her arms and pulled her up to face me. Instead of looking scared, though, she just grinned at me and rested her hands on my bare chest.

"Why aren't you afraid of me?"

"Because I've suffered abuse at the hands of a man. I know all about abusive men, and you, Matt Long, aren't one."

This time, I couldn't fight instinct; I wrapped my arms around her and held her tighter. "Someone hurt you?" I growled into her neck.

She shrugged. "Doesn't matter. I'm here now. Thanks to Beatrix and her Buxom Beauties. What made you choose a mail order bride service, anyway? You have a thing for buxom ladies?"

Fuck. She was teasing me and all I could think about was sliding my dick into her. I looked between us, at the space where my flannel shirt on her gaped open and her tits pressed firmly against my chest, and licked my lips. It'd been too long.

"You're poking a stick at a sleeping grizzly, lady."

She somehow managed to wiggle her body even closer to me. "What are you going to do?"

"*Who* are you?"

"Your mate."

I jerked away from her and glared. "What the fuck do you know about mates?"

"I lived with a family of gators a while back. I heard stuff about mates."

Gators? I grabbed her and swung us both around until her back connected with the wall behind her. I put my forearm across her chest and held her there. "Who the fuck sent you?"

Her eyes grew panicked and she pulled uselessly at my arm. "Stop it, Matt. No one sent me."

I stayed where I was and glared at her. "Tell me."

Tears filled her eyes and as she stretched her neck away from me, I saw bruises on her delicate skin. I moved my arm, but gently placed my fingers over the bruises. Looking over her neck, I spotted teeth marks from someone biting her. I cursed and moved across the room. "Are you already mated? What the fuck is going on?"

7

MATT

My bear roared and fur sprouted along my body. Fury like I'd never felt before overwhelmed me until I had to throw my head back and shake the cabin with a massive roar. When I looked back at her, she was already recomposed with her hands on her hips.

"My ex tried to claim me as his mate. It didn't work, though, because I'm not his true fucking mate. He just... bit me. After the first time, I guess he was humiliated, so he just kept trying. He was insane. This will fade. I'm not bonded to anyone."

Her explanation just pissed my bear off even more. "He hurt you?" What kind of an asshole would do something like that?

She surprised me by walking towards me, facing my anger, despite the slight tremble in her hands. "If you'll sit down and talk to me, I'll tell you the whole story."

Not even my brothers would dare to face me when I was in one of my moods. Here was this small human woman challenging me. My bear wanted her. Bad. He wanted me to claim her. But, I was in no shape to be anyone's mate. Besides, from the way it sounded, she'd already been through too much to have to put up with my crazy wayward bear, or my crazier human. "I'm not sure any of this is a good idea."

She crossed her arms and stared up at me. "I had planned on just coming here and hiding out for a bit before I left again. That's all changed now, though. Now I'm staying and you're going to have to deal with me. Whether you like it or not."

"Look, lady, I'm not looking for a wife. That ship has already sailed. Right into the fucking bottom of the ocean. So, that's a no go."

"What happened?"

I looked down at her big green eyes and felt myself waver. It wasn't the first time since she'd shown up that I'd felt this, but it was definitely the strongest the pull towards her had been. I could have fallen apart right in front of her like a little child whining and complaining about the way things had turned out after my dad died. About the way I hadn't ever told him how important the ranch was to me, or how grateful I'd been to have such a wonderful father. What a fucking bitch I was being. "This isn't happening. I've got to go."

She stepped to the side and ushered me out. "Go ahead, do your bear thing. I'll be here when you get back."

Instead of arguing, I stepped around her and walked to the front door. I dared a glance back over my shoulder at her, at the marks on her neck, and then left. I didn't need anything else on my plate. She deserves to be with a man who can help her through her troubles. I couldn't help her. I couldn't even help myself.

I ran through the woods, turning bear as I went, and headed straight to my brother's place. He was mated and I needed to know what level of hell I'd fallen into. There had to be a way to get out of it, and I was certainly going to try.

8

LEILA

I fell asleep in his bed that night, frustrated and hurt. I knew the hurt was stupid, because I'd just met the big idiot, but I couldn't help it. Every time he denied it and acted as though I wasn't his mate, it felt like a little piece of my heart was being trampled. I just wanted to talk to him and explain things, maybe even tell him that my name wasn't Maggie. Instead, I was alone in his cabin.

The next two days I spent waiting for him to return. Still no sign of him. My hurt had transformed into anger and I was ready to rip him a new one, giant grizzly bear or not.

I'd had my fair share of pacing the cabin alone, so I decided to visit the rodeo that I'd heard about on my trip into town to get a few more things. Normal rodeos didn't start until March or April, but shifters didn't feel the cold the same way that humans did, so they started their rodeo in cold as shit February.

I dressed in jeans, boots, one of Matt's flannels, and a sweatshirt of his. I let my hair do its natural wild tangle of curls around my head before heading outside.

I stood next to the truck for a second and looked around. I couldn't see Matt, but I knew he was there. I could sense him close by. "Hey, asshole! I'm taking your truck and I'm going to the rodeo.

Maybe I'll meet a nice guy and bring him back here, since you're not living here anymore. You won't mind, right?"

A low growl sounded from the trees but I just climbed into his truck and headed towards town. Either he'd show up or he wouldn't. I had a feeling he would, though.

I'd been to rodeos before. I'd grown up in Georgia and there'd been plenty of cowboys running around. Sitting down in the small stadium seats in Landing, though, felt different. People shied away from me and no one seemed inclined to start a conversation. Hell, even if I'd been serious about finding a man there, it would've been damned near impossible since everyone treated me as though I were a leper. Landing residents were even less trusting than I was.

I didn't let it get to me and instead, enjoyed the show. About halfway through, I sensed Matt. I could feel him when he showed up. The whole crowd seemed to go still and when I looked over, he was standing at the end of my row of seating, fully dressed and looking about as delicious as a man could possibly look.

He was dressed in jeans and a flannel. He'd shaved to reveal a chiseled jawline, and he'd cut his hair. He looked incredibly edible, instead of like the wild man I'd first met. He slowly made his way over to me and sat down stiffly avoiding eye contact and staring straight ahead. "You took my favorite shirt *and* my truck."

I stood up and started shrugging out of his coat. "Hold this. I'll just take this off and you can have it back. No harm done."

Matt grabbed me and pulled me back down. "Keep your fucking clothes on, woman."

"Leila. My name is Leila."

He snapped his head in my direction and frowned. "You said your name was Maggie. The emails said your name is Maggie. What's the deal?"

I ignored him and reached up to run my fingers through his shorter hair instead. "You clean up real nice, cowboy. I won't lie and say that I didn't like the wild look, but this is hot as Hades."

He glared down at me. "Why do you insist on antagonizing me?"

Seeing him show up for me emboldened me. I leaned up and

nipped at his earlobe. "Because negative attention from you is better than no attention at all."

Matt's hand landed on my thigh and he squeezed. "I don't have a lot of control, Leila. I haven't been out in a while."

Over the show, and over pretending like I wanted anything more than for him to handcuff me to his bed, I stood up and looked down at him. "Let's go home, then. I'll tell you everything on the way and then, when we get there, you can punish me for being a bad girl and telling you that my name was Maggie."

He looked like he wanted to argue, but I'd worked his nerves enough that he didn't. "This is a bad idea."

I caught his hand and grinned. "Fine then. You can call me Maggie and I'll be your good little school girl. Whatever you want. Just take me home, bear."

9

MATT

I sped up the mountain like the idiot I was. I kept telling myself that I needed to stay away from her, she deserved better than some fuck up with a broken bear, but no matter how many times I said it to myself, I couldn't escape her. She was like kryptonite. I'd spent two days hiding in the woods to avoid her, while never straying more than fifty feet from her, except the vague chat with my brother.

I spent two days sleeping on a pile of leaves to keep myself from being in the cabin with her. I was afraid of making some dumb mistake. Like claiming her. My bear wanted nothing more than to sink his teeth into her beautiful flesh and mark her so the world would know who she belonged to. Bear was relentless, too. He knew she belonged to us. He was pissed at me for hiding from her.

That wasn't that unusual, though. I'd spent years with my bear pissed at me, but I was in control then. I'd spent way too much time in an office, focused on money, and bear had eventually stopped talking to me. It was only in the months after dad died when I'd been avoiding everyone had bear started coming out again. And when he showed up again, he did so with a vengeance. He no longer accepted being pushed down and ignored and I had to appease him by suppressing the human form for months before we came to somewhat of a truce. I was still broken, but my bear didn't hate me anymore and I'd gotten better and faster at the shift than I ever had been.

My bear definitely wasn't quiet now as I swerved around a car that was going too slow and pushed on the gas pedal even harder. He was as eager to claim his mate as I was to be alone with Leila.

I shot a look over at her. She was slipping out of the jacket she'd been wearing. "What are you doing?"

She grinned. "Getting undressed. Are you going to ask me any questions?"

I tried to focus on the road but it was damned near impossible. I had to ask her about her name, though. I needed to find out who the hell she really was. "Who are you?"

She started unbuttoning the flannel and turned to face me. "Leila Harold. Born and raised in Peachpit, Georgia. I spent the last couple of years on a compound full of gator shifters. I dated the wrong guy and ended up getting trapped. After I knew what they were, Steven wouldn't let me go. Last month, I stole lots of his money while he was away on business and escaped. I was on the run when I found Beatrix and her Buxom Beauties. I gave her half of that money so I could pretend to be Maggie and have a way out of the south and a place to lay low for a while."

I stopped the truck in the middle of the road and slowly turned to face her. "What?"

"Yeah. Me ending up at your doorstep was a fluke. I had no clue you were going to be a shifter or that we'd have any kind of connection. I wasn't even planning on sticking around for longer than I had to."

"He held you *captive*?" My blood boiled and I felt the urge to rip something apart with my bare hands. I punched the dash, cracking the heavy plastic, and then pulled my hands down my face roughly. It was still hard to control my anger these days. "Where is he?"

She shrugged her shoulder and my shirt slid down, revealing a smooth satiny shoulder. The marks were faded and I knew in a few more days, they'd be completely gone. "I don't know. Probably looking for me down there somewhere. I'm sure he's pissed and wants to kill me. He can't trace me, though. Beatrix was the only person who knew where I ended up and she said that she was closing up shop and moving to California to be near her grandkids after I gave her the money."

I felt myself starting to turn and held on tight to the steering wheel willing bear to stay buried inside. Leila scooted over next to me and wrapped her arms around my neck. She was too close. She could get hurt if I couldn't control bear and stop the shift. "Get back!"

She just tightened her grip and pressed her mouth against the side of my neck. "No. You're okay."

My bear instantly settled and my dick turned to stone. I sucked in a big breath and turned to face her. A human female with that much power over me wasn't something I'd ever thought possible, but here she was. "You're going to tell me all about this ex later."

"After," she grinned.

I started driving again. "After."

She visibly shuddered and undid another button on the shirt. I hadn't planned on letting things between us get this far, but hearing her threaten to bring another man home had enraged me. Bear was crazy and demanded that I claim her so she couldn't. I was still at odds with bear on most things and had to fight him the entire way to the rodeo. He wanted to run there and scoop her up. He believed her fully and knew that she was our mate. I was slower on the take. The more I sat next to her, though, and the more I felt the connection. I was a goner. The only reason we weren't already pulled over on the side of the road, was because I hadn't been with a woman in a long while and I was slightly worried about hurting her.

I slid the truck into its spot in front of my house and pulled Leila out with me through the driver's side. She squealed as I did and then wrapped all of her limbs tightly around me.

I pushed open the cabin door and then kicked it shut before carrying her over to the bed and dropping her on it. After I did, I backed away and sat at the kitchen table, facing her. I needed a second to calm down or I would hurt her.

"Come here."

I shook my head. I was nervous. My brother, Alex, had tried to convince me that having a mate was the best thing that ever happened to him, but I wasn't so sure. I didn't know this woman. Hadn't even known of her existence a few days ago. How could I trust what seemed like such a good thing when everything in my life had turned to shit?

She stood up and slowly unbuttoned her shirt before opening and revealing that she wore nothing underneath. Her bare breasts called to me and my mind went blank. How the fuck was I supposed to question something like that?

She tossed the shirt at my head and then grinned at me. "Come, bear. I want to play."

I was on my feet in nanoseconds, moving to her. "You're a tease."

"I don't tease. *You're* the tease. You hid from me and only came out when I threatened to bring another guy back here."

I growled low in my throat and reached for her. When she sidestepped me and all I got was a wisp of her hair, I moved faster and caught her in my arms with her back to my chest. "No other guys. Ever again."

She wiggled her body against my dick and laughed. "You're fast."

"It's the bear. When you run, it increases the need to chase." I buried my nose in her hair and breathed her in, delicious. I had a sweet tooth, like most bear shifters, and her vanilla scent with an underlying hint of honey was scrumptious.

"So, if I ran, you'd chase?" She dropped out of my grip and then sprinted out of the front door.

My dick hardened even more, even though it hardly seemed possible. I sprinted after her, feeling a need for her that surpassed any I'd ever felt before. She circled the side of the house and raced through the back yard, heading towards the woods. I cut her off and she ran back towards the front of the house. I kept close enough that she could feel me closing in, but I didn't grab her until she was just outside of the front door.

She turned to see how close I was and I was on her. I tackled her to the floor of the cabin, spinning to make sure she landed on top of me. "Got you."

Her wild laugh was like cupid's arrow to the chest. I rolled us so that she was under me and then I kissed her to stifle it. Except, the plan backfired because feeling her lips on mine dug the arrow in even deeper. I was fucked.

10

LEILA

I opened my mouth to Matt's kiss and gave as good as he was giving. He tasted like wild berries and horny man and it drove me a little crazy. I ran my hands through his hair and held him to me, desperate for more.

Kissing down the side of my neck, he growled out my name and raked my sensitive skin with his teeth. I moaned and lifted my hips, needing to feel him against me.

I jerked at his shirt until the buttons snapped off and went flying across the room. Without hesitation, I pushed his shirt off of his shoulders and down his arms. "Too many clothes."

He sat up and jerked the shirt off the rest of the way and then reached for my boots. He threw them over his head and then grabbed the button to my jeans, before freezing.

I looked up at him and saw that he was staring at my chest. A breast man? I cupped my large breasts in my hands and teased my nipples for him. The feeling was magnified under his inspection. Arching my back, I presented myself to him, feeling dizzy with lust.

Matt's eyes turned gold, glowing and I watched his hands turn more bear than man. He used his massive claw to rip the front of my jeans open. Then, with his hands back to man, he pushed them farther down.

"Hey! Those were expensive."

He lowered his head to take one of my nipples into his mouth and then scraped his teeth over it. "I'll buy you two more."

I moaned. "Matt!"

He devoured my chest, going from side to side, tasting and teasing me until I thought my head would explode from the building pressure. Only when I'd begged him did he trail kisses lower down my belly. He ripped my jeans the rest of the way off of me and then buried his face against my core. His mouth turned me into mush in a matter of seconds.

I gasped as he spread my legs even wider and used his tongue to fuck me. I'd never been treated to such an exquisite thing in my life and it took no time for the sensations to build, getting closer and closer to a massive orgasm.

Matt gave attention to my clit, sucking it into his mouth as he pushed two fingers into me and started an unforgiving rhythm. He twisted his tongue over me and then curled his fingers.

My toes curled and I fell into an orgasm that was so powerful it almost hurt. I cried out and dug my hands into his shoulders, trying anything to stay grounded when I felt like I was going to shoot straight to the moon.

When I stopped shaking, Matt lifted his glistening face and licked his lips before flashing me a grin that sent a jolt to what felt like my very soul. It was the first time I'd seen him smile and I knew right then and there that nothing would ever be the same again. I was his. I now belonged to Matt Long, through and through.

"You taste so sweet. So fucking delicious. I could taste you all day."

As promising as it sounded, I ached for him to be inside me. I scooted out from underneath him and climbed to my feet. "Pants off, cowboy."

He looked up at me and groaned. "Fuck."

I flushed, realizing that he was getting quite the eye-full. I put my hands on my hips anyway, and gave him an impatient look. "Up."

Matt jumped to his feet and easily pushed his pants down. He kicked off his boots and the pants followed. Then, standing naked in front of me, he grinned again and reached for me.

I wanted my chance to worship at the altar of Matt, so I dropped to my knees in front of him and took his large erection in my hands. I sucked in a breath when I saw his eyes once again flash the golden glow.

"You don't have-"

I opened my mouth and took in his shaft, effectively cutting him off. I stroked the inches that I couldn't taste and started what I hoped was the best blow job he'd ever received. I moaned in pleasure. Pleasing him felt almost as good as him pleasing me.

Before I got too far along, Matt grabbed me and pulled me to my feet. He kissed me again, the taste of our juices mingling together, before pushing me towards the bed. "Now."

My excitement soared and I fell against the soft mattress. I started to turn, but Matt was already behind me, using his knee to widen my stance. His fingers pushed into me and I moaned. "Matt, I need you."

He replaced his fingers with the head of his dick and then pushed into me in one solid stroke. My knees buckled from the pleasure of feeling him in me, but he wrapped his arm under my hips and held me firmly in place.

"Fuck, you feel perfect. So good." Matt groaned as he pulled out and then slid back into me.

I dug my fingers into the bedding and cried out my pleasure. I was louder than I'd ever been and couldn't even stop to think about whether or not I was embarrassing myself.

He thrust into me over and over again, fast and then slow, slow and then fast. He pushed me towards the edge and then pulled back so I wouldn't come yet.

I lost track of time, sense of where we were, and even who I was as he continued his movements over me. He surrounded me, never breaking contact. His free hand stroked over my back, tugged at my hair, toyed with my nipples. His mouth nipped at my back and teased my skin. Every part of him branded me until I felt like one giant exposed nerve ending.

When his thrusts did get more erratic, he dropped his hands to my clit and circled it while he whispered against my ear that he wanted me to come on him. The mix of everything pushed me over the edge and I came harder than ever. My toes curled and I ripped the blankets off the bed as I jerked. White hot orgasm washed over me, spilled out of me, and turned me liquid.

Matt came with me as I squeezed tighter around him. He sank his teeth into my neck as he came inside of me. The feeling made my own orgasm last longer and caused it to be even stronger.

I collapsed forward on the bed and Matt followed. Our skin was slick with sweat as he adjusted himself to make sure he wasn't suffocating me. My breathing was wild and in those post-climax moments, I didn't feel like it would ever go back to normal.

11

MATT

I shifted our bodies so that we were laying the right way in the bed and held her against my chest. I'd lost control and claimed her. I'd lost control and hadn't used a fucking condom. I rested my forearm over my eyes and blew out a big breath. I was waiting on the panic to hit. Surely, I'd feel some. I'd realize that I'd fucked up and I'd want to beat the shit out of myself. Leila had fallen asleep with her head on my chest.

I looked down at her and found myself smiling. It didn't make any sense. I'd run away from my own family and hadn't even ventured into town for months. I even ate as bear to avoid it. I'd holed up in the cabin like a hermit wanting nothing but quiet and time to figure out how to control my bear. And my anger. I'd been so angry over the whole thing with Dad's will and the ranch ending up in Alex's hands. Not just the ranch, but my identity. Isolation was supposed to be a way for me to fucking find myself.

Yet, somehow I hadn't found a damned thing until Leila. I'd heard Dad talk about fate bringing a shifter's mate before. He'd ended up with Mom by a stroke of fate, he'd always said. I'd just never bought into the fairytale.

Looking down at Leila, though, recognizing the way my heart

beat for her, I had to think that maybe I'd been wrong all along. Hell, there was no maybe. I'd marked her as my own. She was mine, just as I was hers.

I was worried about how she would react when she realized that I'd claimed her without permission. She had been the one to say it out loud. She told me that first day that she was my mate, but we hadn't talked about claiming. I hadn't been able to help it. Alex told me that he'd had a hard time fighting it, but he'd been able to. I guess I'd just been living with a broken bear for too long. There were times when I could not control the beast.

Leila sighed in her sleep and wrapped her arm over my chest. She buried her face against my side and squeezed me.

A slow grin spread across my face as I realized that as hard as I tried, there was no denying destiny. Leila had belonged to me from the day she arrived, the moment she swiped bear on the nose and stepped around him into the cabin and into my heart.

I'd never stood a chance against her.

12

LEILA

When I woke up, Matt was knocked out beside me. I grinned up at him and slowly edged my way out from under his grip. I'd barely made it out of the bed when he grabbed my arm and hauled me back into it, on top of him.

"Where do you think you're going?"

I giggled and tried to stand up again. "Bathroom."

He kissed me, long and hard, before releasing me. "Hurry back."

I peed and then brushed my teeth. When I made it back to bed, Matt was sitting with his back against the headboard and the sheets pulled up to his waist. I slid under the covers and cuddled into his side. "It's freezing in here."

"Yeah, we might've left the front door open in our haste last night. I just shut it."

I looked over at the closed door and frowned. "So much for privacy."

"Just be glad it didn't happen on the side of the road. I barely got us back here."

I tossed my leg over his and straddled him. Our naked bodies rubbed together as I settled in. "Hi."

He looked like he wanted to stay stoic but then he laughed. The sound sent a jolt of energy straight to my core and the transformation of his face made him look even sexier. I rested my hands on his shoulders and kissed him.

"I have to tell you something that might piss you off."

I grimaced. "I guess it's only fair. *I've* been trying to piss *you* off for days."

He ran his fingers down my neck, causing an erotic chill to arch down my body. "I might have claimed you in the moment last night."

I ran my fingers over the spot he'd been touching and felt the slightly raised mark. It'd already healed and was now just a raised scar-like thing. "Okay."

"You're not mad?"

I shook my head. "No way," I grinned. "This makes me feel safer. Now, you're stuck with me. Even though we're mates, I was afraid you'd still try to get rid of me."

He cupped my ass in his big hands and pulled me farther against him. "I'm still struggling with 'broken bear', but I'll never try to get rid of you. That I can promise."

I lifted my hips and then reached between us to grip him and line our bodies up. "I don't think you're as broken as you say, but I've got better things to do right now than argue with you."

∼

AFTER A MORNING SPENT ROLLING in the sheets, I got dressed and went to town to buy more food. Matt stayed in bed. It'd been quite the visual. He was still naked, the state of dress he was most comfortable in, and lounging with the blanket thrown across his middle.

I'd barely been able to resist staying and staring at him. The man was so sexy that I was almost willing to adapt to his reclusive lifestyle. Almost. I'd only recently gotten freedom back and I wasn't willing to stay in *all* the time. I'd had plenty of that with Steven.

Matt told me about a larger grocery store in the next town over, so I headed that way. I drove with the windows down and listened to an old country station. It was better than nice to be able to get out and go. Steven had been a controlling asshole and hadn't let me go anywhere after I knew about their secret. Even before that, though, I'd been regulated to only leaving home when he could come along.

I'd seen the concern flash through Matt's eyes when he thought about me going by myself, but he hadn't even vocalized it. He understood what being able to come and go as I pleased meant to me. He just kissed me and told me to hurry back. He seemed to know instinctually that it was exactly what I needed.

I found myself shopping faster than I normally would, in my excitement to get back to Matt. I made my way up and down the aisles, tossing items in my buggy as I thought of things I could make for him to impress him with my ninja cooking skills.

For the first time since I'd run from Steven, I wasn't paying attention to my surroundings. Suddenly, my buggy was grabbed and yanked with a force that stopped it in its path. I gasped and looked up, into eyes that were similar to Matt's, but different.

13

LEILA

"Who *are* you?" a gruff voice asked. The man was almost as big as Matt, and his face bore a confused look.

I stepped away and frowned. I didn't feel safe. Not at all like I had that first day with Matt. I was trembling, but tried to appear tough. "What does it matter to you?"

Elizabeth, the woman who'd given me a ride the first day, stepped out from behind him with a baby in her arms. "Jesus, Alex. Get out of her face."

I breathed a sigh of relief when I saw her and then damn near cried when I spotted the baby. I loved babies and for a while, it seemed like the dream that I might ever have one of my own was dead. Now, well, I realized that it could be a reality with Matt. I couldn't help the big smile that accompanied that thought. "Elizabeth, hi! Look at this beautiful baby! Is he yours?"

She held him out to me, despite the big guy's growl. "Would you like to hold him? He's on my short list currently. Little Connor doesn't like sleeping at night."

I wrapped my arms around him and peered down into his tiny face. He looked just like the big idiot next to us and reached up to tug on my hair. I rocked him back and forth, feeling tears well up in my eyes. "Oh, god. He's so cute."

"I know you're the one staying with Matt. His smell is all over you. I'm just curious as to how the fuck you found him. He's been locked up in that cabin for almost half a year."

Little Connor started to cry at his Dad's tone and I reluctantly handed him back to Elizabeth. "That's none of your business."

He stepped closer to me. "It is my business. He might've decided to trust you, but that doesn't mean I have to. You just dropped right out of nowhere. Our family isn't going to suddenly roll over and welcome you with open arms just because you spread your legs for Matt."

I wanted to slap the hell out of him and had to actually rationalize it all out play by play a few times before deciding that it wouldn't go well. Just as I was about to chew him out, Elizabeth beat me to it.

"Seriously, Alex? *I* dropped right out of nowhere and you didn't think twice about it. Leave Leila alone." She winked at me. "I knew you didn't look like a Maggie. Your real name got around."

He shook his head. "That's different. Matt is going through some shit. It would be easy for someone to take advantage of him, by, say, claiming they were his mate. The guy's in a vulnerable position is all I'm saying. Easily fooled."

I pulled down my collar and showed them the scars that were still fading from Steven's bites. "Turns out that you can't actually claim someone who isn't your real mate. It doesn't take. Matt and I *are* mates and I don't want or expect anything from you or your family."

Elizabeth sucked in a rough breath and then punched Alex with her free hand. "Leave her alone. Right now. And we *are* going to welcome her with open arms. We're having a birthday party for Matt's little sister tonight. Please, come."

Alex kept his eyes on my neck and then sighed. "Fine. Come. Bring my big brother if you can get him to come."

"I'll pick you up. If you want to come, that is."

A chance to meet new people and see where Matt came from? I couldn't say no. "Sure. What time?"

Alex pouted while we made arrangements and then stalked off before we were finished. Elizabeth rolled her eyes. "Men. I would ask you if Matt is this moody, but I already know he is."

I smiled and shrugged. "He is moody, but he's a good guy at heart. Maybe he can play nice with everyone tonight."

She frowned. "I seriously doubt he'll want to come. He hasn't been to a family function in a while. After everything that went down with the ranch, he just kept to himself."

I didn't pry because I wanted Matt to be the one to explain everything to me. "We'll see what we can do then, right?"

I hurried through the rest of my grocery shopping and then stopped at a department store, while still in that neighboring town. I quickly found makeup and a few different dresses to wear, as well as new shoes. I didn't want to look embarrassingly plain the first time I met all of my mate's family.

I also wasn't going to let Alex skew my view. Surely, the rest of them were nicer. I hoped.

14

MATT

I hadn't wanted to let Leila go shopping. At all, much less by herself. But, I could tell it was something she needed to do. We'd have to have the unpleasant conversation about her piece of shit ex later, so I'd know better what she needed from me. I wanted make my mate happy. My bear agreed with me, though he'd been pissed that I let her go alone.

I'd paced the cabin until I was dizzy from the incessant circles I'd been making. I thought about everything that could go wrong. Landing was full of bears and they'd all smell me on her, they'd know she was taken, but still. I'd made enemies by being an asshole. Would anyone take their anger towards me out on her?

When I heard my truck coming up the mountain, I practically ran to the door. I needed to see her to calm my bear down.

By the time she parked, I was there beside the truck, opening the door and pulling her into my arms. I held her head and took her mouth in a fierce kiss. My bear instantly relaxed, while my cock stiffened. She was my female.

I stroked my tongue over her lips and growled when she opened her mouth to me. She tasted like a little piece of heaven and I took her for all she was worth.

My hands moved down to her delicious ass and I gripped her hard, pulled her against my body so she could feel just how much I wanted her. She hooked her leg over my thigh and then I had her pinned against the side of the truck.

My bear growled and I had to pull back from Leila's kiss so I could understand what he was pissed about. Then, I got it. A faint whiff of another male came off of her.

I jerked back and growled low in my throat. "Who touched you?"

She rolled her eyes and cocked her hip out to the side while gently touching her mouth in a way that went straight to my dick. "You should recognize the scent. Your idiot brother accused me of being some sort of super spy."

I breathed in deeper and singled out Alex. Fur erupted on my arms and chest and I angrily headed towards the woods. I could be at his place in less than half an hour. I would kill him for touching my mate.

Leila grabbed my arm and clung to my back when I didn't stop moving. "Stop it, you big oaf!"

I shrugged her off and kept going.

"Ow!"

I jerked around and saw her on the ground, holding her knee. Fear overrode my anger and I rushed back to her side. "What happened?"

She reached up and wrapped her arms around me before tugging me down to the ground. She rolled on top of me and straddled me with her hands on my chest. "Nothing happened. I just needed you to stop and listen to me."

I wanted to be pissed at her manipulation tactic, but her ass was perfectly cradling my dick and it was hard to think about anything else. I caught the sides of my shirt that she was wearing and tugged. The buttons flew apart, revealing her perfect bare breasts to me.

She squealed and covered herself. "No. You've got to listen to me first."

I blew out a rough breath. There were *definitely* parts of having a mate that were difficult.

15

MATT

"I ran into Alex with Elizabeth and Connor in the store."

I growled and shook my head. "Don't say his name right now."

She gave me a flat stare. "Fine. I ran into *male* with Elizabeth and Connor in the store. Male is worried about you. He thinks that I may be taking advantage of your current state. Which, according to him, is shit."

I scowled. "Shit?"

She leaned down and nipped my chin. "His words. Not mine. I love your current state."

I lost my breath when she rotated her hips to punctuate her words. I'd had something to say, but when she did that, everything in my brain turned to sludge.

"He was an asshole, but Elizabeth is great. And Connor, oh my god. That baby is adorable. She actually invited me to your little sister's birthday party. Tonight. Both of us, actually."

"No."

She pressed her lips to my bare chest and then stood up. "Yes. I'm going. Elizabeth is going to pick me up at six-thirty, unless you want to drive me?"

I hadn't been with my family, together in a group, in a long time. I still had issues with the way things had gone down after Dad died. There was no way I was going to show up with 'broken bear' at Bailey's birthday party. Maybe I did need to go over and see everyone, but I wasn't going to interrupt her party with bullshit that was sure to arise.

"I'm not going." I climbed to my feet and headed towards the house. "You do what you want."

Something hit me in my back and I turned around to find Leila standing with a handful of pebbles she'd just picked up. She stood there, glaring at me with her shirt open, chest exposed. "Don't be an asshole."

Seeing her like that did something to me and I strode back over to her and scooped her up before she even knew what was happening. I took her into the house and we found a useful way to spend the afternoon.

∼

"Elizabeth is going to be here soon, Matt. Are you sure you're going to stay and pout around the cabin instead of being with your family and me?"

I was in bed, stretched out, gripping the sheets so hard that my fingers were going numb. Leila looked amazing. It physically hurt to turn her down, especially when she looked like that.

She stood there, her body on display in a dress that fell off her shoulder and showed a lot of skin. Skin that I wanted to taste again. Too much skin.

"It's February. Why are you wearing a dress?"

She crossed her arms and tapped the boot she was wearing on the floor. "It's a sweater dress. I'm also wearing tights and boots and I'll also wear a coat. Don't be an asshole just because you're feeling left out. I have begged you, in more ways than one, to come with me. I wear what I want, when I want. You don't ask me questions about it, either. What you could do in this situation is *come with me.* Then, you wouldn't have to stay here and worry that some other big, bad male was looking at me."

I jumped to my feet and stormed across to the door. Of course, she was right. I knew she was right. I should go with her. She was going to my family's and I was letting her face them alone. *Knowing* I was wrong didn't make it any easier to say it, or to go and face them. I shifted, letting bear take over, sand stormed out of the house, feeling frustrated with myself.

"If you're going to be a big brat and shift to avoid me, the least you could do is learn how to close the damn door!" I heard her scream at my back before I heard the slam.

I grunted and went into the woods, making use of the cave that rested a mile back from my house. I looked around at it, feeling disgusted with myself. Not just my actions, but my living habits. Leila had swept into my life like a breath of fresh air and warmed up my cabin- and my life- in a matter of days. She'd organized stuff and even brought a candle home. The fucking place felt like a home already.

Looking around the cave I stayed in when I was bear, made me snarl. It was filthy. There was even some sort of rotting fruit in one corner. I sat back, resting on my ass, and used my paw to scratch my chin. My bear was furious at me, which wasn't really that unusual. He was only happy when Leila was near.

I huffed and tried my best to be stubborn enough to sit it out but every second felt like a million years. I looked at my paws and combed out a knot of fur on my leg. Heaving out another sigh, I shook my head and stood up. I just needed to run through the woods. I went down on four legs and ran for all I was worth.

I ran straight back to the cabin. I could feel that Leila was already gone, but it didn't stop me from throwing open the cabin door, hoping to find her in my bed.

I shifted back and headed to the shower. I'd made a mistake and I was man enough to admit it. For her.

I cleaned myself and got dressed in the nicest button down I owned. I combed my wet hair back and pulled on my cowboy hat before grabbing my keys and getting in my truck.

It didn't take me long at all to reach the property line of the Long Ranch. I stopped my truck there and looked out at the land. Dad and Alex had been convinced that I'd only cared about the ranch for the money. They'd been wrong. I'd been an ass to Alex and Elizabeth when I found out the ranch was going to Alex, just because he'd knocked Elizabeth up.

Looking back, I realized I owed Elizabeth an apology. Hell, it hadn't even been Alex's fault. Somehow, I'd let Dad die thinking that I didn't care about the family business, that I was a man only concerned with money and material things. I'd somehow hidden how much I really cared about the place.

I shrugged off the feelings that settled heavy on my shoulders and drove on towards the house. Leila was inside there somewhere and I knew I belonged at her side.

I parked and walked to the front door. Without knocking, I let myself in and followed my mate's scent to the kitchen. She was standing with her back to me, helping Mom do something. She'd covered the sexy little dress with an apron and had pulled her hair into a messy ponytail.

I knew we were bonded to each other already, but seeing her like that hit me so hard in the chest that it actually hurt. I was the luckiest man in the world I just then in that very second realized that nothing else mattered. Alex could keep the ranch. It just didn't matter. It was nothing when compared to Leila.

16

LEILA

I'd arrived at the party and met Matt's family without a hitch. They'd all heard of me already, and were expecting me, so it wasn't a shock. While some of the brothers had questioning looks on their faces, Matt's mom, Carolyn, was a sweetheart. She'd been eager to have my help in the kitchen and before we knew it, the party had moved there, as we laughed and moved around each other.

Bailey stood between us, watching as we put the final touches on her cake. I'd proved to be an icing wiz and the cake looked beautiful. All of the food was finally ready and everyone was standing around waiting to eat.

"It's so cool that you know all of this stuff. Mom's cakes always look so messed up." Bailey giggled as she bumped me with her hip. "One year, it toppled over! It fell right off the plate and just landed on the floor. Icing went everywhere!"

I laughed, but then shook my head. "Sometimes, the messiest cakes taste the best. Isn't that right, Carolyn?"

She grinned at me over Bailey's head. "Sure do. I'll admit, though, that this is stunning."

I opened my mouth to reply, but suddenly the air around me felt like it was sizzling electricity. I felt my body instantly responding in excitement and blushed. He's here. I cleared my throat and rolled my shoulders, before turning around.

My heart leapt. Matt. He'd come, and he looked amazingly hot. I dropped the spatula I was holding and ran to him, unable to contain my excitement. I jumped into his arms and grinned down at his handsome face. Without a care in the world about who was watching us, I knocked his cowboy hat off of his head and kissed him with everything I had.

Matt wrapped his arms around me and kissed me back with just as much heat. His hands roamed to my ass and then farther down, to slip under my dress.

A throat cleared beside us and I pulled away, suddenly remembering where we were. My blush deepened and I forced Matt to put me down. Sure enough, everyone in the room was watching us with wide eyes.

Carolyn had a huge grin on her face. She wiped her hands and then walked towards us. Her eyes filled with tears and she stared at Matt. "Matt, honey. I'm so glad you're here."

I stepped out of the way and watched with a knot in my throat as she grabbed Matt and hugged him tight to her body. Bailey was right behind her, throwing her little body at him.

I met Matt's eyes over their heads and mouthed a 'thank you' to him. It meant everything to me that he'd come, but I could see that it meant just as much to his family. He raised an eyebrow at me and then nodded to the cake. Instead of answering him, I just grinned. I had lots of secret talents that he was going to find out about eventually.

"Damn, Leila. You know what? Maybe I was wrong about you."

I scowled at Alex. "Of course, you were, asshole."

Matt disengaged from his mother and sister and shoved his brother's shoulder. "You heard the lady. You were wrong. Don't let it happen again."

I stiffened as Alex stood up taller and puffed out his chest. The last thing they needed was a fist fight.

Alex shoved Matt back. "How was I supposed to know that she

wasn't taking advantage of you? You've been depressed and locked away for so long, we were starting to forget what you looked like. You can't blame me for being suspicious. Who would have thought that such a fine woman would fall for a sullen, salty prick like you?"

Matt shoved him back and then locked Alex's head under his arm. "Don't forget that you're still the *little* brother, Alex."

Alex sent a rib shot to Matt and then slipped out of his grip. "Yeah, I remember that you're an *old* man."

I waited with my breath frozen in my lungs to see what Matt was going to do. I wasn't stupid enough to get between the two of them. I liked all of my teeth where they were, thank you.

Matt suddenly laughed and shrugged. "Be nice to my mate. Or, I will make you remember how hard I used to kick your ass."

His smile sent tingles straight to my core and I couldn't help wrapping myself around him. I pressed my face into his chest and grinned. This man impressed the hell out of me, right and left.

"It was a mistake. Won't happen again. Everyone knows she's yours now."

I raised my head. "I'm my own. But, that's nice of you, anyway."

Matt stole a kiss. "You're mine, but we can phrase it however you like."

I gave him a growl of my own and then grinned. "I'm glad you came."

He nipped my ear and grunted. "Keep that in mind later, baby."

I laughed as Bailey faked a gag. I secretly brushed my hand over Matt's already hard dick and winked at him. "Got it covered."

∽

THE PARTY LASTED for several hours. Bailey was having too much fun for anyone to cut out early. Having Matt back seemed to make everyone feel festive. He, himself, seemed to be lighter. He laughed more and every look he sent my way was a grin or a heated one that took my breath away. As much as I was enjoying myself, I was eager to get back home with him.

By the time we were able to sneak away, it was nearly midnight. I was exhausted, but all I could think about was getting Matt out of his clothes and into bed. I wanted to wrap myself around him and stay that way for weeks.

Seeing him with his family, coming out of his shell, made me realize just how much I already cared for him. I'd never been in love before, but I damned well was now. It was scary that it happened so fast, but the feelings were there. No use ignoring them to fit some preconceived idea that I had in my head about the speed at which relationships should progress.

The entire drive back to the cabin, Matt had his free hand all over me. He'd tried to get up my dress, but my tights were in the way. I laughed at the growl he sent my way when he'd realized it.

I slipped my hand into his lap and tried to work at the button while he drove. One sharp tug at the wheel, though, and I stopped that. Turned out that touching Matt's dick directly affected his ability to keep the truck on the road. Who knew?

We got to the cabin, our frustration building until I thought we were going to implode. I wanted him so bad that I was shaking. I jumped out of the truck on my side and ran around to Matt, ready to start our night.

Matt was stock still, though, his nose lifted, taking in the night. I was about to ask him what he was doing when he shoved me to the side just as a mass flew into him, knocking him against the side of his truck.

17

LEILA

I screamed as I hit the ground hard. Matt shifted into a bear in seconds, his claws swiping at whatever was on him. I stared hard in the faint moonlight at the shifting form that was against him, slowly turning into an alligator.

I screamed again as I realized that it was Steven. Seeing his huge alligator form sent terror racing through my body. I watched in horror as his massive jaws snapped down on Matt's leg.

He rolled and dragged Matt to the ground before opening his mouth to clamp higher up on his body. Matt ripped his claws up the soft underside of Steven's massive body and blood spurted.

Steven rolled away and shifted back to his human form before taking off towards the woods. I watched as blood poured from his chest. Matt released a roar that felt like it shook the ground. He raced after Steven, his eyes glowing golden in the darkness.

I scrambled to my feet and chased after them. Nothing could happen to Matt. *Please, please don't let anything happen to Matt.* I couldn't breathe as fear clogged my throat.

Stumbling through the woods, I cried out Matt's name. If I was too late and anything happened to him, I didn't know what I'd do. I couldn't be without him.

I heard another roar and followed it, tripping and catching my hand on a sharp stick. I cried out again but didn't stop moving towards the sounds.

I found Matt's bear hovering over Steven's limp form. He snapped his head towards me, blood dripping from his mouth. I covered my mouth and turned away from the scene. I was glad with the outcome, but the dead body, mauled as it was, wasn't something I needed to keep looking at. Steven was gone. It was over.

Warm arms wrapped around me. "I'm sorry."

I leaned into him. "Don't be. He found me and he attacked you. He would have killed us both if he'd been able to."

Matt easily lifted me into his arms and carried me back to the cabin. "So, that was your ex? Nice guy."

"That was him. It's over, now, though. I don't know how he found us, Matt. I thought...I thought I'd handled it. I thought I'd hidden my tracks well enough. I'm the one who should be sorry."

He put me down on the steps and stared at me. Blood coated his naked body, but it didn't matter. It was his badge of honor. He'd proven that he was willing to fight to the death for me. He was more than I deserved. I ducked my head and noticed that his leg was bleeding and that he was holding it off the ground slightly.

I gasped and dropped to my knees so I could look at it. "He bit you. You're hurt, Matt."

He grunted. "It's not pleasant, but it'll heal soon. Stop it, Leila. You look like you're about to crumble. This wasn't your fault."

I shook my head. "It was. He was here because of me. You got hurt because of me. You had to do...*that* because of me. I'm so sorry, Matt. I'm so, so sorry."

Three massive bears ran into the clearing beside Matt's house. They roared and stood on their back legs before shifting into Matt's brothers. Alex, Michael, and John hurried to their brother's side, while also looking around.

"What happened?" Michael, the third oldest brother, asked with a wild look on his face. "It smells terrible. Like blood and... swamp."

Matt turned to me. "Why don't you go inside and get cleaned up? We have to take care of this, okay?"

I nodded and went inside, feeling worse than I could've imagined.

18

MATT

Leila turned and disappeared inside the cabin with tears still in her eyes.

I swore and turned to my brothers. Lucas was out of town, on some trip across the states, but the rest had come running as soon as they heard my call. I held out my hand and clasped each of theirs in turn. "Thanks for coming."

I told them what happened and led them to the body. I stared down at it, feeling angry all over again. He was the man who'd marked my mate. He came to try and hurt her again. He had to die. I felt no remorse for his life being lost. Shifters had their own law, and their own way of policing it. He was a sick animal and he'd been put down. Simple as that.

Michael stared down at the body with a scowl curling his scarred upper lip. "Piece of shit. He tried to mark her?"

I growled and barely held back the shift. "He did that and worse."

Alex nodded. "Then you did the right thing. Let's load him into the back of your truck and go from there."

"We'll need to be on guard for a while. Who knows if anyone will come looking for this piece of shit. I'd rather us not be caught with our pants down if they do." Michael leaned over and hefted the carcass over his shoulder. "You owe me for this."

"Consider this me owing you all one. Take his body down to the river. Leave him beside it, where the animals can find him and finish him. I've got to get back to Leila. She's convinced herself that this is all her fault."

Alex patted me on the shoulder. "Take care of her. Elizabeth informed me that if I had anything to do with running her off, she'd skin my hide and make a bearskin rug for the bedroom. It seems your mate and mine took a liking to each other. Take care of that leg, too."

I looked down at the reminder that I'd almost lost the fight because I wasn't focused. "Piece of shit caught me off guard."

"You mean with your pants literally down. Couldn't help notice that you two seemed a little eager to get home tonight."

I thumped him on the back and headed towards the house. "You're not all wrong, brother. Leave the truck back at the main house if it's easier. Thanks for this."

Alex gave me one last nod and then joined the others. I made my way inside to check on my mate. I didn't give a fuck what happened to the body of that piece of trash gator. It could've rotted behind my cabin for all I cared. I just wanted to get inside and take care of Leila.

I heard the shower running and stepped into the bathroom. The shower door was steamed up, but I could see her silhouette leaning against the wall, looking defeated. I opened the door and climbed in. "Scoot over."

She turned to face me and tears spilled down her face. "I'm so sorry, Matt."

I quickly rinsed all of the blood off of my body so it would be one less reminder for her. Then, I pulled her into my arms and held her tight. "You didn't do that. I'm glad it's over, if anything. You don't have to hide anymore. You can do whatever you want here."

She rested her cheek against my chest. "I was terrified. I don't know what I'd do without you."

I rubbed her back, soothing her. "You won't ever have to find out.

Everything's okay, Leila. How about we wash up and then go to bed? It's been a long night."

She nodded and silently grabbed a bar of soap. With shaking hands, she took her time washing me. Her eyes moved over me, taking time examining me to make sure I was okay.

My leg was already closing up and any pain was long forgotten, so it was hard for me to keep my body from responding to her movements. I didn't want to push for sex when she was upset, even if I did think it might help. I just remained silent as she washed me, happy to be tormented by my mate.

19

MATT

Leila looked up at me with wide eyes and then looked back down at my leg. "You're healed!"

"I told you I'd heal up. When are you gonna believe me? I'm okay, baby."

She seemed to deflate against my chest. "I knew it, but I just got so freaked out, Matt. I can't lose you. I love you."

Hearing the words made everything right with the world. Nothing else mattered, except being with her for the rest of my life. I could work as a farm hand at the ranch, for all I cared. As long as I got to come home and hear my mate say that she loved me, I'd die a happy man.

I picked her up and held her against me. "I love you, too, mate."

She kissed me, pinning her chest to mine. "Make me forget, Matt. I just want to think about you and me tonight."

I stepped out of the shower, and carried her to our bed. I would do anything she asked of me, but this request seemed like a gift to me.

Her body glistened as water rolled down her soft skin, marking trails that I followed with my lips. I covered her in kisses, tasting her everywhere. She writhed against me, silently asking me for more until her pleas became louder.

I buried my face between her thighs, licking and sucking her until she climaxed. I drove her to orgasm after orgasm, determined to make her forget anything but the small and intimate world that only the two of us shared.

I slipped two fingers into her body and curled them, finding the spot that made her scream when she came. Her liquid flowed freely, coating my fingers and lips. I was a happy man, content in feasting on her body for the rest of the night.

Leila eventually pushed me away, though. She clamped her legs together and used my hair to pull me up to her so she could kiss me. Her tongue slipped into my mouth and she gripped my shoulders so hard I could feel her nails digging into my skin.

"Make love to me."

I didn't need to be told twice. I wanted to be in her more than anything in the world. I settled between her thighs and slowly, carefully slid into her. Her wetness made it easier and then I was home, surrounded by her wet heat. Her body fit mine perfectly as I pulled out and pushed back in.

Leila held on to me, keeping me close as I thrust into her again and again. I kept it slower, making love to her until we were both panting and moaning. Just when I didn't think I could last a second longer, she tilted her hips and I slid deeper, hitting a new spot in her body. She cried out as another orgasm shook her body, clamping down on me.

The feeling of her body sheathing my cock was too much. I thrust into her once more and then buried myself as I came deep in her. I whispered into her neck how much I loved her as our orgasms rocked us.

20

LEILA

After a couple of days full of rolling in the sheets, earth-shattering orgasms, and whispered words of love, I felt much better. Steven was gone and my past gone with him. I didn't have to look over my shoulder any more. Matt was completely healed and everything was going to be okay.

As I spotted my mate outside, roaming in his bear form, I couldn't help but smile. Things were going to be better than okay. I'd found the man who was made just for me. I couldn't believe how lucky I was.

Landing, Wyoming and Beatrix's Buxom Beauties had turned out to be the two of the luckiest finds, and Matt Long was the most perfect man that ever walked the Earth. Perfect for me, that is.

I slipped on my jacket and walked outside to see what he was doing. He'd been going outside here or there, working on something in the shed out back.

At that moment, he was trying to pick up a two by four with his paw. He huffed and swiped at it, sending it skating across the ground a good twenty feet. He stood up straight and growled.

"Hands might work better, Matt. What are you doing?"

He spun around to face me and instantly shifted. His naked body steamed in the cold air. "Hey. I was just...cleaning up."

I raised an eyebrow and moved closer. I couldn't stay away when he was naked. Our bodies worked like magnets. I was drawn to him constantly. "Cleaning up?"

His cheeks actually turned pink. "Yeah, I was building and made a mess."

I grinned and pressed my body against his. His warmth seeped through my jacket. "What were you building, mate?"

He held me and gave me a soft kiss. "It's a surprise."

I grinned. "Is it done?"

Instead of answering, he lifted me into his arms and carried me into the shed. He put me down and moved to lift the tarp off of a big object in the corner. "Your smell changed. I know it's early, but I wanted to make this for you. We'll have to move out of the cabin and get a bigger house, too. I'll have to go back to the ranch, start working again. It'll be okay, though. I'm happy."

I'd never seen him like this, he was rambling nervously. "Matt, slow down. What are you talking about?"

He pulled the tarp off and revealed a rustic crib. "We're going to have a cub."

My knees instantly went weak and I fell into Matt's waiting arms. He sat us on the ground and held me in his lap. Tears fell from my eyes and I was instantly sobbing hysterically.

Matt took my tears to mean I was upset and tried to comfort me. "It's okay, Leila. It's a good thing. We can do this together."

I pushed him back and straddled him. "I know," I blubbered, "I'm so happy. We're going to have a baby, Matt. A baby. A cub."

"You're happy?"

I laughed and then kissed him. My heart was so full, it felt like it would burst. I deepened the kiss and held on as he rolled us over so that he was on top of me. "I am so happy, Matt. All my dreams have come true. You're going to be the best dad."

My big bad bear had a few drops of moisture in his own eyes. He kissed me again and then blew out a big breath. "I was worried there for a second."

I wrapped my arms around him and pulled him against me, taking his weight on top of me. "I am in this forever. You're everything to me. We're going to have a family, Matt. How could I ever be anything but happy?"

"Marry me."

My mouth fell open and it was my turn to stutter. "What?"

He grinned. "Marry me. Be my mate *and* my wife."

I screamed, my excitement getting the best of me. "Yes!"

We celebrated by christening the shed and scaring all the wildlife in the area away with our love sounds. I poured every ounce of strength I had into showing Matt just how much he means to me.

We ended up snapping a piece of the crib off in our excitement. Matt barely noticed and muttered about having plenty of time to fix it, and then we went back to celebrating. The way things were going, I was sure it wasn't the last time we'd break something, and I was completely okay with that.

THE END

The next book in this series is Rancher Bear's Surprise Package.

RANCHER BEAR'S SURPRISE PACKAGE

RANCHER BEARS BOOK 3

After his younger brother inherited control of the family ranch and his older brother went into hiding, Lucas Long got into his truck and hit the open road. Heading out across the country, he was on a mission. A mission to find something that may or may not even exist. After a year and a half of searching, and exhausting almost all leads, he gets an urgent phone call summoning him home ASAP.

Sammie Delaney has worked her ass off to become the tough, hardened U.S. Marshal that she is today. Her last case has left her reeling, though. When her partner and the witnesses they were in charge of protecting were murdered in cold blood, Sammie was left in charge of a frightened four-year-old boy. Only, he's not currently a boy, the kid's transformed himself into a bear cub. Sammie's vow to protect little Mason and do right by him leads her to the small town of Landing, Wyoming. Lucas Long, the man whose name was a whisper on the lips of a dying woman, is her last hope of helping little Mason. Who knew Lucas would turn out to be a hotter-than-hell bear shifter.

When Lucas arrives home to finds a woman who takes his breath away, holding a little boy who smells just like him, he instantly knows that these two are his future. But the beautiful Marshal remains unconvinced. Can Lucas find a way to not only manage a crash course in parenting, but also entice his mate to stay in Landing where their little family desperately needs her?

1

LUCAS

"Honey, you look about as awake as a dead man. Can I get you some more coffee before you go? Anything?"

I looked up at the older waitress. Her hair was a strange shade of 'bluish' and the tag pinned to her beige polyester uniform read *Blanche*. I shook my head. I'd spent enough time in the little Arkansas town, but she was right. I needed something to clear the fog that had invaded my mind.

"Make it a to-go cup, please."

I massaged my left temple and watched her walk away. I didn't have much money left in my savings account. I was traveling on fumes. Money-wise and energy-wise. I'd been on the road for months and all I'd managed to find was a sore back and a never-ending dull throb of a headache.

I dropped my head into my hands and tried to remind myself that I was doing all of it for a reason. A good reason.

"Honey, your coffee's gone cold. I'd let you nap for a while, but my boss is being an asshole. You're going to have to get a room if you want to sleep."

I jerked awake and looked around. It took a minute for my mind to process where I was. I must have dozed off for a second there.

"Poor thing. You can sleep if my car for a while if you can't afford the room."

I grunted and stood up. My legs were stiff and my back gave a painful crack before straightening. I caught a reflection of myself in the window beside me. Jesus, I looked rough.

"I've got to go. Thank you, ma'am." I pulled several bills out of my wallet and folded them into her hand. "I appreciate it."

I grabbed my cold coffee and headed out to my truck. I climbed in and used a felt-tipped pen to X off the town of Hoodwink, Arkansas on the map that was open across my passenger seat. The next stop on my trip was a little hole in the wall in Texas. It was the last place anyone in Mallory's previous town had heard her mention.

I was running out of leads, running out of options. I'd been doing this for almost a year and a half. I started searching as soon as my family found out about Dad's will. My father had left the family ranch to whichever of my brothers and me had a child first. It'd taken me months to even get a line on Mallory. I'd never been able to reach her directly, but I'd been hopeful up until the last month.

It was getting harder and harder to find people who knew her. No one wanted to talk about the pretty brunette with the dark cloud hanging over her head.

I grimaced as I chugged down the cold coffee and then tossed the cup in the back seat. I started my truck and headed west, towards Texas.

My last hope to find her.

*****Sammie*****

SPLASHING WATER ON MY FACE, I sucked in a rough breath and struggled to remain in control of myself. I couldn't afford to fall apart. At that thought, I looked over at the rough pallet I'd laid down on the bathroom floor. Sitting on it was a tiny bear cub looking about as forlorn as could be.

"It's okay, Mason. It's all okay." This whole thing was about as far from okay as one could possibly imagine. I was talking to a bear cub. A real bear cub. A bear cub who a week before had been a little boy.

Nothing was okay.

I slipped out of my soiled clothes and did my best to wash them in the sink before hanging them up to dry. A knock sounded on the door and my chest tightened. "Occupied!"

A young female voice yelled back. "For how long?"

I relaxed and looked down at my mostly bare body and the bear cub huddled on the floor. "A while. I'd go somewhere else."

She kicked the door and mumbled something, but she left.

I picked up Mason and held him against my side. "How about we do a quick wash? Do bears take baths?"

I turned the water on and he made a whimpering sound before trying to climb up my head. I winced as his claws scraped across my skin, but tried to remain gentle with him. "Mason, baby, you've got to be easy with me. I'm not a tree."

I finally pried him off of me and placed him back on the floor. "Okay, no bath. How 'bout a snack?"

He turned away and curled into a little ball.

My heart ached for the little boy. I had no clue what was happening with him, but I knew enough to know that Mason was still in there.

The child had witnessed his mom and her junkie boyfriend shot to death in cold blood. Along with my partner, U.S. Marshal Aaron Givens. Aaron and I were tasked with keeping them hidden while they waited to testify against scumbag heroin distributor Wesley Butler. Something had gone wrong. I'd been out grabbing dinner for everyone. When I came back, the door was wide open and Aaron was sprawled out in front of it, dead.

I gagged as the recent memory flooded my vision, and rushed into the little stall to vomit up a lunch that I'd barely touched. Bile came up and I fought the tears. I couldn't fall apart. I couldn't afford to fall apart, or even to slow down.

Mason needed me. I swore I would do right by the little boy, and the best thing I could think of right now was to get him to his father. The *only* thing I could think of. I'd finally managed to track him down and we had only a few more miles to go. I didn't know anything about his dad, but I was pretty sure his mom had never turned into a bear. I was praying that this was something his dad could explain. Explain and get him to turn back into a little boy so I could stop hiding from my boss.

As a U.S. Marshal, it was my job to keep Mason safe. My boss demanded proof that he was okay, but if I turned up with a bear cub claiming it was Mason Simmons, one of two things would happen. One, I'd get fired for being off my rocker, or two, they'd take little Mason and he'd end up being poked and prodded for God knows how long while they tried to figure out how a little boy could transform into an actual grizzly bear cub.

I wouldn't let that happen. Mason had already been through more than any child should have to endure. I really didn't want to get blacklisted by law enforcement either.

I flushed the toilet and stood up to find Mason sitting up, watching me wide-eyed. I forced a smile. "I'm okay. Let me get washed up and then we'll get back on the road. We're close to finding answers, buddy."

I hurriedly washed my body with a wad of paper towels and the last few squirts of watered down soap. I dressed in my still damp clothes and scooped up Mason.

"Let's get you wrapped back up, shall we? We wouldn't want to start a bear flu, would we?"

He hugged his little body to mine and I sighed. He was warm and soft in my arms. I'd been with him for so long that I couldn't help but love the little boy. Bear or boy, I loved him and needed to make things right for him.

I wrapped him up to made sure he was hidden from prying eyes before picking up our bag and heading out to the car. We had about half an hour to go before we reached Long Ranch.

2

SAMMIE

The town of Landing, Wyoming was already green, despite how early in the year it was, and Long Ranch was breathtaking. I was stunned by its beautiful, mountainous backdrop. Horses ran in a little paddock and, on the other side of the winding driveway, cows grazed with their heads bent low. As I watched them munch on grass, I had the crazy thought that all of those animals could possibly be people.

I parked next to a large, picturesque white farm house that seemed to sprawl on forever. If Mason's dad was as wealthy as it appeared, I was even more confused as to why he'd never been brought up before. Mallory had never mentioned him, not a word, not until literally the very last second of her life. She'd never brought up child support or anything.

I climbed out and debated with myself about taking Mason up to the front door with me. He didn't like to be separated from me, but I didn't know what situation I was walking into either. I couldn't chance his safety. I decided to leave him in the car. I kept the heat on and reached into the glovebox to grab my gun.

Mason whined.

I quickly tucked the gun away out of his sight and smiled back at him. "I'm going to see if anyone's home, okay? You stay where you are. I'll come get you in a minute."

I shut the door and eased up the steps to the front door. I listened for a minute before knocking. My nerves were frayed after everything. I eased my gun out and held it steady at my side, ready to protect Mason with everything I had.

A big guy opened the door and took a long sniff of the air around me. He raised an eyebrow and cocked his head to the side. "Can I help you?"

I nodded. "I'm looking for Lucas Long. Are you him?"

He shook his head. "No, ma'am. I'm his brother, Michael. He's not here right now. Can I do anything for you?"

"I need to see him. It's important. Do you know where I might find him?"

Footsteps came up behind me quickly and I instantly raised my arm to thrust my gun in Michael's face as I twisted my body so I could see who was approaching me. "Touch me and I blow his head off."

A guy equally as big as Michael froze and fur sprouted out on his bare chest. His eyes glowed bright gold and a growl ripped out of his chest. "Lady, you've got about two seconds to explain why you're pointing a gun at my brother's head."

"You're bears, too." I nearly cried I was so happy to see more humans who turned into bears. "Oh, thank God."

The pissed off one raised an eyebrow. "What are you talking about?"

I gradually lowered my gun and stepped back. "Sorry. U.S. Marshal Sam Delaney. I have a package for Lucas Long. I think you should get him here as soon as possible."

*****Lucas*****

I'D BARELY EXPLORED the little Texas town of Gumdrop when Alex called with an urgent message for me to get home. Something about an important package for me. *Important enough for me to rush home?* Said I was needed ASAP. Something in Alex's voice told me not to take his words lightly.

I couldn't deny that there was a feeling of dread in the pit of my stomach that had me pressing the gas pedal a little harder. It felt dire for me to get to the ranch as soon as I possibly could.

I blew through cities and towns without glancing up from the road. I stopped only when I had to and then immediately got back to it. Sleep had become a fond memory.

When I crossed the Wyoming state line, I just sped up. I felt almost sick with anticipation. I knew my brothers; Alex wouldn't have called me home unless it was something huge. Had something happened to mom? My sister Bailey? *A package* Alex had said. Obviously,that was a cover. What the hell could be urgent about a package?

I didn't know what to expect.

By the time I sped down the driveway of our ranch, I'd gone days without sleep and a shower. I'd crossed over from looking rugged to looking like a homeless person, but I didn't think twice about my appearance as I ran up the steps of the porch and burst into the house like a hurricane.

"Alex!"

He stepped out of the kitchen, looking grim. "Took you long enough."

Fury filled my vision and my bear was at the ready. My bear had been compressed inside my truck for months. It desperately wanted to get out and stretch its muscles. "I just sped here from bum-fuck Texas. Don't give me shit right now."

He shook his head. "It isn't the time. Why don't you get cleaned up and come back down here?"

"What the fuck, Alex? This is important enough for me to rush home, but I have time to shower beforehand?"

A prickling of awareness broke through my anger as I breathed in the scent of something like apples and warm cinnamon sugar. It smelled a little like... apple pie? I breathed in deeper and groaned as my dick hardened in my pants. I'd never responded to apple pie that way before. "Who's in there?"

Just then, a beautiful woman stepped out of the kitchen holding a cub in her arms. Her tall frame barely held the little bear's weight, but she didn't show any sign of weakness as she stepped purposefully towards me. Her sweet smell enveloped me until my eyes shut on their own. As I breathed her in, I had to ball my hands into fists to keep from grabbing her.

Underneath her scent, I smelled myself. It caught me off guard and I stepped back as I realized why. My cub. *Naw.* I took a deeper whiff. *Yeah.* The woman was holding my cub.

The shock of it hit me hard. I'd been all over the country looking for Mallory. I'd worn myself thin trying to find her because of a drugged-out call she'd made to me one night four years earlier. I hadn't believed her then, but after everything with Dad's will, I'd gone out scouring the country in hopes that she'd been telling the truth for once.

Seeing him clinging to the woman, practically trembling, I forgot all of the plans I'd made. I had a son.

I moved closer to them and growled when she held him tighter to her chest. No matter how amazing she smelled, she was holding my son. "Hand him to me."

Most humans would've backed down. Not her. She glared at me through narrowed eyes. Belatedly, I realized her hand was dangerously close to a gun holstered to her side. "I don't know you. He doesn't know you. I suggest you back up and give us some time to adjust to you. And your brother's right. A shower wouldn't kill you."

I couldn't help it, my bear had been cooped inside too long, and I shifted right there in front of her. I was still struggling, man against bear, as I towered over her, dwarfing her. Bear wanted to rub his nose against her delicate looking skin but man won and released a frightening growl in her face.

She didn't look frightened, though. She stood her ground.

"You smell worse as a bear."

3

SAMMIE

The bear became a very naked man in the blink of an eye. His clothes rested in shredded piles on the floor and I wasn't the least bit sorry about it. I knew I should look away and give him privacy, but I couldn't. He drew me in like a magnet. The minute he'd stepped into the big house, I'd felt like I'd gained a sixth sense.

I'd known it was him. Lucas Long. The man I'd been searching for. For Mason, of course. My cheeks burned as my mind noted the slip. *I* hadn't been looking for him. I hadn't been looking for any man.

"Who are you?"

I ran my eyes over his body and then cleared my throat. I had to stop staring at him. I was the bearer of bad news. As always. My job didn't usually make me a whole lot of fans.

"U.S. Marshal Sammie Delaney. We have to talk."

His eyes still glowed the same golden shade as Mason's. He stared at me for a few more seconds before nodding. "Fine."

He started to walk towards me and I held up my hand. "Shower first."

He glared at me but quickly ascended the stairs, taking them three at a time. I couldn't help but stare at his muscular ass and legs as they disappeared around the corner at the top of the stairs.

"Want me to take him?" Carolyn, his mother, asked from beside me.

I looked down at Mason and stroked his head. "Mason? You want to go to your Grandma Carolyn?"

He whined and tightened his hold on me. His little claws dug into me, but I kept a straight face.

Carolyn breathed in deeply and gasped. "Oh, honey. He's hurting you. I can smell blood."

I tried to detach Mason gently, but his claws dug in deeper. I sighed and hugged him back to my body. "It seems that I've grown a bear. It's okay. It barely even stings."

She looked at me with a worried expression, but let it go. "Well, when he's ready, you just send him right to me. I've got a whole load of toys left from when the boys were little. They're dusty, but I'm sure we can find something great. Just let me know when you're ready to play, Mason."

He whimpered in my ear and I rubbed his back, trying to comfort him. "It's okay, buddy. These people are your family. You don't have anything to worry about here."

At least I hoped that was true. I immediately felt like I could trust the others, but Lucas gave me weird feelings that had me on edge.

Just then, he walked back into the room, sporting flannel pajama bottoms. He hadn't bothered with a shirt and I swore silently.

Laughter came from my right and Alex grinned at me. "Heard that."

My cheeks burned and I groaned. "Yeah, well, keep it to yourself. Remember, I'm armed."

He just rolled his eyes and looked around at his brothers. "Come on, guys. Let's give them a little privacy."

Everyone slowly left the room after slapping Lucas on the back and telling him they'd missed him. I watched with weariness, trying to pinpoint what it was about the man that had my nerve endings on high alert. There was something about him that made my insides feel chaotic, but something else that I found calming. Weird.

I circled the couch, putting it between us. "You've been gone for a while?"

He matched my steps and faced me head on from across the couch. I felt a little bit like prey being stalked. "I was out looking for Mallory."

A little sting of jealousy bit at me. *What the hell was that?* I shrugged it off. It made no sense. Not that it mattered. Mallory was gone. "And Mason?"

"Mason." He smiled as he said the name. "I didn't know he actually existed. Mallory was never honest. You never knew what to believe about anything she said, and she only mentioned anything about him existing once, while she was high out of her mind."

I covered Mason's little ears and kissed the top of his head. "Watch what you say. That's his mother you're talking about."

Lucas growled. "I'm not going to make her out to be a saint. She's always been an addict and always will be. It's amazing that Mason looks as healthy as he does. Why is he still bear, though?"

I adjusted Mason on my hip and he clawed me deeper. "Mason, baby, you've got to be careful."

Lucas circled the couch in an instant and held Mason's paws. "Mason, *stop*. You're hurting her."

Mason scrambled to get back to me while Lucas pulled him into his own chest. I watched with my hand over my mouth, feeling helpless and vulnerable as Mason fought to get away from his father. Lucas kept his arms gently around Mason, being careful to not hurt him, while keeping him pressed to his chest.

Claw marks appeared and then vanished on Lucas's chest as Mason scratched him. He didn't seem bothered by the pain and, as I watched on in a stupor, he healed immediately.

Mason wore himself out and drooped against his father's chest. Lucas wrapped his arms tighter around his son and blinked down at the top of his head with watery eyes and a pained expression.

When he looked back at me, he was wide-eyed and confused. "What happened to him?"

I turned away to gather myself. When I faced him again, Lucas had folded his large body onto the couch and was holding Mason tightly, gently stroking his fur. The image touched me to the core and I clutched at my chest for a moment. Tears threatened to gather in my own eyes, but I quickly composed myself. I was supposed to be way more put together than to blubber over a father-son reunion.

"Mallory and her boyfriend got into something bad." I swallowed and prayed I'd get through the story without falling apart. "They were busted and rolled over on a bigger fish to stay out of jail. My partner and I were assigned to keep them safe and hidden until the trial."

Lucas shook his head and looked disgusted, but remained silent.

"She was doing better. Frank, her boyfriend, was a piece of work, but Mallory was…better. She was doing better." I cleared my throat. "A week ago, I came back to the house and found them all… *gone*."

He sat up. "Gone?"

I stared at him, my eyes pleading with him not to make me say it. "*Gone*. Frank, Mallory, and my partner, Aaron."

"Jesus. Where was Mason?"

I looked at the little boy and sucked in a deep breath. "He was there. He was hiding but I'm fairly certain he saw everything. Before… he was talkative. A regular chatterbox. Now, he, well, he's been like this since that night. He's terrified."

4
LUCAS

I tore my eyes away from Sammie and looked down at my son. He was hurting. It wasn't normal for a bear shifter to remain bear at that age. He still trembled slightly in my arms.

"No one's going to hurt you, Mason. I'm your dad. I'll protect you. I'll make sure no one hurts you, buddy."

He held onto me tighter and I took it as a good sign. My heart ached for him, for this little boy that I wasn't even sure really existed. The life he must have already had.

I looked back at Sammie and felt another tugging at my chest from the look of pain on her face. She was obviously tough, but whatever she'd seen had hurt her badly, too. I wanted to reach for her and pull her down beside us and soothe them both.

"I... I didn't know what to do," she continued, "I just found this beautiful bear cub and it took me a bit to figure out it was Mason. I didn't know he could do that, turn into a bear. I just knew that I couldn't let anyone else find him like that."

I nodded. We were a private community for a reason. "How did you find me?"

"Mallory... She was still hanging on when I got there." Sammie stopped and looked away. "She said your name. I didn't know what it meant, but I went through her stuff and found that she'd kept a piece of paper with yours and Masons name on it. It wasn't hard to put two and two together. I just hoped that you were… umm, like Mason, so you could help."

I couldn't help but formulate a mental picture of the scene. My stomach twisted and I had to fight the urge to grab Sammie and pull her into my arms. My bear was agitated, more riled than I could ever remember him being. The sight of her in pain had him rumbling in my chest with the need to comfort Mason while also comforting Sammie.

"Thank you for finding me."

She nodded and stood up. "I just need to go wash my face. I'm feeling a little-"

"Sammie!" Before I could lunge for her, she melted sideways and slumped to the ground. Her head made an awful thud as it landed on the floor.

Mason cried out and flung his little body on top of hers. I rushed to her side, ignoring the way he growled at me. "I've got to make sure she's okay, Mason."

I could smell blood, but her head was dry as I brushed my fingers over it. I scooped her into my arms and looked down at Mason. "Come on."

Mom was already racing into the room. "What happened?"

"She just collapsed. Where's Michael? Is he still here?" My bear threatened to push forward. He raged inside of me, pissed that I'd let her get hurt. "Where is he?!"

Mason clawed at my legs, fighting to get to Sammie. He roared pitifully and got under my feet until I nearly fell.

"Mason! We have to get her to Michael to make sure she's okay. I know you can understand me, little man. Walk beside me and you can sit with her when we get there."

He pouted and huffed, but did as I asked.

Mom rushed ahead of us and yelled out of the front door for Michael. He was there in seconds.

He looked at Sammie in my arms and then pointed to the kitchen.

"Get her on the table."

I laid her out on the table and snatched up Mason so he could sit on the table next to her. He immediately curled up beside her and laid his head on her stomach.

Michael ran his hands over her body and it twisted something deep in my stomach watching him touch her. I was growling at him before I even knew what I was doing.

He looked up at me with a frown. "Now's not the time, big brother. Tell me what happened."

I fisted my hands and leaned on the table as he continued his examination. I told him what happened through gritted teeth. "Is she okay?"

He rolled her over onto her stomach and flinched when both Mason and I sent a warning growl at him. He gently lifted her shirt from her shoulders and frowned. "The only thing I can see wrong with her is a knot on her head from falling, and just about a million little holes and scratches on her shoulders from Mason. He's practically torn her shirt to shreds back here. Everything else seems normal. Honestly, I think she just passed out. Let's give her a little while to rest and then see."

Michael was a natural at medicine. He'd completed several years of schooling before returning to the ranch. I trusted him.

I moved over to look at her shoulders and frowned. Mason had done quite the number on her. The upper part of her shirt was in tatters. Her shoulders were covered in claw marks, some scratches deeper than others. There was dried blood in spots and fresher droplets in others.

My eyes rested on my son. I'd just been handed him and I didn't know how to parent a kid, but I knew that he couldn't be hurting her like that. "You have to be careful with her, Mason. She's not like us. She won't heal like we do."

He whimpered and buried his face into her side. His body shook and I could tell he was crying.

I scooped him up and held him against my chest. His little body was heavy in my arms and I glanced back at Sammie, impressed by her strength. "She'll be okay, Mason."

He didn't fight me, but instead wrapped his paws around my neck and held on. My chest felt heavy and I sunk down onto one of the kitchen chairs. My family moved around me, being sure to keep a wide berth around Sammie, but to me there was just the three of us in that room. Only three of us existed. I had never experienced anything like the feeling that surrounded us.

I sat staring at Sammie's unconscious form until I'd memorized every line and curve of her, while Mason breathed deeply in my arms. When I realized he'd fallen asleep in my arms, I stood up and looked around. I wanted to be alone with them.

Mom appeared at my side and held out her arms. "I'll carry him up to a guest room so you can carry Sammie. We'll put them together."

I nodded and handed Mason to her before scooping Sammie into my arms. She made a whimpering noise, not unlike the ones Mason made, and curled into my chest. I held her tighter and prayed that she'd wake up soon so I could be assured she was okay.

Mom and I secured them in one of the guest bedrooms and Mom patted me on the shoulder before leaving. She came back to the room a few minutes later with a first aid kit. "You may as well take care of her shoulders while she's asleep. She doesn't seem like the type to let you when she's awake."

I couldn't help the smile that touched my face. "Did you get to talk to her much before I got here?"

She nodded. "She's a tough one. She loves Mason, that's for sure. I don't know how she'll leave him."

I growled. "She's too weak to leave."

Mom ruffled my hair, the same way she had when I was little. "Who knows? Maybe you'll give her a reason to stay."

I glanced over at her but she was already out the door. The door closed softly and I was alone with Mason and Sammie. They were both on the king sized bed, curled into one another. Mason had nuzzled his head into her stomach as soon as they were both on the bed. He loved her, too. It was clear.

The thought of her leaving had my bear pushing through. I let the shift take over and paced the room before leaning against the wall, watching them.

5
SAMMIE

I woke up and stretched. My shoulders ached, but I'd grown used to the stinging pain. Mason had definitely left his mark on me. I opened my eyes and took in the unfamiliar ceiling above me.

Mason was curled up next to me, his wet nose shoved against my stomach where my shirt had ridden up. He stirred and looked up at me, blinking the sleepiness out of his little bear eyes.

I heard his belly growl and sat up. My head hurt, and as the memories flooded back and I remembered the reason for the headache, it worsened. I buried my face in my hands and groaned. I'd passed out. I'd never passed out before in my life. What the hell?

A low snore sounded from my left and I jerked my eyes over to the giant sleeping bear across the room. His large furry body was sprawled in front of the door. I felt warmth creeping through my body. I knew it was Lucas. I'd seen him as a bear and recognized the huge beast.

"Let's see if we can get out of here without waking your Daddy." I stood up and crept across the room. My body ached and I wondered how long I'd been out.

Mason seemed lighter as he jumped down from the bed and

hurried behind me on all fours. He sniffed at Lucas and then climbed up on the sleeping bear's back.

I laughed, enjoying seeing Mason act more like a kid than a sulking, sullen animal. I leaned over to scoop him off of his Dad's back, but suddenly found myself being grabbed.

Lucas was on top of me in a second, a man again, completely naked. He'd changed so fast that I'd just seen a blur as he pulled me under him. Mason still clung to his back, making excited sounds.

My heart pounded away in my chest, attempting to break free from its own body. I couldn't find words as I felt Lucas's muscular body pressed firmly against mine. I looked into his golden eyes. A lock of his curly hair had fallen across his forehead. The man was even more visually pleasing up close.

I felt like I was on fire. Everywhere his body touched, I burned with the ache of wanting more.

He leaned on his forearms on either side of my head and slowly smiled at me. "Don't you know never to wake a sleeping bear?"

His voice was deeper than normal, rough from sleep, and it sent chills down to my core. I bit my lip and tried to remember what I was doing at his house. It was hard, though. I could hear Mason actually playing on his father's bare back. He was obviously safe. Without him to worry about, my body had all of its energy back. To focus on Lucas.

"What happens when a sleeping bear is awakened?"

His grin was fierce as he leaned closer. "You owe that bear a kiss."

My eyes went wide and an embarrassing little gasp escaped my mouth. "A kiss?"

Lucas nodded. "Yep. A kiss. Sometimes, it has to be paid at a later date, due to little bear circumstances, but yes. *You* owe *me* a kiss. I'll collect it later."

I nodded before I realized what I was doing. Then, I moved under him, attempting to slide myself free. I brushed against his very hard length of manhood and felt my face go red. "Mason's hungry."

"Scaredy-cat." Lucas immediately rolled over, though. He laughed as Mason tumbled off of him and bounced off the wall behind him. "Watch out, little cub."

I scooped Mason up and practically ran from the room. Everything about Lucas left me feeling completely out of control. It wasn't horrible, but it was insane. I'd just met the man. I didn't know him from any stranger on the street, yet my body reacted to him like a silly schoolgirl.

Carolyn was in the kitchen, grinning to herself over the stove. There were massive piles of food spread out on the counters around her, enough to feed a small army.

"Wow. Are you having a party?"

She turned her bright sunshiny smile on me and called me over. "Kind of. Most of the family will be coming over this morning. They're excited to meet Mason and you."

I frowned. "Me?"

She laughed. "Yes, you. The woman who pulled a gun on Michael and faced Alex down like he was a teddy bear. They're all impressed by you. You'll get to meet the girls, too."

I looked down at my outfit and frowned. "I don't know if I'm exactly dressed for a party."

"I've got it covered. Elizabeth will be here shortly with an array of clothes for you. You two are similar in size. You're a little taller than she is, but I think it'll work."

I nodded and sat Mason down. I watched Carolyn offer him a piece of bacon which he greedily snatched. "Manners, Mason."

He grunted and inhaled the bacon before holding out his paws for more. Carolyn held the second piece closer to her and he inched over. He took the second piece slower and let her stroke him behind the ears.

"He's an adorable cub. I'd love to see a little boy soon, though. I've got so many toys that won't work for a little bear, but would work amazingly well for a little boy."

Mason gestured for more bacon and then slowly nuzzled his head against her legs. Carolyn was a goner. Her eyes flooded and she wiped away a tear, trying to hide it by giving him more food.

I snagged a piece of sausage and shoved it in my mouth. I couldn't remember the last time I'd eaten. I'd been so focused on keeping Mason safe that I hadn't taken care of myself.

Carolyn saw me and slid a plate towards me. "Eat. We won't tell the boys that I let you eat early. They never get to. I noticed you didn't eat at all yesterday, though. No wonder you fainted"

I greedily scarfed the food down, not stopping to remember my own manners. When I finished the plate, I came up for air and laughed roughly. "Sorry. I guess it's been a few days."

She put a large bowl of milk on the floor for Mason and then suddenly grabbed me and pulled me in for a hug. "Thank you for keeping him safe and finding us. He's safe now, though, so you can focus on your own needs."

Before I could reply, she winked. "*All* of them."

Lucas chose that moment to strut into the kitchen, freshly showered, in a faded pair of jeans and a flannel. His hair was curling around his face as it dried and he was cleanly shaven. He looked and smelled so delectable that I had to force my eyes away from him.

"Is that an empty plate I see?" He moved behind me resting his hand on the small of my back as he leaned over and tried to grab a biscuit.

Carolyn smacked his hand. "You know the rules."

A pretty woman came in, carrying a large baby. She immediately pushed the baby into Carolyn's arms before turning to me. "Hi! I'm Elizabeth."

I couldn't help but grin at her enthusiasm. "Sammie. Nice to meet you."

She grabbed my arm and pulled me away from everyone. "I am so glad you're here. Leila, Matt's wife, is pregnant and her hormones have been all over the place. She's about as mean as a rattlesnake right now."

I looked back to find Mason and caught Lucas staring at me. I blushed and turned back around hurrying after Elizabeth.

6

LUCAS

I stood at the kitchen counter, watching Mason warm up to Mom for a while. My mind was elsewhere, though. I couldn't stop thinking about Sammie and the way she felt under my body. The woman was driving me crazy. Even my bear, who usually looked at my conquests with disdain, was sitting up and howling.

Mom leaned over and picked Mason up in her free arm. He struggled for a second and then quieted down when she shoved a piece of bacon at him. "That's it. We're going to be good friends, aren't we?"

"You could bribe *me*, you know. I'm standing right here."

She narrowed her eyes at me and shook her head. "You don't need bribing. You need to get your head out of your backside."

Mason made a sound that was dangerously close to a laugh. I glared at both of them. "What's that supposed to mean?"

"It means that you'd better not let that woman get away." She fed another piece of bacon to Mason and then turned the stove off. "Let's go find a toy before everyone else gets here, huh?"

She left with Mason and Connor so I grabbed one of the chocolate croissants she'd made. I shoved it into my mouth and stared after them. I didn't know what she was talking about. I didn't especially feel like my head was up my ass. And how the hell did she expect me to keep Sammie around? What was I supposed to do? She'd done her job. I was assuming she'd probably leave soon.

That thought had my bear pacing frantically inside of me, demanding that I go to her. I headed towards the stairs. *Beg her to stay.*

I took the stairs quickly and then stopped. What the hell was I doing? What the hell did I plan to say to her? I spun and headed back down the stairs, feeling like an idiot. With my foot on the bottom step, I turned around again. How could I not say anything? I felt such a strong pull to her. What if she felt it, too?

I made it halfway back up the stairs before pivoting and heading down them again. I argued with myself back and forth until I felt completely mentally exhausted. I finally stopped moving and sat down on a stair.

"Well, hell." I'd been sitting there for a little while before Elizabeth passed me. "Don't you look utterly confused. What's wrong?"

I frowned. It hadn't been that long ago that I was an asshole to Elizabeth. She'd been the reason that control of the ranch went to Alex. It seemed now that, if Dad's will was still in force, I was the rightful heir. I had the first child. The ranch was technically mine. I wasn't as excited as I thought I would be in that moment, though. I had a son to raise. A scared, scarred son. Hell, I had a son I didn't even know. A son who didn't know me. I needed to spend a lot of one-on-one time with him, if the way he clung to Sammie was any indication. Sammie. Could Mason let her go? Is there any way we could keep her?

"Earth to Lucas?" Elizabeth waved her hand in front of my face. "You in there?"

I nodded. "Yeah, sorry. How is she?"

"Sammie? She's fine. Seems a little weary right now. I like her. Do *you?*"

A growl escaped my chest.

"I'll take that as a yes. She should be out of the shower soon. Good luck, Lucas."

I waited a few minutes and then headed up to Sammie's room. My chest tightened and I realized I was desperately nervous. It was pathetic, but I was terrified to screw this up by saying or doing the wrong thing. I knocked on the door and leaned closer so I could listen for a reply.

I heard soft, muffled cries from her side of the door and I didn't think twice about pushing it open and letting myself into the room. Something was wrong.

The sounds grew louder near the bathroom and I rushed in. She was huddled in the corner of the shower, sobbing. My heart twisted and I ran to her.

Sammie gasped when she saw me and tried to cover herself, but I just grabbed her and pulled her into my chest so I could wrap her in my arms and hold her. She struggled feebly at first, but I rested my chin on her head and held her tighter.

"It's okay. Just let me hold you."

She instantly went lax and slumped into my body. I could hear how hard her heart was beating and she shook as I held her.

"I've got you, Sammie." I stroked her hair and back, forcing myself to ignore all the bare skin and soft curves pressed against me. I just wanted to take away her pain, help her get through, make it okay.

Water saturated my clothes, but I didn't care. I held her until her tears quieted and then she stiffened against me once more. I pulled back slightly and looked down at her face. "Better?"

Her cheeks were flaming red. "I'm naked."

I groaned. "Don't remind me. I didn't come in here to sneak a peek, sweetheart. I heard you crying. You okay now?"

She snaked her arms around my waist and gently moved her hands over my back. "You're soaked."

I nodded. "I'm fine. Are *you* okay?"

She rested her forehead against my chest and shivered against me. "Not really. I don't want to think about it, Lucas."

I couldn't have missed the sudden change in her demeanor if I'd been blind, deaf, and completely stupid. Her body squirmed against mine. Her thighs rubbed together and then her hands slowly edged to the front of my body running up under my shirt. She lifted it until she could pull it off.

When she backed away, her naked body was completely on display for me. Her breasts were full with tight rosy-pink nipples, her soft stomach let down to a small patch of brown curls. I was already hard, but I felt myself growing even harder when the scent of her arousal reached my nostrils.

Sammie's knuckles brushed my lower abdomen as she unbuttoned my jeans. "Help take my mind off of it."

7
SAMMIE

I hadn't meant to cry. One thought had led to another and the next thing I knew, I was falling apart like a blubbering fool in the shower. I would've gathered myself eventually. But, then Lucas barged in and took me in his arms, and in that moment everything about him soothed and comforted me. Until it didn't. I hadn't meant to beg him to screw me like a love-starved harlot.

Lucas gently lifted my face so I was looking at him. "I can distract you in other ways. We don't have to do this if you don't want to."

"You don't want to?" Had I misread the situation?

"Of course I do; I just want you to be sure."

I was sure. There was something about the man that had me yearning for him more than I could ever remember wanting anyone or anything else.

"I'm sure."

He slid his mouth over mine and growled softly. With ease, he lifted me and sat me down on the bathroom counter. "I don't know if this first time is going to be slow and romantic."

I tugged his jeans down and wrapped my legs around him. "Don't care."

He moved back and lined our bodies up and then slid into me.

His size surprised me, and I had to stretch to accommodate, but he filled me so fully that I couldn't help but cry out. He captured my cries in his mouth and stroked my tongue with his until everything in me felt like it belonged to him. Everything felt so right.

Lucas slid almost all the way out and then thrust back into me harder. His big hands gripped my ass and lifted me when he pulled out again. "Fuck."

I bit his bottom lip and raked my nails down his back as he thrust faster. "Lucas, yes. Don't stop. Don't stop."

He picked me up and held me in the air as we spun and slammed up against the wall; he pummeled in and out of me. I wrapped my arms around his head and tugged on his hair. We were forehead to forehead. He filled me more than I thought possible, but my body responded to his like it'd been made for him.

Our chests rubbed together and his fingers tightened on my ass. "I don't think I could."

I caught sight of us in the mirror and moaned. Seeing his hard body, tight with tension, pumping into mine was nearly too much. I let my head fall backwards, arching my back slightly and the new angle hit a different spot inside me.

Lucas swore and reached his fingers down to brush lightly against my clit. He grunted as my walls squeezed around him in response. "This isn't going to last if you do that again."

I kissed him as he circled my clit with his fingers. My legs were wrapped around his waist. I was so lost in him, his tongue, his fingers, his cock.

Warmth budded in my core, blossoming and spreading out to my limbs as I edged closer and closer. My nails dug into his shoulders and I clung to him for all I was worth as the first wave of my orgasm hit. It rolled over me, slowly drowning me in pleasure.

Lucas stumbled as he growled and thrust himself deeply into me. My back hit the cool tiles of the bathroom wall and a second later I felt his warm shooting ejaculations filling me. I cried out as my body came apart around him. My head rolled and I moaned his name. I'd never orgasmed so hard in my life. Even as I was coming down from it, as the last tremors were still rocking my body, I felt shell-shocked from its power.

Lucas gently pulled out of me and sat me back on the counter. He planted his hands on either side of me and hung his head against my shoulder. I watched curiously as my nail marks slowly healed themselves from his back.

"Jesus. What was that?" he breathed.

I stroked his hair absently. "I don't know."

He lifted his head and stared at me. "You're my mate."

I raised my eyebrows. "What?"

He pulled his hand down his face roughly and shook his head. "It makes sense. Holy shit. Holy shit!"

I scooted off of the counter and grabbed at the towel I'd hung up. "What are you talking about, Lucas?"

He suddenly laughed and then grabbed me again. He pulled me to him and kissed me hard on the mouth before pulling back. "I thought Mallory could be my mate. But, it's you."

Apprehension filled my stomach. "What's a mate?"

"A mate. Soulmate. Bears find their mates, their one and only, if they're lucky, and they claim them and then they live happily ever after."

"And you thought Mallory was yours?"

He nodded, not noticing that I was starting to get upset. "Yeah. I went searching for her, and then you showed up on my doorstep."

I gulped in a big breath. "You went looking for her?"

He hesitated, as if sensing I wasn't feeling the slightest ounce of the joy he seemed to be feeling. "I thought maybe she was my mate. But, it wasn't about her. I just needed a mate because of this thing with my father's will."

My heart ached, and then I was pissed. I was pissed because I didn't want to feel anything for him. Where was this heartbreak coming from? He'd been out looking for Mallory, the woman he thought was his soulmate.

Jealousy reared its ugly head and I stomped out of the bathroom and into the bedroom. I suddenly wanted to be as far from him as possible.

Lucas wrapped his arm around my waist and pulled me into his chest. "What's wrong?"

I shrugged him off and grabbed the clothes Elizabeth had brought for me. "Get out."

"Whoa. What happened?"

I didn't want to be jealous of Mallory. I'd grown to like her. She'd finally cleaned up and started getting her act together. She was trying to be a good mom to Mason. Yet, when he said he thought she was his mate just now, I'd wanted to time travel backward and rip her hair clean out of her head. What the hell was wrong with me? I should be ashamed thinking such thoughts about a dead woman.

"Get out of this room. I am not some poor man's Mallory. Some sad, sorry, second choice. Thanks for the fuck. Thanks for taking my mind off of everything. Now, GET. OUT."

He actually looked hurt and that made me feel terrible. Which pissed me off even more. He still wasn't moving, so I opened the door and then pushed him out of the room using all of my strength. After he was out, I slammed the door shut and locked it.

In the quiet of the room, without Lucas standing there looking at me, I could finally think again. Unfortunately, my thoughts didn't make me feel any better.

I GOT DRESSED and went downstairs to find Mason. I just wanted to hug him and forget about what I'd just done. I'd taken a few minutes in my room to try to make sense of what had happened, but I couldn't. I couldn't grasp onto any logic that made sense of *any* of it. It wasn't like me to have sex with someone I just met. It *definitely* wasn't like me to have sex with someone I just met minutes before sitting down to breakfast with his family.

I hadn't even been upset when Lucas had started talking about soulmates. I got upset that he thought I was a good backup choice.

My emotions were all over the place, and this wasn't like me at all. I had always been cool, steady, and level-headed.

Loud voices echoed from the kitchen and I groaned when I thought of all the people that were in there. I just wanted to go back up and hide in my room with Mason.

"Come on in here, Sammie. We all heard that." Alex called.

I looked up at the ceiling and shook my head. Life was just getting stranger and stranger.

8
LUCAS

Sammie walked into the kitchen and I snapped a chunk off of Mom's wooden dining table. I'd been holding onto it out of frustration, but seeing her in the tiny dress and smelling my scent on her sent me overboard.

Mom spotted the chunk in my hand and shrieked. "Lucas! Not my table! Dammit! You boys. This is why I should've had more girls. Look what you did!"

I winced. "Sorry, Mom."

Alex snorted. "And the plot thickens."

Elizabeth giggled when she saw Sammie coming in. "Oh, Sammie. I accidentally gave you a mini-dress. I didn't realize how much taller than me you are."

Sammie shrugged. "It's okay. Thank you for the dress. I'll have to be careful when I sit or bend, but it's still nice."

Michael turned to look and I let out a vicious growl. "Keep your eyes to yourself, little brother."

He raised his eyebrows at me. "You're serious?"

I glared at him. "Deadly."

Sammie noticed the empty seat next to me and then went to

stand in the kitchen with Mom. She wouldn't even meet my eyes and it was driving me crazy. "Where's Mason?"

Mom grinned. "He's playing with Bailey. Come see."

I gritted my teeth and made myself stay where I was. I wasn't going to push her. I groaned. I'd fucked up. I hadn't even realized what I'd said until I was out of her room. She had every right to be pissed at me, but I still didn't like it.

"How did you fuck that one up so royally, brother?" Alex pulled Elizabeth into his lap and laughed at me.

I got up, forgetting about my decision to give Sammie space. "It wasn't hard, believe it or not."

I followed her scent into the small playroom behind the kitchen and found her sitting next to Mason on the floor. She was tickling him behind the ears and whispering to him that she was going to tickle him until he told her all of his secrets. My heart felt like it grew a couple of sizes in my chest. That could be my family. That *would* be my family. No way was I going to let her slip through my fingers.

I sat down next to them and focused on my son. I wanted to will him to change back to a little boy. I wanted to see the signs that he was comfortable enough here. He'd already made progress, just in letting Mom hold him, and my sister Bailey play with him. I wanted to be able to bond with him as a man, but if it took me being a bear, I'd do it.

I stripped out of my clothes and then shifted. My bear immediately moved closer to Sammie and nuzzled her hand, where it was resting on her lap. My nuzzling was a little rough and forceful and she tipped backwards, laughing.

"You silly bear. You're a little bigger than me." She sat back up and gently stroked my fur. "Don't think this means that I'm not mad at you anymore. It just means that I'm a sucker for bears. You two are just really cute like this."

I gently nipped at her fingers and she popped me right on the nose. Mason watched us and rolled over onto his back, making a laughing sound. Sammie caught on and waited until Mason was watching again to lightly swat me.

I moved to his side and ran my nose across his little belly before gently nipping him and then moving to the other side of the room in a game of chase. He ran after me, knocking over everything in his way. Bailey quickly shifted, and Mom followed, and then the game moved from the playroom to the kitchen and then out the front door. I heard Alex give a mighty *whoop* and run after us.

Before long we were all in the yard, chasing each other. I stuck close to Mason and let him catch me a few times before chasing after him. He was fast for his age and gave me his all. I'd never felt prouder of anything in my life. This amazing little life had come from me. My heart ached for how many years and how much time I'd missed with him, but I'd make it up to him. He'd never have to worry about anything again.

I felt Sammie watching us from the porch and stood on my hind legs to get her attention. I let out a mighty roar and hit my chest, showing her how much of an idiot I could really be. She shook her head, but when she looked away, I saw a smile on her lips. I was going to win over my son and Sammie too. There was no turning back.

I smelled Matt coming up the drive and turned to him just as he was stripping down to shift and join the fun. He tackled me to the ground and we rolled into Alex, taking him down with us. Michael stood off to the sidelines, watching. I felt my brother's pain in that moment and crawled out from under Matt to go to him.

Michael wasn't much for shifting, not for fun. It had been years since he shifted for anything other than emergency situations. An accident when he was younger had scarred him, physically and mentally. We were all still connected to one another in our own way, though, and I felt the unhappiness rolling off of him in waves.

I stood up in front of him, watching him as he frowned at me. I huffed and then shoved him by the shoulder. My bear wanted our brother to play.

"Knock it off, Luc." He ground his teeth together and then turned and headed off in long strides.

I roared at him and then heard the same noise come from below me. I looked down at Mason and forgot my brother's troubles for the moment. My son was trying to imitate me.

Sammie came towards us, holding berries. "Look what I found for my bears."

Mason ran towards her and reached for the berries, but she held them over his head and shook her finger at him. "That's not how we take food from humans. Unless you want to eat my fingers, too."

Mason made a gagging sound and gave his own little huff at her.

"What? You want to eat my fingers?! This little bear is a wild man!" She leaned down and tickled his belly. "If you eat my fingers, how will I tickle you?"

He laughed and then suddenly, Mason wasn't a bear anymore. My jaw dropped as I watched him become a scrawny little kid with shaggy brown hair and the gangliest looking limbs I'd ever seen.

Sammie dropped the berries she was holding and screamed. She scooped him up and held him tightly to her chest. I watched with my heart in my hand as the biggest tears I'd ever seen rolled down her cheeks and her body shook from her silent sobs.

"I don't want to eat your fingers, Sammie. You're silly."

I shifted back and almost fell to my knees. Seeing him as bear was one thing, but seeing him as a little boy knocked the air out of my lungs. I ran over to them and pulled them both into my arms. Mason struggled against being smothered by us, but it quickly turned into a bout of giggles.

9
SAMMIE

"What's so funny, boy?" Lucas's voice shook with unshed tears and I had to remember to keep breathing. Everything in me was overwhelmed with emotion and feelings that I couldn't make sense of.

"You're naked and you're hugging Sammie."

I felt my cheeks turn red and lightly pulled out of his embrace. I sat Mason down and cupped his soft cheeks in my hands. "I've missed your little boy face so much."

He moved into the touch, smiling at me. "You smell good, Sammie."

I fell to my knees and held him against my chest. I kissed his head and cheeks and said a prayer of thanks all over again that nothing had happened to him. "You smell good, too."

He suddenly pulled away and frowned. "You're crying."

I touched my face and realized that I was. So much for keeping it together. As excited as I was about Mason being a little boy again, I couldn't help but think about what it meant for me. I would have to leave him, return to work. I would show my boss that he was okay and with his father and then I'd have to go home. Away from Mason.

Away from Lucas. The thought sent a pain through me that was so harsh it felt like a dagger in my chest. I whimpered.

Lucas knelt beside me and stroked my face, almost the same way I was stroking Mason's. "What's wrong?"

I felt another breakdown coming on and realized I had to get away from them. I didn't want Mason to see me sobbing. "Mason, why don't you play with your Daddy some more? I've got to go check on something."

He looked like he wanted to argue, but finally nodded. "Okay, Sammie."

I stood up and hurried inside before Lucas could stop me. I didn't fail to notice that we'd had an audience for that whole show and it just fueled me to make it to my room even faster.

I shoved the door closed behind me and threw myself on the bed like I was in some bad teenage drama. I wanted to keep it together, but everything was too much. I cried for what Mason had endured, I cried for Mallory whose life ended far too soon, and I cried for Aaron, a fine man who would be sorely missed.

I didn't know how I was supposed to go back to doing my job without Aaron at my side. We'd worked together since I joined the Marshals. He'd become my best friend pretty much instantly. He had a wife, and a young baby that would grow up without him. Their loss was much greater than mine, so I cried for them, too.

When I thought I'd cried everything that I had out, my thoughts turned to my leaving Mason. And Lucas. My chest ached and I rolled over in my bed. Staring at the ceiling, I blew out a rough breath and tried to make sense of what I was feeling about Lucas.

Any anger I'd felt towards him had dissipated when he'd nearly cried over Mason. I was still hurt that he thought of me as second-best. I didn't even fully know what it meant, though.

I groaned and pulled a pillow over my face, just as someone knocked on the door.

"It's me, Elizabeth. Can I come in?"

I sat up and called for her to come in.

She crept into the room and smiled at me before shutting the door. "Hi. You okay?"

I nodded, embarrassed. "I must be getting my period."

"Or you've got a shit-ton going on and you've had a really hard time lately. Don't minimize your feelings, Sammie."

I couldn't help but laugh. "You're right. I'm not getting my period. I'm just a hot mess."

She sat on the bed and pulled her feet under herself. "Talk to me. I'm a great listener."

So I talked. I told her everything that had gone on and all the reasons I had for releasing my tension through tears. By the time I got to the end, I was standing and ranting around the room like a lunatic.

"And then he said he'd thought that Mallory was his mate. But now he thinks it's me. I guess now that she's dead? I don't even really know what that's supposed to mean, but I do know that I don't like coming in second place."

She rolled her eyes. "He's an idiot. If he said you're his mate, then *you're* his mate. You're not second to anyone. That's not how it works. They, shifters, know immediately when someone is their mate. She'll smell different, everything will feel different, and it's like they can't keep their hands off of her. And, speaking from personal experience, being the human counterpart is almost as intense. As soon as I met Alex, I didn't even wait a whole two hours before we were rolling around in the sack."

My cheeks burned and she laughed. "Yeah, we all know you slept with him already. Bears have insanely great hearing."

I gasped. "No!"

She laughed even harder. "Yep. That's what I'm saying, though. No judgement. It's insane how the mate bond works. It's virtually instantaneous."

"Then why did he think Mallory was his mate?"

She rolled her eyes again, so far back in her head that I was afraid they'd get stuck facing the wrong way. "When their Dad died, he left this crazy will that said that the first son to have an offspring inherited control of the ranch. I don't know if Lucas just *hoped* Mallory was his mate, or what. It was weird. He just left one day and said that he was going to find her. None of us knew what to make of it."

I groaned, surprising myself. "I hate that he went looking for her."

Elizabeth grinned. "That's the mate bond. You become insanely jealous. When I see a woman look at Alex, I can't help but visualize myself scratching her eyes out."

"This is all too much. What do I do about it?"

"You just... accept it and deal with it. Life gifted you with a soulmate who was made just for you. Fate sent you to one another. That's pretty special. You shouldn't ignore it."

I didn't think I had a choice. "I can't stay here."

She stood up and stretched. "Then maybe you can stay at Lucas's house."

I started to correct her, but she cut me off. "I know what you meant, but I'm unwilling to lose a partner in crime. Leila is too hormone-crazy right now. I need a sane counterpart."

"I don't know what's going to happen, Elizabeth."

She nodded. "It'll work out. Mates are bound together by larger forces than our own silly fears and anxieties. Alex would move mountains to get to me. Just like Matt would move mountains for Leila. Just like Lucas will move mountains for you. No matter how big you build them."

She moved towards the door. "Come downstairs soon. You don't want to miss time with that cute little boy running around down there."

10

LUCAS

I could barely stand it. Sammie spent the rest of the day avoiding me. No matter what I did, when I got close to her, she moved away. I was ready to throttle her, just to get her to look at me. She'd busied herself with Mason, coddling him until I'd wanted to scream. I was actually jealous of a four-year-old.

When she'd stood up later that night and said she was going to bed, I stood up to follow her, but Alex caught my arm. "We need to talk, bro."

I growled at him and watched as Sammie quickly disappeared up the stairs with Mason hot on her heels. The boy was in love with her. He stared at her with so much adoration that everyone noticed. All day long, there'd been the comments about how attached he was to her.

Like I didn't know. My own son had just left me without a second glance.

As if on cue, I heard Sammie's soft voice correcting him. "Go and tell your Daddy that you're going to bed with me. Give him a hug, too. He's had a hard day."

Mason ran back down the stairs and sprang his sweaty little body into my arms. He wrapped his sticky hands around my neck and pressed a kiss to my chin. "Night. I'm going with Sammie."

I cleared my throat of the emotion that had lodged there. "Yeah, well, tell Sammie that you're sticky from all the candy she fed you earlier. You could probably use a bath."

He wrinkled his nose and shook his head. "I'm not telling her."

I swatted his backside as he jumped down and ran away from me. "Tell her!"

I stood there, watching my world disappear up the stairs and shook my head. I couldn't go to bed without talking to Sammie. She could only ignore me for so long.

Alex called me to the kitchen table, where he, Matt, and Michael were sitting. Only John was missing. "We've got to discuss something."

I sat down, but looked towards the stairs. I wanted to be with my mate and my son. "Can we make this quick?"

Matt snorted. "You in a rush to get ignored some more?"

"I don't want to hear it."

"Well, if you said what I heard you said, you deserve it. What the hell's wrong with you, man?"

I let my head fall to the table and hit it relatively hard. "I'm an idiot."

Alex called a stop to the picking and brought up what was on his mind. "According to Dad's will, Lucas is now the rightful heir to the ranch. Mason is four. You brought an offspring into this world before any of us."

I was still staring at the stairs. "What?"

"The ranch is yours."

I looked at the three of them and sighed. Before today, I had wanted it so much that I'd spent months frantically searching for Mallory. Now, as it was being thrust into my lap, all I could think about was that it would keep me away from my son and my mate. The platefull of responsibilities that came with running a working ranch would command time and energy that I'd rather spend with my family.

"Well, what do you say?"

I shook my head. "I don't want it."

They all stared at me in shock.

"I need to develop a relationship with my son and I want to convince Sammie to be with me forever. I don't want to spent eighty hours a week running this place."

"More. I don't know how Dad did it." Alex shook his head. "It's a lot of work for one man."

Matt nodded. "Why don't we come to some sort of agreement to run it together? It's what we were doing before the will was read. Even back then when we were fighting each other like cats and dogs, it still worked better than with one of us trying to do everything."

Michael cleared his throat. "It's cool with me. John will agree. He's been so focused elsewhere that I know he has little interest in running this place full time."

I stood up. "Then it's settled. We share as a family. Like we should. How about we hammer out the details later, boys?"

Alex laughed. "Go on."

I RACED up the stairs and knocked on the door. "Sammie, it's me."

There was a long silence and then a muffled sigh. The door opened a crack and then her pretty face was looking out at me. Mason peeked out from below, his curiosity getting the better of him.

"Hi."

Mason grabbed my hand and pulled me closer. "Daddy, can you sleep in here with us?"

Sammie bit her lip and then moved out of the way. "Come on in."

I wasn't about to argue with him. I wanted desperately to be close to them both. "I'll take the floor again. How about that?"

Mason pulled me towards the bathroom. "It's bath time first."

Sammie caught him just before he jumped into the water in his pajamas. "Did you forget you're wearing clothes, little man?"

He looked down at the offending things and then shifted into a bear cub right in her arms. The additional weight took her by surprise and she ended up dropping him into the water. The splash soaked her and left a once-again-human Mason giggling hysterically.

"You're wet, Sammie!"

I couldn't help but smile watching the two of them.

Sammie turned to me and narrowed her eyes. "If you're going to be in here, you're going to help. He's surprisingly wigglier as a little boy."

I laughed and knelt down beside her. Instantly, a big splash soaked my shirt and face. I sent a playful growl his way and then reached in and tickled him. "Did you forget how to take a proper bath?"

By the time we got him washed and redressed for bed, we were all three tuckered out. Mason climbed into bed and curled up right in the center of it. "Daddy?"

My heart flipped over in my chest. "Yeah?"

Mason patted the mattress beside him. "Stay here."

I looked at Sammie and saw the hurt flash over her face for a brief second before she attempted to hide it with a half-smile. "Where's Sammie going to sleep?"

He patted the bed on the other side of him. "Here, silly."

Her cheeks burned, but instead of fighting it, she nodded. "Okay, kiddo. Whatever you want."

I got a nervous feeling in the pit of my stomach and couldn't shake it. Something was up with her. She got in bed and crawled to Mason's other side. I laid down next to him and turned to face them.

Mason yawned widely and then shoved his little butt into Sammie's ribs. "Goodnight, Sammie. Goodnight, Daddy."

I kissed his forehead. "Night, buddy."

Sammie pressed her lips into his hair. "Night. Love you."

"Love you, too."

In seconds, Mason was out and Sammie squeezed her eyes shut, pretending to be asleep.

I stretched my arm out and lightly flicked her on the nose. "I can tell you're faking, Sammie. You're going to have to talk to me at some point."

11

SAMMIE

I groaned. I didn't want to talk to Lucas. Every second I talked to him was just a little bit farther I fell for him. Watching him with Mason was like torture. I had to leave, but everything about the two of them tethered my heart and called me to stay.

"I said the wrong things earlier, Sammie. I didn't mean it like it sounded. I'd like the opportunity to explain."

I shut my eyes and tried to block out his deep voice.

"When my father passed, we were all surprised by his will. At the time, I thought that taking over the ranch was what I wanted most in the world. I had no one around that I was willing to have a kid with, but all of a sudden, I was plagued by a memory... almost five years ago, I got a late-night call from Mallory. I hadn't seen her in months and she was higher than a kite on something. She was almost completely incoherent. She was babbling but I distinctly heard her say that she was pregnant. I freaked out. I knew she and I weren't supposed to be together."

My eyes flew open and I stared at him. He'd known about Mason?

"I tried calling her for weeks after that, but she never answered. I had all but given up when I finally managed to get ahold of her. She laughed and told me that she'd just been high that night and wanted to mess with me. Said she didn't even remember telling me that. She also said she'd met another guy and was happy. I believed her."

He frowned and shook his head. "This next part is not flattering. After dad's will was read, I decided to find Mallory. I... I thought that maybe she had been my mate and I'd just been too big of a dumbass to notice. And, yes, I also thought that if she'd been telling the truth that night, if she had been pregnant with my child, I had a chance to get control of the ranch."

I withheld judgment because of the pain etched across his face. He brushed Mason's hair off of his forehead and his frown grew even more severe.

"I went looking for her, in hopes of finding a child who could be my ticket to a huge inheritance. I know now how misguided I was. I honestly didn't have a clue until I saw him. I realize now that everything I was doing was for the wrong reasons." He met my eyes. "I'm going to make it up to him. I'm going to be the best father a little boy-cub could ever dream of. It's different now. I'm different. When I saw him, I didn't think about the ranch. I just saw this little bear who smelled like me and who made my heart feel like my body was too small for it.

"And then there was you. As soon as I saw you, Sammie, I knew I'd been stupid to ever wonder if Mallory could've been my mate. As though I could come face to face with my mate and not be a hundred percent certain. But, hell, I didn't know what it actually felt like to meet a mate. That there's no way I could be anywhere near her and not notice, because the feeling would be so indescribably all-consuming. That every part of my mind, body, and heart would buzz with hyper awareness. That I would want to be near her every second of every day. That I would have a constant and overwhelming need to possess her completely. That I would think of nothing but claiming her so I could shout it to the world, tell everyone, that this amazing woman is *mine*. I didn't know. Until I saw you"

I sucked in a breath. As much as I wanted to hear what he was saying, I didn't. I had to leave. I couldn't stay. I had to make sure Mason was safe and go back to work.

"I know that the feelings are slower for you, probably. I just wanted you to know."

I looked at him with tears in my eyes. "I have to leave, Lucas."

Panic filled his face. "Why?"

"I have a job, a life, outside of this. I have an apartment in Cheyenne. I have family that I haven't seen in months. I have to make sure the man who did that to Aaron and Mallory pays for it."

"You don't want to stay with us?"

My heart felt like shattering glass. "I have to go. Tomorrow. I have to."

He looked like he wanted to argue, but I turned away and faced the wall. Mason rolled over and I got a knee in the back, but I ignored it. I couldn't help the tears that fell from my eyes. I knew Lucas could tell I was crying, but I couldn't help it.

He rested an arm on my hip and left it there even after I'd stopped crying and as I fell asleep.

I LEFT the next morning after quietly kissing a sleeping Mason on the forehead. He was warming to his family so well and so quickly that I wasn't worried about him being okay. He'd probably need therapy after what he'd endured, but he was going to be okay. He had a top-notch support system. I left him in bed with Lucas and crept out of the house. I was on the road back to Cheyenne before the sun had come up over the mountains.

I WALKED AROUND in a daze the first day. With the exception of the calls I made to my boss, letting him know I was back in town, and to the pizza shop closest to my apartment, I couldn't stop the tears. My emotions were a mess. I had cried more in the last two days than I had in the previous five years.

I knew that what I had done was necessary. I had a meeting with my boss bright and early first thing the next morning and we were going to go over what to do about the man who'd killed Aaron and

Mallory. I had to get it together and make sure that their killer wasn't running free. I had to. Mason deserved as much from me.

Sleep didn't come easily. I would eventually doze for a while only to be awakened with dreams of Lucas and Mason fresh on my mind. My heart ached. I desperately wanted to go back to them and pretend like nothing was happening outside of Long Ranch. I was a U.S. Marshal, though. I had a job to do.

The meeting with my boss went like shit. He saw right through the concealer I'd layered over my under-eye bags, and my bloodshot eyes. If that wasn't bad enough, when he told me there was nothing we could do about Wesley Butler, I'd lost my cool. Unless Mason had witnessed it and could actually point Wesley out in a line up, saying that Wesley was the man who'd killed his mother, there was nothing we could do. Our jobs were done with him. The case would go back to the FBI who would try to catch him at something else. Without witnesses, we didn't have a case, and now that Mallory and her boyfriend were dead, the original case we'd had against him was thrown out.

It wasn't pretty, but yes, I had a serious freak out. After seeing how unhinged I became about the case, my boss refused to let me come back to work until I'd been cleared by a psychologist. It pissed me off because I couldn't stop thinking about the fact that if I had to stay at home all day long with just my sadness and heartbreak over leaving Lucas and Mason, then my freak out today was nothing. I was going to absolutely lose it. I was also furious. Wesley Butler got off scott-free.

It was final, though. My boss wouldn't budge. No work until I received clearance. I made an appointment immediately and went back to my apartment to drown in the emotional mess that was now my life.

12

SAMMIE

My phone rang in the middle of the night and I sat straight up in bed, fearing the worst. The phone never rang in the middle of the night unless someone was dead or dying. I tripped over the blankets in my haste to get up and ended up slamming to the ground. My head ricocheted off the hard wood floor. Instant head pain.

I raced to the phone. "Hello? Hello?"

Lucas's voice filled my ear and I collapsed into one of my kitchen chairs. "Sammie? Are you okay?"

"Yes, of course. What's wrong? What's going on?"

He let out a big sigh of relief and swore under his breath. "The house was just attacked. I can't say too much, but I think you should come."

I was already grabbing my keys and running out of the door. "Is everyone okay?"

"We're okay. Be careful."

I wanted to beg him to stay on the phone with me. Just a couple of days away from them had me longing to hear more of his voice. "I'll be there soon."

I hung up and sped towards the ranch. I realized half way there that in my haste I'd forgotten to grab my purse. I didn't have my purse, my gun, or my badge. I prayed that I didn't get stopped doing twenty over the speed limit.

*****Lucas*****

I SLAMMED my fist into a tree trunk and felt a sick satisfaction at the cracking I heard coming from the tree. I wanted to rip it from the ground, roots and all, and throw it across the ranch. My body was raging and my head was pounding from an adrenaline hangover. The bullet wound in my side was healing fast, but still stung like hell. The worst pain was the pain in my heart that hadn't stopped aching for days.

Michael still growled from across the yard. He'd shifted and ripped the head off of a man named Wesley Butler. The man who'd dared to come onto our property and attack us while we slept. I knew that it was the same man who'd killed Mallory by the way Mason reacted to him. He'd instantly turned back into his cub and had hidden behind me shaking uncontrollably. He'd even wet himself in fear.

The man had shrieked like a little girl when he'd seen Mason shift. When he ran, I chased. I'd gotten several damning blows onto the man's body before he remembered he had a gun and shot me. That was when Michael had come out of nowhere and ended him.

Michael was still in his bear form, growling viciously anytime anyone got near him. My worry for my brother was only overridden by my worry for my mate. She'd sounded so panicked when she'd answered the phone. I'd worried that the man had sent someone to attack her, as well.

My mom was inside with Mason and had sent my little sister Bailey to tell me that he'd calmed down and had asked for Sammie before falling asleep. He'd been asking for her since she left. Damn her. My blood started boiling again and I had to force my bear back down inside. He'd been raging since she left. I'd never heard from him so much. He was a quiet bear, only sounding out when absolutely necessary, usually. Sammie leaving us had him screaming in my head, clawing at my insides constantly.

It was another hour before Michael had calmed down enough to shift back. He still stood away from our brothers and kept his back to the man he'd killed.

"When did you call her?" Alex asked from beside me.

I glanced at the road and felt the air around us change. "She's here."

Soon after, we heard her car speeding towards the house. I shifted, unable to hold bear inside, and let out a big roar. My bear was happy. Our mate was home. I was still angry with her. I didn't know which one of us was going to win this tug-of-war.

Matt waved Sammie over and she sprinted across the wide expanse of lawn in just a thin T-shirt and a pair of barely-there shorts. I forced myself to shift back and slapped Matt and Alex on the back of their heads.

"Don't fucking look."

Sammie closed the gap between us and threw her body at mine. I was already hard watching her run, but feeling her barely-covered, soft, curvy body up against mine did me in. I growled low in my throat and squeezed her into me, despite the pain.

She must've felt the dampness of my blood against her, though. She pulled back and looked down. Her face went pale and she let out a gasp. "Lucas! You're hurt!"

I shook my head. "It'll heal soon. I'm fine, Sam. The other guy isn't, though."

I had to get her attention off of me or I was going to fuck her up against a tree, right then and there. My bear was roaring so loudly in my head, demanding I mark her so she couldn't leave us again, it was all I could do to keep my teeth to myself.

She looked over at the spot where I was pointing and shuddered. I `expected her to blanch and turn away, but instead, she walked over to the body and looked closer. "I don't know how the fuck he found this place. I covered my trail. I'm so sorry to have brought him to your doorstep."

Alex stepped forward. "It's okay, but we need to know, is it over now? Is there going to be anyone else coming here to find him?"

"He works alone. This is the end. And the cops aren't coming either. He doesn't deserve anything resembling a proper burial. Is there a place here where we can get rid of his body?"

Michael came forward, still looking shaky. "You can call the cops, Sammie. I killed him. I didn't mean to, but I did. I killed a human and that's outside of the boundaries."

I had to grit my teeth and hold my bear in when she turned to him and cupped his face in her hands. I knew she could tell he was hurting and just wanted to comfort him. If she could do what we couldn't, I'd let her. Even if it was making me crazy watching her touch him.

"Michael, he wasn't human. He was a monster. He came here to kill a little boy. You did what you had to do and I would have done the same. Even if he hadn't come here, I would've found a way to end him. You protected my mate and you protected my boy. I'm forever grateful to you for that. There's no way I would bring cops here to poke around. I've got all the answers I need already."

He nodded and walked into the woods behind the house, still looking haunted.

Sammie turned to Alex and Matt. "Is there a place to get rid of him?"

Alex nodded. "We know a place. We'll take care of it."

She tilted her head and then shook it. "I'm not going to ask. Just make sure all traces of him are gone."

As they both moved to follow her orders, she came to my side. "Are you the only one who got hurt?"

I nodded but didn't say anything. I was fluctuating between anger and lust so strong that I could barely see straight.

"Is there somewhere we can be alone for a few minutes?"

I looked down at her and nodded again. "Follow me."

13

LUCAS

I led Sammie through the trail in the woods that led to my house on the other side. It was small and cozy, just big enough for a little family to start out in, if my mate ever chose to stop running from us.

I let us inside and then shut the door behind her. "My house."

She looked around and smiled. "I love it. Rustic and cozy. Mason will be very happy here."

I turned to face her and pinned her with a look. "You left."

She nodded. "I did."

"Why?"

"I had a job to do. I needed to make sure Mason would be safe. Turns out it was all for nothing." She hesitated. "I... I thought I had to."

I frowned. "But?"

"I am miserable without you and Mason. I couldn't think of anything else. All I wanted every second of every day was to come back here and be with you. I knew I messed up. I *know* I messed up."

I edged closer. "And?"

"And I took some time off. I was planning... to come back here tomorrow." She gave me such a goofy grin at the end of her declaration that my heart skipped a beat.

I'd never seen her look so light. "You were coming back?"

She grinned again and nodded, sending her hair flying around her head. "I don't have all the answers here, but I know that I want to be with you and Mason. You two are my heart."

I grabbed her by the wrist and pulled her closer. I was still naked and it took me no time to strip her down to nothing. When her bare breasts were smooshed against my chest, I felt something uncoil in me that had been wound up tightly for as long as I could remember. "Mine."

She nodded. "Hopelessly."

I kissed her then, ending the conversation. I needed to possess her, be inside of her. I needed to mark her. I slid my tongue into her mouth and stroked hers. It was a messy kiss, full of teeth and nips, but it told me how eager she was to be with me too.

I picked her up and groaned as my dick rested right up against her already damp core. I wanted to plunge into her, but I also wanted to give her more the second time around, take my time a little, so I carried her to my bed and placed her on top of it.

She crawled backwards until she was in the middle of the bed and then spread her legs wide for me. "Come on."

I growled and crawled up the bed until I was hovering over her. While she trembled with need, I lowered my mouth and took one long lick from her. She bucked and cried out like she'd never experienced anything like it before. Wanting to give her more, I pressed my face between her thighs and inhaled her scent before working her over with my tongue.

She came before I was ready to be finished, so I kept going, working her to another orgasm before stopping and crawling the rest of the way up her luscious body. I sucked her nipples into my mouth, one at a time, and teased them while she writhed under me.

"Stop playing with me, Lucas!" She grabbed a handful of my hair and pulled me higher so she could kiss me. Her teeth bit down on my bottom lip and then my chin and neck before she raked them across my shoulder. "I need you inside me."

I grabbed the back of her hair and pulled her neck to the side, exposing her neck. Then, I plunged my dick and teeth into her at the same time.

Sammie screamed and tightened on my dick almost painfully as an orgasm shook her. She raked her nails down my back and clung to me as the power of it rocked her.

I was struggling not to come so soon. I didn't want to embarrass myself, but her walls were doing everything they could to milk me dry. I waited until she'd relaxed slightly to start moving.

I licked the mark on her neck, knowing that it would be extra responsive, and then gripped her ass as I thrust into her. Sammie moved under me, lifting her hips to meet mine, rolling them in a way that damn near had my eyes crossing. Her chest moved against mine, letting me feel her soft breasts and pebbled nipples over and over again. Her nails found a new home buried in my back, but I liked the sting.

Thrusting harder and faster into her, I felt the heat gathering and reached one hand down to gently stroke her clit so she would come with me again. She clenched around me tightly as she cried out and locked her legs around me. My body gave in instantly to a climax more powerful than I've ever felt before. I filled her with my seed as I continued to thrust into her a few last times.

Sammie locked her teeth against my shoulder, leaving her own, less permanent, mark on me as we came together.

I didn't feel like I could move as I came down from the high of claiming her. I knew I was heavy on top of her, though, so I rolled to the side and brought her with me.

She rested her head on my chest and ran her hand over my stomach. "Let's never stop doing this."

I stroked her back and pressed my lips to her head. "How about when I'm old and gray?"

I'd meant the question as a joke, but even as the words left my mouth, I heard the insecurity in my voice. I wanted to laugh it off, but

I had to know. Even with the mark on her, I still needed to hear her say that she wouldn't leave again.

She looked up at me with wide eyes and nodded. "Even when you're old and gray. Even when my boobs sag."

I looked down at the objects in question and grinned, feeling a world lighter. "You mean they won't always be this perfect?"

She slapped my chest and I grabbed her hand and lowered it to my dick, already hard again. "That's what you do to me."

Her eyes widened and then she leapt from bed, grinning hugely. "You can't keep me here all night, you beast! We've got a kid to go see."

I jumped from the bed and got ready to give chase. She was right. We did have a kid to go see, but he was asleep and tonight was all mine to show her just how much I loved her. Because I did. Without a doubt.

"You'd better run, little Goldie Locks, because the big, bad bear found you in his bed and he's never letting you go."

She laughed and ran.

I gave her a head start because I knew that I'd always catch her.

She was mine.

THE END

The next book in this series is Rancher Bear's Secret

RANCHER BEAR'S SECRET

RANCHER BEARS BOOK 4

Michael Long has scars, both physical and emotional. He's damaged. His bear is broken and dangerous. In fact, the only time his bear comes out is to viciously maim and kill. So when the woman he knows is his mate shows up, right there on his family's ranch, his best course of action is to avoid her. But, Daisy Hawkins is unavoidable.

Daisy isn't taking no for an answer. As sweet as her name, Daisy is Landing, Wyoming's newest kindergarten teacher. She's not sure what came over her when she set eyes on the tall, muscular rancher at the annual field trip to the Long Ranch. Daisy has never hit on a man before, but Michael Long is the sexiest thing she's ever seen. The connection between them is almost palpable.

  Why does the guy keep running away from her?

As if chasing down a reticent cowboy wasn't stressful enough, Daisy's period is late. She's always wanted to be a parent, but she hadn't planned on meeting the man of her dreams while pregnant with another man's baby.

1
DAISY

"Your kids are so much sweeter than mine. Look at them!" Maggie Budding pointed to several of my children who were gathered around a goat, showering it with love. "I have such a rotten group this year."

I smiled at my kids and waved when one of them looked over at us. "They love animals. They've been so excited about this trip. I think they knew more about it than I did, honestly."

One of my little boys, Davey, pressed a wet kiss between the goat's eyes and it nibbled his chin. He fell backwards, in a fit of giggles, and then squealed as the goat moved on to nibbling his belly.

Maggie laughed along with me. "I can't imagine dealing with five-year-olds all day, every day, but damn, they're cute."

"Don't let them fool you. Last week, Davey cut off Mary Jane's ponytail. When I asked him why he did it, he said he wanted it to make a tail for his puppy."

She winced. "Yeah, not so cute."

I shook my head. It wasn't. My class of ten five-year-olds was a handful. They had more energy, more stubbornness, and knew more ways of manipulating an adult than any children I'd ever met. Landing, Wyoming sure raised them differently.

I'd been teaching at Landing Elementary for a little over a month now and I'd learned almost instantly that I had my hands full. I couldn't help but fall in love with the children, though. Despite their somewhat animalistic behavior at times, they were sweet in moments that stole my heart. Again, manipulative.

"I'm going to head over to the snack carts. Do you want me to grab you something?" I couldn't stop looking at the funnel cake sign.

The Longs had gone all out. I heard they did it up like this every year, and I could certainly understand now why my kids had been looking forward to the trip since the first day of school. I'd probably be the same way in future years. The Long family had turned their ranch into a carnival, full of food, games, animals, and even a photo booth.

Every grade, from kindergarten to high school seniors, was in attendance and from the looks of things, having a blast. The air had even turned slightly cool, as though it was working in harmony with the Longs to provide the most magical day ever for the kids.

"No. Go ahead and take a break. You can take over for me later."

I looked back at the funnel cake sign and nodded. "That sounds perfect. Thanks, Maggie."

I said hello to fellow teachers as I passed by making my way to the food, not wanting to appear rude. They'd been a little closed off towards me, the whole town had, really, but I figured it was just their way. I'd only gotten this job offer because the previous teacher, Mary Ellen Simon, had run off with her boyfriend to Mexico. I was a last minute hire and, from what I'd heard, everyone had loved Miss Simon. I was determined to make them love me, too. I planned to stay in Landing for as long as I could, so they'd get used to me eventually.

I joined the line for the fried batter and when it was my turn, I smiled at the attractive older woman and winked before speaking. "I'm going to ask for two and say that I'm sharing with someone, but I'm not. I could smell these from across the ranch, even over the animal scent."

She grinned and sprinkled powdered sugar generously on both

plates. "We all have those days. Would you like chocolate sauce drizzled on top?"

I thought about it for a second and then nodded. "I've never had a funnel cake with chocolate sauce, but it sounds divine. Thank you so much."

She passed me the plates. "Feel free to come back through to get more for your other friends, honey."

I laughed and headed off towards the picnic tables to eat in peace. As much as I loved children, eating while they were underfoot was a chocolate sauce smeared across the front of my dress disaster waiting to happen. I sat down and hungrily shoveled food into my mouth. I'd skipped breakfast in my eagerness to get to school early to prepare for my kindergarten class's first ever field trip.

I people-watched as I ate, taking the time to make sure none of the adults looked like they needed help with any of the students, before relaxing and watching just for fun. All of the students seemed to be having a blast.

I'd worried that the older students might find it boring, but the Longs were a smart bunch. I guess the ranch was run by several brothers who all appeared to be quite good looking. I spotted at least three of them, positioned at activities, with long lines of teenage girls waiting to do whatever they were offering.

I couldn't help but giggle at one little girl who demanded one of the Long brothers hold her in his arms the whole time. She was probably eight, but she seemed to know quality when she saw it. The rancher was being a team player and going along with it.

I caught movement out of the corner of my eye and turned to catch a very tall, very muscled man disappearing behind one of the barns. Something about him startled me and I suddenly felt a rush of heat spread over my skin and a crackle of something like an electric pulse surge through me. *Wow.* I continued to stare at the spot where he'd disappeared until I'd convinced myself that he wasn't going to reappear.

A few minutes later, though, I spotted a few older kids walking off in the same direction. No one had specified that any part of the ranch was off limits, but it worried me nonetheless to see them going off by themselves.

I quickly downed my funnel cake and tossed the plates in the trash barrel before heading off after them. I'd worn flip flops and I had a hard time not announcing my arrival with click clack they made.

It turned out that I didn't need to worry. The kid's laughter was more than loud enough to conceal my sounds. I rounded the corner of the barn and spotted them, leaning against the barn wall, lighting cigarettes, and staring at the hunk I'd seen earlier.

He was a distance away from them, completely ignoring them as he chopped wood like a madman. His T-shirt clung to his back and shoulders in a way that made my body pulse a little harder. He had longish, dirty blonde hair that was partially covered by a large cowboy hat. As I watched, he stopped what he was doing, pulled off the hat, and pulled up the bottom of his shirt to wipe his face free of sweat.

I nearly gasped as the move left the bottom few inches of his defined abs showing. Instantly, I felt my panties dampening. I sucked in a sharp breath. *That* had certainly never happened to me before.

Almost immediately, the cowboy tilted his head back and took a deep breath in with his eyes closed. Then, he turned and focused on me. His eyes bore into me with a fierce intensity, his expression was... something that I couldn't quite place.

Even from where I was standing, I could see how stunningly handsome he was. If that word even covered it. Just watching him sent sparks of flaming passion to every nerve ending in my body as though, at the slightest breeze, I'd become a blazing inferno. *Wowza.* I'd never experienced an attraction on that deep a level before.

"Look at that scar. Jesus, he's like Frankenstein." One of the teens was making fun of him as she lifted the cigarette to her mouth.

They hadn't noticed me yet, but I was about to make my presence known. There was nothing I abhorred more than meanness.

2

MICHAEL

I'd smelled her the second she stepped foot on our property. I had an idea that it was no coincidence that she smelled like strawberries. It was my favorite sweet, after all. I'd felt her presence immediately, and the closer she got, the more painful it was to avoid her. But, I did.

I kept to the shadows and stayed out of her way, even as she got closer and closer. I never let myself look at her, worried that if I did, I might lose my barely maintained control.

But, when I'd smelled her arousal, not fifty feet from me, I couldn't help but look. There she was. *Right there.* Wet, ready, and... perfect.

Her long blonde hair curled softly around her angelic face. She couldn't have been more than a few inches over five feet tall, with soft curves that I desperately wanted to trace with my tongue. Bright blue eyes widened when I looked at her and her cheeks flushed pink. The long dress she was wearing got caught in a breeze and it danced, revealing a slit up the side that teased my cock more than any lover had ever been able to do with hands or mouths.

I wanted her. My bear came to life in that instant and I damn near shifted right then and there. *Mine.*

My bear was a nasty bear, dark and unable to remember that we were part human, as well. I gritted my teeth and did every breathing technique I knew to keep the change from happening.

Just as it passed and I dropped my hat back on my head, she turned a hard look on the kids who were smoking against the barn wall. I'd heard them laughing about my scars, but it had barely penetrated the lust-filled fog she created around me.

I watched as she stomped her little feet over to them, her breasts swaying in a way that made me feel like I could shoot my load just from watching them.

"You know, it's bad enough that you snuck away to smoke a cigarette, but to hear you making fun of someone, too? You should be ashamed of yourselves. Being nasty to other people isn't cool. It just makes you look trashy and ugly. Put the cigarette out and get back out there with the rest of your class, or I'm taking names and having your teachers assign you detention."

Her voice was sweet, too sweet to scare a rowdy bunch of bear shifter teens. They just stared at her with blank expressions before laughing and rolling their eyes.

My blood boiled and I dropped the ax I'd picked back up. There was no way they were going to treat her like that and get away with it. My bear foamed at the mouth at any chance for violence.

"Are you kidding me? Don't be jerks, guys, go back to the carnival." She put her hands on her hips and frowned, her lips going ridiculously pouty.

They still didn't listen to her, but I stepped up behind her and growled at them. "*Now.*"

My voice was hoarse from not being used often and the order came out more like a deep bark, than an actual voice. It did the job, though. Every one of them could sense my dominant bear. The kids scattered faster than bugs in the light, leaving me alone with a woman that I shouldn't be alone with.

She spun around and grinned up at me. Up close, she looked even more like an angel than she did from far away. Her big blue eyes could've made Bambi look threatening. Her nose was tiny and cute, but her mouth... Her mouth made my dick harden painfully in my pants.

"Thank you. Apparently, I'm not threatening to teens. Kindergarteners are much more intimidated by me, I promise."

I frowned down at her, feeling things that I shouldn't be. I should be running away. It was dangerous to be so close to her. Dangerous for her. "I'm not so sure."

She giggled and tucked a piece of hair behind her ears. "I'm Daisy. I just moved to town a couple of months ago."

I breathed in her scent and growled again. My bear wanted to sink his teeth into her sweet little body. "I gotta go."

Without hesitation, she reached out and put her hand on my chest. "Thank you. For helping me with those kids. Maybe I could repay you."

My dick was about to explode, straining to get out of my pants, and I couldn't help but lean into her touch. People didn't touch me. It'd been months since anyone had. "You want to...repay me?"

Her cheeks blushed bright pink and she giggled sweetly before ducking her head and letting her hair hide her face. Then, she looked up at me through her thick eyelashes, and her blue eyes sparkled. "I could make you dinner. I'm a great cook."

Her smell was driving me insane. Under the strawberry scent, I could smell chocolate and sugar. To a hungry bear, she was a wet dream. And I wasn't just a hungry bear. I was the *hungriest*.

I couldn't move away from her. I was using all of my physical and mental control to keep my bear placated, so the man in me could do nothing but stand there, eating up all of her attention.

She ran her hand up to my shoulder and the pads of her fingers pressed into my skin. "I'll make you dinner tonight. Do you have a phone?"

Before I could even think about what I was doing, I'd reached into my back pocket and handed her my cellphone. Daisy kept her hand on my shoulder and used her free hand to type something. Then, she slipped the phone back into my hand and smiled at me again.

"I put my address in. Is eight good?"

I couldn't open my mouth without releasing a growl, so I just nodded.

She let her hand drop and backed away from me with the sweetest smile on her pretty face. "I'll see you then."

I balled my fists at my side and struggled to keep breathing as she backed away. My chest felt like it was going to cave in as she swayed her hips away from me.

Right when I thought she was done lighting the fuse to the bomb that was my life, she looked at me over her shoulder and winked. "I didn't add my number so if you want to cancel, you'll have to come to my house to do it."

3
DAISY

I walked back to my kids completely astonished with myself. I didn't understand how in the hell I'd managed to talk in complete sentences to the sexy stranger I'd just invited to my home. I'd been so busy tripping over my brain that my mouth had just moved on its own. I'd never, ever asked a guy out, much less in such a smooth way. I wanted to high-five myself, but I didn't want to lose any cool points that I'd just acquired.

I rushed back to Maggie, uncertain of how much time I'd lost lusting after the cowboy. The cowboy, whose name I hadn't bothered to catch. *Darn.*

Maggie was standing in the same spot, a frown on her face as she watched a few of her kids playing. She glanced up at me and gave me a concerned look. "Are you okay, Daisy? You look all flushed."

I nodded, too quickly for it to be considered normal. "I'm fine. I didn't keep you waiting too long, did I?"

"Not at all. I was enjoying watching your kiddos play, until mine came closer and I remembered my misery."

I forced a smile and took a quick stock of my class. "Were they any trouble?"

"Well, one of my boys peed on one of my little girls. That's my trouble, though, isn't it?" She shot me a look. "Let's switch grades."

I shook my head. "No thanks."

Just then, I caught a flash of my cowboy stalking around the crowd and into the main house. I quickly pointed him out to Maggie. "Who is that?"

She followed my finger and grunted. "Michael Long. He's the middle brother."

"What's with the grunt?"

"He's a little weird, I guess."

I turned to face her. "Weird?"

Maggie's eyebrows scrunched together. "Yeah. He was in some sort of accident when he was younger and it left him all scarred up. He stays to himself, mostly."

I watched as she hesitated and wanted to shake her to get more information from her. "Tell me."

She looked around and leaned in close. "There are rumors about him. People are tightlipped here, but if you listen, you can overhear little snippets here and there. There's talk that he killed a man."

I gasped and tried to find him. "Surely, that's just some vicious rumor."

She shrugged. "I don't know. I just know that he gives me the creeps when I see him. He always looks pissed off. Plus, that scar running through his lips is too intense for me."

I thought of the man who'd come to my rescue against a mild group of teenagers. He wasn't a murderer. His scar wasn't too intense, either. It took the feminine edge away from his otherwise too pretty lips. It made him different, rugged and mysterious.

"Why? Did he bother you?"

I caught sight of him again and grinned when he looked my way. I bit my lip and then looked at Maggie. "Nope. I invited him to dinner at my house tonight. I think he's sexy."

I could've sworn I saw a blush tint his cheeks, but there's no way he could have heard me from this distance. He stared at me for a few more seconds before heading off again. I had to fight the urge to follow him.

"Really?"

I nodded. "That man doesn't get the credit he deserves."

~

AFTER WORK, I rushed to the market and bought groceries to cook for Michael. Then, I raced home and put a pot of boiling water on the stove for the start of my grandmother's chicken and dumplings recipe. I wanted to impress him with my culinary skills.

My cheeks warmed as I thought about what I really wanted to do with him. The man had a physical presence that beckoned me and every time I thought about him, I imagined taking his shirt off with my teeth. I'd never fantasized about a man this way, and in such vivid detail. I'd never felt so lust-filled.

I wasn't a virgin, by any means, but my experiences in the bedroom had been less than stellar. I had a feeling that Michael Long could show me a thing or two.

I showered and then changed into a white lacy dress that emphasized my curves. It stopped mid-thigh and dipped lower in the cleavage area than anything I'd ever wear to school. While waiting for the chicken to cook, I painted my toenails a pretty pink color and waddled around while they dried.

I'd gotten sun that day at the carnival, so I skipped most of my makeup and just applied mascara and a lip stain. I was ready early, so I stood in the kitchen, over my stove, and waited for eight o'clock.

Michael was right on time. I'd just tossed the dumplings into the pot when the doorbell rang. I stripped off my apron and raced to the front door.

There he was, so tall, that his face was dangerously close to my lit porch light. His eyes were pure gold in the light and I sucked in a breath as his male scent washed over me. Mmm... I didn't know what it was he was wearing, but it reminded me of the woods. It also made me lust after things that I had no business lusting after from him. Yet.

"Hi."

He braced his hands on my doorframe and I heard the wood creaking under his big fingers. "I shouldn't stay."

I pouted before I could stop the childish reaction. "You don't want this, do you?" *Why did I feel so heartbroken?* "I'm sorry for pushing you, Michael. I just...got carried away, I guess."

He shook his head. "I didn't say that I didn't want it."

I tilted my head to the side and bit my lip. Confusion played at the edges of my conscious, but first and foremost was hot lust. "Michael, do you want to come inside?"

My doorframe creaked. "Yes."

I stepped back to allow him to enter. When he didn't move, I reached out and grabbed the front of his black T-shirt. I tugged him inside before kicking the door shut. "Well, look at that. You're inside."

He growled low in his throat and I forgot that I'd been cooking. I forgot Maggie's whispered warning. I forgot that I'd only just met the man hours ago. I forgot that my momma had raised me to be a good girl.

I still had his shirt in my fist and I used it to pull him closer to me. When he wouldn't budge any more, I brought my body into his and blinked up at him with wide eyes. I'd never been so attracted to anyone in my entire life and all I could think about was getting naked with him. Something was going on here, this wasn't my normal reaction to any man, no matter how sinfully good looking he was. I was a kindergarten teacher for goodness sakes!

"What is this?" I wondered aloud.

His muscles tensed under my fingers and the muscles in his jaw worked as he stared down at me. "It's dangerous for you."

My heartrate spiked, but it didn't stop the playful smile from quirking up one side of my lips. "Yeah?"

He grunted and backed up a step. "I'm serious. I should go."

I matched his step and nodded. "If you want to."

His back hit the door and he groaned as my body pressed against his. "Daisy..."

Hearing my name uttered in his rough voice sent chills down my spine. "Michael?"

Something flashed in his eyes and his expression changed from controlled to wild. He wrapped his hands around my forearms and tugged me higher against his chest. When just my tip toes were touching the floor, he lowered his mouth to mine.

4
MICHAEL

I'd come to cancel. What the fuck was I doing?

Daisy was just too tempting. I couldn't leave. Not when I could smell her sweet scent and feel the warmth of her hand on my chest. Not when she was looking at me, the sweet, demure, kind-hearted teacher with passionate carnal desires written clearly across her face.

Before I even knew what I was doing, I'd grabbed her and had my mouth on her. She tasted even sweeter than she smelled. I dipped my tongue between her lips and my dick hardened to steel when she moaned into my mouth. Her fingers tugged at my hair and knocked my hat off.

I stumbled farther into the room with her in my arms, barely on her feet. Her teeth sank into my bottom lip as we stumbled again but she made no apologies for it. Instead, she moaned and stroked her tongue across it. *Mine.*

I reached down and grabbed her ass, lifting her. Then, I dropped us both onto her couch. I covered her, being sure to keep my weight on my knees on either side of her, and found her mouth again.

Daisy was hot passion and lust under her reserved exterior. She writhed under me like a belly dancer, twisting her hips all around until she had me gripping the arm of the couch behind her head with all of my might. I pinned her hips down with the weight of mine and rubbed into her.

She wrapped her arms around me and moaned louder. "*Michael.*"

Hearing my name on her lips, sounding thick and heavy with desire, nearly did me in. I pushed into her kiss harder and then moved down her throat until I was poised over her neck with my teeth bared.

Daisy stilled under me and then made a whimpering sound. "Michael? Michael!"

I snapped to attention seconds before I sank my teeth into her neck. I realized that I'd started shifting on top of her and jumped off. I was across the room in a fraction of a second, staring at her, panic etching my features into something I was sure wasn't pretty.

"Fuck. Fuck!" I pulled my hands down my face roughly and blew out a shaky breath. My dick was still rock hard, straining against my jeans, my heart was racing painfully in my chest, and I was breathing like I'd just run a marathon.

There was Daisy, spread out on the couch like some kind of virginal sacrifice. Her little lacy white dress was pushed up her thighs and her mouth was red and swollen from our kisses. Her blue eyes were wide with shock, and trained on me like laser beams.

I didn't know what to say. I didn't even know what to do. I hadn't shifted without there being a huge threat of danger in years. Not since I was twelve. My body was so revved up. My bear, who never did anything but kill and destroy, was scratching at my skin, trying to get out. He'd almost succeeded while I was distracted. I shuddered at the thought of what he'd do to a sweet little thing like Daisy.

"Michael, what just happened?"

I felt trapped. I had to get out of here. I moved towards the door, terrified that I wouldn't be strong enough to keep him inside. "Nothing. I have to go."

She stood up and started to come closer to me, but I held up my hands. "Stay over there, Daisy. Please. I'm sorry."

I rushed out of her house and to my truck. I needed as much

distance between us as possible. It was all too much. Too much feeling and too much danger for me to be close to her. I should've known better. *Dammit!* I *did* know better. I was stupid to think that I could have a mate. I was more monster than man. I didn't deserve a mate.

Just as I pressed down on the gas pedal to get the hell out of there, I glanced back and saw Daisy watching me from her front door. A sharp pain stabbed my chest and I knew I was fucked. I couldn't be with her because I'd hurt her, but being away from her would slowly kill me.

*****Daisy*****

I watched as Michael high-tailed it away from my house and I let my fear get the best of me for a second. I slammed the door shut and rested my back against it. My chest was heaving and it wasn't from the sexual excitement. Michael was different. I didn't understand it. I couldn't make sense of it. But, I knew it as sure as I knew my own name.

I'd seen his eyes change a different color and fur erupt all over his arms. His teeth had come forward and he'd been growling like some sort of wild animal. Mostly, though, he'd immediately looked so terrified and alarmed that I couldn't help but feel sorry for him.

I went to the kitchen and turned the stove off before grabbing a bottle of wine from my fridge and pouring myself a glass. Had I really seen that? Was Michael not...human?

I thought about all of the paranormal romance books I read in my free time and shook my head. No way. Werewolves and things like that didn't exist. My mind prodded me, sending images of Michael over and over again.

Maggie said people whispered about him being a killer. What if he was some kind of werewolf?

I tried to carry on like nothing had happened, but I couldn't focus. After trying to store my dumpling leftovers in my blender, I decided I needed to face whatever had just happened head on. I couldn't get his face out of my head. I just wanted to talk to him and figure out the truth, otherwise, I was going to drive myself insane thinking all kinds of craziness.

I pulled on a cardigan to keep warm in the cool air outside and packed a large Tupperware container full of our missed dinner before heading out. I drove to the ranch because I wasn't sure where he lived. If he didn't live there, hopefully someone at his family's house would be willing to help me.

THERE WERE SEVERAL CREWS OUTSIDE, cleaning up from the day's events, when I pulled up. Immediately, Lucas Long walked over to me with a concerned look on his face. "Ms. Daisy? Everything okay?"

His son, Mason, was one of my students, so I should've realized that he might think I was here about his child. "Of course. I'm sorry, I was actually wondering if you've seen Michael."

He cocked his head to the side and his eyebrows furrowed. "Michael?"

I wrapped my arms around my stomach and nodded. "Yes, Michael."

When I didn't give him more information than that, he looked over his shoulder, towards the barn. "He came racing in here about half an hour ago. Far as I know, he's in the barn, mucking out the stalls."

I forced a smile. "Thanks, Lucas."

He hesitated and I couldn't help but stare at his face. He was Michael's brother. If Michael was different, was Lucas? Were all of the Long brothers werewolves? My heart started racing and I found myself edging away from Lucas.

He noticed and frowned. "Is everything okay?"

I nodded. "Of course. I... I'm going to find Michael."

Without realizing it, I was practically running across the ranch.

As much as it scared me to suddenly think that everyone around me was some sort of non-human creature, I wasn't afraid of Michael. I'd been freaked out earlier, who wouldn't be, but I'd still felt comfortable with him, for whatever reason.

I let myself into the barn and headed towards the back, where I heard movement. "Michael?"

A low growl was my answer and then Michael stepped out of a stall, his eyes glowing as he looked at me. "You shouldn't have come here, Daisy."

Looking at him, hearing him say my name, I knew without a doubt that I would accept him no matter what. Even if he was a…werewolf.

5

DAISY

"You didn't really give me an option." Michael ran his hand through his hair blew out a deep breath. "I gave you an out, Daisy. You'd be smart to take it."

I stepped closer to him. "I need to talk to you. I need to know what happened."

He frowned and leaned against the pitchfork he'd been using. "I don't know what you're talking about."

I moved closer, all traces of fear gone. I wanted the man in front of me, and to have him, I needed to figure out what was making him act so strangely. "You act like you're afraid of me, Michael."

He gave a low growl and stepped closer to me. "I'm not afraid of you. But, you should be afraid of me."

My body wasn't reacting in fear, though. I was feeling way more turned on than I should be, all things considered. "I'm not. You don't scare me."

He gently pushed me away from him. "Go home. I mean it. You don't understand, Daisy. I'm not good. I'm not safe."

I gritted my teeth and set my hands on my hips. "Do not push me away again. Come with me for a walk. Please. We can talk."

He looked like he was going to argue again, so I leaned up and kissed him. One soft kiss and then I was back on my side of the conversation. "It's just a little walk, Michael. What's the big deal?"

He grunted. "Fine."

Even though it was his land, I led the way. I walked down the little dirt road, past all of his brothers, who eyed us with curious gazes, and only stopped when we were at the edge of the property. The woods were across the street and a fenced in pasture on the other.

"This is going to sound crazy. I know it is. I have to ask, though." I sucked in a big breath and blew it out slowly. "Are you a... werewolf?"

Michael laughed. "You're kidding."

I frowned at him. "I'm not."

He actually bent over, he was laughing so hard. He slapped his knee. His deep belly laughs both surprised me and turned me on. "A werewolf?"

I put my hands on my hips and stared at him. "You don't have to laugh at me, Michael."

When he still didn't stop, I reached out and slapped his arm. "You're being a jerk. Stop laughing."

He straightened and tried to get his face in order, but I could tell he still wanted to laugh. "I'm not a werewolf, Daisy."

"Then what *are* you?"

There was a long pause while he looked out into the woods and all traces of his smile disappeared. "Nothing that you should be around."

A chill went down my spine but still I moved closer to him. I just wanted him to wrap his arms around me, but he was holding strong to his conviction not to touch me. "I don't agree. I may not understand it, but there's something between us. I've barely said a hundred words to you, but I feel connected to you in a way I've never felt with any person before. I know it sounds insane, but I *know* that there's something here, Michael."

*****Michael*****

Hearing her say it didn't help me any. Knowing that she felt the connection almost as intensely as I did made it feel like it was impossible to walk away from her. She was my mate. How was I supposed to walk away?

"I just need to know. I saw what happened. I saw your eyes change and I saw the fur. I'm not going to freak out."

I turned away from her and looked back at my family. I could hear my brothers talking about Daisy chasing me down. They were also talking about me. They were worried about me. It'd been months since everything happened with Lucas and Sammie. Months since I'd killed a man.

My shifter hearing was excellent and with the light breeze blowing their voices our way, I couldn't help but hear them.

"Should he be alone with her?"

"Dammit, I'm not sure. He's been so different lately."

"We're going to have to do something soon if the chick is going to be sniffing around him."

I growled in their direction. It pissed me off to hear them thinking my mate wasn't safe with me, even if it was the same thing I'd been thinking. At least John wasn't around to give me grief. Three of my brothers talking shit about me was bad enough.

"What are you growling about? Are you sure you aren't a werewolf?"

I looked down at Daisy, into her sincere eyes, and made the decision to be truthful with her. I couldn't have her thinking that we were some strange family of werewolves. "I can hear my brothers talking. They're worried that you're not safe with me."

She rested her hands on my chest and stood closer to me. "You're not going to hurt me."

My dick was working against me. It hardened painfully at her touch. I could smell her arousal and all I wanted to do was bury my face between her legs. "You don't get it, Daisy. I could. I'm not... I'm not just the man you see in front of you."

She nodded and her blonde hair fell into her eyes. She blew it out of her face and frowned. "I know you're something else. I don't care."

"Bear. Not werewolf, bear. I'm a bear shifter, Daisy. Not just a normal bear shifter. A bear shifter with issues who can't control his beast. I'm a monster."

Her eyes widened, but I still couldn't sense fear. "A bear? Wow. A little bigger than a werewolf, huh?"

I wrapped my arms around her waist and brought her into my body. I knew what I should do, but it didn't matter. "You keep ignoring the part where I tell you that I'm no good, that I'm dangerous."

She reached her hands up and grabbed me by my hair pulling me down to her level. "I don't care if you're a bear or a gosh darn unicorn. You *are* good and you *won't* hurt me."

"How are you just accepting all of this without blinking an eye?"

"Honestly? I don't know. Maybe I'll freak out later, but I just... Being next to you makes me feel alive, Michael. Colors are brighter, sounds and scents are enhanced, everything feels electric when I'm near you. Like suddenly someone flicked on the light switch to my life. Are you doing that? Is it some sort of bear power?"

I shook my head. "We're mates. We're fated to one another."

"I want you *now,* Michael." Her, soft, sweet, full lips pressed into mine and she forced her tongue into my mouth. Her taste exploded on my lips and I had her ass in my hands in a second. When I lifted her, she wrapped her legs around my waist and locked on.

"Don't freak out this time, Michael." She held my face in her hands and peppered kisses all over it. "I need you."

I wasn't strong enough to walk away from her again. Her taste and smell enveloped me and I couldn't control my overwhelming desire. I crossed the road, headed for the trees. I ran with her in my arms, bouncing up and down against my dick with every stride. When I found a secluded spot deep in the woods, I stopped and dropped to my knees.

"I'm sorry this isn't a better place."

She was already tugging her cardigan off. "I don't care. I just need you."

I yanked it off of her shoulders and threaded my hands into her hair. It was so soft it reminded me of silk. I ran the strands through my fingers and watched it slip over my rough hands. "Beautiful."

6

MICHAEL

Daisy grabbed the bottom of my shirt and pulled it up. I expected the hiss of air that came out of her mouth, but I didn't expect the rush of her arousal that hit my nose.

I ripped the shirt off and then grabbed her hair again. "I was in an accident when I was younger."

I knew that what she was seeing wasn't pretty. I was covered in scars. Not just the one on my face. There were multitudes of the faint white and silver lines covering my body, some thicker than others. I usually kept myself covered because no one had ever seen my scarred body without becoming a little unnerved.

"What?" She trailed her mouth across my chest and raked her nails across one of my nipples. "What are you talking about?"

I pulled back and looked down at my chest. "The scars."

Her blue eyes were heavy with longing, but as she traced the scars, her eyes became heated. "Did someone do that to you?"

I swallowed around so much desire that I didn't think I'd ever be the same again. She wasn't repulsed by me. She was angry for me. She looked like little bear herself as she met my gaze. "Yes."

"I hope you gutted the sonofabitch." She leaned forward and flicked her tongue over my throat. "No one else will ever look like you, Michael. There are probably millions of blonde haired, blue eyed guys out there, but no one on this planet will ever come close to you. You're special."

An unexpected wave of emotion hit me and I looked up at the sky as I blinked away tears. Then, Daisy's little hands were on my belt buckle and I was sucked back to the present with a narrow minded focus. *Mine.*

She fumbled with it and growled. "Come on!"

I grinned at her eagerness and worked at removing her little dress from her shoulders. She wasn't wearing a bra and I got an eyeful of beautiful, pale breasts. I dipped my head and took one of her nipples into my mouth. The little pink bud hardened to a peak and pushed its way into my mouth even more when she arched her back.

I growled and as she whimpered, I felt my control slipping. I tried to pull back, but Daisy caught my head. "Don't. Stay, Michael."

"I don't know if I'm going to hurt you. I don't want to lose control."

She pushed her dress down, as far as it would go, and then placed my hand into her tiny panties. My fingers stretched them out and I almost felt bad for ruining them. Her hot wetness coated my fingers immediately and as the top of my thumb brushed against her clit, she cried out.

"Don't leave me, Michael. I feel like I'll die if you don't screw me right now. Is this the mate bond?"

I didn't know. I was just as lost as she was. My bear was raging in my head, trying to push forward. It took everything I had to keep it together. I couldn't stop. I'd passed the point of no return and I couldn't leave Daisy. I had to be in her.

I slid two fingers into her tight body and groaned at the noises of pleasure she made. Her body squeezed my fingers like a vice grip, and I knew if I didn't get her used to a bigger size, I'd rip her apart when I entered her.

Daisy's nails raked down my chest as she came apart in my arms. I could tell her orgasm surprised her by the look on her face. She screamed and then shoved her own hand into her mouth to quiet herself.

"Let it go, baby. I want to hear you." I pushed another finger into her and then kissed her open mouth.

I looked down at myself and found that I was covered in a thin coating of fur. My bear was screaming at me. He wanted our mate. *Mine.* I fought him back and withdrew my fingers from Daisy. I stood up to take my pants off, desperate for her. I didn't know how much more control I had, but I needed to be inside of her.

"Michael?"

I stripped my clothes off and picked her up. Her dress fell to the ground at her feet and I easily ripped the already ruined panties from her body. "I'm not leaving."

I could smell that she was aroused by the way I manhandled her. Her juices were coating the insides of her thighs and I swore to myself that I'd taste her soon. First, I had to be inside her.

I turned her around and she put her hands on a thick tree trunk. "Stay there."

She arched her back and pushed her soft, round ass out at me. "I need you to fuck me, Michael. Please." My demure goddess was a sex kitten!

I grabbed my dick and poised it at her entrance. I knew I should go easy, but my control was slipping fast. I thrust into her in one stroke and didn't stop until I was balls deep. She screamed out, in pleasure, and clamped her body down around mine.

I reached around and cupped her breasts in both hands as I started fucking her. It wasn't soft or romantic, like I knew she deserved. It was rough, hard, she'd be walking funny when we were done. The animal in me wanted that. I wanted everyone around to know she'd been given one hell of a ride and that she was mine. She *was* mine. My bear agreed with me for the first time in as long as I could remember. He settled down and let me take our mate.

Daisy screamed my name and pounded her small fists against the tree. In just a few seconds, she was coming again. Her body was so damn responsive to me. She shuddered and convulsed.

I tilted my head back and roared, unable to use words to express how goddamn amazing it felt to be buried in my mate. I pulled out until just the tip of my dick was in her and then slammed back inside. Her walls squeezed me, almost painfully.

"Michael!" She rotated her hips in a figure eight pattern and I saw stars.

My balls tightened painfully and I knew I was close. My thrusts got even wilder and I slipped one hand between her thighs to caress her clit. I grabbed her hair with my other hand and bunched it together so I could tilt her head to the side.

With her neck exposed like that, my bear roared louder than ever. He wanted us to bite her. I recoiled at first, regarding him as the monster he'd proven himself to be, but then I realized what he wanted. He wanted us to mark her, claim her as ours.

Daisy's pussy started spasming right then, her strongest orgasm yet, and I knew I was done for. I couldn't hold off my own climax any longer, just like I couldn't leave her neck bare. I needed to mark her and stake my claim to her just as much as my bear needed it.

I tilted my head back and roared at the darkening sky. My bear came forward just enough and that we sank our teeth into her neck. The enchantment that flowed through that bite finished me off. I came harder than I'd ever come in my life, filling Daisy with my semen until she overflowed.

She screamed and her knees gave out as her orgasm intensified. Her body sagged and I caught her and pressed her body against mine as the last waves of our orgasms washed over us.

I didn't know if I'd ever breathe normally again. My body trembled as I slipped from her, spent and exhausted. Her whimper had me scooping her up and hugging her into me as tightly as I could without hurting her.

Daisy mumbled something incoherent, so I released her slightly and looked down at her. When she met my eyes, she gave me a satisfied smile and moaned. "What. Was. That?"

I kicked my jeans into something resembling a blanket and sank onto them. I pulled her on top of me and held her. "Are you okay?"

7
DAISY

Was I okay? Was that even a real question? I was so far better than okay that I didn't think I'd ever come down to Earth again. Michael had just sent me soaring to the heavens. I'd never had rough sex before, but if that was what it was like every time, I'd been missing out. Truly.

"I'm fantastic."

He leaned down and ran his tongue over the spot he'd sank his teeth into. Wild chills of arousal washed over my body at the sensation. He grinned down at me and did it again. "I can smell what that does to you."

I played it coy. "What it does?"

He reached down and slid his finger over my slick core. I moaned, unabashed, and kissed him. I was helpless. My body was sore and exhausted, already, but it was still willing to go another round with him. Him, a *bear*.

"If I'm dreaming, don't wake me up. I want to stay here and keep having the best sex of my life."

Michael grinned, pleased, but then his face turned serious. "I'm sorry if I hurt you. I... It was hard to keep myself in check."

I sat up and giggled as his eyes lowered to my bare pussy. I'd never been so bold with anyone else I'd ever slept with, but I felt so safe with him. For whatever insane reason. "You bit me. Did you leave a mark?"

He winced and nodded. "A big one."

I tried to catch a glimpse of it. "I have work in the morning. Am I going to be able to hide it?"

Another wince. "It's...permanent."

My eyes widened. "What? What do you mean, permanent?"

"I mean that... well, it's a claiming mark."

"Ok-ay, a claiming mark?"

"A shifter will usually mark his mate. To show that she's his, that they are mated. The urge to claim you was so strong... I... Normally, a couple will discuss the marking before it happens. I'm sorry. I just... lost control."

I was hearing a lot of stuff that amounted to him basically peeing on me. "What does the claiming mark do?"

"It makes the connection stronger. A bond. It's also like a homing beacon. I'll always be able to find you."

I swallowed. "It lasts... forever?"

He winced yet again. "Yeah."

I took a deep breath in and rolled back onto his chest. His arms immediately wrapped around me. "You're sorry as in, you regret it?" *Please say no, please say no.*

He tightened his arms and grunted. "No. You're my mate. We were made for each other."

"You were so scared at first. You kept running away from me."

"Yeah, well, no one ever said I was brilliant."

I took a deep breath. "Are you going to continue to run?"

"I don't think that's an option anymore."

~

WE LAID like that for a while, in the woods at twilight, listening to the sounds of nature, our naked bodies warming one another against the chill. We were both lost in our own thoughts, each processing what all of this meant. It was peaceful and comforting to be lying next to him and I needed that while trying to figure everything out. He was my mate. He was a bear. He'd marked me with a bite that meant he'd claimed me as his. I squeezed my eyes shut and took deep breaths. My body got it. My body was all kinds of on board. My brain was the hold up. As much of a connection as I felt towards him, I didn't know what to think about all of this. I was tied to him forever, if what he was saying was true. Had we just more or less gotten married?

It was overwhelming, but with his arms wrapped around me, everything felt right. The world made sense. For the moment.

Eventually, we stood up and got dressed. Michael shot me heated looks the whole time I clumsily slipped into my dress, trying not to let on that I was aware of his ogling. I still wanted him. Despite the aches in my body, I craved him.

He walked me back to my car and I handed him the chicken and dumplings while trying to avoid his brother's stares. I didn't feel awkward being with Michael, but I felt awkward thinking that his brothers could've heard us. And knowing they were bears too, probably.

"Thanks. It smelled delicious earlier."

I leaned against my car and sighed. "I'm confused."

He rubbed the back of his neck and then put the food down on the roof of my car before leaning in close to me. "I know."

I noticed the air change around us and felt his brothers drifting closer. I looked around and watched as they each approached slowly with worry in their eyes. When I looked back up at Michael, I noticed his eyes had changed. "Your brothers are worried about you."

He shook his head. "They're worried about you. They don't trust me."

I heard the pain in his voice, even though he tried to sound flippant. It made me angry to see him hurting. I glared at each of his brothers, who were still drifting closer. "We're fine. We don't need a bunch of babysitters. Go on back to your chores and leave us be."

Michael rubbed his nose into my throat and chuckled. "You're fighting for me, now?"

I pushed him away and opened my car door. "It would seem so. I'm going home. I've got work in the morning."

He held the door and leaned in after I was seated. "I left my hat at your place."

I closed my eyes and thought of him being in my house again. There was no way he would just be retrieving his hat and leaving if he came over. No way. I looked up at him and blew out a breath. I fought back a grin that tried desperately to pop itself out onto my face. "I guess you should come on by and grab it then."

His smile was overwhelmingly charming. "See you, soon."

I pulled the door shut and drove back to my house, butterflies in my stomach knowing he'd soon be following. I was also trying to ignore the very real ache that grew in my chest proportionately with the increased space I put between us. It didn't make any sense. None of it made any sense. Yet, it did.

8

MICHAEL

I woke up early the next day, in Daisy's bed. Everything was frilly. Her pillows had pillows, all of them ruffled in pink and white fabric so soft that I couldn't help but rub my beard over it. I stretched my legs out and sighed when my ankles and feet hung off the bed. I'd have to buy her a bigger bed.

I could hear her shuffling around in the bathroom and the whole scene felt comfortable. I'd heard stories about the mating bond for ages, but I never realized how instantaneous it would be. I felt like I'd been doing this same thing with Daisy for years. Her and I just felt right. Something about her soothed me, and I hadn't hurt her. My bear had just wanted to claim her and after we had, he'd been silent.

I sat up and leaned against her headboard, waiting for her to come out. If I was lucky, I'd get a quickie before she left for work.

Only, when she came out, she looked pale and sick. She spotted me and groaned. "Don't look at me."

I was at her side in an instant. "What's wrong?"

She rubbed her stomach absently. "I just feel so nauseous. I can't remember ever feeling this sick to my stomach. Ever."

"Was it the dumplings?"

She glared up at me and climbed under the covers. "That's not funny. There was nothing wrong with my dumplings. I thought you liked them."

I climbed in behind her and slid my body against hers. "I loved them. I didn't mean to imply-"

"I'm not having sex with you."

I wrapped my arms around her and pulled her even closer to me. I knew my hard-on was pressing against her thighs, but I was okay with it just resting there. I could only imagine how sore her body was. "I'm just trying to hold you, Daisy."

She groaned and then made a crying sound. "I'm sorry. I'm not trying to be mean. I just feel so awful, Michael."

"Tell me what all's going on."

"Why? Are you a doctor?"

"Nope. I got about half way through medical school, though. I'd planned to become a doctor, but there was an... incident, and I left. Tell me your symptoms."

She rolled over to face me and stared up at me, her eyes round and curious. "Incident?"

I frowned. "Tell me your symptoms, and I'll tell you."

She shook her head. "No way. You first."

"Fine. I was halfway through med school when a guy tried to mug me on my way home one night." I let out a long breath before continuing, "I lost control and shifted. The guy lived, but I knew I couldn't be around normal humans anymore. Not regularly. Sometimes, if the threat isn't directly in my face, I can kind of direct my bear. But, under any threat of real danger, he takes over. He isn't cuddly."

She stroked my chest and frowned. "Are all bears like that?"

"No. Mine is just... broken."

"Is it from the accident when you were young?"

I rolled over onto my back and stared at her ceiling. I liked recalling the memory about as much as my bear did. Which was nil. "Yeah."

She curled into my side and pressed her lips to my shoulder. "You don't have to talk about it."

As difficult as remembering was, and as much as I hated it, I found myself wanting to tell her. "When we were kids, we had an Uncle Max. My dad's brother. He'd found his mate when he was very young and he and my Aunt Mary were together for many years before she died in a car accident. For a bear, losing your mate can be the thing that ends you. Some bears manage to handle it okay, like my mom. She's strong. But, Max, he wasn't strong.

After Mary died, he lost it. He went off the deep end and started thinking all of this insane shit. He thought that someone had murdered her."

I took a deep breath and let it out slowly. "I went to his house one day to fetch him for my Dad, but when he saw me, he snapped. For whatever reason, he thought that I was the one who'd killed Mary. I was only twelve. My bear wasn't very strong yet.

"He tore me apart. My bear didn't understand and he was scared. He retreated. Shifters, all of us, have an excellent capacity to heal, but Max tore me to shreds. The damage was so extensive I nearly bled out before someone heard my screams and came to help. And my dad, well, he had to kill his own brother. He was so far gone, it was really a mercy killing. Max wasn't there anymore."

Daisy held me tightly in her arms. "You must've been so scared."

"At that point, I was so close to death, I didn't feel anything. I just knew that my bear was gone and that I was never going to be the same. My brothers, they're all normal. They shift and play. They shift and intimidate. They shift and hang out in the woods, just to do it. I can't, though. Most of the time, it's like I'm human. My bear just comes out in emergencies, but when he does, it's like he has something to prove. He's angry and it's nearly impossible to get him to remember that I'm here, too."

I groaned and sat up, needing to stretch out. I suddenly felt constricted, the memories and sadness welled up in me. It was easy to say it all to her in a distant, emotionless way, but in reality, I was definitely feeling the emotions. "I...I'm a monster at times, Daisy. When the bear takes over, all I can do it watch. Someone came to our house a few months ago and tried to hurt Lucas and Mason. He shot Lucas and before I knew what was happening, I ripped his head off. Literally. A human. I killed a man without even getting to have a say in it. My bear is a cold-blooded killer."

I don't know why I told her that part. I don't know if I wanted to scare her, or what. I usually tried not to think about that night. It had been a turning point for me. A realization that I couldn't be trusted around anyone. I could turn and kill before I was even cognizant of it.

"You protected your brother and that sweet little boy. That doesn't sound like a monster to me." She sat up and rubbed at her stomach. "If anything, I think it makes you a hero."

I growled and turned away from her. "No. I'm a killer. Dangerous. I hurt people. This is stupid. I don't want to talk about it anymore. Your turn, tell me your symptoms.

"If I had your physical strength and abilities and someone attacked my family, I would've ripped them to shreds. I know I shouldn't say that, because I'm supposed to be this sweet kindergarten teacher, but it's the truth. This world can come at you viciously at times. When it does, it's our responsibility to protect our own, Michael, no matter what. What if you hadn't killed him and he'd gotten to Mason? What if you followed the laws and he was arrested, and released in ten years? What if he'd come back while no one was around and killed someone you love? I refuse to believe that you're a monster for protecting your family.

"Maybe your bear is a little out of control, but he's been through a lot. He wasn't able to protect you all those years ago, when you really needed him. Maybe he's trying to make up for it now."

I closed my eyes and shook my head. I wasn't ready to deal this now. "Symptoms, Daisy."

She sighed. "I've been nauseous lately, when I wake up mostly. I think it's just nerves with school. Teaching at a new place is challenging, but especially here. People are closed off here more than anywhere else I've ever lived."

"What else?"

"Um, tired. I've been tired a lot."

I turned to face her and tried to remove any judgment from my face. "Are you pregnant?"

I watched her laugh and then grow still. Her face lost whatever color it'd regained and then she lurched for the bathroom again. After several minutes, I heard her faint crying.

"No, no, no. That's not possible."

I pushed into the bathroom and my stomach dropped at the sight of her. She was on the side of the tub, her head in her hands, her shoulders shaking with her sobs. "Daisy?"

She snapped her head up and met my gaze. "I... I didn't know. I guess I haven't had a period in a couple of months, but that's not unusual for me. I can't be pregnant. I just can't. This is too much."

I tuned into my senses as much as I could and took a deep breath in. Sure enough, I could now sense what my brothers had probably picked up on right away. Daisy was pregnant. Anger radiated up from within and I had to grip the doorframe to keep myself still. Another man had touched my mate. "How?"

Huge tears fell down her face as she looked up at me. "I went to a party a while ago. I got drunk and made the stupid decision to go home with a friend of a friend. We used protection, though. I was safe. This doesn't make any sense."

My chest felt like it was going to crack open. Another man had dared touch my mate. Of course, realistically, I knew that she'd been with others. Knowing it and seeing the physical embodiment of it, though, were two different things.

My bear was suddenly very present and very pissed off. I growled and forced myself to turn away. My movements were jerky from trying to contain it.

"Michael?" Daisy followed me. "I'm sorry. I honestly didn't know."

I moved as fast as I could to the front of the house, needing to get out of there. I could feel the bear clawing its way out and I didn't know how long I could continue to fight it off. Boiling hot rage was pouring through my body and I was fighting a losing battle.

"I didn't mean to suck you into a situation like this. I didn't know!"

I spun around on her and winced when I saw the fear flash across her eyes. I spit the words out as best as I could. "Not...you. I'm going to...turn. Bear...pissed...run."

I wanted to console her, but I felt the bone snapping shift begin and roared out in pain. It was happening. I was too late.

9
DAISY

All panic about pregnancy flew out of the window when I watched Michael disappear amidst cracking and popping, and turn into the biggest grizzly bear I'd ever seen. The whole process took seconds. As asinine as it was, all I could think about was this giant bear sculpture I'd seen in a natural history museum when I was a little girl. I'd been mesmerized by how large it was. Michael was bigger. His bear didn't even seem possible. He didn't fit in my house, that was for sure.

Then, he roared again, and I snapped back to reality. There was a giant grizzly bear in my house. One that Michael seemed afraid of. I watched as it lowered its face to mine and then pulled back its lips in a snarl.

My heart seized and I screamed before I could stop myself. The bear roared back at me, its spittle flying everywhere. I turned and made a beeline for my bedroom door in an attempt to put space between us. Even though it was Michael, I was starting to worry that I'd been wrong about him not hurting me. Maybe this bear hadn't just been protecting him and his family.

I slammed the bedroom door closed and ran to the other side of the bed, praying that it would give up and go away. I didn't want to be eaten. I didn't want Michael to have to deal with the aftermath of that, either.

My door snapped from its frame and slammed into the wall across from it. The bear had to squeeze through the doorway, but thudded into my room and locked onto me. Panic and fear kept me frozen in place.

As it came nearer, I prayed. I tried to calm down enough to talk to it. "Michael? I know you're in there." My voice came out in a shaky, cracking whisper.

The bear roared and I figured it wouldn't be the best response to roar back. So, instead, I tried talking. "Bear, let's figure this out, okay? Don't hurt me. I know you don't want to hurt me," I used my best kindergarten teacher voice. "I'm not a threat to Michael. He's safe with me. You're safe with me."

It inched closer and huffed out a blast of breath that blew my hair back.

"I'm your mate. I don't really know what it means, yet, but I know it means that we're supposed to be meant for each other. I don't think that it means I was just meant for Michael. I think I was meant for you, too. Doesn't it?"

It was standing over me, now. I closed my eyes and waited for the first blow to happen. I was talking to a giant grizzly, trying to make sense of it all, but it didn't seem like anything made sense. At all.

Another growl came from right beside my head and I started crying softly. I was a goner. Then, something strange happened. I felt something wet land on my shoulder and tried not to freak out. Was it tasting me before eating me?

But then, a lighter huff came from it. It licked me again and nudged me with its cold nose. I opened my eyes and found myself staring right into the big gold eyes of the bear. It huffed again and then nuzzled into my side with its big head.

I tentatively raised my hand and stroked the top of the bear's head. "Is that okay?"

It licked my hand and then nudged it with the top of its head so I would pet it again. I laughed lightly, not wanting to startle it, and then rubbed it more firmly behind the ears.

"Is this okay?"

It made a sound eerily similar to a purr and then flopped onto its side. My whole room shook and the nightstand next to it was crushed, but then it rolled over onto its back and wiggled around. I laughed and reached down to pet its belly.

Another blur of motion and then Michael was lying in front of me. He looked up at me with a range of emotions playing out over his face. Shame and horror seemed to be the most prominent. He jerked upright and started rummaging for his clothes. "I'm sorry, Daisy." He yanked on his jeans.

I looked around at my destroyed room and shrugged. "It can be fixed. Are you okay?"

He paused before buttoning his pants and I took a moment to enjoy how stunning he was. I should've been afraid, if his reaction meant anything, but I wasn't. I was slightly turned on and a whole lot amazed.

"I don't mean the fucking room. I could have killed you. I... I'm not safe to be around. I can't do this. I'm sorry. I thought I could, but I can't. I need to be alone."

I frowned, feeling frustrated with him. "I'm not going to chase you down this time, Michael. If you want me, you have to stop running from me. You're not going to hurt me. I believe that with every fiber of my being. You need to believe it, too."

He shrugged into his shirt and then swiped his hat off of my bedpost. "I'm sorry, Daisy."

I let him walk out. I heard the door slam a few seconds later and then I heard his truck speeding away. My heart ached and my stomach soured at the same time. I barely made it to the bathroom before the dry heaves took ahold of my insides again.

I still had to make it in to work somehow, and put on a face of patience and cheeriness for the children. All I wanted to do was cry on my bathroom floor. My life had been perfectly normal until that stupid field trip to the Long Ranch.

It didn't feel like the carnival had just been yesterday. I felt like I'd lived half a lifetime between then and where I was now, lying on cold bathroom floor tiles, pregnant by a stranger, and mated to a man-bear who kept running away from me.

I did the only thing I knew how to do. Carry on. I got up and dressed, while trying desperately to quiet my brain. I kept thinking in circles, attempting to comprehend everything that recently happened. Just yesterday, I'd thought that every human I saw was just human. I never would've guessed that all those romance novels were onto something. I'd also thought that soulmate was just something that people told themselves about their significant others to make their relationship feel more special. My world had been rocked in less than twenty-four hours and I hadn't found my footing, yet.

Dealing with Michael made it damn near impossible to get my footing. He was so wishy-washy. I wanted to smack him, to knock some sense into him. He was so terrified that his bear was going to hurt me, but it was too late for that. He'd claimed me and, according to him, that meant forever. It was too late to run from me now.

I knew I couldn't stop him, though. He was set in his way of thinking, which was that his bear was a monster who wanted to kill. I had to give him time and hope that while I waited for him to figure stuff out, I could adjust to what his world meant for me.

For me and the baby growing inside of me, I thought with a sigh. I'd better get myself to a doctor to be sure that I really was pregnant. How ironic that I'd waited to have an accidental pregnancy until meeting the man who was supposedly made for me, my soulmate. I couldn't have just done it as a stupid teenager. Nope. Leave it to me to be an adult making teenage mistakes.

10

MICHAEL

It'd been two weeks since I ran out of Daisy's bedroom after nearly tearing her throat out. My bear had turned nice at the last moment, but I hadn't been sure before then. I was terrified that I was going to watch my mate die by my own claws. I'd spent my time away from her thinking of her, watching her when I could, and working until there were blisters on my hands. Every day I spent away from my mate was torture, but I had no choice. I couldn't put her or her baby at risk.

I'd finally talked to Matt about what happened. I figured he was most likely to understand at least a little of what I was going through. There'd been a time when his bear wasn't exactly friendly. But, when I finished telling him everything, he just called me a dumbass and walked away.

John finally came home. He was just shy of a year younger than me and he and I had always been close. Irish twins, is what my father had called us. He was quiet and more reserved than my other brothers and he'd never made me feel bad when I didn't go out and hang out with the rest of them as bears. He just let me be.

He'd been on the road, trying to convince the woman he loved to give Wyoming a chance. I personally felt like if you had to beg a woman to try out Wyoming, she probably wasn't meant for the bear shifter lifestyle. Plus, there was the fact that she wasn't his mate. He'd been in LA for months, after making a deal with her that he would give city life a try for a while.

He was the only one of my brothers who hadn't already settled down. We were both having women trouble. Although, I guess mine was less woman trouble and more bear trouble.

We sat on the back porch step at the ranch house, a shared bottle of whiskey between us. John listened to me without interrupting and then thought quietly to himself.

"I barely know anything about her. I've been…watching her. Just to make sure she was safe. Well, that, and honestly, I felt like I would die if I didn't see her at all. She's kind and sweet. She does everything for the people around her and I know she cried when she went to the obstetrician. I couldn't even go to her and comfort her. I'm a horrible mate. I can't give her what she needs and deserves because I'm too goddamned dangerous."

John took his hat off and rested it on his leg. "You're stalking your mate instead of talking to her?"

I grumbled. "I'm not stalking her. I just like to keep an eye on her."

He shook his head. "Michael, I know you've always been different. I don't fully understand what happened with you and I wasn't here for all that shit that happened with Lucas, but I know you. And I know you're making a mistake."

I started to speak, but he continued on. "You didn't hurt her. Your bear wouldn't have. He couldn't. He loves her just as much as you would if you gave yourself the chance."

My stomach twisted and I knew that I didn't need the chance. I already loved her. I *wanted* to be with her. It tore me apart not being next to her, getting to know everything about her, spending every second she'd allow right beside her, making love to her every night.

"He already proved that he isn't going to hurt her. You're hurting yourself, and your mate, because of some fears that you need to realize aren't based in reality. You wanted to be a doctor, to help people, to save lives. You're not the monster you think you are. You're one of the most gentle guys I know. All of our brothers would say the same."

I snorted and poured myself a hefty glass of whiskey. "Yeah, right. You should see them when I'm around the kids. They nearly pushed me away from Daisy when she was here. They don't trust me."

"Michael, they aren't worried that you're going to kill one of their kids or Daisy. They're worried about you, in general. You've been through a lot and you're not the best at handling things, if this isn't evidence enough for you. When that guy shot Lucas, you did what any of us would've done. Your bear knew to protect its brother bear. You just got to him faster. Matt said he would've done worse. But, no matter how many times you hear us say that, you only manage to think that you're some monster."

I threw back the whiskey and poured another glass. "You guys just say that shit."

"No, we don't. We've never coddled you. None of us are the type. And I'm not going to coddle you now. You're terrified of your bear. I don't know if it's because of what Uncle Max's bear did to you, or what, but you're so fucking scared of your bear that you've convinced yourself that his normal reactions are all vilified. But your bear's not broken, Michael, he's fine. You're just afraid of him.

"We all see it. You flinch every time one of us shifts. I could shift right now and I bet you'd be so uncomfortable that you'd run off. We never called you on it because there never was a good enough reason, but you're about to throw away a chance with your mate. How long do you think she's going to sit around waiting for you?"

I swallowed the whiskey and put the glass down so hard it shattered in my hand. "I'm not fucking afraid."

"Then what is it? You don't like the idea of raising another man's child? Can't look past the fact that someone else fucked your mate before you found her?"

I roared at him, feeling the need to rip *his* head off. "Don't say that about her!"

He kept poking. "Are you afraid you're not bear enough to handle a mate? Maybe I should go get one of those unmated bears working down at the rodeo to see if they can handle your mate for you."

"John! Fucking stop!"

"Why, brother? Too scared of your bear coming out to play? Bring it. You may be a chicken shit, but I'm not."

My anger was getting the best of me and I couldn't stop it. "Get out of here, John! I don't want to hurt you."

He ripped his shirt off and shoved his pants down. "I've been in fucking LA for months. I need this. Show me how scary this bear of yours is, Michael. It's been so long since I've seen him. I can't remember. Tell me, is he as scarred up as you?"

That was it. My bear ripped forward, faster than I expected, and slammed into John's still shifting form. Before we hit the ground, John was bear. He turned his head and nipped my shoulder before kicking me off of him and standing up.

I ran at him full speed and slammed into him again, knocking us both to the ground. We rolled back and forth, swiping at each other with our paws, snarling and nipping each other. With his words still running through my head, I tried to see my bear in a different light.

John wrestled me off of him, but then another bear jumped into the fray. Matt. He let out a happy roar and dove into John's body. Then, another landed on my back. I could smell Alex clear as day and something strange happened in that moment.

I wasn't fighting to kill them. My bear was…playing with his brother bears. I felt like the rug had been pulled out from under my feet. I hadn't played with my brothers since we were kids.

I gave a mighty roar, deciding to think it all through later and instead enjoy the gift I was being given. We rolled and wrestled until we were all flattened in the grass, outside of the barn, four panting grizzly bears.

John was the first to shift back. He pulled himself up and made a show of spinning in front of me. "Not a scratch. You're telling me that I'm just so amazing at dodging that I managed to escape a fight with the most vicious bear in Wyoming without getting a single little scratch?"

Well, shit.

11

DAISY

I'd waited as long as I was going to wait. I had a baby growing inside of me and my baby needed someone who would commit to being its daddy. No matter what happened with Michael, I wasn't going to pretend like the two hours I'd spent with that random sperm donor qualified him to raise my child. I didn't even know his last name, and I was sure he would be perfectly fine if he never knew about the secret I was carrying. I didn't want him. I wanted Michael. This kid would have the best home and the most loving parents if I could just get my mate to stop being a first class imbecile.

I'd seen him following me around. I knew he was checking on me. He cared enough to do that, so I know he was feeling our bond as strongly as I was. He was just a blooming idiot.

I was done. Some might say my hormones were driving me, but I knew better. I just wanted my mate. I thought I could outwait Michael, but I couldn't. He won that game. I surrender.

I didn't care about him being a bear. I didn't care that he thought he was some monster. I just wanted him back. We could sort out all the details later. We could play four hundred questions and he could read my journal from my teenage years, but right then, I just needed him back.

I'd driven to the ranch, expecting a fight, but the one I witnessed was not what I'd been expecting. I drove up just as Michael and another man turned into bears and started fighting. What looked rough at first quickly turned into something fun and lighthearted. I parked and watched as more bears joined into the party and they all wrestled each other to the ground multiple times.

Michael seemed to actually be having fun. If anything, his bear looked gentler than the rest of them. I easily tracked his movements until he was flat on his back, just like the rest of his brothers.

For someone who hadn't known shifters existed until very recently, I took it all in easily enough. I was fascinated by it, but mainly I just wanted to run and comb my fingers through Michael's fur while he was still a bear.

I got out of my car and walked around the front end of it. I'd barely gotten ten feet closer when Michael's bear sat straight up and turned its golden gaze on me. He roared and ran at me. I knew the gig, though. I didn't run. I just stayed where I was and smiled.

I noticed that his brothers remained calm. "Michael. I came here to yell at you, but look at how cute you are like this. I can't get over it."

His brothers snickered, but Michael slowed down and then eagerly bent to rub his head into my stomach. The massive creature was easy with me, delicate almost. Then, he was man again, naked and kneeling in front of me. "Daisy."

I put my hand on the center of his forehead and pushed him backwards. "You are in trouble. I'm tired of you running away from me. I have been waiting on you to come to your senses for too damn long, Michael. You're making me eat my pride and come out here to get you, and that's just so... annoying!

"I don't care that you think you're a monster. *I* don't. I want my mate. I don't know everything about you, but I know that you are mine. You said it yourself. So, stop being a butthead and *act* like my mate. I mean it. I have a lot of pent-up stress right now and I'm willing to release it on you."

He stood up and grinned at me. "Butthead? I thought you were supposed to be sweet?"

I opened my mouth to yell at him but he his lips descended over mine before I could get words out. His kiss tasted wild and then dark, like whiskey. His tongue swept into my mouth and I moaned as all of my tension seemed to seep right out of me.

When he pulled back, Michael was still grinning. He looked like all of his tension had faded, too. "Come with me."

I tried to keep up with him, but he was too excited. His naked steps were twice as long as mine and eventually, he just turned around and picked me up. "Where are we going?"

"To my favorite spot. I need to be alone with you."

My body reacted immediately. My nipples pebbled, my panties soaked a wet spot right through, and I was suddenly panting against him. "Don't leave me again. I can't do it."

He broke into a run and then finally stopped beside an overgrown lake. "This is going to be cold for a second."

I shrieked as he waded with me into the water. The water was chilly, but his body was steaming hot against mine. "What are you doing?"

He adjusted me in his arms until I was pressed against him like a second skin. His big hands reached inside of my skirt and effortlessly ripped my panties apart so he could dig his fingers into my bare ass cheeks. "I'm trying to make it right."

"How?" I moaned as he pushed my skirt up farther, and discarded the scrap of panties. His shaft brushed against my bare core. "By freezing me to death?"

He easily pulled my shirt off and then leaned forward and nipped at my chest when he saw that I was wearing a lacy bra. It'd been a matching set until he ruined the bottoms. "By warming you up."

I wrapped my arms around his neck and pressed my chest into his. "We have to talk."

He wrapped his arm around the back of my thighs and expertly slid a work-roughened finger into me. When I released a moan, he inserted another finger. "After."

I grabbed onto his hair and let my head fall back. "After, it is."

"I want this to last longer, but we've got forever to do that. Right now, I just need to be in you."

I gasped when he replaced his fingers with the hard shaft of his dick and thrust himself into me. He stretched me just past the point of pleasure, but something about the light sting made it even better. I arched my back and took another inch of him in. "Yes!"

Michael gripped my ass and lifted my body until he was almost completely out of me. Then, he pulled me back to him fast, starting a rhythm that had my head spinning. "Tell me if I hurt you."

I let him work my body up and down on his manhood, the water making gentle waves around us and lapping against my lace-clad nipples. I was enjoying every second of it. When I arched backwards so he'd hit a certain spot, his mouth closed on one of my nipples over my sheer bra and he devoured it with his tongue and teeth. Then, he moved to the other one, building me up, higher and higher.

He moved up my throat, to our mark, and flicked it with his tongue. "You're mine."

I lowered my mouth to his and kissed him for all I was worth. "Then act like it."

The provocation worked. He growled and then swiftly moved us up to the bank. He laid us down and wrapped his arms around my shoulders. With his eyes glowing, he looked absolutely wild. When he pushed back into me, his movements were fast and hard.

I could feel the pressure building in my body as he kept up his uninhibited pace. It started at my core and worked its way out until my entire body felt like a rubber band that had been stretched to capacity.

He reached between us and rolled his finger over my clit. "Come for me, Daisy."

The rubber band snapped. My walls squeezed around him and pulsed in tune with my pounding heart as my orgasm flooded my body and tingled my every nerve ending. It was too much for Michael. I felt him jerk and shudder and then he was orgasming with me. I raked my nails over his shoulders and bit my bottom lip to keep from screaming loud enough to alert the entire town to what we were doing.

It was needless, because the roar Michael let out as he came surely did the job.

12

MICHAEL

My mate had tried to suck the life right out of my cock. Her body was too tight, too hot, and too willing, for me to last longer than it took for her to reach her climax. I rolled off of her and let my arm fall across my eyes. My chest was heaving and I didn't know if my heart would ever calm down. My mate was one hot lady, that was for sure.

It'd been different. Without the anxiety about my bear, I'd felt everything a little clearer. It was a double-edged sword, because I didn't know if I'd ever last longer than a few minutes with her.

Daisy trembled next to me, her body still reeling from her own climax. I wanted to crawl between her thighs and taste her, but I didn't know if I could move.

She rolled into me and I wrapped my arm around her. Her soft breath on my chest had my dick hardening again, but I ignored it. If I listened to him, I'd screw myself stupid, or my mate lame.

"You never answered me earlier. I asked you not to leave me again and you didn't answer."

I looked down at her and frowned. "I don't deserve you."

She started to argue, but I rolled onto my side so we were facing each other and cut her off. "I don't deserve you, but I'm going to have you. I'll work at being worth your time, and I'll work as hard as I've ever worked at anything. I can't stop this thing between us. I was an idiot to try."

She blinked. "You're done running?"

"I'm done running. I know this is a little crazy and I can only imagine how weird it is for you, but we belong together. I barely know you, but I... know the things that matter. You're passionate and willing to fight for a man you don't owe anything to." I took a deep breath in. "I already love you, Daisy."

She hauled off and landed a smack on the side of my head. "Shit. That wasn't exactly what I was expecting."

"That was for giving me such hell." Then her eyes welled up with tears. "You love me?"

I laughed and nodded. "Yeah, I do. I have a lot of things to try to understand about myself, but that's one thing I know for sure."

She swallowed. "I think I love you, Michael. I let you stay away for longer than I should have because I was trying to make sense of all of this, but I don't think I have to. We can learn along the way."

My chest felt like it was going to fly away. "You think you love me?"

I had a lot of exploring to do with my bear and I knew everything wasn't as simple as John had made it sound, but hearing her say that she even *thought* she loved me made me feel like I could conquer anything.

"I don't know why I said that." She cupped my face. "I *know* I love you."

I crushed her mouth in a hot kiss and then lowered my hand to cup the tiny bump that was her stomach. "And this little guy or girl?"

She blinked back tears. "I'm keeping my baby. I want you to be the father, Michael. I know you'd be a good one and I want us to be a family."

"I can't...have kids of my own. Because of the attack." I looked down at her belly. "This would make me unbelievably happy, Daisy. Being a family with you and your child."

"Our child."

I rolled us over so I was hovering on top of her. I needed a moment away from the heavy stuff. I wasn't great at it, and I knew we had plenty of time for me to learn. "So, tell me, mate, what does a bear have to do to get some attention around here? It took you two weeks to chase me down. My poor ego is wounded."

Her eyes flashed and she crawled out from under me. She backed away slowly, engaging both me and my bear to chase. "I don't want to hear about your poor ego. I want to see *you* work for *me* for a change."

She ran and I easily chased her down. When I caught her, I pinned her against a tree for the second time in our very short relationship and showed her that I was willing to put the work in for her. In fact, I'd give her as much of me as she could stand.

THE END

The next book in this series is Rancher Bear's Desire

RANCHER BEAR'S DESIRE

RANCHER BEARS BOOK 5

John Long has his life under control. Everything is going according to plan. His girlfriend, the beautiful, vivacious socialite Mandy Scott, has finally agreed move with him from L.A. to his family's ranch in Wyoming to give the 'simple life' a chance.

All's well.

Until Bunny St. John enters his life in the form of personal assistant/pack mule for Mandy and suddenly, John's small tranquil world erupts. There's no denying Bunny is John's mate.

Bunny's divorce papers are barely dry.

She's fed up with men, doubly fed up with bear shifters, and doesn't care one iota about this whole 'mate' crap.

All she knows is she doesn't want to be the 'other woman', and she needs her job as Mandy's assistant to get back on her feet.

She is not going to let any man mess this opportunity up for her, including the hot-as-Hades bear shifter, John Long, who continues to claim that she is his mate.

The two can only dance around the flames of desire for so long, though, before someone ends up getting burned.

1

BUNNY

"How soon can you start?" The voice on the phone was breathy and seductive in a way that would probably make any man take notice. It was also fake.

I knew that, of course, because I'd once used that voice, too. Back when I was naïve enough that getting hitched to a man was the most important goal in my life. With a severe eye roll, I barely stopped myself from sighing. I didn't have room to be a pessimist. Ms. Seductive Voice might be my ticket out of here.

"Um, I can start immediately. Wouldn't you like to know a bit more about me first, though?"

I'd spotted the job advertised on line exactly thirteen minutes after it was posted. It'd taken me eight minutes to rearrange things on my resume and submit it. Another fifteen, and I'd gotten the call.

"Not necessary. Your resume is adequate. I don't need a miracle worker, Mrs. St. John. I just need someone capable of being an assistant. It's not at all difficult." She blew out a long breath and I didn't have to try very hard to picture Jessica Rabbit smoking a Virginia Slim. "Really, you're just going to be answering calls and picking up my dry cleaning. It's not rocket science."

I bit my tongue hard to keep from telling her where to stick her condescending attitude. "It's Miss. I'm not married," I countered in a sickly sweet voice.

"Good for you. Anyway. My name is Mandy Scott. I'll be in Wyoming in three days. I'll need you to go ahead to the house I'll be staying in to set up my things. I'll send you a list of everything I need, and your transportation instructions. Just text me after you get it and let me know when you begin working. Also, I'll add the number of my father's accountant. Call him and he'll get your salary set up right away."

"Okay, I-"

The phone clicked off in my ear and I slowly pulled my cell away from my ear and glared at it. "What the hell is wrong with her?"

Even though I would've loved to call her back and tell her to take her job and shove it, I couldn't. Truthfully, despite her shitty attitude, I was more than excited about the job.

It came with a hefty salary, probably because Mandy was a miserable witch to deal with, a car, and a place to stay. Nothing could be better for me at this current time.

Things hadn't exactly been going superbly lately. Well, they were great in some ways and not so great in others. I'd finally gotten away from my lying, cheating, wretch of a husband, officially ex-husband. But, the only way he'd agree to a quickie divorce was if he got to keep everything. And he did mean *everything*. I left the marriage with only what shards remained of my dignity. While it was plenty for me, it sure as hell wasn't enough to keep a roof over my head.

After a couple of weeks on my best friend's couch, I was more than ready to have a real bed to sleep in. Even if it meant working for a woman from LA who had about as much sweetness to her as a bowl of lemons.

I slipped my phone into my pocket and went back inside to tell Star, my friend and temporary roommate, the good news. "I got the job!"

Star raised her eyebrow at me. "The one you applied for like five seconds ago?"

I nodded. "You're looking at the personal assistant of Mandy Scott, from LA."

That eyebrow shot up even higher. "Mandy Scott? *The* Mandy Scott?"

I shrugged. "I don't know about *'The'*. Is she famous, or something?"

"Well, I've seen her on the cover of several magazines while I'm waiting at checkout counters. In fact, Mandy Scott is a regular tabloid fodder. She's a socialite. Doesn't do much of anything, from what I can tell. Just parties and looking stunning on a red carpet."

"She must do something. Why else would she need a personal assistant?"

Star laughed. "You've got to get out more. Rich people don't have to do anything to need a personal assistant. They want someone to handle their planner, their miniature dogs, their wardrobe, and probably even their diets. You're about to become maid, cook, stylist, and dog walker."

I rolled my eyes and went to the kitchen to grab a bottle of water. "Are you sure you just see covers of these tabloids? You seem to know a lot about this sort of thing."

"I may have flipped through a few pages, here or there. That doesn't matter. I just want to make sure you're prepared to do that kind of work for some rich brat."

I shrugged. "Maid, cook, stylist, dog walker? Sounds a lot like marriage and I did that just fine."

"You just got divorced. I'm not sure that classifies as fine."

"You know what I mean. I did the work part just fine. I'm divorced because my ex-husband couldn't keep his junk in his pants. That, and he was, and is, a complete and total asshole." I took a deep breath. "Anyway, I don't have any other options right now. The pay and the perks are too good to pass up. I have to get off of your couch. I'm starting to become one with it."

"Honey, you know you're welcome to stay on my couch for as long as you need to. I love having you around."

"I saw your latest man in all his glory last night. He walked right past me on the couch where I was laying, reading. He spotted me and, naked as a jaybird, continued on to get some milk. Which he drank straight from the jug, by the way. Then he nodded at me, looked down at his dick, and licked his lips. It's time for me to go."

She laughed. "Oh, god. No wonder you want to leave so badly. I knew Frank was an asshole, but I didn't realize he was *that* big of one. I'm sorry, Bunny."

I shook my head. "Don't apologize. You've been so gracious in letting me stay here. I love you even more for it. I'm just in the way. Even if you love having me here, I'm still in the way. It's time for me to get my shit together. And if that means scooping well-to-do Chihuahua doo-doo for a while, then so be it."

Star wrapped her arms around me, in a big hug. "I'll miss you. I hate that you won't be on my couch when I need you."

"You can call me, and I'll call you. I'm sure I'll have plenty of shit to get off my chest. After one conversation with Mandy Scott, I already don't like her."

"Look on the bright side. At least you'll get a fresh start. You might actually get a chance to meet a nice, stable, boring guy who wants nothing more than to see you smile."

I held up my hands and backed away. "Not interested. I can smile, live, and orgasm without a man's help. I've got everything I need right here." I waved my hands, motioning up and down the length of my body, "I'm not falling into that trap again."

2

JOHN

I watched the sun set over the lake beside my house and did my best to squelch the growing anxiety in my chest. As a bear shifter, I shouldn't be freaking out like a little boy. I was a *man,* a *bear,* and I had things under control. Only, a nagging doubt in the back of my head warned that maybe I didn't have *everything* under control.

A bird swooped low and plucked a fish straight out of the lake and then hurriedly flapped away with it. A breeze gently floated the scent of water and pine over to me. My dog, Whiskey, snored lightly at my bare feet. Things were peaceful. I should've been dozing in the warm sunshine.

Yet, I couldn't relax. I hadn't been able to in months, but I'd chalked that up to living in LA. I wasn't cut out to be a city boy. I didn't like big buildings, tight spaces, smog, or even people, really. I'd stayed with my girlfriend, Mandy, in her penthouse apartment for more months than I cared to remember. It was part of our deal, but most of the time I spent feeling like I was beating my head against a wall. I got nothing done, felt sick from the air quality, and grew to despise take out.

We had agreed that I would try out LA for a while and then she would try out Wyoming for a while. Looking out over the water and trees, I couldn't imagine having to make a deal with anyone to coax them into coming here. Landing, Wyoming had been home for me since birth. My family owned the ranch where I worked, when I wasn't off in LA. Wyoming was beautiful, and to me, it was everything.

Mandy hated the idea of it, though. She was a city girl. She'd been weaned on red carpets and luncheon dates with A-list celebrities. She acted as though Wyoming was a death sentence. Part of me knew she was only giving Wyoming a few months simply to say she'd tried it. She was also supposed to be working on a book, so the time away from the hustle and bustle of the city would be good for her.

No matter how much I knew that Mandy wasn't my mate, I also thought that she was, maybe, the girl for me anyway. Not every shifter is fortunate enough to find his true mate. My brothers were enigmas. All four of them had found their mates fairly recently. Somehow, all of their mates had just ended up in Landing.

I knew that wasn't going to happen for me, though. It was just a gut-deep feeling that I couldn't get rid of. I'd had it since I was a kid. When I heard stories about bears finding their mates, about my parents finding each other, I just knew, for whatever reason, that it wouldn't happen for me.

It was why I was okay to settle down with a woman who wasn't my mate. I loved Mandy enough. It wasn't the kind of unbreakable bond of love that my brothers had, but I wasn't my brothers. I didn't need that kind of wild and passionate love. I just needed enough.

Mandy wasn't ideal. There were things that I wished were different, but she was a nice enough girl underneath, besides being attractive and vivacious. I liked the woman that stayed in with me and cuddled on those rare Tuesday nights in LA. She was soft and she smelled good. I was a simple guy.

When I'd finally talked her into following me to Landing, though, the tightness in my chest just clenched harder. My bear became more restless than he'd ever been in LA, and I couldn't remember the last time I'd spent so much of my days as a bear.

I'd spent the last couple of weeks fixing up the house so she could enjoy her time there, but I wasn't too blind to know I had a bad case of cold feet. A part of me wanted to call it off. I didn't know what my end game was here. Did I expect her to fall in love with Wyoming and choose to stay? Did I even really want her to stay?

I had never before been so confused and wishy-washy. I was the level-headed brother. This back and forth wasn't me.

Yet, as I sat drinking my beer, my mind was playing ping pong with my thoughts. I looked over my shoulder at my house. It was *my* space. I hoped Mandy would be pleased and excited when she arrived, but I was slightly skeptical that it was going to happen that way.

The tension in my body too strong for me to relax, I went back inside and sat down at my desk. I had a hundred pages due soon and the deadline was sneaking up on me. My editor would be pissed if I asked for another extension. He didn't seem to understand that my brain couldn't function properly in the blaring horns and chaos of LA.

I opened the document I'd been working on earlier that morning and started typing out the story that'd been trapped in my brain the entire time I was in the city. I had a whole lot to do and not much time before Mandy arrived, so I got busy.

*****Bunny*****

WORKING for Mandy had already proven itself to be a pain in the ass. She texted me at all hours with new demands. Her latest texts had nearly sent me to LA to slap the hell out of her. She had no manners and I doubted she'd ever been taught to play nice, especially not with the hired help. Barely two days in and I want to throttle her. Two days.

When I thought about it, I envisioned Star's couch and felt warm tingly feelings for it. *It* never sent me to Rodeo Drive just after midnight so I could be standing outside of Gucci first thing when it opened for the purse she already had in two different shades. *It* never put me in a rental car and sent me driving through the middle of nowhere to find the house she'd be moving into. And *it* never forgot to mail me the key to said house but asked me to break in instead.

She was scatter brained and disorganized, but that was okay with her because she wasn't the one who had to suffer for it. I, on the other hand, was *not* okay with it. I had a feeling that Mandy and I were due for a long conversation about how she ran this operation.

As it was, Mandy was still in LA, and I was standing at the bottom of a steep driveway that I was afraid my tiny rental car wouldn't drive up. It was barely six in the morning and I'd driven all night on zero sleep.

The sun wasn't even up yet. That was a good enough sign to me that I should still be in bed.

I just had to keep reminding myself of the money I'd be making. I wouldn't have to work for Mandy forever.

I started my hike up the driveway and kept an eye out on the woods surrounding me. The last thing I needed or wanted was to get mauled by a wild animal, or an animal that wasn't wild.

With my heart pounding in my ears and that thought racing through my brain, I picked up the pace and raced up to the large porch of the house. My aversion to breaking in was suddenly gone and all I wanted to do was get into the relative safety of the inside. I went around the porch, pushing on windows until I found one that creaked open. That was the only invitation I needed, I thought, as I wedged my body through the gap and quickly closed it behind me.

3

BUNNY

I knew the house would be empty because Mandy was still in LA, so I wasn't stealthy in my movements. I looked around, not thoroughly, and then headed upstairs. There were several bedrooms, but I picked the one that smelled the best. It reminded me of sunshine on a fall day. I kicked off my shoes and pants before climbing under the sheets.

Mandy might have won the battle by getting me out and about at god-awful hours, but my phone was downstairs in my purse, and I didn't have anything else to do right now. She wouldn't be arriving until the following day and the tasks she had for me, I could do after a nap.

I wrapped myself in blankets and curled into myself. The bed was more comfortable than I could ever remember a bed being and the delicious scent was even stronger in the bed. I was going to have to find out what kind of detergent the cleaners used.

I yawned loudly, and was unconscious in seconds.

THE SOUND of a door opening and slamming shut downstairs had me sitting up so fast I immediately got the hiccups. I swore under my breath and tried to do the breathing thing Star had taught me to get rid of them. Movement downstairs sent me scrambling from the bed, to the door. I pushed it mostly closed and then crept over to my pants. I searched the pockets before remembering that my phone was downstairs. *Shit!*

I knew the moment whoever was downstairs heard me because a loud roar of anger practically shook the house and then doors started flying open. I went to the window and looked out, but the drop was too far down. There was a bathroom attached to the room, but there was nowhere to hide it there. It had to be the closet.

I snatched up my clothes as I went and backed into the closet. I pulled the door closed and pressed my back against the wall opposite the door. I still had the hiccups, but I was keeping my mouth closed, so they weren't as loud. Maybe the intruder wouldn't hear me.

Heavy footsteps pounded up the stairs and trekked from room to room until they got to the one I'd been in. I balled up my fists and tried to ready myself for a fight. The person was, without a doubt, about to find me. In the back of my mind, I couldn't help but notice the enticing scent I'd been noticing earlier was stronger in the closet. The clothes that were hanging all around me were teasing my nose.

What happened next was a mess. The door was yanked open and, without looking, I bolted forward. I smashed into what felt like a solid rock wall and fell on my ass, in a heap of clothes from the closet that I yanked down in my fall. The metal bar that kept the clothes hung came off of its hooks and smacked me right on top of my head.

I was, by no means, a tiny girl. I stood nearly five foot ten inches tall, and I had plenty of curves. My weight caused the bar to come down with so much force that it felt like I'd been shot in the head. Not that I necessarily knew what being shot in the head felt like.

I grabbed my head and swore vividly. "Son of a bitch!"

I completely forgot about the person I'd been hiding from as I rubbed my head and smacked the ground with my other hand. I didn't feel blood, but I almost would've felt better if I had. At least then, the pain would've made sense.

"You broke my closet."

I snapped my eyes up to the man with the gravelly voice standing over me. Immediately, I forgot about my head. My body reacted with a mixture of fear then arousal. I was ashamed to admit that the second reaction was stronger than the first.

"Your closet almost broke my head."

He offered me his hand and when I took it, jerked me up and around, pressing my back to his front. He locked his arms around me and held me tight. "Why the fuck are you in my house?"

I tried to break free of him, realizing that maybe I shouldn't be thinking about how hot he was and, instead, focus on getting away. I only managed to wiggle my hips against him, which earned me a low growl and a slight shake.

"Talk."

I tried to look back at him, but he just held me tighter. His arms across my ribs were steel bars. I wasn't making any progress whatsoever. I tried the thing I always used to use against my older brother. I went completely limp, becoming dead weight in his arms. Instead of dropping me, the way my brother had always done, he just continued to hold me. I slipped down a couple of inches, just enough that his arms ended up right under my breasts.

"Let me go!"

He easily picked me up and walked across the room. He tossed me down on the bed and glared at me. "Fine. Now, talk."

I bolted for the door, but he grabbed me. He tossed me onto the bed again, as easily as someone would a rag doll.

"I've got all day."

I crawled away from him, to the other side of the bed, but he caught my ankle and dragged me back towards him. I kicked out at him, but he caught that leg, too. I had moved past fear. I was pissed that I couldn't get away from him and even more turned on. There was something about him that was affecting me more than it should. His smell, his hands, his strength.

I rolled over, onto my back, and went still. "Why are you here?"

He let one of my legs go and frowned down at me. "I live here."

It finally hit me what he was saying. "What?"

He'd grown still, though. He was staring at me with wide eyes and I could've sworn his nose flared. The hand that was on my ankle became softer, more of a caress. "Who are you?"

I squeezed my thighs together as desire raced through me. I'd never experienced anything like the immediate lust I was feeling for this man. He was a stranger, but just his touch was making me feel things that didn't make any sense.

"Bunny."

"Bunny?" His hand moved up my calf slowly, his large hand easily encompassing my leg.

I nodded. "Yeah."

"You smell like wild cherries." His voice went even deeper and his grip tightened. "God, it's good."

His hand brushed against the back of my knee and I couldn't help but moan. It hung out there, in the air between us, in silence for what felt like forever. I wanted to die of embarrassment, but then he dragged me to the side of the bed and wedged his body between my legs.

He wrapped his arm around my thighs and held them steady as he shifted and brushed his rock hard erection against me. In just panties, I had no protection against the onslaught of desirous feeling.

I couldn't seem to think straight as I arched my back and moved against him. *What the hell was I doing?* He leaned forward and pressed himself firmly into me as he rocked back and forth. I moaned again, throwing caution to the wind. "What is happening?"

He bucked into me firmly as he met my wide eyed gaze and growled again. "I'm not stopping to ask questions."

4

JOHN

I moved my hips, rubbing the hot little strawberry blonde to get her to moan again. I hadn't planned on pinning her to the mattress. Jesus, I hadn't planned on anything. When I saw her shit downstairs, I'd been pissed. I hadn't even stopped to breathe in her scent until I had her against me. My bear was roaring like he'd lost his mind and I wasn't far behind him.

I wanted to shove her panties to the side and make her mine. I gripped her thighs harder to keep from just doing it. I didn't know this woman. Even though I could smell her arousal, that didn't mean that she was ready to actually allow me in her body. My bear raged for me to take her, though.

I closed my eyes and took a second to try to regain some control. Then she moaned and I was lost. I grabbed a handful of the front of her shirt and dragged her up to my mouth. When our lips touched, I felt warmth fill my body and groaned.

She *tasted* like cherries, too. I slid my tongue into her mouth and gripped her head.

"Too many clothes."

I tried to pull her shirt off, but she pushed my hands away and pawed at my clothes.

"These. Off." Her hands ripped the two sides of my button down apart and buttons flew in every direction.

I worked at my belt buckle and then shoved my pants down, all while still trying to kiss her. My boots sailed across the room and knocked something over, but I didn't care. Only when I was naked in front of her did I stop.

Her dark green eyes trailed down my body and stopped on my dick. Her pupils dilated and she licked her lips. I laughed, feeling proud that I could solicit that type of reaction from her.

She gripped the bottom of her T-shirt and yanked it over her head, leaving her naked from the waist up. Her mostly bare body took my breath away. Pale with a light dusting of freckles over her shoulders and chest, she was a sight.

I grabbed the sides of her panties and pulled them down while staring up at her. She lifted her legs for me, one at a time, and then she was naked. Her hair just brushed the tops of her shoulders and it was already rumpled from my hands. Her lips were red from our kisses.

She scooted up the bed and hooked her finger to call me closer. I was already on my way. I knelt in front of her on the bed and gripped her knees. With a grin, she kept them locked together.

"What's your name?"

I leaned forward and pressed my lips to her knee. "John. Open up."

She did and then grabbed the back of my neck and pulled me down for a kiss that left me panting.

I kissed down her throat and chest so I could take one of her nipples into my mouth. Her breasts were large and soft, perfect for my hands. When I kissed across to the other nipple, I was happily surprised by a tiny tattoo of a wildflower between her breasts. I ran my tongue over it and was rewarded with a shiver from her.

She rotated her hips under me and my dick rested right against her. She gasped and dug her hands into my scalp. "John, I want you so bad. What is this? What is going on between us?"

Her wet heat was calling to me. I gripped myself so I could slowly enter her. I didn't want to hurt her. It was a challenge to maintain control, though. Both me and my bear were dying to be inside of her. "Heaven."

She laughed, but it was cut short when I slowly pushed into her. Her legs immediately locked behind my back and she dropped one of her wrists to her mouth in an attempt to quiet herself.

I wanted to hear how she felt, though. I pulled out and nudged at her wrist. "I want to hear you."

Her cheeks reddened, but she obliged. She tilted her hips and I slid in another inch or so. A low moan fell from her lips.

I pushed the rest of my cock into her in one thrust and growled as she screamed my name. My bear purred like a fucking kitten at the sound and I dug my hands into her hips to keep myself from pounding into her. She didn't give me much of a chance to regain my control, though. She tightened around me and dragged her nails down my back before rotating her hips again.

I cursed and then pulled out before driving back into her. I lowered myself so I could kiss her and nearly died when she sucked my tongue into her mouth. The taste of cherries exploded in my mouth and I moaned.

"More." Her voice broke and she tilted her head back, exposing her neck to me.

For the first time in my life, my bear demanded I claim someone. He wanted to sink his teeth into her soft neck and mark her as our own. Realization slammed into me, but it was too late to stop.

I teased myself and her by raking my teeth down her neck. Thrusting into her harder, I did everything I could to make it last longer. She was so tight, though. Her body squeezed me so perfectly. I met her gaze and held it as we both got closer to coming apart.

My control slipped as she started to orgasm and I felt my eyes start to glow as my bear got closer to the surface. I turned my face away, but Bunny caught my face and pulled it back towards hers.

"Bear!" Her eyes widened.

I thrust into her once more and then came with her. My orgasm was stronger than any I could ever remember having and I knew I'd just given a piece of myself to a woman I didn't even know.

She clung to me and I let my weight rest on her as I calmed down. My heart was still trying to beat its way out of my chest and all I could think about was that she was my mate. A random woman that broke into my house, was my mate. It didn't make any sense. My bear didn't need it to make sense, though. He was still demanding that I claim her. He didn't care that she was a stranger, possibly a thief. He knew that she was our mate and that was enough.

5

BUNNY

As I came down from what felt like a drug induced high, I blinked up the ceiling. The stranger, John, had his head buried in my neck and his lips were moving against my throat in a way that threatened to send me back into that fog of lust. I'd just had sex with a complete stranger. What the hell was wrong with me?

I pushed at his shoulder until he rolled to the side and then I stood up and searched for my clothes. I didn't know how it'd happened, but I clearly wasn't where I was supposed to be. Even through the lust-filled fog, I'd eventually been able to process that we were in *his* home, that I was in *his* bed, and that he smelled just as delicious as his laundry.

"Do you normally break into people's homes and have sex with them?"

Spinning around, I glared at him while tugging my panties up. The first thing I spotted was his dick, still hard and slick with our juices. Heat consumed my face and I turned away again. My body instantly reacted to the sight, but I had my wits about me now. "I didn't break into your home."

A low growl had me spinning back around to find him standing right behind me. He reached for me and growled again when I moved out of the way. "I can smell your reaction to me. It's driving me fucking insane."

Bear. I'd found another bear. "Don't smell me! I have to go."

"Why are you in my home?"

I snagged my shirt off the ground and jerked it over my head. "I didn't mean to be in your home. When I got here, it was still dark. I'm starting a new job and I was told this was the right address."

I had to walk past him to get my pants and shoes out of his closet. I thought about leaving them to save some pride, but I didn't know how much pride I'd save if I had to walk down his driveway in just a T-shirt and panties. I moved around him and his naked body carefully, muttering to myself. "Of course, I find a damn bear. What the hell is wrong with me?"

"What'd you just say?"

I hopped into my jeans and slipped my shoes on. "Nothing. I said nothing. At all. I have to go."

When I tried to walk around him again, he hooked his hand around my arm and pulled me into his chest. "How do you know what I am?"

I fought the attraction to him as best as I could, but it was insane. I'd never in my life felt anything like the zapping, zinging pulse of electricity that shot through me in response to him. This man was sucking me in without even trying. Hell, I'd just rolled around in the sheets with him even though I thought he'd been an intruder.

"I've known plenty of bears. My ex-husband was one."

He growled and wrapped his other arm around me. "Who is he?"

I shook my head. "Why do you care? I have to go, John. I have to find the right house."

"I care because you're my mate. You were married to someone else, another bear, and I want to know who it was. Is it someone from around here? What's his name, Bunny?"

My heart felt like it was going to beat out of my chest. "*Mate?* Did… did you say *mate*?"

"Yeah, mate. You're mine."

My ex had told me all about mates. Actually he'd thrown in my face over and over again, the fact that I wasn't his. He'd repeatedly told me about how great the connection and sex would be if we were true mates. He'd used it as a weapon against me. To have John standing in front of me using that word, felt like a punch to the stomach.

"No. No, I'm not your mate. I have to go!" I ripped myself away from him and headed towards the stairs. "Do you know where Mandy Scott lives? I was supposed to be at her house this morning. I'm going to get fired."

John grabbed me again, but this time the look on his face was pure shock. "You know Mandy?"

"I work for her." He looked like he was going to be sick, so I moved away again. "Why? Do you know her?"

"Fuck." He ran his hand over his face and then started getting dressed. "Yeah, I know her."

I didn't like the look on his face at all. My stomach filled with dread and my palms started getting clammy. "How?"

He tried to put his shirt on, but I'd ripped all of the buttons off. Instead, he just stood there, looking like he'd prefer to shift into a bear and run away than actually have this discussion.

When he didn't answer, I had flashbacks of my ex being unwilling to talk when I confronted him about his cheating. John had the same shifty look on his face. I groaned and shook my head. "This *is* the right house, isn't it? She's your girlfriend, isn't she?"

I hurried down the stairs and tried to remember where I put my bag. "It just figures! I needed this job, you cheating ass! God, I hate men who can't keep their dick in their pants. What is it with you bears? You think you can just treat women like shit? Mandy seems like a real bitch, but even she deserves better than this."

I kept yelling at him, figuring he was still on the stairs. "Goddamn you, John! You made me the other woman. Shit. I'll just leave the damn bag. I can't find it."

I head for the door, but John was already there, his arms crossed over his massive chest. I motioned for him to move, but he just stared at me. "Come on, I need to go."

"I need to figure this out, but I'm not letting you just leave. You're my mate. That means something. You must feel it too?"

I rolled my eyes. "Yeah, it means you get to cheat on your human girlfriend and use the word 'mate' to excuse it. I can't tell you how many times my ex thought he found *his* mate. Of course, he absolutely had to take each of these so called mates for a test drive."

A low growl rolled out of his chest and his eyes glowed bright gold. "You were made for me. Your ex sounds like a liar and an asshole. Bears know their mates immediately when they see and smell them. I knew almost instantly that you were meant for me. You smell and taste just like the wild cherries that I've loved since I found a tree growing at the back of my family's property. I've never smelled anything sweeter or more enticing than you. I couldn't possibly be confused by that."

My chest ached, my heart was stupid enough to enjoy the words he was saying, but my brain had seen and heard it all before. "I'm not meant for you. One, I don't want to be with another bear shifter. Two, I don't want to be with someone who cheats on their girlfriend. Three, there is no three."

"Fine. I'll call and break it off with her."

I screamed. Frustration bubbled up in me until I couldn't handle it. "I need this job! I need to work. I gave up everything I own just to get away from my ex. I'm broke, homeless, and I've gained ten pounds since we divorced because all I can afford to eat is ramen. Do you know how much sodium is in ramen? Do you? I want to be able to afford a freaking salad! So, don't you dare call her and break anything off!"

6

JOHN

I stared at my mate, wondering what the hell game life had decided to play with me. She was screaming at me, something about ramen noodles. She was also pretty intent on pissing me off by calling me names and mentioning her ex. I wasn't the jealous type. I just wasn't. I knew Mandy cheated on me all the time with pretty little Hollywood types, and I didn't care. But something about hearing my mate talk about her ex set me off. I wanted his name. I wanted to rip him open with my bare hands.

My bear was clawing uneasily under my skin. He was pissed at me for making our mate angry. He was even more possessive than I was feeling right now.

"So, you want me to stay with Mandy?" It was asinine to even toy with the idea of not ending things with Mandy. All the tension I'd been feeling for the past few days was gone. My mate had miraculously found her way in my life against all odds, and I was ready right now to tell Mandy to stay in LA. I cared about her as a person, but whatever I felt for her was vastly overshadowed by the powerful feelings that flowed through me at the sight of Bunny.

Bunny. My mate's name was *Bunny*. Who named their kid that?

"Yes. I need this job!"

"So, now you want to keep the job? I thought you were pissed at me because I'd cost you the job?" I made a big show of scratching my head and scrunching my brows. I knew I shouldn't bait her, but she looked fucking delicious when she screamed. Her chest heaved and it made her breasts sway and jiggle in a way that had my dick straining at my jeans trying to break free.

She didn't disappoint with her anger. She poked me in the chest and stomped her foot. "I *have* to keep this job. I'll be back on my friend's couch if I don't. I can't quit. I'm going to have to stay here, even after what happened."

I bit my lip and fought a smile. I was being an asshole, but I couldn't believe the gift fate had placed in my path. I had a mate. She was here. I was overjoyed, no matter the details that needed to be ironed out. "Good. You're staying with me, then."

Her cheeks burned and those dark green eyes flashed. "I'm not staying with you."

"Also, *what happened* might be a little ominous. Why don't we just call it what it was? We had amazingly good sex. The best I've ever had."

Her cheeks blushed even darker and the blush traveled down her throat and chest. Her hands fisted and she looked like she wanted to punch me. Her mouth gave her away, though. She chewed on her lower lip, her tongue flicking out to wet it when her teeth released it. "The best?"

I tried to reach for her, but she realized what she'd asked.

"I didn't mean to ask that. What I meant to say was that it definitely wasn't the best for me, so there's no reason to think about it again. We'll just pretend like it didn't happen."

I did catch her that time. I pulled her into my bare chest and let her feel how hard I was for her. I ran my hands down her back and over the curve of her ass. I cupped each cheek in my hands and squeezed. Immediately, I could smell her arousal and I groaned as my dick hardened even more.

She panted against my chest, the reaction immediate for her, as well. Her fingers dug into my chest and her lips parted when I lifted her until she was on her tip toes and I was nudging her core. "John..."

I leaned down and sucked her lower lip into my mouth. "Bunny, this happened and it's certainly nothing that we can pretend didn't. Even when you're screaming at me, all I can think about is touching you. I assure you, the mate bond isn't some excuse to fuck freely until you happen to stumble upon the right one. It's real and it's special. It's going to turn us both into animals for each other. More animal than I already am.

"It's already happened. I thought you'd broken into my home and instead of calling the police, I couldn't get past the idea of being inside of you. It was all-consuming. I forgot everything else. I'm pretty sure my mother could've been standing there with me and I would've still let that go down the way it did."

"I can't."

My heart ached and my bear threatened to shift. "You can. You feel it, too. You must."

She pulled out of my arms and spotted her bag across the room. "It doesn't matter what I feel. I can't be with you. You *have* to be with Mandy. I need this job."

I started to actually get angry. "No fucking way am I going to pretend to still want to be with Mandy. I couldn't. I don't even want to so much as look at another woman right now, Bunny. I want you. *Only* you."

I had to step to the right as a book came sailing at my head. I turned an exasperated look on her. "You're serious? Are you sure your ex's cheating was the only problem with your marriage? You've got a real anger issue."

She threw her hands up and huffed at me. "I'm going to find myself a room and I'm going to get my things set up for when Mandy gets here."

"Mandy isn't going to be getting here." I shook my head at her stubbornness. "I'm going to call Mandy as soon as you're upstairs. There's no point in her coming."

"Don't you dare! I told you, I need this job!"

"Fine. I'll pay you."

"For what? Sex?"

I might've missed the mark with my joke, because it didn't go over well. "Sure. How much do you want?"

She threw another one of my books at me and then looked down at the title of one still in her hand. "James Smith? You read James Smith?"

I didn't just read James Smith. I wrote James Smith. "Yeah, why?"

She tucked the book under her arm and headed towards the stairs. "If you call her and tell her not to come, I will never forgive you. Mate or not."

"What the fuck do you want me to do? Should I romance her and fuck her right here? Right next to you?!"

Bunny flipped me off. "I don't care what you want to do but I need this. Don't mess this up for me. I'm serious. I'll never forgive you."

7
BUNNY

Shit, shit, shit! What the hell was I doing? I should've been back on the road to Star's place. What I definitely didn't need to be doing was putting my bag down on one of the guest bedrooms in John's house. I was an idiot.

My blood pressure was through the roof and I was pretty sure I was going to have a heart attack. I should've just grabbed my stuff and ran. My car was waiting at the end of the driveway. I could've been on Star's couch in a few hours.

This job wasn't the only decent paying job. It was the easiest to get, sure, but there were others. Probably. Besides, I didn't even like Mandy. Why would I want to stick around and work for her after everything?

The only honest reason I could come up with as to why I'd decided to stay, was one that made me want to bang my head against a wall. John. I, apparently, didn't know as much as I thought I did about the mate bond. The sex had been amazing and I couldn't stop my body from responding to his touch, but there was also something deeper happening. The idea of driving back to Star's and never seeing John again made me want to throw up.

None of it made any sense. He was a cheater. A bear shifter. And, kind of a jerk. He kept pushing my buttons until I'd resorted to throwing things at him. I hadn't done that since I was a child. It took John less than ten minutes to get me into full blown temper tantrum mode.

I threw myself onto the bed and groaned. "What the hell are you doing, Bunny?"

My blood was still boiling at the last words John spoke to me. The idea of him sleeping with Mandy in the same house as me made me irate. As if I needed another reason to not enjoy the woman. Although, after sleeping with her boyfriend, I wasn't sure that I had any right to think poorly of her anymore. I'd officially crossed a line, accidentally or not. In choosing to stay, despite what happened with John, I was crossing even more lines.

My phone dinged and I reached into my bag to get it. I saw that I had a collection of texts that I hadn't checked. After checking them and reading through all of Mandy's new demands, I blew out a breath and decided that I was okay to still think poorly of her. She was terrible.

I cleaned up in the attached bathroom and stared at myself in the mirror while I changed into a long teal colored maxi dress. My skin seemed to be glowing and my eyes were bright. I grunted in disgust at myself. Where was my self-control?

I grabbed a notepad from my purse and made a list of all the things she wanted. Fresh flowers. White linens on all the beds. Candles in a particular scent. A grocery list with ridiculously specific items on it. I was even supposed to buy her a few fresh towels and other shit like that. Her father's accountant had overnighted me a credit card, so paying for the things were fine, but I'd have to go and find them all.

Standing at the door, I couldn't help but feel nervous at potentially facing John again. My body was a traitor and tightened at the idea.

Finally, I made myself do it. I opened the door and headed downstairs. John was sitting at the kitchen table with his phone on the table in front of him. He was frowning at the thing, like it'd done him some great disservice. When he saw me, he took in my dress and a sly grin crooked his lips.

"You're beautiful."

I frowned at him, even while a warmth blossomed in my chest. "I have to go shopping for Mandy. I'll be back."

He stood up and nodded to the stairs. "Let me get a shirt on and I'll come with you."

I just kept walking towards the door. "No, thanks."

I made my way down his driveway, thinking of all the places I would need to go in order to get everything that Mandy wanted. I considered the conversation with John over until he suddenly appeared at my side, dressed in a simple black T-shirt.

My mouth watered at the same time I felt my panties grow wet. John was hotter than hot in the simple shirt. It fit snugly against his chest and arms and I knew that if he reached for something, I'd be able to see a sliver of his abs when the shirt rode up. I wanted to make him reach for every top shelf item in that shirt. I wanted to see the alluring hip V I'd seen earlier, and the thin trail of hair that pointed to his impressive package.

He was a giant of a man, as most bears were. Even at my height, he towered over me. His arms were massive, as well. With dark, buzzed hair and a five o'clock shadow that made me want to cry it was so devastatingly sexy, he was my dream man. My dream man who was completely off limits if I ever wanted to get back on my feet.

"As much as I love the way you're looking at me, unless you want me to drag you back up to my bed, I suggest you close that pretty little mouth."

I snapped my mouth shut and grunted. "I'm not looking at you any kind of way. Get over yourself."

He grinned at me. "Come on. I'll drive you around."

"No, thanks. I'll drive myself. My car is right… Where is my car, John?" I looked at the ground where I'd parked it and then back at him. "What did you do to my car?"

"I didn't know it was your car. You had the entire driveway blocked. I had it towed."

"You *what*?" I glared at him. "Why would you do that? I have a million things to do today and thanks to you, I wasted enough time already!"

"Now I'm a waste of your time? Ouch." He pointed to where his truck was parked. "Even though you wound me grievously, I'll still drive you around."

I marched over to his truck and yanked the door open. "Fine. You can drive me around, but this doesn't change anything. I'm not your mate and Mandy is still on her way here. Nothing happened. Nothing is going to happen."

8

JOHN

I drove my heated little mate all over the place while she refused to look at me and angrily stared at her phone. She'd finally told me that she'd only recently accepted a job as Mandy's assistant. From the way she looked at her phone, I could tell that Mandy was probably being her typically demanding self. I shook my head and tried to work through what plan of action I was going to take.

I'd tried calling Mandy already, but she wouldn't answer. I knew what Bunny said, but I wasn't willing to have my mate watch me with another woman. Hell, I couldn't stand the idea of touching Mandy, or any other woman for that matter, now that I'd found my mate. I felt slightly sorry for her, but only slightly. Actually, Mandy would be fine. She'd probably be relieved that she didn't have to hang out in Wyoming.

I didn't want her arriving smack dab in the middle of a breakup. It looked like that was potentially the way things were going to go though. I was getting a headache that felt like a vice around my head. All I wanted to do was be with my mate. I was with her, sure, but she was about as warm as a block of ice towards me. I wanted the pretense gone. She knew about bears, knew about mates, she was perfect. Except for the whole not wanting anything to do with me thing.

I went in with her to every store, eager to watch out for her. My bear didn't want anyone else near her. He was coming alive, full of constant growls and always at the surface.

Whenever I tried to touch Bunny, she practically hissed at me and jerked away. It was killing me.

"I still need fresh flowers." She was sitting in my truck with her notepad in her lap and her phone in her hand. She had a pen gripped between her teeth and lines between her eyebrows from bunching them together all day.

"There's not a florist around here, but I can take you to my family's ranch. I need to talk to my brothers, anyway."

She tapped the pen against her lips and frowned. "There'll be flowers there?"

I nodded and pointed the truck in that direction. "Yep."

She closed her notebook and shoved it into her purse, with the pen that I was feeling massive amounts of jealousy towards. "Fine. To the ranch we go. Then, you take me back to your house and I get everything ready for your girlfriend's arrival."

I stopped the truck at the edge of the ranch. "It's not going to work, Bunny. She's no longer my girlfriend. I'm not going to be with her and I'm not going to lie to her about being with you. She deserves to know the truth and I deserve to be happy. Finding your mate is special. I don't want to start it off hurting you, or myself, by pretending that I'm still with Mandy. What would be the point?"

"We talked about the point. The point is that I need this job."

"Not really. You're my mate, Bunny. That means that I would do anything for you. I will take care of you."

Her cheeks turned red and I'd already learned that it wasn't going to be as cute as it looked. "What the hell is it with you bear shifters? You swoop in and take care of everything so I'm completely dependent on you and then you snatch it all away. I'm not doing it again. I don't want to be with a *bear*. I don't want to be with a *man*. I don't want to be with anyone. I want to be alone."

I felt my bear clawing through my skin and did everything I could to stop the shift from happening. "How can you ignore the pull? I know you feel it."

She looked out the window, her face redder than ever. "I don't feel anything. I'm not going to be mated to a bear."

I shoved the truck back into gear and headed towards the main house. I needed to get out of the truck and away from her for a few minutes. I needed to hit something and I had a feeling one of my brothers would be down for a fight.

I slid to a stop in front of the house and jerked my thumb to the right of it. "Walk that way for a bit and you'll find a small gathering of flowers. Honk the horn when you're finished and back here."

Before she could even get her door open, I was out of the truck and striding across the property in search of one of my brothers. I shucked clothing off along the way, shifting as soon as I could. Once my bear was free, he tried to turn me around and run me towards the smell of wild cherries, but I refused. Instead, I roared as loud as I could and charged my brother Alex.

Alex shifted immediately and wasted no time in returning the attack. He was going easy on me at first because I'd never instigated any kind of fights, but once I tackled him to the ground hard enough to piss him off, he gave as good as I was giving.

We rolled around and lashed out at each other until we were both panting and covered in muck and dirt. Alex shifted back first and glared up at me.

"What the fuck was that about?"

I shifted back and sat down next to him. "Found my mate. She works for Mandy. She hates bear shifters and doesn't want anything to do with me. That pretty much sums it up."

Alex shook his head and grunted. "Fuck. Did you do anything to piss her off?"

I thought about everything that'd happened in the few short hours we'd been together. "Probably. But she asked me to go ahead and have Mandy come tomorrow. Act like nothing ever happened between us."

"And something did happen between you?"

I shot him a look. My character was changing when it came to my possessiveness, but I was still a gentleman. Mostly. "I'll just say that I can't in any way, shape, or form pretend like I still want Mandy. God. I can't even imagine touching Mandy now. The bond just fucking sucker punches you, doesn't it?"

He laughed and smacked my arm. "Yep. And there is no fighting it. Your girl can say that she isn't interested all day long, but no matter what, she'll give in eventually."

"Her name's Bunny and she's anything but the sweet, timid picture the name brings to mind. She's stubborn as a fucking mule."

"Glad to know what you really think of me, jackass." The woman in question stood several feet away with her hands on her hips. "I got the flowers and I'm ready to go."

I watched her stomp away and felt my dick turn to stone. I tried my best to cover it in my naked state and groaned. "That woman will be the death of me."

Alex laughed harder than I would've liked and nodded. "One thing's for sure, she does *not* like you. Good luck, brother."

"What the fuck am I supposed to do?"

He shrugged. "Give her what she thinks she wants. Pretend like you're with Mandy and see how insane she gets."

"It doesn't feel right to do that. Not to Bunny and not to Mandy."

"Mandy doesn't give two shits about you. You know it, I know it, hell the whole world knows it. She's with you because of the mysterious writer thing and because it's easy for her to be with you. You're never in her business and you let her do whatever she wants. I'm not completely convinced the woman even feels normal human emotions. She's intense."

I pulled myself to my feet and looked out at my truck. I could see Bunny sitting in the passenger seat, talking to herself. "Doesn't seem like a good idea, Alex."

"Nothing seems like a good idea when the woman who was made for you isn't receptive. Elizabeth left me at first. It took her months to come back and I honestly felt like I was dying at times. You'll figure it out."

I sure as hell hoped so.

9

BUNNY

I watched a very naked John strut across the dirt like he wasn't in his birthday suit, stopping to pick up articles of his clothing as he went. He stopped in front of the truck and casually got dressed. I couldn't look away. I couldn't ignore the pull I felt towards him as much as I wanted to.

Spending the whole day with him, running errands, had been a bad idea. The more time I spent around him, the more I was drawn to him. I really needed to call Star and talk to her about mates. I had to know if it was something I could avoid or if I was ruined.

John got back in the truck without saying a word. He remained quiet the entire drive back to his house and still didn't say anything when he helped me unload everything. In the truck, I accepted it because I thought he was just trying to get to me, but after he unloaded everything and still served me the silent treatment, I was beyond annoyed.

I got to work and tried to ignore the fact that he wasn't speaking to me. It was hard, though. I felt awkward being in his house, close to him, and not speaking to him. It was driving me crazy.

I'd changed the sheets in his bedroom with a bright red face and then rushed around to find his washing machine, so I didn't have to look at the incriminating evidence of what we'd done. I found the laundry room and was just starting the machine when I spotted John through the window. He was outside on the porch.

I stepped closer and inched the curtain aside. He was completely naked again and staring out at the lake behind the house. He moved with grace and lifted himself over the porch railing like he weighed nothing, shifted in mid-air, and landed softly as a bear before diving into the lake. My ex had never moved so smoothly. He was more bumbling bear. John was easily all apex predator.

He swam, coming up just to breathe and then dove under again. His dark fur looked black while wet and I couldn't help but be awed as I watched him.

Eventually, I tore myself away from the window and finished the tasks I needed to do. I was dreading Mandy's arrival. I didn't know what was going to happen. I didn't know if I could keep a lid on my emotions.

I made my way around the house, looking at everything to make sure it was done the way Mandy wanted it, and then settled in my room with the James Smith book I'd grabbed earlier. I tried to read, but knowing John was somewhere nearby was too distracting. I let the book fall over top of my face and groaned.

It felt like there was a battle raging between my brain and heart. I was the same Bunny who'd just managed to escape a bear shifter with a cheating problem and an ability to scream so loudly the house would shake. I didn't want a man. I didn't need a man. But, I couldn't deny the feelings that were taking over. I wanted to talk to John. I wanted to argue with him, anything, just to spend time with him.

Not to mention the way my body reacted to the man. I'd never experienced anything like that. My ex hadn't made me orgasm in years. John had done it in minutes.

I tossed the book aside and went to the bathroom. I started the water in the shower and turned it towards the cold side. I just needed to cool down.

"Or maybe drown yourself, you idiot." I muttered as I stripped down and climbed under the cold spray.

If I'd acted like I had any decency and hadn't slept with him, maybe things would be easier. They definitely would be a lot less awkward. I didn't know where I stood. He kept saying things about me being his mate, but he wasn't even talking to me anymore, so... Besides, he'd cheated on Mandy and she was perfect. I'd looked her up in my spare time. How could he cheat on a woman who looked like perfection? I sure as hell wouldn't be able to hold his attention if a stunningly gorgeous woman like Mandy couldn't. I couldn't even hold my ex's attention.

I got out of my shower and towel dried my hair. I left it down to curl naturally and the pulled my dress back on.

My stomach growled so I slunk downstairs to try to find something to eat, hopefully without running into John. It was a useless attempt, though. He was sitting at the table with a laptop in front of him, typing away, until I entered the room. Then, he snapped it closed and pulled out his phone.

I decided that two could play that game. If he was ignoring me, I could ignore him right back. I grabbed a bag of cherries out of the fridge, just to mess with him, and leaned against the counter to eat them. I ate around the pit slowly and noisily, then dropped them into the trashcan, while staring at him.

He just kept typing on his phone, ignoring me.

I lost my patience and tossed the cherries back into the fridge before going out to the porch and sitting in one of the deck chairs. "Stupid man."

It seemed he was over me. That whole mate thing didn't last very long. I angrily punched Star's number on my phone and waited while it rang.

"Hello?"

"Star! I miss your couch."

She laughed. "You've been gone for no time at all. Also, thanks for missing my couch and not me."

"Anytime. How are things?"

She snorted. "How are things? What are we? Desperate Housewives? Tell me everything. I can hear in your voice that you have plenty to tell me."

I breathed a sigh of relief. "I messed up big time."

She paused. "Well? Get on with it."

"Well, apparently Mandy Scott is moving in with her boyfriend whom she neglected to tell me about. I got here, broke into his house pretty much and had sex with him." I said the last part super-fast, hoping she wouldn't understand me.

"You *what*?" She screeched. "You had sex with a stranger? Your boss's boyfriend?!"

"It was an accident. It just… happened. He says I'm his mate, but I don't believe it." I laughed. "Oh yeah, he's a damn bear shifter!"

Star screamed, a scream that was ten times worse than her usual screech. "Oh, my god! That's amazing! I'm so happy for you!"

"No! No, no, no! It's not amazing. I told him I didn't want him and now he's over me. Mandy is still coming tomorrow to be with him."

"It doesn't work that way, Bunny. You can't just ignore your mate and he can't just be over you."

"Well, it sure as hell seems that way."

"Well, it's not. Didn't you learn anything about mates while living here?"

I groaned. "I guess not. I was too busy being cheated on by an asshole who swore every time he cheated that he simply thought she'd been his true mate. It was a big guessing game for him, so he said."

"That's not how it works. There's no guessing involved, mates just know. Don't you just feel crazy about him when you see him? Mates are just… well, there's instant physical lust, sure, but you're smitten… forever. It's amazing that you've found your mate, Bunny."

I sighed. "There's no getting out of it?"

"Not at all. He's your mate, babe. No matter what."

"Well, shit."

10

JOHN

Sleep that night was damn near impossible. I was still giving Bunny a cold shoulder, hoping she'd crack and talk to me, but she had disappeared. After her cherry eating seduction attempt in the kitchen, I thought she was warming up to me, but then she'd run off.

I tossed and turned, feeling like an asshole for not telling her goodnight. I should've at least said goodnight. She was my mate. I shouldn't be treating her like this.

Then there was the fact that Mandy was going to be arriving relatively soon. I couldn't wish her farther away if I tried. And I had tried. I'd also tried calling her time and time again, but she was the same old Mandy. She only got in touch with people when she wanted to.

The sun was almost up when I gave up on staying away. I padded down the hallway and tried Bunny's door. It was locked. I swore and was about to move away when the door opened.

Bunny looked up at me and a frown turned her pouty lips down. "Is everything okay?"

I shrugged. "I hate my new sheets."

"That's why you came to my door?"

I shook my head and put my hand on the door to push it open farther. "No. I needed to see you."

She immediately stepped back and let me into her room. She hadn't switched her sheets and I was jealous of the worn flannel. The old sheets from my parents' house and they were insanely soft.

Bunny stood in front of me wearing nothing but a large T-shirt. Her hair was piled on the top of her head in some strange blob with pieces falling out all over. She was absolutely stunning. Her body was tall and curved in places that made my mouth water. Soft. I couldn't stop thinking about the way those delicious curves had felt so soft under me.

The T-shirt hid most of her curves and I found myself getting angry about the idea that it was some other man's shirt. I wanted to pull it over her head and make sure that she only ever wore mine.

"What do you need?"

I stared into her eyes, shadowed in the dark room. "I need you. This is crazy, Bunny. I don't want to do this shit with Mandy. I've tried calling her about a hundred times today. At the risk of you being pissed at me, I am planning to tell her to stay in LA. She hasn't answered, though."

She walked over to the window and looked out of it. "I talked to a friend about this whole mate thing. Apparently, we're stuck with each other."

I felt like ripping my hair out. She made being my mate sound like a prison sentence. I tried to remain calm, though. "Yeah, basically."

"I spent five years of my life with my ex-husband. Five years feeling like I was trapped in the relationship. Dealing with his bullshit and feeling like I had no other choice, no way out. When I finally saw my chance to leave, I did. I left with just the clothes I could fit in a suitcase. That still feels like yesterday. I don't think I can do this with you. At least not now."

"I don't want to force you into anything, Bunny. I know you're feeling what I'm feeling, though."

"So, what? I'm attracted to you, sure. Insanely attracted. But, I want to be free. I can see the way you're already looking at me. This shirt makes you sick, doesn't it? You glared at it. You already want to control me."

My claws came out and I held them behind my back. "I don't want to control you. I just want a chance."

She shook her head. "I can't give you that. I'm sorry, John."

I wanted to fight her on it. I wanted to scream at her. My bear was ready to come out and claim her so she was given no choice. That wasn't me, though. That was the mate bond. I wouldn't let it control me. If she wanted to go her separate way, then I had no choice but to get out of her way.

If she expected me to hang around with her and Mandy, she was crazy, though. I wasn't going to torture myself. "Okay. I'm not staying here, though. I'll fill Mandy in about why I'm gone. I won't put your job at risk, don't worry."

Bunny fisted her hands at her sides and stepped towards me. "You don't have to leave, John."

"Yes! I do." I stepped out of her room and forced a smile. "Good luck, Bunny."

Leaving felt like I'd taken an icepick and driven it straight through my chest. Life could be so shitty at times. I'd gone my whole life being okay with not having a mate. Then when I find her and don't want to live without her, she ends up being okay without me. It wasn't like I didn't understand what she was saying. I'd just hoped that the bond would be enough to outweigh her fears and objections.

I couldn't seem to get the doubts out of my head, when I wasn't overwhelmed by the pain of being rejected by my mate. I kept overthinking everything. My brothers would never believe it, if they could see me falling apart like this. I'd always been the calm, rational, level-headed one.

That guy was so far gone, I couldn't even see him in my rearview mirror. He'd vanished. Replaced with some weak sonofabitch who couldn't imagine life without a woman he'd just met. A woman who clearly wanted nothing to do with him.

I left messages with Alex, Michael, and my publisher, letting them know I was taking a few days off. I needed to clear my head. The only way I knew to do that was to spend some time in the sun, so far south that no one would ever expect to see a giant grizzly bear roaming around.

11

BUNNY

Six Months Later

"Tell Robin that Mr. Scott is expecting those papers on his desk by three P.M. sharp. No later or he'll find someone else to take care of it." I hung up the phone and sighed. I had no clue who I'd just yelled at, but I was pretty sure they didn't deserve it.

That was the job, though. Ramsey Scott was intense. He had his fingers in a lot of pies and they were all sticky. I yelled at people more than I'd ever thought possible. Most days I barely had a voice by the time I got home. Which wasn't exactly early.

I'd been working for him for three months and I'd already made myself at home in his business. I handled anything he needed me to, but I couldn't help remembering the days I'd worked for Mandy fondly. She'd been an angel compared to her father, and that was saying something.

"Barbara!" Mr. Scott's voice rang out from his office. That was another thing. He refused to call me Bunny.

I gritted my teeth and calmly walked into his office. "Yes, sir?"

Mandy was sitting in front of his desk with a couple of samples from the clothing line she was working on resting across her lap. "Bun! Hi!"

I tried to avoid a mouth kiss as she moved her face around mine, air kissing like a damn bird. "Hi, Mandy. How are you?"

Mr. Scott waved his hand at us in a way that said he couldn't be bothered with whatever was happening around him. "Girls. I'm busy. Catch up on your own time. I need you to run these samples across town, Barbie. Take them by Tom's. You know the place?"

I nodded. "Yes, sir. Anything else?"

He handed me his half-finished coffee. "Do something with this, would you?"

I took the samples in one hand and then the coffee in the other. "Sure. I'll be back soon."

"Be careful with those, would you? I only have the ones you're holding."

I forced a smile to Mandy. "Of course."

"Oh, do me a favor. Pick up the new James Smith novel. Stop by the store that carries the latte that I like. They'll have the book in the back. Tell them it's for me."

I nodded so damn much that I felt like a bobble head and then hurried to finish with my tasks. It was almost the weekend and I was eager to just sit at home and have girl talk phone convos with Star.

She'd been busy lately, getting to know her very own mate, so it was the first time we would get to really talk in a while. I couldn't wait to catch up with her.

When Mandy arrived in Landing, Wyoming, she'd been surprised to find her boyfriend gone, but not too phased about it. When he'd called to end things with her, she'd thrown a hissy fit and refused to leave his home until she was done with her book. He hadn't seemed to care, so I'd stayed in his home with Mandy for two months. I'd never felt such sheer torture. I didn't even like to think about it. That was one of the many blessings of working for the Scotts.

Mandy liked me and offered me a job in LA with her. After two months of walking around John's house, feeling like my skin didn't even fit me right with him gone, I'd jumped at the chance. It paid incredibly well and she provided me with a home, a car, and a phone. After a month, though, it was obvious to Mr. Scott that I was being wasted with Mandy, so he'd offered me even more money and stolen me from her. Not that Mandy cared.

Being in LA was strange and didn't fit me all that well, but I was so busy most days that I couldn't think about anything. Not much, anyway.

After dropping off the samples, I crossed town and stopped at the bookstore Mandy liked. I had to argue with the manager for a few minutes before she finally relented. Then, instead of buying one copy, I bought two. I loved James Smith's writing and I wouldn't be able to talk to Star every minute of the entire weekend.

In the Uber on the way back to the office, I cracked my copy and started reading. Almost immediately, I felt my chest tighten. Something about the book felt darker than the other mysteries. I even asked the driver to circle the block twice so I could read more. I didn't want to put it down. I thought about asking for another circle around, but I saw what time it was. Mr. Scott hated when I took too long.

I hopped out and ran into the building, feeling excited for the first time in forever. I was hungry for more of the book. I needed to know what was going to happen.

As expected, I found Mandy in Mr. Scott's office, impatiently waiting for her book. She snatched it from me as soon as I walked into the office and frowned at me. "Jesus, did you take the stairs? Why are you breathing so hard?"

My tongue had grooves from me biting it.

Mr. Scott gave me his signature stinky face and wave me away with a gentle flick of his wrist. "Please, return Monday with a more urgent nature, Miss Brooks."

I thought about correcting him on my name for the one millionth time, but decided it wasn't worth it. I just wanted to get out of there.

I hurried home to the tiny apartment that Mr. Scott supplied with the job. Once there, I stripped out of my professional clothes and pulled on a T-shirt and pajama bottoms. I had a date with Mr. James Smith and then, later on, with Star.

For the first weekend in forever, I felt almost normal again.

12

JOHN

I threw the newest draft across the room and felt a little better when it slammed into a lamp and shattered the glass shade. "It's shit. Fucking hell. I've written better things while drunk off of my ass!"

My agent cut me a look. "That lamp was a Tiffany."

"Look at me, not giving a shit about your lamp. You've read what the critics said about the latest book. It was darker, weirder than the rest of the books. They didn't like it. Now, I'm trying to write something lighter again, but all I want to do is fucking kill off my main character."

I walked over to the mess I'd made and snatched the draft off the ground. "This draft I wrote in a week. You want to know why? Because it ends at page one hundred with Thomas getting murdered."

"Well, change it, John. I don't know what else to tell you. You're the damn writer." Mark Stump shook his head. "You used to be a real pleasure to work with. Now, I can't even have you over without expecting to have to replace something when you leave."

I headed towards the door with the draft tucked under my arm. "Yeah, well, I'm darker now. Haven't you heard?"

Without waiting for him to reply, I stormed out of his office and slammed the door behind me. It wasn't his fault that I was completely stuck in a rut. It was my own. That wasn't to say that I didn't have some help getting myself into such a miserable state. I couldn't stop thinking about one little hellion in particular.

I got in my rented truck and navigated my way through all the convertibles and electric cars that filled the streets. In Wyoming, I usually liked to ride with my windows down, but traffic was shit here and the air just wasn't the same in LA.

I didn't even know why I *was* in LA. I'd been here more times than I could count since Bunny moved. So, maybe I did actually know why I was in LA. I was slowly going insane and all I could think about was the possibility of something happening to her out here while I was in Landing.

It wasn't healthy. Nothing that I'd been doing was healthy. I never made the effort to contact her because one rejection from my mate was enough, but I liked to make sure she was okay. It was torture, though. She wasn't aware of it, but I saw her every time I came to LA. Just once. That was all I allowed myself because it felt as tough as my heart was being ripped out each time.

Bunny never looked happy. I knew that she couldn't be. The mate bond kind of took over after a while. Your body craved your mate for survival. Denying yourself time with your mate made it easy to become depressed and lonely.

I'd already made my one visit to see Bunny, so I knew it was time to go home. I wanted to drive by her job again to catch her leaving, but I wouldn't do it. I saw her once and that was it.

I headed towards the airport and tried my hardest to direct my thoughts to anything else in the world. Nothing had been able to take my mind off of her so far, but I had to keep trying.

I'd spent the first couple of months after leaving Bunny, completely alone. I'd broken it off with Mandy right away and then she'd informed me that she wasn't leaving my home. I was over it, so I just agreed to whatever she wanted and stayed gone. When I found out they'd moved on, I went back home.

What I found was painful, though. Everything smelled like Bunny. The whole house had her touch, her scent, everywhere. She'd changed the sheets back to my flannel ones and she'd left a note saying I could throw the new ones out if I wanted. It was like she'd rubbed herself against all of my shit.

I'd nearly gone insane after one night, rolling around in her smell, so the next day I opened all of the doors and windows, hoping to get some relief. So far, no relief.

There I was again, headed home to sit in silence with the smell of wild cherries wreaking havoc on my brain and the piece of shit book that I couldn't seem to figure out. I didn't know how much longer I could handle this.

*****Bunny*****

I SPENT the weekend talking to Star and finishing reading the book. I ended up even reading parts of it aloud to her, to her dismay. She just wanted to talk about her new mate and how she couldn't imagine not being with him for so long, because just the weekend away from him was killing her. She wasn't exactly the best audience for a girl like me, who was currently suffering.

I was almost glad when it was time to head in to work on Monday morning. Star's mate would have returned and I could get back to trying to pretend as though my life wasn't one big revolving door of sadness over him. Him, whom I couldn't even name. It hurt to say his name and I'd been avoiding it.

I'd finished the James Smith book and it had also left me reeling. For some reason, I felt about as helpless about it as I did about *him*. I felt a strange attachment to the thing. Maybe, it was because one of the few memories I had at his house was of me throwing James Smith books at him. I didn't know. I just knew that it left me oddly anxious.

Mandy came in for lunch and plopped down across from my desk. "I almost wish I hadn't asked you to get that book for me on

Friday. I can't get it out of my head. I don't think I've ever finished a book so fast."

My chest tightened. "I read it, too. It's definitely darker than his other books."

She frowned and shook her head. "It's just really sad. If I'd known he was taking it so hard, I would've stepped in and tried to help him."

My eyebrows slammed together as confusion riddled me. "What do you mean?"

"It's just so obvious that this book is so dark because he is in a bad head space. He's hurting. It's because of our break up. I figured he'd have a hard time with it, but I didn't realize it would be quite this bad. Did you read the message at the front?"

I nodded. It'd been one of the parts that hit me the hardest.

Mandy recited it. "Come back home."

My chest ached again and I stood up from my desk and walked over to the window. "You think that's because of a break up?"

"Well, duh."

"I didn't know you'd dated anyone since-"

"John. Yeah. He's who I'm talking about. You can't tell anyone this, but John is James Smith. It's a big secret. I signed some kind of legal form saying I wouldn't reveal it, but really? Who are you going to tell? You don't know anyone."

I spun around to face her. "What did you say?"

She rolled her eyes. "Don't be so sensitive. I didn't mean it in a bad way."

I waved her off. "No, before that. *John* is James Smith? John, your ex? From Wyoming?"

She gave me a weird look and nodded slowly. "Yes. John is James Smith. He's apparently really torn up about our separation. I'd heard some of the early reviews were saying that he got really dark and something must be going on, so I had to read it as soon as possible. He was such a hunk. Maybe I'll call him. He clearly is devastated by losing me."

I felt like my knees were going to give out so I rushed back to my desk chair and fell into it. John was James Smith.

Was the mate connection so strong that I could feel him through the book?

Did he mean his message to me?

Did he still want me?

My heart was pounding so hard that it drowned out whatever else Mandy was saying.

Wasn't it too late?

13

BUNNY

I drove myself crazy for a week. A week spent questioning myself and debating with myself about whether or not John's cryptic message was even meant for me, or if I could even do it. If I could go back and try to have something with him. My ex had left such a bad taste in my mouth that I couldn't imagine life with any man again, much less another bear shifter. I couldn't stop thinking that things would turn out the same as with my ex.

Star assured me that it wouldn't be like that. She'd started to settle down nicely with her bear. I just didn't know if that could be possible for me.

I didn't know John. I knew that my body wanted him and I couldn't deny that there was something about him that called to me on an emotional level, but I was terrified of it.

There were so many fears and doubts. I hardly ate that week because my stomach was always tied in knots. My anxiety was through the roof and I messed up more at my job that week than ever before. I made the mistake of not recognizing a pretty well-known actor and the guy flipped out on everyone in the office. Which led to Mr. Scott flipping out on me. I barely noticed, though. My mind was definitely somewhere else.

At the end of the week, Mandy came in and sat in front of me again, this time a lot less cheerful. She wiped at her eyes, even though there were no tears, and pouted until I asked her what was wrong.

"Well, you know how I told you about John obviously being depressed about our relationship ending?"

I'd been holding a paper coffee cup and when she mentioned his name, my fingers twitched and I ended up crushing the cup. Coffee went everywhere on my desk, and my lap. I jumped up and grabbed a roll of paper towels from the kitchen next to my office and rushed back in to clean it up. I couldn't meet Mandy's eyes as I blotted at my once white shirt.

"I remember."

"I called him and we talked for a while. He had the nerve to tell me that the message wasn't about me. He said he met someone else- and it was about her!"

I coughed and continued to work on my desk. My heart was racing. Did he mean me? "That's uncomfortable."

She scoffed. "It was embarrassing as hell. He said he met the little bitch right around the time we ended and she left him. It broke his heart, yada, yada, yada. I think he cheated on me."

Mandy didn't need me to look like I was actively listening to her, so she went on. "She left him and they haven't spoken since, but apparently, he's hoping she comes back to him. He told me all of that like I was supposed to care. I'll tell you one thing, Bunny, he was never that sentimental when he was with me. It's such bullshit. What was so wrong with me that he didn't feel that way about me?"

I tried to answer, but my tongue felt like it had swollen up to the size of a golf ball. John wanted me back.

"I'm attractive and I'm nice! I'm also a lot of fun! What does a guy like that not see in me? It's infuriating. I have half a mind to out him. Wouldn't that just serve him right? Having a crowd of reporters show up at his front door. He'd die."

Irrational anger threatened to erupt out of me. I chomped down on my tongue and gripped the back of my chair.

"I'm better than that, though. Just like I'm sure I'm better than the woman he cheated on me with. It was probably some little backwoods hussy he found in Wyoming. A mountain-dwelling nobody whose uncle is also her brother."

I slammed my hand down on my desk. "Mandy. This is a man you broke up with months ago. There's no need to dwell on him. He's clearly depressed enough, as it is. You're better than this."

Her eyes lit up, forever the self-help addict. "Oh, my gosh. You're so right. It's just so easy to get caught up in the negative. I just need to forget about all of this. Maybe I'll burn his book to clean out my energy."

I just wanted her out of my office. "That would really be good. Just don't do it in here."

She rolled her eyes and stood up. "Duh. I'll see you later. Thanks, Bunny."

After she left, I sat there, contemplating my next move. I couldn't just ignore him. Not anymore. I had to make some sort of concrete decision. I also had to find a way to apologize to Mandy for what happened with John. Despite everything, I still felt bad for what I'd done.

I contemplated my life and kept coming up with the same answer. I hated my job and I hated living in LA. LA was nice, but it wasn't for me. I had plenty of money saved up. I could take my time looking for a job in Wyoming and not have to rush into something I hated. Even if in the end I decided that I couldn't be with John, I would be closer to Star and in a place I enjoyed living.

With that realization in my head, I walked into Mr. Scott's office and tried to smile at him. I was beyond nervous, but I knew what I had to do.

"What is it, Bonnie?"

"I need to talk to you, Mr. Scott. About working here."

He looked up from his cell phone and sighed. "Are you giving me two weeks to find someone else, at least?"

I nodded. "Yes, sir. I wouldn't leave you empty handed."

He barked out a rough laugh. "I'm never empty handed, Bailey.

Alright. Two weeks it is. Have you told my daughter? She seems to like you. I'm sure she'll be sad to see you go."

I didn't actually believe that. Mandy didn't like anyone who didn't get her more views on her social media sites. "I'll email her. Thank you, sir."

He waved me away. "I'll contact HR and have them draw up paperwork and some sort of package."

I turned to leave but he cleared his throat. "Yes, sir? Anything else?"

"Don't think I'm going to expect any less of you for the next two weeks. You slack and you're out of here, on your ass, with nothing but the trash bag you came to town with."

It was an exaggeration. I'd come with suitcases. Instead of correcting him, I nodded and left.

Just two weeks. Two weeks until I had to make a final decision about what to do with John.

14

JOHN

"Jesus, John." Alex was flat on his back, breathing heavily after a round of fighting. "You need to figure this shit out. I can't keep fighting with you every day. I'm getting too old for this."

"You're younger than me." I was on my back next to him, aching in places that I hadn't ached in a while.

"I don't fucking care. This is getting out of hand. Elizabeth is pissed at you. She's already planning to slap the hell out of you the next time she sees you. If I come home exhausted from wrestling with you one more night, we're both dead men. Her words."

"You know what? I may consider putting my head on the chopping block for her." I blew out a rough breath and sat up. "How the fuck did you manage this, Alex?"

He threw his arm over his face and grunted. "I didn't beat the shit out of everyone constantly, that's for sure."

"I just want the incessant pain to go away. I keep hoping that one of these days, you're going to hit me hard enough to make me forget. I should pick a fight with Matt. He'd probably fucking do it."

"You're never going to forget, asshole. She's your mate. There is no forgetting. I'll tell you one thing, though. This pain you're feeling?

She's feeling it, too. She'll come back. Or you'll finally give in and go get her."

I pulled myself to my feet and staggered for a few steps. We'd really let each other have it this time. "I'm sorry I keep doing this to you, brother. I just feel like I'm going crazy."

"I get it. Why do you think I'm back here for more every day?"

I helped him up and then we both made our way to my truck. "I'll figure it out. It's got to hurt less eventually, right?"

Alex gave me a look that said that he doubted it. "Why don't you come inside and have dinner with us? Everyone's here."

I looked up at the house and imagined sitting at the table with my four brothers, their mates and their children. No way. I looked away from Alex and shook my head. "Thanks for the offer. I'm heading home. A nice long swim in the lake sounds good right about now."

He patted me on the shoulder. "Take care of yourself. Come on back tomorrow, too, if you need to. I'll handle Elizabeth."

I nodded and drove into town. I needed to grab something for dinner, so I stopped at the general store. I drew plenty of stares in my still healing state. I was sure I looked a lot like death warmed over, but I didn't give a shit.

I grabbed a case of beer and a loaf of bread, resigning myself to a night of peanut butter sandwiches. I was just putting my stuff on the counter when I looked up and caught a glimpse of a tall strawberry blonde strolling past the store.

My stomach dropped into my boots. I felt light headed. It couldn't be her.

"You going to pay for that?"

I looked back at the cashier and grunted. "I'll be right back."

I couldn't not check it out. I had to be sure that it wasn't her. I rushed out of the store and looked in the direction she'd gone. Nothing. It was like she'd vanished. It didn't stop me from walking down the street, peering into stores and down alleys.

When I realized she wasn't there, and probably never had been, I trudged back to the general store to paid for my things before heading home. My heart was heavier than ever. I was almost ready to check myself in somewhere because I felt a little bit like I was going insane.

I was doing the same old song and dance in my head, trying to think of something, anything, to lessen the pain. When I pulled into my driveway, there was already a truck parked there. I didn't see anyone in it and there was no one on my front porch, but I got a strong whiff of wild cherries.

I dropped my beer and bread and rushed around the side of the house. There on the porch, sitting with her back to me, was Bunny. My heart stalled out and I was pretty sure I was going to have a heart attack and die right here in front of my mate.

"This is probably my favorite place in the entire world. You have the best view I've ever seen." She stood up and turned to face me. Her eyes went wide and she touched her own face. "What happened?"

I couldn't get the words to come out. I knew what I wanted to say but I couldn't get anything out. I was choking at the worst possible moment.

She was stunning. Her hair was longer and she'd gotten a little bit of sun. Her toes were bare and she'd wrapped a blanket around her shoulders to keep out the evening chill.

"At the risk of making a fool out of myself, I'm just going to talk. You're doing great at just listening, so far." She hugged herself tighter. "There are things that I won't negotiate on. I don't want to get married again. I don't want to feel trapped. I am going to work and I'm going to support myself. I'm not just some woman you can keep under your thumb and at your beck and call. I'm my own person and I want to be treated as an equal.

"No cheating or lying. No bossing me around. No pushing me around. I want the freedom to go and see my best friend, whenever I want. Essentially, I want to be free. But, I want you."

She stopped and laughed. "Man, this is going to be awkward if you don't want me, too. I guess I should've led with that question."

I closed the gap between us and held her face in my hands pressing my lips against hers, letting her know how much I still wanted her. Her body fell against mine and I lost any sliver of chance I had at ever being okay without her.

"Whatever you want."

She ran her hands through my longer hair and then across my full beard. "This has to go. It's tickling me."

I shrugged. "Fine. What else?"

She brushed her shaking fingers over my eyebrow. "No more fighting. Your poor face."

"Done."

"I missed you. It's crazy. I don't know you, but I missed you. Even right now, I don't feel like you're close enough."

I caught the backs of her legs in my hands and lifted her into my arms. Her legs locked around my waist and I let my eyes drift closed at the sensation. "I missed you. More than I could ever explain."

"Can you deal with my list?"

"Bunny, I can agree to anything as long as it includes you being here with me."

She kissed me again. "I rented a house. I want to get to know you first, before we live under the same roof."

"Fine." I tasted the skin at her throat and grinned as she writhed in my arms. I had no real intentions of letting her out of my bed for a couple of weeks, so we could sort out the details then. "It was hell without you."

She pulled her nails across my back and moaned. "Eventually, we have to do more than this. We have to talk."

"Okay, sure."

"Later, though."

I grinned. "Definitely later."

15

BUNNY

The world was back on its axis. All of the anxiety I'd felt over the past six months had faded the second I saw John. A new tension had formed south of my stomach in its place. I'd made the right decision. I knew it as much as I knew the sky was blue. I belonged next to him.

John carried me into the house and up the stairs, to his bedroom. With ease, he lowered me onto the bed and then stepped back. His bruises were quickly fading, leaving perfect, tan skin behind. His hair was longer and messily brushed back from his face, and his beard had grown fuller. I liked the way it made him look, even if it tickled my face.

"What are you thinking about?"

I looked up at his golden eyes and smiled. "I don't hate the beard."

He laughed while pulling his shirt over his head. "I like your hair like that."

I shook off the blanket that'd been around my shoulders. "Mandy told me you're James Smith. I'm sorry I threw your own books at you that first day."

He undid his belt buckle. "I probably deserved it. I wasn't quite myself. See, I'd just met my mate and slept with her within ten minutes of finding her hiding in my closet. It was a busy day."

I sat up and leaned forward on the bed so I could grab the front of his pants and pull him closer to me. "She sounds easy."

"Ha! No, she is not easy. She is anything but easy!" He leaned over me and grabbed the bottom of my dress before easily pulling it off. When he saw that I wasn't wearing anything under the dress, he groaned. "Not easy at all. But worth it."

I ran my hand down his length, through his jeans. "Well you're pretty hard yourself. We should do something about that."

"We'd better not. I'd like to last longer than last time."

I unzipped his pants and pushed them down enough to get him out. "Apparently, we have a while. Being mates and all. I'm told that's forever."

He twitched as I held his erection in my hands and stroked. "Damn, Bunny. Say that word again."

"Which one?" I flicked my tongue over the head of his dick and looked up at him. "Forever?"

John opened his mouth to talk, but I opened my mouth and took as much of him as I could in. I moved my tongue along the underside of his shaft and curled my lips over my teeth as I bobbed my head. He growled and buried his fingers in my hair.

Just when I was finding a good rhythm that had his grip tightening in my hair, he moved away from me. "On your back," he growled.

I moved to the middle of the bed and pressed my thighs together as John undressed. Seeing him naked turned me on more than anything else ever had. My mate was sexier than should've been allowed. His body made me stupid.

He knelt in front of me and rained kissed all over my legs, working his way up my thighs. "You have no idea how many times over the past six months I've regretted not tasting you that day. I was in such a hurry to be inside of you that I missed out."

I gasped as he pulled my legs apart and kissed my inner thighs. "Have you thought about this a lot?"

"I've fantasized about you every single day." He lowered his face until his breath fanned out over me and then he extended his tongue and ran the tip from end to end of me.

I cried out, feeling just as wild as I had the first night. I wondered if it would always feel so unhinged with him. I constantly felt like I was out of control, but I loved it.

John rolled his tongue again, diving deeper with that stroke. Again and again, he caressed me with his tongue, working me into a frenzy in no time. He stiffened his tongue and thrust it into me, fucking me with it.

I gripped his hair and held on as I felt like I was flying away. When his tongue found my clit, I was lost. His beard rubbed it in just the right way that had an orgasm shooting through me before he'd really even started. My hips twisted and left the bed, but he held me steady.

"John!" I screamed his name, letting go.

"I need to be in you. Fuck, Bunny." He moved up my body, kissing as he went. Stopping at my breasts, he took a few seconds to tease my nipples until I was writhing under him again.

I opened my body to him, invited him in, and was surprised when he rolled me onto my stomach. I looked back at him over my shoulder and felt the weight of his erection rest between my thighs. My core clenched and I bit my lip.

John's eyes were bright and I could see his bear right under his surface. "Mark. I want to mark you."

I knew what he meant, thanks to Star. He wanted to claim me as his own. I couldn't fight it, even if I wanted to. His desire to do it was as natural as the sun rising. I lifted my hips and shifted so I could reach under me and line our bodies up. "Do it."

He surged forward, flattening my hips into the bed as he filled me completely. He held onto my hips and pulled out so he could slide back home again.

That angle was magical. He was hitting me in a place that had my eyes crossing. I gripped the pillows under me and begged him for more.

Not needing to be asked twice, he started an unforgiving rhythm. Each thrust forced my hips into the mattress. Each little growl of his had my heart pounding away.

John shifted forward, leaning his body onto mine, covering me. He held himself up with his fists planted on the mattress on either side of my head, as he rocked into me again and again. Just when I thought I couldn't take anymore, he whispered in my ear about how he wanted to make me come for him. His deep voice tickled my ear, but it had my core clenching in an impossible way.

John growled and moved his hips faster. It was too much for me. I sank my teeth into his arm and fell into an earth shattering orgasm. My whole body shook as heat spread through me. At the same time, I felt John's teeth close on my neck and then he shot his seed into me. I opened my mouth and screamed as white hot pleasure scorched every nerve ending I possessed.

I lost track of time. I didn't know how long I was orgasming or how long it'd been since John marked me. I just opened my eyes and then he was beside me, pulling me into his chest. He dipped his head and ran his tongue over his mark, causing ripples of my orgasm to move through me.

"What happened?"

John chuckled and held me tighter. "I marked you. And you marked me."

I looked at his arm and saw my teeth marks. "Oops."

"I don't know how I survived the last six months without being able to hold you. This is amazing."

I closed my eyes and let myself enjoy him. "Let's never do that again."

"You have me forever, Bunny."

I rested my leg across his and traced his stomach muscles with my fingernails. "I changed my mind."

He stiffened. "About?"

I leaned up and kissed him. "The beard. It can stay."

EPILOGUE

*****John*****

One Year Later

"I told you we didn't have time for this! Everyone's going to know what we just did."

I tucked my dick back into my pants and slapped Bunny on the ass. "Yep. And it's all your fault. This dress has been driving me crazy all day and you've been prancing around here, wiggling your hips at me."

She gave me a wicked grin. "I can't help it. I'm horny constantly these days."

I pulled her into my chest and kissed her. It was a little awkward with the belly between us, but we were making it work. I cupped her perfectly round belly and knelt in front of her. "Do you hear that, baby? Mommy's blaming this on you now."

There was a knock on the door and Alex's voice rang out. "If you two are finished, you may want to get out here. The show's about to start without you."

I kissed Bunny once more and opened the door. My little brother was standing with a big grin on his face as he looked at us. I smacked him on the back of the head. "We are the show."

Bunny gave me the evil eye. "I told you they were all going to know."

We hurried towards the ceremony, where soft music was playing and our family was waiting for us. Everyone was there. All of my brothers and their mates, and their children. I could already hear a baby squealing.

"Who thought it would be a good idea to do this when I was nearly nine months pregnant?"

Alex moved on as I stopped and rested my hands on Bunny's shoulders. "You did. You wanted this to happen before the baby came. If you'd rather not do it, just say the words, Bunny. I'll do whatever you want."

Tears filled her eyes and she shook her head. "No, I want to. I just feel awful. Look at me."

I did look and I felt myself hardening again. "Baby, you're fucking sexy as hell. I can go again if you need proof of how I feel."

She laughed and let me wipe her tears away. "I'm sorry. I'm all over the place. I'm just nervous."

I pulled her into my chest and held her. "I love you, Bunny. I love you more than any man has ever loved any woman, I'm pretty sure. I don't need this ceremony. I know what we have. If you'd rather just have the party, no one is going to blame you."

She straightened herself and shook her head. "No. I know what I want. Come on."

I let her lead me to the field of flowers and couldn't help feeling a little relieved that she wanted to do it. We joined the rest of our family, because they were her family, too, and I couldn't help feeling like I was the luckiest bear there. I stood back and watched as all of my brothers' mates rushed towards my mate, to fawn over her and her very pregnant belly. My heart felt like it couldn't take anymore. I knew it could, though. Soon, my son would join us.

Our whole family was complete. Of course, Bailey was still too young for her mate, but she seemed happy just taking care of all the new babies. I knew Dad would be pleased with how we'd turned out. We finally understood the crazy will. This, this spectacular thing, was all he'd wanted for us. It'd taken us losing him to get our heads on straight, but here we were. Better than ever.

Bunny suddenly cried out and I rushed to her side. She looked down and growled. "My water broke!"

Elizabeth grinned. "The baby's coming early!"

Bunny shook her head. "No. No way. We have to do this first."

I grabbed her arms. "No fucking way, Bunny. We're getting you to the midwife and the tub. We can do this later."

She grabbed the front of my shirt and yanked me closer. "We're doing this. Now."

And so we did. We committed our lives to each other in a commitment ceremony- not a wedding- while my mate was in labor. She screamed as I slid her ring on and threw mine at my head when I suggested we skip the rest and go ahead to her midwife. It was messy, with everyone gathered around us in a tight circle of worry and laughter. Bunny cursed me, while also telling me how much she loved me. It was us. It was perfect.

And then we all lived messily, and happily, ever after.

THE END

The next book in this series is Rancher Bears' Merry Christmas

RANCHER BEARS' MERRY CHRISTMAS

RANCHER BEARS BOOK 6

Lettie Jay was born and raised in Landing, Wyoming. She knows everything about everything that goes on in the town. So when three kids show up at her office looking a little rough around the edges, she knows something isn't right. It's Christmas Day. Kids should be wrapped up tight with their family, getting ready to open presents. She heads to the local sheriff, Tucker Long, to get them some help.

Tucker is just heading out the door on his way to his family's Christmas party. After hearing the children's plight, he decides that they could use some holiday cheer, at least until he can figure out what to do with them.

An old-fashioned Christmas with the Long family warms the children and warms Lettie to Tucker. Somewhere between singing carols and carving the turkey, something clicks. Could he be her mate? Is it possible? She's already fallen head over heels for the three kids, alone and afraid of being put back out in the cold. She can't help but think about her big house going to waste with no one in it but her and her cat.

1

LETTIE

If my mother had still been living, she would've lost her cool on me. I couldn't get that thought out of my head as I sat behind my desk on Christmas day. Mom was big on traditions and spending Christmas with family was one of them. Unfortunately, she and Dad had only one child, me, and their brothers and sisters didn't have kids nor did they stick around Landing, Wyoming. So, here I was, sitting alone in my office on Christmas day. No family around to speak of, and all my friends were spending time with their own families today.

My office sat on the corner of Main Street and Second Avenue and if I rolled my chair to the left corner of my desk, I could just see the giant decorated Christmas tree in the center of town square. It was early in the day, but the lights were already twinkling. A thick layer of snow blanketed the town, undisturbed except for the twin tracks on the road where people had driven over it. It felt magical, serene, and silent like the song.

I rolled my chair back in front of my laptop screen and tapped the space bar to get it to come to life. I didn't have anything to do. What was a travel agent supposed to do at her office on Christmas day? All of my clients were either already enjoying their holiday vacations, or tucked away cozy and warm in their homes celebrating with their families. I opened my email, anyway, then refreshed it a few times when nothing new appeared. Still, nothing.

A heaviness was beginning to settle over me at the realization that I was feeling, well, a little bit lonely. I had nothing to do on days like today but think about how alone I was in the world. Dad died when I was in college and Mom followed him a few years later. At twenty-seven, I'd been on my own for a number of years already and I was no stranger to holidays spent alone, yet each year around this time felt more and more depressing.

I'd received invitations to join people over the years, but I didn't want to be the orphan at the party. It always felt like I was being invited out of pity, because everyone knew I was all alone. Eventually, the invitations quit coming. People knew I wanted to be alone. Or, that's what they assumed, anyway.

I leaned back in my chair and closed my eyes. Instantly, a post-card perfect image popped into my head. My friend, Helen, had sent me the picture from her mother-in-law's living room. Helen, her husband, perfect children, cute dog, and a perfect backdrop of a fireplace, stockings, hot cocoa mugs, and even more family photos. I couldn't help the jealousy I felt. I was happy for her, but I truly wished I had something like that for myself.

I'd proven to myself that I was okay being alone. I was healthy enough to sit alone in a silent room without going insane. Didn't that mean I was ready for someone to love? Wasn't that what people said? Once you were okay with yourself, the right person would come along? So far, that wasn't true for me.

I opened my arms, looked up at the ceiling and said aloud, "I'm okay, world. I'm okay with me!"

I refreshed my email again and sighed. At the rate I was going, I'd be dead from boredom by nightfall.

The shrill sound of my office phone interrupted my thoughts and I practically dove at it. "Hello? Jay Travel. Can I help you?"

"Busted!" Leila Long's voice barked into my ear. "I knew you'd be at the office. Dammit, Lettie, that's no way to spend Christmas."

I made a face at the phone. "I just had to run in and finish up with something. Jeez. Do you harass all of your friends this way?"

She laughed, and then I heard others talking in the background. "Just the ones I love. Are you going to be free later?"

I'd had my back to the front door of my office, so when the bell rang, it startled me. I spun around and froze at the sight in front of me. Three children stood, without jackets, shivering, and staring at me. The oldest one, who was probably twelve, rubbed her hands over her arms and gave me a forced smile.

"I've got to go, Leila. I'll talk to you later."

She was talking when I hung up, but she'd be fine with me hanging up on her if she knew what I was looking at.

"Hi."

The oldest, a girl, gave me another forced smile. "Hi. You're the only shop open on this street."

I nodded and jumped into action. I didn't know what was going on, but these children had to be freezing. "I am. C'mon in, kids, here, let's get ya'll warmed up. I have a heater over here. Huddle on up to it, you'll all be able to feel the heat."

They rushed over to it, the smallest one getting pushed right up against it. He looked up at me with the biggest brown eyes I'd ever seen and stuck out his full bottom lip. He couldn't have been much older than three and everything about his sweet little face broke my heart.

"Why are you open?"

"I'm... not quite sure. Why are you walking out here alone?" It was direct, but I couldn't help it. I knew everyone in Landing. Everyone and everything. It was a small town and people talked. Yet, I didn't recognize these children. In fact, if I were a betting woman, I'd wager I'd never seen these kids before.

The middle boy, only about five, started to cry. "Mommy left us."

His big sister nudged him. "Be quiet, Joey."

I knelt in front of them and smiled up at the girl. "You in trouble?"

She sucked her bottom lip in between her teeth and roughly shook her head. Her messy brown hair matched her brothers' and they all shared the same huge brown eyes. Their pale skin was slowly turning rosy as the warmth returned to their little bodies.

"What's your name?"

Joey struck again. "Abby. And I'm Joey. This is Bear."

The small one's eyes turned bright and fur started spouting out on his little body. He let out a little sound that sounded more kitten than bear. Abby grabbed his arm and shook it.

"Stop it! Stop it, Bear!" She looked at me with panicked eyes and pushed him behind her body. "Don't hurt us. Please."

I reached around her and pulled her hand away from Bear's little arm. "It's okay. You don't have to stop him here, Abby."

"You... You know what he is?"

I nodded. Landing was made up mostly of shifters and their partners. Everyone in Landing, for the most part, knew about shifters. "I do. How did you kids get here?"

Abby looked more relieved than anyone I'd ever seen. Tears filled her eyes and she hugged herself. "We walked. From the bigger road."

"It's okay, sweetie. We'll get this sorted out."

2

TUCKER

"You know it ain't right to leave a man in jail on Christmas day, Tuck." Jeremiah Hawthorn called from the holding cell behind my desk. "I barely did anything wrong."

I kicked my feet up on my desk and sighed. "You know, I wouldn't have to be here right now if you hadn't decided to get drunk and show your bare ass to every woman at Sally Farm's meeting."

"Aw, come on, Tucker! You know how that lady is. She puts that red hat on and she thinks she's the freaking queen of England. I was just joking around."

I wanted to laugh, I did. I knew exactly what a pain in the ass Sally Farm could be. She called me to report anyone and everyone, sometimes daily. Someone's music was too loud, someone else's dog peed on the edge of her grass, so and so's daughter looked suspicious. I still had a job to do, though. And Sally Farm hadn't just seen Jeremiah's ass. He'd bent over a little too far and she'd caught a glimpse of his dangling set.

"Well, your joking is costing me a day with my family. I could be at the ranch right now, sipping on Aunt Carolyn's special egg nog. Next year, remember to keep it in your pants, would you?"

He grumbled some more, but eventually grew quiet. I figured I'd let him out in another hour or so, so he could go home and be with his family for dinner. Hell, his momma was going to punish him much more than I ever could.

The bell over the door tinkled and I looked up to see Lettie Jay hurrying my way. She'd shed her normal professional attire for a pair of dark jeans and a thick sweater that couldn't hide her ample curves. Tall, beautiful, and smelling like the most delicious coconut cake I'd ever gotten a whiff of. Her normally sleek black hair was piled into a rumpled bun on top of her head and her green eyes were wide.

I stood up, worried that something had happened to her, and noticed the three rag-tag children shivering behind her. "Lettie?"

She gestured to the kids and then opened her mouth, only to have no sound come out. Finally, she clamped her lips shut and took a deep breath before trying again. "This is Abby, and her little brothers Joey and Bear."

I smiled at the kids and rounded my desk. "Hey, guys. What are ya'll doing out here on Christmas day?"

The kids moved closer together and looked up to Lettie. She twisted her hands together and frowned. "I think they were...abandoned." She mouthed the last word silently.

My bear stirred inside, angry at the idea that someone would hurt the innocent looking children in front of me. "Walk me through it."

She turned and knelt in front of the kids, a sweet look on her face that suddenly caused my bear to stir in another way. "Abby, I'm going to go to Sheriff Long's office and tell him what you told me, okay? Why don't ya'll sit right here and try to let your toes thaw out some?"

I looked down at their feet and, sure enough, they were wearing house slippers. The fuzzy things were wet and dirty from the snow and I could only imagine how uncomfortable they were to wear. "I have a really awesome blanket you might like."

I found the emergency kit I stored in the corner of the station and grabbed it. Inside, there was an emergency blanket that would work wonders to warm the kids up. I made a show of flipping it open, letting the silver foil-like material crinkle loudly as I did.

Joey and Bear's eyes widened and they stared at it with a wary eagerness written on their faces. Abby looked more wary than either of them. She edged closer to Lettie and looked up at her, seeking advice on whether or not to trust me.

"It's okay. It'll be warmer than any jacket I could hope to find around here. Sit here on the bench and cuddle up."

Abby cautiously took the blanket from me and the boys rushed to get into it. Lettie tore her eyes away from them and then looked at me. Being the focus of her attention was almost alarming, but I held her gaze and nodded towards my office.

"After you."

She walked ahead of me and I had a hard time keeping my eyes off of the snug fit of her jeans. The woman had curves that made me want to drop to my knees for her.

Once we were in my office, she spun on me and grabbed my shirt. "Bear, the little one, is a bear shifter. He's the only one. His mom saw him do it, and decided to leave them all at the highway on the edge of town. They're not from anywhere around here, Tucker. They walked all the way here from the highway after their mom had them in the car for hours and hours. She just left them there to freeze to death. What kind of mother would do that to her children? They're terrified and freezing. What do we do?"

I rested my hand on top of hers. "I'll try to find their mother. Try to talk some sense into her. After that, it's not great. They go into the system until we can figure out where they belong."

"Bear can't go in the system!"

I ran my hands over my hair and blew out a breath. "It's not for me to decide, Lettie. Let's find out their mom's name and then put out a search. We'll start there and then figure out the rest later."

Lettie blinked away tears and nodded. "Abby told me her name is Danielle Thomas. They'd just moved up here from a town called Greenwich, in Kansas. Has no clue what the new address is."

"That's good. I'll put it in the system now." I walked around to my desk and sat down. "Did they have anything else on her?"

"No. They're just so scared and cold right now. What's the protocol here? Can I take them and find them clothes and stuff?"

I met her gaze and grinned. "Like you'd listen if I told you no."

"I'm going to take them, then. Just let me know what you find out."

I blocked her path from leaving and caught her hand. "Why don't we take them to the ranch? The party could be good for them. They could play with the other kids."

She looked up at me and hesitated for a second. Her pupils dilated slightly before she looked down at our hands. "Are you sure that would be okay with your family?"

"It'd be fine. Come on."

3
LETTIE

The kids looked scared as we arrived at the Long's ranch. I couldn't exactly blame them. The place was huge and the family was large and loud. They had every reason to be excited, as well, though. The entire place was decorated. Snow covered everything, but bright white icicle lights sparkled, despite it not being dark out. Garlands, that I was willing to bet were fresh, curled around the columns at the front of the sprawling farm house, garnished with big red bows. The front yard held a large statue of Santa and his sleigh, all lit up and being pulled by his reindeer.

Even from Tucker's truck, I could hear the faint notes of Christmas carols being played. The music made me feel like a kid again, complete with all the excitement that came with singing those songs. Caroling, drinking hot cocoa to stay warm, even snowball fights with friends while our parents conversed after we sang.

Tucker looked over at me and smiled. "It's beautiful, isn't it?"

I nodded. "Stunning. They're very lucky."

He looked back at the kids and smiled even bigger at them. "You guys ready? I heard Santa stopped by this morning. Maybe he's still hanging around?"

Joey looked up at Abby and tugged at her hand. "Santa? Abby, *Santa!*"

She just nodded and gazed up at the house. "Who's that?"

I looked up and watched as Bailey, the youngest Long child, came rushing out to the truck with a bundle of coats in her arms. I opened my door and jumped out to greet her. "Bailey! You're going to freeze out here, honey."

She rolled her eyes. "I'm a bear, remember? It's good to see you, Lettie. Mom told me all about your friends here and I thought I'd help. I found some extra jackets that we had around the house."

I took them from her and wrapped her in a tight hug. "You're an angel. Help me get them on the kids?"

She nodded and climbed into the truck, through the door I'd just left. I heard her talking to the kids and by the time I got the back door open, she'd already gotten them warmed up to her. Joey was staring up at her with big, puppy dog eyes, and Bear was sniffing at her hands when she came closer to wrap him up.

Abby, though, was still leaning away. I gently tugged her hair and grinned at her. "Bailey's okay, Abby. She's like Bear. Most of the people inside are like Bear."

She froze. "Will they hurt us? Mom said they're dangerous."

Bailey paused in helping Joey into his jacket to listen to my answer and I could feel Tucker standing behind me, listening as well. I cupped Abby's face and leaned down so we were eye to eye. "Bear isn't dangerous, is he? He's just special. These people are the same, Abby. They're special. They wouldn't hurt you. Ever. You can trust them. I do. A couple of my best friends are inside and they're married to bears. Apparently, they can be quite cute, even."

That gained me a smile from her, the first one yet. "I'm old enough to think boys are cute, now."

Tucker chuckled from behind me and rested his hand on my lower back. "Come on, ladies. Let's get ya'll inside before you freeze."

I shivered at the contact, but ignored it as I wrapped Abby in the too big jacket and helped her out. Joey and Bear were already racing to the house with Bailey, seemingly eager to forget their troubles for the moment.

"They don't know Mom isn't coming back for us." Abby tucked her hand into mine and looked up at me. "Should I tell them? I don't want to make them sad, but they keep asking me about Mom coming back."

Tucker squatted in front of her. "We don't know for sure that she isn't coming back, yet. I'm going to try to find her."

Abby's face hardened and she shook her head. "Don't. She doesn't want us. She hates us. I don't want to go back with her."

My heart ached and I blinked back tears. "We'll talk about it later, okay? Right now, let's go see what your brothers are getting into."

She let us lead her into the house and I watched the anger on her face slip away as she took in the Long's home. Her eyes went wide and no amount of twelve-year-old cynicism could put a damper on the amazement of the winter wonderland we'd walked into.

There was a two story tall tree in the living room loaded down with lights and ornaments. Beneath the tree were mountains of gift-wrapped presents with ribbons and bows and a toy train circled its way around them on a track. Delicate looking snowflakes hung from the ceiling, making the whole place feel like a snow globe. Garlands and more red bows wrapped around the staircase and stockings hung from above a fireplace that crackled with dancing flames. More music drifted throughout the rooms, creating a scene not unlike a picture perfect Christmas card.

For a few moments I felt nostalgia, like I was back with my mom and dad again. The warmth the Long family home emitted was impossible not to feel deep in your bones. Laughter rang out from the kitchen and I was immersed in a big, happy family. Then, the pitter-patter of little feet racing across the hardwood floor preceded a string of tiny kids running through.

Tucker scooped one of them into his arms and grinned at the boy. "Caught you. What do you think you're doing?"

Mason, Lucas' son, laughed as Tucker tickled him and then put him down. "Come play, Tucker!"

"In a little bit, I will. Go, have fun."

I heard Elizabeth's voice and then took the brunt of her weight as she threw herself into hugging me. I sucked in a large breath of air and pushed her away. "Are you trying to kill me?"

She grinned from me to Tucker. "It was so nice of you to bring Lettie, Tucker. We've been working on her for weeks trying to get her to agree to come today. Apparently, I wasn't cute enough for her."

My cheeks heated and I grabbed her arm. "Elizabeth, this is Abby. Abby, this is one of my best friends, Elizabeth. She's married to Alex. You'll meet him soon."

Abby stared at Elizabeth's swollen belly. "You're having a baby."

"Yes, ma'am. The third one. This little kicker is going to be our first girl. I'm looking for help naming her. You want to give it a try?"

I could see Abby immediately warming up to Elizabeth, so I squeezed her hand and let go. "Try to come up with something ridiculous. I'd love for her to have to call her newborn baby girl something crazy."

"Like watermelon?"

I laughed. "Exactly. You're on the right track now."

4

TUCKER

I watched as Elizabeth led Abby off towards the couch, towards her stack of baby naming books. I already knew she'd been pestering everyone all morning long with them. Alex had made it more than clear that he needed backup to help him escape Elizabeth's baby naming obsession.

I breathed in the smells around me and groaned when all I got was coconut cake, and nothing else. I turned to Lettie, unable to help myself. "You smell amazing."

She turned to face me with pink cheeks. I couldn't tell if it was the cold or my words. "Sherriff, why are you smelling me?"

It was a good question. We'd known each other for years and I'd never smelled her that much before. Sure, I'd noticed the woman in front of me. I would've had to have been blind to not notice her. I'd never taken the time to really look at her, though. Finding your mate as a bear was supposed to be instantaneous and I'd never been too interested in getting serious with a woman who wasn't my mate. Yet, looking at Lettie, I had to reconsider.

"I don't know. I can't seem to help myself."

She took a step back, which my bear interpreted as a challenge. When I stepped closer to her, her lips parted and her tongue darted out to wet her lips. Dang, just when I thought she couldn't get any hotter.

Lettie's eyes moved to my lips and then back up to my eyes. "What-"

Leila, Matt's wife, chose that moment to step into the foyer. She looked at us and then grinned at Lettie. "Come with me, girlfriend, I want to hear all about this."

I watched Lettie get pulled away, all the while stammering about there not being anything to tell. I couldn't help but feel like that wasn't true. There was definitely something. I just didn't know what it was yet.

I went to find my cousins, eager to catch up with them. I'd been busy at the station lately, and they were all busy with their growing families. We'd always been close growing up, so not seeing them for a couple of weeks was a big deal.

Matt and Lucas, the oldest two brothers, were sitting on a couch in the living room, their eyes glued to the TV, watching a parade. Michael was sitting with his wife, Daisy, in his lap. She was holding their squirming two-year-old, Sean, in her arms. Alex was on the floor, trying to set up a princess castle with John. Sammie, Lucas's wife, was on the floor alongside, arguing with them about how to put it together. Bunny must've been in the kitchen, with Aunt Carolyn, because I hadn't spotted her. There were kids everywhere, climbing on their parents and running around in circles.

I spotted my two little guys, playing on the floor with Mason. He was doing a pretty good job sharing the new toy cars he'd gotten from Santa. It was a stark reminder that I'd need to find something for Joey and Bear. They couldn't celebrate Christmas with a family like mine, who spoiled their children, and not get a single gift.

Just as I realized that I'd thought of them as *mine*, Matt spotted me. He gave me a big grin and came over to hug me.

"Well, look what the cat dragged in. Hey, little cuz. We were hoping you'd be able to make it. Your mom's in the kitchen, cooking out her frustrations that you might dare not show up."

I hugged him back and sighed. "I should go say hi. Keep an eye on the boys, will you?"

He looked over at them and cupped me on the shoulder. "As soon as you called, mom went a little nuts. She went through everything and made sure we had gifts for them. She also rounded up some clothes, so whenever you want, there's a big pile of stuff up in the guest room."

My chest tightened and I nodded. "Thanks, man. I'll be sure to thank Aunt Carolyn, too."

"We couldn't believe anyone would do that to their kids. We're here for whatever you need. If you can't find their mom and need a place for them to stay, we've got you covered."

I thought of Lettie and laughed. "Man, you'd have to fight Lettie for them. She's lost already."

He raised an eyebrow. "Lettie, eh?"

Lucas chose that moment to join the conversation. "I always thought you two might have something."

I raised my hands in the air and backed away. "Gotta go check on Mom. You kids try not to have too much fun in here."

Joey looked up at me and pouted. "We can't play?"

I laughed. "Of course, you can. I was talking to the grown-ups. *You* can have all the fun you want."

Lucas grunted. "Cute little things, aren't they? Kind of makes me want another one."

Sammie looked up from the floor with wide eyes. "Really?"

"Really."

I thumped Lucas on the back and nodded towards his wife. "I hope they look like their mother."

I left them to it and made my way to the kitchen. Mom was standing at the stove, her back to me, but her head tilted to the side. I knew she knew I was there, so I went up and gave her a hug. "Hey, ma."

She turned to face me and patted my cheek. "You came. With Lettie. Are you two finally going to wake up and smell the coffee?"

"Mom, we talked about you getting involved in my love life."

"Are you saying that you have a love life with her?"

"Mom."

"Tucker."

I sighed. "What are you cooking?"

She patted my cheek, rougher that time, and sighed. "Look at my sister. She's getting grandkids left and right. She's the lucky one. I get a son who refuses to open his eyes. He's too busy arresting mooners and drunks."

"Good talking to you, too, Mom. I love you."

Melissa Long was anything but a softie, but hearing me tell her that I loved her always warmed her up a bit. She hugged me quickly and then pushed me away again. "Get out of here. You're stressing me."

I made my way over to Aunt Carolyn and gave her a big hug. "Thanks for having us all over and for doing everything you've done for the kids so far."

She squeezed me. "Of course, Tuck. We've been trying to get Lettie here for forever, so you're a miracle worker. Plus, no kid deserves to be alone on Christmas. This is a very special day. Those kids need to feel that. Not abandonment."

I nodded. "Hopefully, I can find their mother."

She gave me a look, like she knew more than I did. "Lettie's good with them, I hear."

"She is. They like her a lot."

"And you're good with Lettie."

I caught on to where she was heading and decided to keep it short. I stole a chocolate chip cookie from behind her and smiled. "Better go check on them."

She laughed and shook her head. "You Long men are all the same. Chickens, all of you."

5
LETTIE

I managed to hold off Leila's questions about Tucker by introducing her to Abby. She was instantly in love. Bailey, Elizabeth, and eventually Leila, sat around a bedroom on the second floor, talking with her. Abby seemed shy at first, but eventually opened up. She'd even suggested a name for Elizabeth's new baby that Elizabeth loved.

I sat beside Abby, quietly brushing and braiding her hair to get it off of her face. Bailey had made a big fuss over bringing Abby some of her own older clothes, so Abby was adorned in a beautiful red dress that was slightly too big for her, but obviously made her feel like a princess. She'd wanted her hair to be special to go with it. Bailey also found the pile of clothes for her brothers and picked them out two outfits that I thought the boys would hate, but would look so cute in.

Tucker appeared in the doorway and leaned against the frame, like he didn't have a care in the world. I couldn't relate. I had a heavy feeling in my belly and couldn't stop thinking about him finding their mother. Should they even be with a woman who would leave them to freeze on the side of a highway? There was something else nagging at me, too. Tucker, himself.

Something about his wavy brown hair and pale blue eyes was speaking to me. He was drawing me in and I didn't understand it. We'd known each other for years, and while I'd always found him attractive, I'd never reacted in such an...intense way.

"Hi, Tucker." Abby smiled at him and then looked over at me. Her eyes widened and then she giggled. "Leila said Lettie has a crush on you, Tucker."

I sucked in a huge breath and felt my face going bright red. I felt like I was suddenly in middle school again. "Leila's got a big mouth."

Leila gasped. "Now, is that anything to say about your best friend? And on Christmas, to boot. For shame, girl. For shame."

Before I could say anything back, Carolyn was yelling up the stairs. "Ya'll come on down here. I need someone to set the table. Then, we're ready to eat."

"I'll set the table."

Tucker looked at me. "I'll help you."

Something fluttered in my stomach and I nodded. "Thanks."

We left the room to a chorus of childish kissing sounds. I did my best to just ignore them but while setting the table, I glanced up to find Tucker staring at me. I couldn't help the laugh that escaped my mouth. He immediately joined in.

"They're ridiculous." I shook my head. "I was just waiting for them to start singing about us kissing in a tree."

His eyes flashed brighter and I got the very clear impression that he wouldn't mind a little kissing in a tree. Or anywhere. "Have you ever thought about us?"

Nervous energy coursed through my body as I took in a deep breath. "Have you?"

His grin was alarmingly handsome. He was systematically laying down silverware at each place setting until he made it to the setting right beside me. As he reached over to put the last of it down, he met my eyes. "I've thought about you. This is new, though. Today is...different."

I was starkly aware of the fact that he was mere inches from me. He'd straightened and his long frame towered over me, but it was comforting beyond belief. Comforting and also disorienting. My body was suddenly pulsing, acutely aware of him. "What is it?"

"Tucker! Lettie! Are you done yet? We're going to have a toast in the living room."

I jumped like I'd been scolded and hurried to put the last two plates down before rushing from the room. My heart was racing and I felt jittery. Something was definitely different between Tucker and me. He knew it and I knew it. His honesty about it was almost off-putting. Tucker'd never been a man to waste words, but having it directed at me was shocking.

We joined the rest of the family in the living room and I almost got teary eyed at the scene before me. The whole family was standing around the fire, talking, while the children laughed and played in front of them. Even Abby had found a coloring book and was showing little Connor how to color inside the lines. The room felt like a Christmas post card and I knew that this was exactly the kind of Christmas Mom would've wanted for me.

I glanced over at Tucker and he was looking back at me. Without saying anything, he took my hand in his and nodded towards Bear, who had shifted at some point and was batting at ornaments on the bottom of the tree. No one seemed to mind and Abby wasn't freaked out by it. Everything felt so close to perfect in that moment that I had to blink away tears.

They weren't my kids, but I felt like they could be. Hell, I would take better care of them than their mother ever would. I had felt an instant connection with them. Then, there was Tucker. It wasn't instant with Tucker, but our connection had transformed when I walked into the police station earlier in the day. I'd been alone for what felt like so long and suddenly my heart was filling so quickly that I found myself reeling a little bit.

"I'll give the toast." Carolyn called as she ushered everyone closer. "This Christmas, I'm reminded of how incredibly blessed we all are. When you're a Long, you're almost never alone. There's always another Long within throwing distance and that's been one of the things I've loved most about our family. Seeing that sometimes people aren't as lucky, makes me realize that we should never take family for granted.

"I'm so thankful for my family, for all of you being as wonderful as you are, for giving me these little rugrats and for constantly bringing new people into our lives that just keep stealing little bits of our hearts. Lettie, I'm so glad you're here. You've practically been family your whole life. It's about time you showed up to dinner."

I laughed and felt myself sway from emotion, but Tucker positioned his body next to mine and wrapped his arm around my back. "Thank you for always welcoming me in. And now, for welcoming my little friends."

Carolyn looked at the kids and then back at me. "I have a feeling this won't be our last Christmas together. Anyway, I'm just thankful for each and every one of you. I love ya'll. More than you'll ever know."

Everyone took a turn hugging her, letting the joyous feelings bubble over. Even Abby rushed over to hug her. When it was my turn, she held me a bit longer.

"Your parents would've been so proud of you, Lettie Jay. And I know your Mom is thrilled to see you away from your office today."

Tears filled my eyes and I nodded. "I was just thinking that earlier. She never would've been okay with me sitting in my office on Christmas day."

Carolyn looked over at where Joey and Bear were tugging on Abby's braids. "Maybe, just maybe, she sent you a Christmas miracle to make sure you never do it again."

I looked at her, confused. "What do you-"

She grinned as she cut me off and moved away. "Alright, everyone, it's time for my Christmas meal."

Tucker's mom, Melissa, snorted. "*Your* Christmas meal? I've been slaving away in there for hours. But, no, go ahead, Carolyn, and take all the credit. That's just like a big sister."

Carolyn wrapped her arm around her sister and led her away. "If I was being just like a big sister, I'd push your head into the toilet and give you a swirlie again like the old days. Want to try me?"

6

TUCKER

After devouring heaping plates of the delicious meal that our moms had prepared, everyone was useless for a while. Bears, being bears, gorged themselves and then found couches to stretch out on before falling into naps. I was tempted, but I had other things on my mind. I was too keyed up to nap. The kids were all passed out on the living room floor with throw blankets and afghans, sleeping to the sounds of the football game playing on the television. The women were spread out. Some were helping with clean up, while some were lying next to their men, napping alongside them.

Lettie was in the kitchen, fielding questions from my mom while doing the dishes. I would've been worried for her, but she'd known my mom for years. She'd be fine. Instead, I walked out to my truck and made a few calls to check on the status of the kids' mother.

"Found her, boss."

My heart sank to my feet. "Already?"

Steven Hannity made a scoffing noise. "Not a lot of good it did. She freaked. Said she had no interest in ever seeing the little heathens again. Went on and on about the little one being a freak of nature."

I growled. "Where is she?"

"Already in Colorado. Headed towards a boyfriend in Alaska, apparently. You know I read people pretty well. She's not coming back for those kids, Tuck."

A big part of me felt devastated for the children. Losing your mother, especially by her choice, couldn't be easy. Another part of me felt something strangely similar to relief. No way should a woman who is capable of leaving her kids out in the middle of nowhere to freeze to death on the side of a highway be allowed to have said children back in her care.

"You want me to start a file on them so we can get them into the system?"

"No." I looked up and saw Lettie step out onto the porch, her arms wrapped around her to ward off the chill. "No, don't do that. I think we're going to do something different with them. I'll call you tomorrow, okay? Thanks for working today, and thanks for getting that information so quickly."

"Anytime, boss."

I put my phone away and then made my way up to Lettie. She shivered against the cold so I took my jacket off and slipped it around her shoulders.

"Don't. You're going to freeze."

I pulled it closed around her and smiled. "I'm a bear. Remember?"

She rolled her eyes and then looked down at our feet. "Was that a call about the kids?"

"Yeah."

When she looked back up at me, her eyes were brimming with tears. "She can't have them back, Tucker. It isn't right. She's awful. You saw how she left them on the side of the road! She doesn't deserve those babies."

I pulled her down the porch steps and across the property, to the barn. It was closed up, so it was warmer than just standing out in the cold. I let us in and then pushed the door closed behind us. "I don't want Bear hearing this. He's going to be able to hear anything and everything with his shifter hearing."

She stepped closer to me, her eyes wide. "What is it? What happened with their mom?"

"My guy found her but she doesn't want anything to do with them. She kept going, heading up to Alaska for a boyfriend."

"So, you're going to put them in the system?"

I sighed and shook my head. "I'm supposed to, but with Bear being a shifter, it's not safe. We would try to get him placed someplace local, but there's just no telling where he'd end up."

"What are you going to do?"

I pulled my hands down my face and then shoved them into my pockets. "Let me think about it tonight."

Lettie moved even closer and rested her hands on my sides. "Please, Tucker. I know it sounds crazy, but I feel a connection to them, like we were meant to find one another. I have loads of room in my house and I make plenty of money. I can take care of them."

I growled low in my throat and had her in my arms in barely a second. Having her touching me was too much. Right now, I was feeling more like bear than man and all I wanted to do was take her. "I'll think about it tonight, Lettie."

She made a sound close to a whimper and then locked her arms around my neck. "We don't have a choice now."

I raised my eyebrow and looked up when she nodded that way. Hanging above us was a perfectly positioned sprig of mistletoe. Weird. In the barn? Not one to look a gift horse on the mouth, I looked back down at her and wound my fingers into her hair. "It would be in bad taste to just walk away."

"Bad luck and all that."

I stepped forward, tipping her back, and then lowered my mouth to hers. When our lips met, my chest fluttered. My bear roared and I ended up growling into the kiss. Her lips were soft and plush, her skin smooth. Everything about the kiss felt perfect. She felt perfect. I knew I should've been gentle, but I couldn't stop myself from sliding my tongue between her lips and tasting her mouth.

She kissed me back with fire. Her hands tugged at my hair and she worked her tongue against mine with unbridled lust. I knew she could feel my erection digging into her stomach, but she just held me tighter against her.

I kissed across her jaw and down her neck, biting at her skin until she moaned and worked her body against mine. My bear scratched and clawed against my skin and I'd almost sank my teeth into her neck when I realized what I was doing and jerked my head back.

Lettie saw my face, my teeth exposed, and moved away from me. "What just happened?"

I'd almost marked her, that's what the hell just happened. I'd almost fucking marked Lettie Jay as my mate. I looked into her wide blue eyes and realized that I wasn't freaked out that I'd tried to claim her, only that I'd almost done it without any kind of consent from her. Lettie was my mate. My *mate!*

Holy shit, I'd been blind.

7

LETTIE

Tucker led me back to the house without answering my question. He just kept looking over at me. I was feeling self-conscious and a little concerned that maybe the kiss that had just rocked my world didn't have the same effect on him. I'd seen his teeth coming out. Was he that displeased with what'd happened? Was it that bad?

I stayed silent and tried to give him his jacket back once we were inside. "Here. Thanks for letting me use it."

"Keep it. You still look cold."

I sighed and shrugged it off anyway. The smell of him was driving me insane and I didn't want people to assume that we were together, especially when Tucker so obviously was not that into me. My chest ached painfully at that thought. Something in me had changed today and I was realizing that I really, really wanted him to want me back. With the same intense desire with which I wanted him. I'd felt the earth move when he kissed me. Apparently, it was one sided.

I went to the living room and found Carolyn slipping in a DVD. She looked back at us and smiled.

"There you two are. I'm putting in a Christmas movie. I want the kids to wake up to it." She nodded towards the loveseat. "You two sit down."

I sat at the edge of the couch and tried to be as small as possible. Tucker looked over at me, yet again, and frowned.

"You okay?"

I nodded. "Just feeling tired."

He leaned in closer. "You're a terrible liar."

I frowned at him and looked towards the TV. "The movie's starting."

He leaned back and let me silently stew in my thoughts while the movie played. I stared at the screen, but didn't see anything. My mind was trapped in thoughts of Tucker rejecting me and the kids being taken to a shelter. Halfway through the movie, Bear woke up and crawled into my lap and I realized for a second that I would be devastated if they were taken away.

The kids had all woken up by the time the movie ended, but Carolyn quickly put in a second to distract them while she got gifts together. She'd explained to me earlier, while we were in the kitchen, that they'd only let the kids open a few gifts that morning and still had a ton to go through. They waited until Christmas night and gathered around the tree to open the majority of them. She'd also mentioned that Abby, Joey, and Bear had plenty of gifts to open, as well.

I owed her so much. Without batting an eye, she'd made Christmas special for three abandoned kids, like they were her own.

Abby crawled in between me and Tucker and rested her head against me. "It's nice here."

I looked up at Tucker and he smiled. "Yeah?"

She nodded. "I know Joey and Bear want to go back home because they're little, but I don't want to. Mom is mean. She never did stuff like this for us. I want to stay with you."

I hugged her to my chest and squeezed her. "We'll figure something out, Abby."

She sighed. "Okay. Miss Carolyn brought in a lot of presents."

I wanted to kiss Carolyn, I was so thankful that she'd thought of the kids. "Some of them are even for you and the boys."

"Really?!"

I nodded. "Yeah. You'll have to be sure to give Miss Carolyn a big hug and tell her thank you. You can make the boys do it, too."

She jumped up, pulled Bear up with her, and ran over to Carolyn, leaving me alone with Tucker again. Everyone was waking up and moving around, so the couch felt much less secluded.

"Want to come get a snack with me before they open presents?"

I raised an eyebrow. "Sure. If that's what you want."

He gave me a weird look but caught my hand and pulled me after him. In the kitchen, a Christmas CD played and the smell of freshly popped popcorn hung around.

I leaned against the island and toyed with an unlit Holiday candle. When I looked up, Tucker was just staring at me. "What?"

He took in a big breath and then moved closer to me. "How have I never noticed the way you smell before?"

I pressed my back harder into the counter, feeling completely at a loss. I knew what I wanted, but I was confused about what he wanted. When he stared at me with so much fire in his eyes, though, I couldn't help but imagine that the flames were for me.

He stepped into me, his body just a hair's width away, and took a deep breath in again. "You're intoxicating."

I dropped the candle in my hand and it hit the floor with a loud crashing sound. I knew it'd shattered, but I was frozen there, pinned to the counter our eyes locked and the hint of Tucker's body brushing against mine.

"What do I smell like to you?" he asked.

The light blue in his eyes was glowing, like he was going to shift. I'd been around enough male shifters to know it meant he was aroused. I swallowed so loudly that he had to hear it and then blinked a few times. I could hardly remember what planet we were on. "You want me to smell you?"

His tongue flicked out and then was gone. "Yes."

I had no way of stopping it. Not that I wanted to. I wanted Tucker with everything in me. I needed him, for some insane reason. I'd never felt anything like the heat building in me and he wasn't even touching me.

I adjusted myself just enough so I could move my face closer. I already knew what he smelled like, but I wanted the chance to get closer. I brushed my nose over his neck and then to his ear. My voice came out sounding hoarse and barely above a whisper. "You smell like the ocean. Like a wave hitting the beach. Fresh."

Tucker shivered under me and it caused his chest to brush against mine. A groan escaped his lips and his hands clasped my hips and yanked me into him completely. "I need you."

I couldn't have walked away from him if I wanted to. My body was screaming at me to jump his bones right there on the kitchen floor. "Let's go."

8

TUCKER

"Well, you kids seem to have your hands full." Aunt Carolyn stepped into the kitchen with Mom and grinned. "If you'll watch out for that glass on the floor, I'll take care of that. You two should go for a walk... or something."

Mom's eyes were practically glowing, she looked so excited. "Yeah, go for a walk or something."

Having my aunt and my mom walk in on a moment like this should've killed my raging hard on that was pressing into Lettie's stomach, but no. I moved so that she was standing in front of me. "How are the kids?"

"They're entranced with the movie right now. We'll keep an eye on them. We're opening presents as soon as it's over. Don't make us send one of the boys out looking for you."

I had to get out of there. It was too much. A conversation with them was the last thing I wanted to do. "Okay, we'll be back soon."

Lettie seemed frozen, so I slid my hand up from her hip and gently squeezed. She wiggled, effectively torturing me. The way she looked at me cemented the fact that I wanted her, and I wanted her now. My brain sizzled, and I gave up trying to be a gentleman.

I scooped her into my arms, praying no one saw my erection, and headed out of the room. "Keep an eye on the kids, please!"

Lettie wrapped her arms around my neck and groaned. "They know. They know exactly what's going to happen."

I liked the way she implied that it was still happening, no matter what. It was a big green light and I couldn't wait to go. "Does it bother you? Because when we come back, you're going to smell a whole hell of a lot like me and then everyone is going to know."

She twisted and I thought she wanted down, but instead she wrapped her legs around my waist and pressed her plump lips to my ear again. "Take me wherever we're going. *Fast.*"

The front door opened and I took it as my chance. We passed Matt coming back inside and he just raised his eyebrows and held up his hands. "Don't let me get in your way."

I carried Lettie to the barn and then set her down next to the ladder that led to the loft. "Up."

She squealed when I slapped her ass and sent a dark look over her shoulder at me. "Watch it."

I pushed the barn door shut and grinned. "Don't worry. I am."

She'd barely gotten her feet under her when I was hurrying over the ladder and into the loft. It was a pretty modern barn and the entire backside of the loft was a large window that looked out over the farmland. I knew the view was beautiful but I was focused on my mate. For every step I took towards her, she grinned and took one backwards.

"Come here, little Lettie. The big bad bear has something for you." I called to her softly and watched as shivers rocked her body.

Her nipples pebbled under her sweater and she bit her lip. She didn't listen, though. "I haven't seen your bear. What's he look like?"

He wanted to come out and show her, that was for sure. I couldn't trust him not to charge at her in an attempt to claim what was ours, though. "Big. Hungry. Dangerous."

Her butt pressed against the bottom of the window. "Should I be worried?"

I growled low in my throat and pinned her in place with just my hips. "Very."

She reached out and unbuttoned my shirt before slipping her chilled hands inside and stroking my chest. She pushed it off and then ran her eyes down my body. "Sheriff Long, you've been hiding quite a lot in that uniform."

I caught the hem of her sweater and pulled it over her head. In just her bra, she looked delicious. I took the tiny front hook and made quick work of it. As the material fell away, her perfect breasts tumbled out and into my hands. "So have you, Ms. Jay."

"Why does this feel so right? Why now? We've know each other… forever."

I pulled her into my arms and kissed her, hard and long. Then, I turned her around and rested my chin in the crook of her neck. "Look at it. A Christmas snowfall. The first white Christmas we've had in Landing in years."

She backed her ass into me and rocked her hips back and forth. "Is that what this is? Just some holiday fun?"

I tilted my face and let my teeth scrape over her vulnerable neck. "No."

A strong shiver shook her. "What is it?"

"It's nature, little mate. Slow and somewhat confusing nature."

A little gasp was the only response I got from her. Her hips didn't stop moving, though. Steady and strong, she rocked them into me, driving me absolutely insane.

"After all these years of knowing each other, it seems it just took three kids and a mistletoe to get us together."

She looked back at me and her eyes were bright. "You're my mate."

I moaned as her hips continued their torture. "I am. I nearly marked you earlier, but I figured you might prefer to be asked first."

Lettie groaned. "Yes. Mark me. I want you to claim me as your mate, Tucker."

I reached around her waist and quickly undid her jeans and

yanked them down. I shoved her panties down with them and then stroked her dripping core with my fingers. "You're mine, Lettie."

I knew that I should do other things our first time, but I was a desperate man. I needed to be inside her. I pushed my own pants down and lined our bodies up. I eased into her, despite her being so wet.

Lettie grabbed my hand that was on her hip and pressed her other hand against the window. She tipped her head back and moaned. "Tucker..."

I pulled out and slowly pumped back into her, trying to extend both of our pleasures for as long as possible. My heart hammered away in my chest, but that was nothing to the pulsing in my dick. Lettie was trying to squeeze me to death.

I took her like that, slow and hard, over the best view on the ranch. I thrust into her again and again until I was close to losing it. All of my senses were on fire. Her smell surrounded me. The way she looked with her pants around her knees, legs slightly spread, hair completely wrecked had me right on the edge.

"I'm close, Tucker." Her voice broke and she balled her fist up, her nails scraping against the window as she did.

I wrapped my arm around her and found her clit with my fingers, while nuzzling my mouth into her neck. "Come for me, Lettie. Come for me, little mate."

The second her body squeezed my dick, I felt my own release shooting from deep inside. I let my bear's teeth come out and sank them into her neck, marking her, claiming her as mine for the rest of our lives.

My orgasm seemed to grow stronger and I came so much that I was barely standing by the time it finished. Lettie screamed, her face so close to the window that her breath fogged it up. Her body pulsed around me as she came, hard and long.

I felt the bond grow immediately, felt myself grow warm with the realization that I'd just marked my mate. *My mate*. Lettie Jay was mine and I was hers. And the kids? The kids were definitely ours.

9

LETTIE

I was barely conscious when Tucker's hand moved from my side and he used his finger to draw a couple of stick figures in the fog my breath had created. I smiled, but then he kept drawing. Three more, smaller, stick figures appeared and then faded as the fog receded.

Tears filled my eyes and I looked at him over my shoulder. "Say it."

He pulled out of me and helped me get dressed again. Once we were both wrapped up, he pulled me into his arms. "I want to keep them with us. Fate had to have meant for it to happen this way. You're my mate and they're our family."

I threw my arms around his neck and squeezed. "Tucker, I... This is too perfect. Are you sure?"

He laughed. "Yes, Lettie. You're my mate. Those kids are our kids now."

I thought of how lonely I'd felt that morning, how much I'd wished for something more. My house was too big, too cold for me to stay in it, even on Christmas day. Yet, there I stood, at the end of the same day, complete with a mate and three kids who I was overjoyed to take responsibility for. It truly was a Christmas miracle.

"I'll figure out how to work it out with the system and we'll figure out how to work it out with three new kids."

I buried my face in his chest and sighed. "We'll have to work out some special time for the two of us to do this."

He grunted. "I'll always find time for this, little mate."

I unwrapped myself from him and moved towards the stairs. "Come on. Let's tell the children."

He caught my arm and pulled me back into a fierce kiss. "I am so glad that you're my mate, Lettie. This is the best Christmas gift anyone could've ever given me."

I gave him a wicked smile. "Just wait until later, after we figure out where the kids are staying and get them off to sleep."

He followed me down the ladder and then chased me back to the house. "You didn't get enough?"

I laughed and spun around just as he grabbed me. Standing in the snowfall, freezing but happy, I shook my head. "I don't know if I'll ever get enough."

"I'm a lucky man."

The door opened behind us and Alex stuck his head out. "Oh, thank God. I was terrified I was going to have to interrupt something. Come on in. We're opening gifts."

I couldn't keep the grin off my face when Tucker took my hand and led me in. Everyone looked up at us and the expressions on the adults' faces said it all.

I blushed, but ignored them as I sat down behind Abby.

She looked up at me and grinned. "We got presents!"

I looked at the big pile in front of her and felt my heart swell in my chest. "You did!"

Joey popped up next to her and pointed to his pile. "How are we even going to get these home?"

Abby suddenly frowned. "We don't... I don't know, Joey."

I scooped her into my arms and pulled her onto the couch between myself and Tucker. "We need to ask you something."

She looked at the both of us, her eyes still round and sad. "What?"

"Would you like to live with me? I have a big house and a cat named Tony. I promise I will take care of you and your brothers. And...Tucker would be there, too."

She was instantly in my lap with her arms around me. Giant tears rolled down her cheeks. "You want us?"

I nodded and shed a few of my own tears. "Of course, we do. No matter what happened with your mom, Abby, you and your brothers are the best gift I could've ever hoped for. I promise that I'll do my best to make sure you're all happy."

Her little body shook in my arms and she let the tears fall freely. Joey and Bear rushed over to join her in my lap. They hugged their big sister, clearly worried about her. She gathered herself, though, and smiled at them. "We're going to live with Lettie, guys. She's going to take care of us. And Sheriff Tucker. They'll keep us safe."

Joey tilted his head. "Do you have cartoons?"

I nodded. "All kinds of them."

Bear gave a pitiful roar. "Can I be bear?"

I nodded. "You can be bear."

That was all it took. The boys jumped down and went back to their presents. Abby was slower. She hugged me for a long time before hugging Tucker and then crawling back to her gifts.

Tucker pulled me into his chest and kept me there. "They seem happy."

I looked down at them, opening the piles of gifts, each one seemed to be perfect for them. I didn't know how Carolyn did it, but she'd made their Christmas. She'd made everyone's Christmas. I looked around at the beautiful scenery with the snow falling outside and the Christmas carols being played, and I felt almost like a little kid myself. Then, Melissa brought out a big tray of cookies and the scene was complete.

Matt and Leila sat together, holding their two children. Lucas and Sammie were cuddled up, staring at each other with so much love it would've made me jealous to see if I hadn't had Tucker at my back, holding me. Mason was on the floor with Joey, racing their new cars. Michael and Daisy were on the floor with their boy, watching him try to walk. John was sitting behind Bunny, on the couch, rocking their crying baby. Then, there was Alex, pacing as Elizabeth tried to find a comfortable position for her belly while their two boys ran wild around everyone.

Carolyn stood back and watched her family with a twinkle in her eye, Baily at her side taking pictures, making sure the memories lasted.

It couldn't have been more perfect. I felt like I'd stepped into a framed Thomas Kinkaid painting. My own Christmas miracle.

At least I thought so until Tucker leaned forward and nibbled my ear. "You said you have a cat named Tony?"

"Yes. Why?"

He laughed. "I have a dog named Thunder. This should be interesting."

I turned to face him and frowned. "Thunder likes cats, right?"

"Hmm... sure."

"My house is going to be destroyed, isn't it?"

He pressed a kiss to my lips. "Welcome to motherhood, little mate."

I looked back down at my three precious gifts surrounded by their new toys. Abby glanced up at me and flashed a big smile before going back to fastening her new charm bracelet.

I settled back against Tucker's chest and sighed happily. "So, we'll have a few messes. How bad could it be?"

I had no idea what I'd gotten myself into, but I knew that no matter what, it would be worth it.

JOIN OUR GROUP

Please join our Facebook group.
Receive ARCs, notifications of new releases, giveaways and hang with friends.

Click to join Lovestruck Insiders on Facebook.

P.O.L.A.R.

(**P**rivate **O**ps: **L**eague **A**rctic **R**escue) is a specialized, private operations task force—a maritime unit of polar bear shifters. Part of a world-wide, clandestine army comprised of the best of the best shifters, P.O.L.A.R.'s home base is Siberia...until the team pisses somebody off and gets re-assigned to Sunkissed Key, Florida and these arctic shifters suddenly find themselves surrounded by sun, sand, flip-flops and palm trees.

1. Rescue Bear
2. Hero Bear
3. Covert Bear
4. Tactical Bear
5. Royal Bear

∽

CYBERMATES

As bunny shifter, Parker Pettit, struggles to get her new online shifter dating site, Cybermates, off the ground, she's matching up shifters and their mates left and right. (This series is a spin-off of the **P.O.L.A.R.** series.)

1. Cherished Mate
2. Charmed Mate

∽

BEARS OF BURDEN

In the southwestern town of Burden, Texas, good ol' bears Hawthorne, Wyatt, Hutch, Sterling, and Sam, and Matt are livin' easy.

Beer flows freely, and pretty women are abundant. The last thing the shifters of Burden are thinking about is finding a mate or settling down. But, fate has its own plan...

1. Thorn
2. Wyatt
3. Hutch
4. Sterling
5. Sam
6. Matt

∾

SHIFTERS OF HELL'S CORNER

In the late 1800's, on a homestead in New Mexico, a female shifter named Helen Cartwright, widowed under mysterious circumstances, knew there was power in the feminine bonds of sisterhood. She provided an oasis for those like herself, women who had been dealt the short end of the stick. Like magic, women have flocked to the tiny town of Helen's Corner ever since. Although, nowadays, some call the town by another name, **Hell's Crazy Corner**. (This series is a spin-off of the **Bears of Burden** series.)

1. Wolf Boss
2. Wolf Detective
3. Wolf Soldier
4. Bear Outlaw
5. Wolf Purebred

∾

Other books from Candace Ayers...

DRAGONS OF THE BAYOU

Something's lurking in the swamplands of the Deep South. Massive creatures exiled from their home. For each, his only salvation is to find his one true mate.

1. Fire Breathing Beast
2. Fire Breathing Cezar
3. Fire Breathing Blaise
4. Fire Breathing Remy
5. Fire Breathing Armand
6. Fire Breathing Ovide

RANCHER BEARS

When the patriarch of the Long family dies, he leaves a will that has each of his five son's scrambling to find a mate. Underneath it all, they find that family is what matters most.

1. Rancher Bear's Baby
2. Rancher Bear's Mail Order Mate
3. Rancher Bear's Surprise Package
4. Rancher Bear's Secret
5. Rancher Bear's Desire
6. Rancher Bears' Merry Christmas

Rancher Bears Complete Box Set

KODIAK ISLAND SHIFTERS

On Port Ursa in Kodiak Island Alaska, the Sterling brothers are kind of a big deal.
They own a nationwide chain of outfitter retail stores that they grew from their father's little backwoods camping supply shop.
The only thing missing from the hot bear shifters' lives are mates! But, not for long...

1. Billionaire Bear's Bride (COLTON)
2. The Bear's Flamingo Bride (WYATT)
3. Military Bear's Mate (TUCKER)

Kodiak Island Shifters Complete Box Set

∼

SHIFTERS OF DENVER

Nathan: Billionaire Bear- A matchmaker meets her match.
Byron: Heartbreaker Bear- A sexy heartbreaker with eyes for just one woman.
Xavier: Bad Bear - She's a good girl. He's a bad bear.

1. Nathan: Billionaire Bear
2. Byron: Heartbreaker Bear
3. Xavier: Bad Bear

Shifters of Denver Complete Box Set

Printed in Great Britain
by Amazon